THE NOVICE

The Black Magician Trilogy: Book Two

TRUDI CANAVAN

orbit

www.orbitbooks.co.uk

This book is dedicated to my mother, Irene Canavan,
who always said that, with hard work and determination,
I could be anything I wanted to be.

An *Orbit* book

First published in Great Britain by Orbit 2004
Reprinted 2004 (three times), 2005 (four times)

Copyright © 2002 by Trudi Canavan

The right of Trudi Canavan to be identified as author of this
Work has been asserted by her in accordance with the Copyright,
Designs and Patents Act 1988.

A CIP catalogue record for this book is available
from the British Library.

ISBN 1 84149 314 7

Typeset by Palimpsest Book Production Limited,
Polmont, Stirlingshire
Printed and bound in Great Britain
by Mackays of Chatham plc, Chatham, Kent

Orbit
An imprint of
Time Warner Book Group UK
Brettenham House
Lancaster Place
London WC2E 7EN

ACKNOWLEDGEMENTS

In addition to those people I acknowledged in *The Magicians' Guild*, I would like to extend an extra thank you to:

The friends and family who generously gave their time to read and critique this book at short notice: Mum and Dad, Yvonne Hardingham, Paul Marshall, Anthony Mauriks, Donna Johansen, Jenny Powell, Sara Creasy, Paul Potiki.

Jack Dann, for launching *The Magicians' Guild* with such flair and enthusiasm. Justin Ackroyd for letting me take over his bookshop, and Julian Warner and the staff at Slow Glass Books for their assistance.

Fran Bryson, my agent and hero. Les Petersen for painting yet another brilliant cover. And the publishing team at HarperCollins for turning my stories into such lovely, attractive books.

The first half of *The Novice* was written during a residency at Varuna Writers' Centre, granted by the Eleanor Dark Foundation. Thank you to Peter Bishop and the Varuna team for an inspiring and productive three weeks.

And finally, thank you to everyone who has emailed me with praise for *The Magicians' Guild*! Knowing I gave you all a few hours' enjoyment and escape makes it all worthwhile.

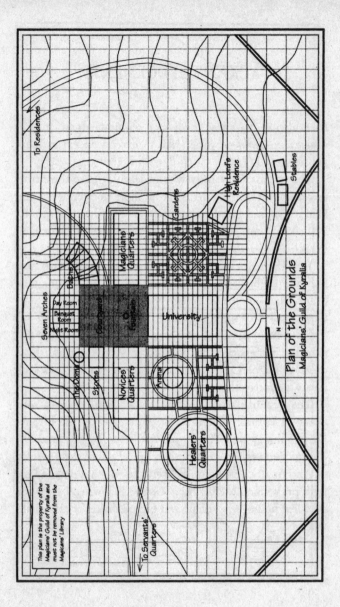

Plan of the Grounds
Magicians' Guild of Kyralia

To Residences

Seven Arches

Day Room
Banquet Room
Music Room

Baths

Magicians' Quarters

Gardens

High Lord's Residence

Stables

The Dome

Stores

Courtyard

Old Foundation

University

Novices' Quarters

Arena

N

Healers' Quarters

To Servants' Quarters

This plan is the property of the Magicians' Guild of Kyralia and must not be removed from the Magicians' Library.

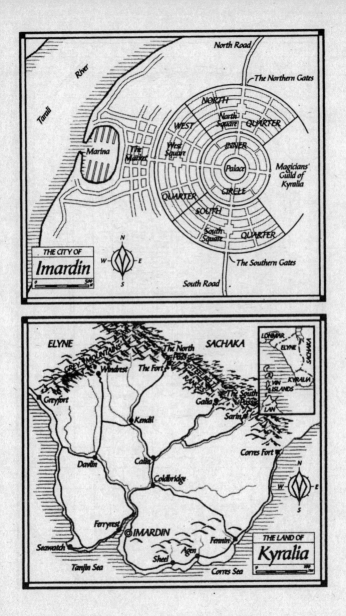

PART ONE

CHAPTER 1

THE ACCEPTANCE CEREMONY

For a few weeks each summer, the sky over Kyralia cleared to a harsh blue and the sun beat down relentlessly. In the city of Imardin, the streets were dusty and the masts of ships in the Marina writhed behind the heat haze, while men and women retreated to their homes to fan themselves and sip juices or – in the rougher parts of the slums – drink copious amounts of bol.

But in the Magicians' Guild of Kyralia these scorching days hailed the approach of an important occasion: the swearing in of the summer intake of novices.

Sonea grimaced and tugged at the collar of her dress. Though she had wanted to wear the same simple, but well-made clothes she had worn while living in the Guild, Rothen had insisted that she needed something fancier for the Acceptance Ceremony.

Rothen chuckled. 'Don't worry, Sonea. It will all be over soon and you'll have robes to wear – and I'm sure you'll get sick of those soon enough.'

'I'm not worried,' Sonea told him irritably.

His eyes brightened with amusement. 'Really? You don't feel even a little nervous?'

'It's not like the Hearing last year. *That* was wild.'

'Wild?' His eyebrows rose. 'You *are* nervous, Sonea. You haven't let that one slip in for weeks.'

3

She gave a small sigh of exasperation. Since the Hearing five months earlier, when Rothen had won the right to be her guardian, he had given her the education that all novices must attain before starting at the University. She could read most of his books without help, and she could write, as Rothen put it, 'well enough to get by'. Mathematics had been harder to grasp, but the history lessons were fascinating.

During those months, Rothen had corrected her whenever she spoke a word of slum slang, and constantly made her rephrase and repeat herself until she sounded like a lady of a powerful Kyralian House. He warned her that the novices would not be as accepting of her past as he was, and she would only make things worse if she drew attention to her origins every time she spoke. He had used the same argument to persuade her to wear a dress for the Acceptance Ceremony, and though she knew he was right, it did not make her feel any more comfortable.

A circle of carriages came into view as they reached the front of the University. Beside each stood a set of primly dressed servants, all wearing the colours of the House they served. As Rothen appeared they turned and bowed to him.

Sonea stared at the carriages and felt her stomach turn over. She had seen vehicles like this before, but not so many together. Each was made of highly polished wood, carved and painted with intricate designs, and in the centre of each door was a square design indicating which House the carriage belonged to – the House incal. She recognised the incals for Paren, Arran, Dillan and Saril, some of the most influential Houses in Imardin.

The sons and daughters of those Houses were going to be her classmates.

At that thought her stomach felt as if it were turning inside out. What would they think of her, the first Kyralian from outside the great Houses to join their ranks for centuries? At the worst they would agree with Fergun, the magician who had tried to prevent her joining the Guild last year. He believed that only the offspring of the Houses should be allowed to learn magic. By imprisoning her friend, Cery, he had blackmailed Sonea into co-operating with his schemes. And those schemes would have proven to the Guild that Kyralians of the lower classes were lacking in morals and not to be trusted with magic.

But Fergun's crime had been discovered, and he had been sent away to a distant fort. It did not seem to Sonea like a particularly severe punishment for threatening to kill her friend, and she could not help wondering if it would deter others from doing something similar.

She hoped that some of the novices would be like Rothen, who didn't care that she had once lived and worked in the slums. Some of the other races that attended the Guild might be more accepting of a girl from the lower classes, too. The Vindo were a friendly people; she had met several in the slums who had travelled to Imardin to work in vineyards and orchards. The Lan, she had been told, did not have lower and higher classes. They lived in tribes and ranked men and women through trials of bravery, cunning and wisdom – though where that would place her in their society she couldn't guess.

Looking up at Rothen, she thought of all he had done for her and felt a pang of affection and gratitude. Once she would have been horrified to find herself so dependent on, of all people, a magician. She had hated the Guild once, and first used her powers unintentionally when

5

throwing a stone at a magician in anger. Then, as they searched for her, she had been so sure they meant to kill her she had dared to seek the Thieves' help, and they always extracted a high price for such favours.

As her powers grew uncontrollable, the magicians convinced the Thieves to hand her over into their care. Rothen had been her captor and teacher. He had proven to her that magicians – well, most of them – were not the cruel, selfish monsters that the slum dwellers believed them to be.

Two guards stood at either side of the open University doors. Their presence was a formality observed only when important visitors were expected at the Guild. They bowed stiffly as Rothen led Sonea into the Entrance Hall.

Though she had seen it a few times before, the hall still amazed her. A thousand impossibly thin filaments of a glass-like substance sprouted from the floor, supporting stairs that spiralled gracefully up to the higher levels. Delicate threads of white marble wove between rails and stairs like branches of a climbing vine. They looked too fine to hold the weight of a man – and probably would be if they were not strengthened by magic.

Continuing past the stairs, they entered a short corridor. Beyond this was the rough grey of the Guildhall, an ancient building protected and enclosed by an enormous room known as the Great Hall. Several people were standing outside the Guildhall doors, and Sonea felt her mouth go dry at the sight of them. Men and women turned to see who was approaching and their eyes brightened with interest as they saw Rothen. The magicians among them nodded politely. The others bowed.

As he stepped into the Great Hall, Rothen led Sonea

to one side of the small crowd. Sonea noted that, despite the summer warmth, all but the magicians were dressed in layers of opulent clothing. The women were draped in elaborate gowns; the men wore longcoats, the sleeves decorated with incal. Looking closer, she caught her breath. Every seam was sewn with tiny glints of red, green and blue stones. Huge gems were set into the buttons of the longcoats. Chains of precious metals looped around necks and wrists, and jewels sparkled on gloved hands.

Looking at one man's longcoat, she considered how easy it would be for a professional thief to divest him of his buttons. There were small hinged blades available in the slums for that task. All it took was an 'accidental' collision, an apology, and a hasty retreat. The man probably wouldn't realise he'd been robbed until he got home. And that woman's bracelet . . .

Sonea shook her head. *How am I going to make friends with these people if all I can think of is how easy it would be to rob them?* Yet she could not help smiling. She had been as skilled at picking pockets and locks as any of her childhood friends – except maybe Cery – and though her aunt Jonna had eventually persuaded Sonea that thieving was wrong, Sonea had not forgotten the tricks of the trade.

Gathering her courage, she looked at the younger strangers and saw several faces quickly turn away. Amused, she wondered what they had been expecting to see. A simpering beggar girl? A workwoman bent and coarsened from labour? A painted whore?

Since none of them would meet her gaze, she was able to examine them freely. Only two of the families had the typical Kyralian black hair and pale skin. One of the mothers was dressed in green Healer's robes. The other held the hand of a thin girl who was gazing dreamily up at the glittering glass ceiling of the hall.

Three other families stood together, their short stature and reddish hair typical of the Elyne race. They talked quietly among themselves, and occasionally a laugh echoed in the hall.

A pair of dark-skinned Lonmar waited in silence. Heavy gold talismans of the Mahga religion hung over the father's purple Alchemist robes, and both father and son had shaved off their hair. A second pair of Lonmar stood on the far side of the waiting families. The son's skin was a paler brown, hinting at a mother of different race. The father, too, wore robes, but his were the red of a Warrior and he wore no jewellery or talismans.

Hovering near the corridor was a family of Vindo. Though the father was richly dressed, the furtive glances he directed at the others hinted that he felt uncomfortable in their company. Their son was a stocky youth whose brown skin had a sickly yellow cast to it.

As the boy's mother rested a hand on his shoulder, Sonea thought of her aunt Jonna and uncle Ranel and felt a familiar disappointment. Though they were her only family, having raised her after her mother died and her father left, they had been too intimidated by the Guild to visit her there. When she had asked them to come to the Acceptance Ceremony they had declined, saying that they would not leave their newborn son in another's care, and that it would not be proper to bring a crying baby to such an important ceremony.

Footsteps echoed in the corridor and Sonea turned to watch another grandly dressed trio of Kyralians join the visitors. The boy sent a haughty look around the circle of people. As his eyes swept around the room they fell upon Rothen, then slid to Sonea.

He looked directly into Sonea's eyes and a friendly smile curled the edges of his mouth. Surprised, she began to smile in reply, but as she did his expression slowly twisted into a sneer.

Sonea could only stare back at him in dismay. The boy turned away dismissively, but not so quickly that she didn't catch a smile of smug satisfaction. Sonea narrowed her eyes and watched as he turned his attention to the other entrants.

It appeared that he already knew the other Kyralian boy, and the two exchanged friendly winks. The girls were treated with dazzling smiles; while the thin Kyralian girl responded with apparent disdain, her eyes lingered on him long after he had turned away. The rest received polite nods.

A loud, metallic clunk interrupted the social game. All heads turned toward the Guildhall. A long, tense silence followed, then excited whispers filled the air as the enormous doors began to swing outward. As the gap widened, a familiar golden glow flowed from the hall within. The light came from thousands of tiny magical globes floating a few feet below the ceiling. A warm scent of wood and polish spilled out to welcome them.

Hearing gasps, Sonea turned to see that most of the visitors were gazing into the hall in wonder. She smiled as she realised that the other entrants, and some of the adults, would not have seen the Guildhall before. Only the magicians, and those parents who had attended ceremonies for older children, had been inside. And her.

She sobered as she remembered her previous visit, when

the High Lord had brought Cery into the Guildhall, ending Fergun's hold over her. For Cery, part of a dream had been fulfilled that day, too. Her friend had made a promise to himself that he would visit all of the great buildings of the city at least once during his lifetime. The fact that he was a low-born street urchin had only made fulfilling this dream a greater challenge for him.

But Cery was no longer the adventurous boy she had hung about with as a child, or the mischievous youth who had helped her evade the Guild for so long. Each time she saw him, when he visited her in the Guild or she had met him in the slums, he seemed older and less carefree. If she asked what he was doing with his time, or if he was still working for the Thieves, he smiled slyly and changed the subject.

He seemed content, however. And if he *was* working for the Thieves, perhaps it was better that she didn't know what he was up to.

A robed figure strode forward to stand in the Guildhall doorway. Sonea recognised Lord Osen, the Administrator's assistant. He raised a hand and cleared his throat.

'The Guild welcomes you all,' he said. 'The Acceptance Ceremony will now begin. Would the University entrants please form a line. They will enter first; parents will follow after and take seats on the floor level.'

As the other entrants hurried forward, Sonea felt a hand touch her shoulder lightly. Turning, she looked up at Rothen.

'Don't worry. It'll all be over soon,' he reassured her.

She grinned in reply. 'I'm not worried, Rothen.'

'Ha!' He gave her shoulder a gentle push. 'Go on, then. Don't keep them waiting.'

A small crowd had formed before the doors. Lord Osen's lips thinned. 'Form a line, please.'

As the entrants obeyed, Lord Osen looked over to Sonea. A quick smile touched his lips and Sonea nodded in reply. She fell in behind the last boy in the line. Then a quiet hiss to her left caught her attention.

'At least that one knows her place,' a voice murmured. Sonea turned her head slightly to see two Kyralian women standing nearby.

'That's the slum girl, is it?'

'Yes,' replied the first. 'I told Bina to keep away from her. I don't want my sweet girl picking up any nasty habits – or diseases.'

The second woman's reply was lost as Sonea moved away. She pressed a hand to her chest, surprised to find her heart beating rapidly. *Get used to it*, she told herself, *there will be more of that*. Resisting an urge to look back at Rothen, she straightened her shoulders and followed the other entrants down the long aisle in the centre of the hall.

Once through the doors, the high walls of the Guildhall surrounded them. The seats on either side were less than half full, yet nearly all magicians living within the Guild and the city were present. Looking to her left, her eyes caught the cold gaze of an elderly magician. His lined face was set in a frown, and his eyes burned into hers.

Dragging her gaze back to the floor, Sonea felt her face heating. She realised, with annoyance, that her hands were shaking. Was she going to let herself tremble over the glare of an old man? She schooled her face to what she hoped was calm self-possession, and let her eyes skim across the rows of faces . . .

. . . and nearly stumbled as all the strength drained from

11

her knees. It seemed that every magician in the hall was looking at her. Swallowing hard, she fixed her eyes on the back of the boy in front of her.

As the entrants reached the end of the aisle, Osen directed the first to the left, then the second to the right, and continued in this pattern until they stood in a line across the width of the hall. Finding herself in the middle of this line, Sonea faced Lord Osen. He stood silently, watching the activity behind her. She could hear a shuffling and a tinkling of jewellery, and guessed that the parents were moving into the rows of chairs behind them. As the hall quietened, Osen turned and bowed to the Higher Magicians sitting in the tiered rows of seats at the front of the Guildhall.

'I present the summer intake of entrants to the University.'

'This is much more interesting now there's someone down there that I know,' Dannyl remarked as Rothen took his seat.

Rothen turned to regard his companion. 'But last year your nephew was among the entrants.'

Dannyl shrugged. 'I hardly know him. I know Sonea, though.'

Pleased, Rothen turned back to watch the ceremony. While Dannyl could be very charming if he wanted to, he did not make friends easily. This was largely because of an incident that had happened years before, when Dannyl was a novice. Accused of 'inappropriate' interest in an older boy, Dannyl had endured speculation from novices and magicians alike. He had been shunned and taunted, and this was the reason, Rothen believed, that Dannyl didn't trust or befriend many people even now.

12

Rothen had been Dannyl's only close friend for years. As a teacher, Rothen had regarded Dannyl as one of the more promising novices in his classes. When he had seen the ill effects the rumour and scandal were having on Dannyl's learning, he had decided to take on the boy's guardianship. With a little encouragement, and a lot of patience, he had turned Dannyl's quick mind from gossip and vengeful pranks back to magic and knowledge.

Some magicians had expressed doubts that Rothen could 'straighten Dannyl out'. Rothen smiled. Not only had he succeeded, but Dannyl had just been appointed Second Guild Ambassador to Elyne. Looking down at Sonea, Rothen wondered if she, too, would one day give him a reason to feel this smug.

Dannyl leaned forward. 'They're just children compared to Sonea, aren't they?'

Looking at the other boys and girls, Rothen shrugged. 'I don't know their exact ages, but the average for new entrants is fifteen. She's nearly seventeen. A few years will make little difference.'

'I think it will,' Dannyl murmured, 'but hopefully it will be an advantage to her.'

Below, Lord Osen slowly walked along the line of University entrants, announcing names and titles according to the custom of each boy or girl's homeland.

'Alend of the family Genard.' Osen took two more steps. 'Kano of the family Temo, Shipbuilder's Guild.' Another step. 'Sonea.'

Osen paused, then moved on. As he announced the next name, Rothen felt a pang of sympathy for Sonea. The lack of a grand title or House name had publicly declared her an outsider. It could not be helped, however.

13

'Regin of the family Winar, House Paren,' Osen finished as he reached the last boy.

'That's Garrel's nephew, isn't it?' Dannyl asked.

'Yes.'

'I've heard that his parents asked if he could join last winter's class three months after it had started.'

'That's odd. Why did they do that?'

'I don't know.' Dannyl shrugged. 'I didn't catch that bit.'

'Have you been spying again?'

'I don't *spy*, Rothen. I listen.'

Rothen shook his head. He might have stopped Dannyl-the-novice from indulging in vengeful pranks, but he hadn't yet managed to discourage Dannyl-the-magician from gathering gossip. 'I don't know what I'm going to do when you leave. Who will keep me informed about all the Guild's little intrigues?'

'You'll just have to pay more attention,' Dannyl replied.

'I have wondered if the Higher Magicians are sending you away to stop you "listening" so much.'

Dannyl smiled. 'Ah, but they say the best way to find out what is going on in Kyralia is to spend a few days listening to gossip in Elyne.'

Echoing footsteps drew their attention back to the hall. University Director Jerrik had risen from his seat among the Higher Magicians, and was descending the stairs to the front. He stopped in the centre of the floor and swept his eyes across the line of entrants, his face set in its usual sour and disapproving scowl.

'Today, each of you takes the first step to becoming a magician of the Guild of Kyralia,' he began, his voice stern. 'As a novice you will be required to obey the rules of the

University. By the Treaties that bind the Allied Lands, these rules are endorsed by all rulers, and all magicians are expected to enforce them. Even if you do not graduate, you are still bound to them.' He paused, looking intently at the entrants. 'To join the Guild you must make a vow, and that vow has four parts.

'Firstly, you must vow never to harm another man or woman unless in defence of the Allied Lands. This includes people of any class, station, criminal status, or age. All vendettas, whether personally or politically motivated, *end here today*.

'Secondly, you must vow to obey the rules of the Guild. If you do not already know these rules, make it your first task to learn them. Ignorance is no excuse.

'Thirdly, you must vow to obey the orders of any magician unless those orders involve breaking a law. That said, we treat this with some flexibility. You are not required to do anything that you feel is morally wrong or conflicts with your religion or traditions. But *do not* presume to decide yourself when and how flexible we should be. In such a circumstance you should bring the matter to me, and it will be dealt with appropriately.

'And finally, you must vow that you will never use magic unless instructed by a magician. *This is for your protection*. Do not perform *any* magic without supervision, unless you have been given permission to do so by your teacher or guardian.'

Jerrik paused, and the silence that followed was devoid of the usual shifting and shuffling. His expressive eyebrows rose, and he straightened his shoulders.

'As tradition states, a Guild magician may claim guardianship of a novice, to guide his or her training in

15

the university.' He turned to face the tiers behind him. 'High Lord Akkarin, do you wish to claim guardianship of any of these entrants?'

'I do not,' spoke a cool, dark voice.

While Jerrik posed the same question to the other Higher Magicians, Rothen looked up at the black-robed leader of the Guild. Like most Kyralians, Akkarin was tall and slim, his angular face accentuated by the old-fashioned style of wearing his hair long and tied at the nape of the neck.

As always, Akkarin's expression was distant as he watched the proceedings. He had never shown any interest in guiding the training of a novice, and most families had given up hoping that their son might be favoured by the Guild leader.

Though young for a High Lord, Akkarin had a presence that inspired respect from even the most conservative and influential magicians. He was skilled, knowledgeable and intelligent, but it was his magical strength that earned him the awe of so many. His powers were known to be so great that some estimated he was stronger than the rest of the Guild combined.

But thanks to Sonea, Rothen was one of only two magicians who knew the real reason behind the High Lord's immense strength.

Before the Thieves had handed her over, Sonea and her thief-friend, Cery, had explored the Guild late one night. They had come in the hope that, by watching magicians using magic, she might learn to control her powers. Instead, she had witnessed the High Lord performing a strange ritual. She had not understood what she had seen, but when Administrator Lorlen had truth-read her to confirm Fergun's crimes, during the guardianship Hearing, he had seen her memory of that night and recognised the ritual.

High Lord Akkarin, leader of the Guild, practised black magic.

Ordinary magicians knew nothing about black magic, except that it was forbidden. The Higher Magicians knew only enough to recognise it. Even *knowing* how to perform black magic was a crime. From Sonea's communication with Lorlen, Rothen now knew that black magic enabled a magician to strengthen himself by drawing power from other people. If all power was taken, the victim died.

Rothen could not guess what it had been like for Lorlen to discover that his closest friend not only had *learned* about black magic, but was *using* it. It must have been a shock. Yet at the same time, Lorlen had realised that he could not expose Akkarin without endangering the Guild and the city. If Akkarin chose to fight, he could easily win, and with each kill he would grow stronger. So Lorlen, Sonea and Rothen must keep their knowledge secret for now. How hard must it be, Rothen wondered, for Lorlen to pretend friendship when he knew what Akkarin was capable of?

Despite this knowledge, Sonea had agreed to join the Guild. This amazed Rothen at first, until she had pointed out that if she left with her powers blocked – as the law required for magicians who chose not to join the Guild – she would have been a tempting source of power for the High Lord. Strong in magic, but unable to use it to defend herself. Rothen shuddered. At least, in the Guild, it would be noticed if she died under strange circumstances.

Even so, it had been a brave decision, knowing what

lay at the heart of the Guild. Looking at her, standing among the sons and daughters of some of the richest families in the Allied Lands, he felt both pride and affection. In the last six months he had come to think of her more as a daughter than a student.

'Do any magicians wish to claim guardianship of any of these entrants?'

Rothen jumped as he realised that his turn to speak had come. He opened his mouth, but before he could say anything another voice spoke the ritual words.

'I have made a selection, Director.'

The voice came from the other side of the hall. All the entrants turned to see who had risen from their seat.

'Lord Yarrin,' Jerrik acknowledged. 'Which entrant do you wish to claim guardianship of?'

'Gennyl, of the family Randa and the House of Saril, and the Greater Clan of Alaraya.'

A faint murmur of voices rose in the ranks of the magicians. Looking down, Rothen saw that the boy's father, Lord Tayk, was sitting forward in his chair.

Jerrik waited until the voices subsided, then tilted his head expectantly toward Rothen.

'Do any other magicians wish to claim guardianship of one of these entrants?'

Rothen rose. 'I have made a selection, Director.'

Sonea looked up, her mouth tight as she tried not to smile.

'Lord Rothen,' Jerrik replied, 'which entrant do you wish to claim guardianship of?'

'I wish to claim guardianship of Sonea.'

No murmuring followed his choice, and Jerrik merely nodded in acknowledgment. Rothen returned to his seat.

'That's it,' Dannyl whispered. 'Your last chance has gone. There'll be no getting out of it now. She's got you well and truly wrapped around her finger for the next five years.'

'Shush,' Rothen replied.

'Do any other magicians wish to claim guardianship of one of these entrants?' Jerrik repeated.

'I have made a selection, Director.'

The voice came from Rothen's left, and was followed by the sound of chairs creaking as people turned or shifted in their seats. The hall echoed with excited chatter as Lord Garrel rose.

'Lord Garrel,' there was surprise in Jerrik's voice, 'which entrant do you wish to claim guardianship of?'

'Regin, of the family Winar and the House of Paren.'

The chatter changed to a collective sigh of understanding. Looking down, Rothen saw that the boy at the end of the line wore a grin. The voices and creaking of chairs continued for several minutes until Jerrik raised his arms for silence.

'I'd keep an eye on those two novices and their guardians,' Dannyl murmured. 'Nobody usually selects a novice in their First Year. They're probably doing it simply to prevent Sonea having a higher status than the rest of her classmates.'

'Or, I've started a trend,' Rothen mused. 'And Garrel may have already seen potential in his nephew. That *would* explain why Regin's family wanted him to start classes early.'

'Are there any other guardianship claims?' Jerrik called. Silence followed, and he dropped his arms. 'Would all magicians intending to claim guardianship come to the front.'

Rothen rose and made his way to the end of the seats, then down the stairs. Joining Lord Garrel and Lord Yarrin, he waited beside Director Jerrik as a young novice, flushed with excitement at having a role in the ceremony, came forward carrying a stack of brown-red cloth. The magicians each selected a bundle.

'Would Gennyl please come forward,' Jerrik ordered.

One of the Lonmar boys hurried forward and bowed. His eyes were wide as he faced Lord Jerrik, and as he spoke the Novices' Vow his voice trembled. Lord Yarrin handed the boy his robes, and guardian and novice stepped aside. Lord Jerrik turned toward the entrants again.

'Would Sonea please come forward.'

She walked stiffly toward Jerrik. Though her face was pale, she bowed gracefully and spoke the vow in a clear, unwavering voice. Rothen stepped forward and handed her the bundle of robes.

'I hereby take guardianship of you, Sonea. Your learning is my concern and task until you graduate from the university.'

'I will obey you, Lord Rothen.'

'May you both benefit from this arrangement,' Jerrik finished.

As they moved aside to stand next to Lord Yarrin and Gennyl, Jerrik called the still smiling youth from the end of the line.

'Would Regin please come forward.'

The boy strode confidently to Jerrik, but his bow was shallow and hurried. As the ritual phrases were repeated, Rothen looked down at Sonea, wondering what she was thinking. She was a member of the Guild now, and that was no small thing.

She looked at the boy to her right, and Rothen followed her gaze. Gennyl stood with his back straight and his face flushed. *He's just about bursting with pride*, Rothen mused. To have a guardian, especially at this point, was proof that an entrant was exceptionally gifted.

Few would believe this about Sonea, however. He suspected that most magicians assumed he had chosen to be her guardian simply to remind all that he had been instrumental in finding her. They would not have believed him if he told them of her strength and talent. But they would find out, and knowing it gave him some satisfaction.

After Regin and Lord Garrel had spoken the ritual words, they moved to Rothen's left. The boy kept glancing at Sonea, his expression calculating. She either did not notice, or was ignoring him. Instead, she watched intently as Jerrik called the rest of the entrants forward to speak the vow. As each accepted their robes, they formed a line next to the guardians and their novices.

When the last of the entrants had joined the line, Lord Jerrik turned to regard them.

'You are now novices of the Magicians' Guild,' he announced. 'May the coming years be prosperous for all of you.'

As one, the novices bowed. Lord Jerrik nodded and moved to one side.

'I extend a welcome to our new novices and wish them many years of success.' Sonea jumped as Lorlen's voice rang out from behind her. 'I now declare this Acceptance Ceremony concluded.'

The Guildhall began to echo with the sound of voices. The rows of robed men and women stirred as if caught by a strong wind. They rose and began to descend to the floor, filling the hall with the clatter of footsteps. As the new novices realised the formalities were over, they moved in all directions. Some rushed to their parents, others examined the bundle in their hands or gazed around at the sudden activity. At the end of the Guildhall the great doors began to open slowly.

Sonea turned to look up at Rothen. 'That's it, then. I'm a novice.'

He smiled. 'Glad it's all over?'

She shrugged. 'I get the feeling it's only just begun.' Her eyes flickered over his shoulder. 'Here's your shadow.'

Rothen turned to find Dannyl striding toward him.

'Welcome to the Guild, Sonea.'

'Thank you, *Ambassador* Dannyl,' Sonea replied, bowing.

Dannyl laughed. 'Not yet, Sonea. Not yet.'

Sensing someone new at his side, Rothen turned to find the University Director standing next to him.

'Lord Rothen,' Jerrik said, giving Sonea a tired smile as she bowed.

'Yes?' Rothen replied.

'Will Sonea be moving into the Novices' Quarters? It never crossed my mind to ask until now.'

Rothen shook his head. 'She'll be staying with me. I have plenty of room for her in my apartments.'

Jerrik's brows rose. 'I see. I will tell Lord Ahrind. Excuse me.'

Rothen watched the old man walk over to a thin, hollow-cheeked magician. Lord Ahrind frowned and glanced over at Sonea as Jerrik spoke to him.

'What happens now?' Sonea asked.

Rothen nodded to the bundle in her hands. 'We see if

these robes fit properly.' He looked at Dannyl. 'And I think a little celebration is in order. Coming?'

Dannyl smiled. 'I wouldn't miss it.'

CHAPTER 2

THE FIRST DAY

The sun was warm on his back as Dannyl stepped up to the carriage. He drew on a little magic to lift the first of his chests onto the roof. As the second settled next to it he sighed and shook his head.

'I suspect I'm going to regret taking so much,' he muttered. 'Yet I keep thinking of things I wish I'd packed.'

'I'm sure you'll be able to buy anything you need in Capia,' Rothen told him. 'Lorlen has certainly given you a generous allowance.'

'Yes, that was a pleasant surprise.' Dannyl grinned. 'Perhaps you're right about his reasons for sending me away.'

Rothen's eyebrow rose. 'He must know it would take more than sending you to another country to keep you out of trouble.'

'Ah, but I'm going to miss fixing all your problems, my friend.' As the driver opened the carriage door, Dannyl turned to look at the older magician. 'Are you coming to the Marina?'

Rothen shook his head. 'Classes start in less than an hour.'

'For both you and Sonea.' Dannyl nodded. 'Then this is it – time to say goodbye.'

They regarded each other solemnly for a moment, then

24

Rothen gripped Dannyl's shoulder and smiled. 'Take care of yourself. Try not to fall overboard.'

Dannyl chuckled and returned the clasp. 'Take care, old friend. Don't let that new novice of yours wear you out. I'll be back in a year or so to check on your progress.'

'Old friend, indeed!' Rothen pushed Dannyl toward the carriage. After climbing inside, Dannyl turned to see a thoughtful expression on his friend's face.

'I never thought I'd see you running off on such glorious escapades, Dannyl. You seemed so content here, and you've rarely set foot outside the gates since you graduated.'

Dannyl shrugged. 'I guess I was waiting for the right reason.'

Rothen made a rude noise. 'Liar. You're just lazy. I hope the First Ambassador knows this, or he's in for a nasty surprise.'

'He'll find out soon enough.' Dannyl grinned.

'I'm sure he will.' Rothen smiled and stepped away from the carriage. 'Off with you, then.'

Dannyl nodded. 'Goodbye.' He tapped on the roof of the carriage. It jerked into motion, drawing him away. Sliding to the other side of the seat, Dannyl pulled back the screen covering the window and glimpsed Rothen still watching before the carriage turned again to pass through the Guild Gates.

He leaned back in the cushioned seat and sighed. Though he was pleased to be finally leaving, he knew he would miss his friends and familiar surroundings. Rothen had Sonea and the elderly couple Yaldin and Ezrille for company, but Dannyl would have only strangers.

Though he was looking forward to his new position, he was a bit intimidated by the duties and responsibilities he was taking on. Since the hunt for Sonea, however, during which he had located and negotiated with one of the Thieves, he had grown increasingly bored with his easy, mostly solitary life of study in the Guild.

He hadn't realised just how bored he was until Rothen had told him he was being considered for the role of Second Ambassador. By the time Dannyl was summoned to the Administrator's office, he could recite the name and position of every man and woman in the Elyne court and, to Lorlen's amusement, numerous scandalous tales as well.

Deep into the Inner Circle the carriage turned onto the road that circled the Palace wall. Little could be seen of the grand Palace towers from this angle, so Dannyl slid to the other end of the seat to admire the elaborately decorated homes of the rich and powerful. At one street corner a new mansion was being constructed. He remembered the old crumbling structure that had once stood there, a relic from before the invention of magician-made architecture. The application of magic to stone and metal had enabled magicians to build fantastic buildings that defied normal structural limitations. Before the carriage moved past, Dannyl glimpsed two magicians standing beside the partly built new home, one holding up a large plan.

The carriage turned again and passed more grand homes, then slowed and rolled through the Inner Gates into the West Quarter. The guards barely glanced up as it passed, only pausing to note the Guild symbol painted on the side of the vehicle. The road continued through the West Quarter, between large and regal houses of a plainer style than those of the Inner Circle. Most belonged to merchants or crafters, who preferred this part of the city for its proximity to the Marina and Market.

As the carriage passed through the Western Gate, it entered a maze of stalls and booths. People of all races and classes filled the roads on either side. Stall holders called out their wares and prices over the endless buzz of voices, whistles, bells and animal calls. Though the road remained wide, sellers, customers, street performers and beggars crowded both sides so that carriages had barely enough room to pass each other.

The air was heavy with a confusion of smells. A breeze sweetened by the smell of bruised fruit was followed by another reeking of rotten vegetables. The fibrous smell of rush matting was swamped by the acrid, suffocating odour of something unwholesome as two men carried a vat of oily blue liquid past the carriage. Finally, the briny tang of the sea, and the subtle, pungent scent of river mud reached Dannyl and he felt his heartbeat quicken. The carriage turned a corner and the Marina came into view.

A forest of masts and ropes lay before him, dividing the sky into ribbons of blue. On either side of the road an endless river of people hurried past. Muscular carriers and crewmen hauled boxes, baskets and sacks on their backs. Carts of all sizes, drawn by all manner of animals, trundled by. The cries of sellers were replaced by shouted orders and the bellowing and bleating of livestock.

Still the carriage continued, taking him past larger and larger boats until he reached a row of sturdy merchant ships resting by a long pier. There it slowed and stopped, rocking back on its springs.

The door opened and the driver bowed respectfully.

'We have arrived, my lord.'

Dannyl slid across the seat and climbed out. A swarthy, white-haired man stood nearby, his face and bare arms well

27

tanned. Behind him stood several younger men, all heavily built.

'You are Lord Dannyl?' the man asked, bowing stiffly.

'Yes. You are . . .?'

'Piermaster,' he said, then nodded at the carriage. 'Yours?'

Dannyl guessed that he was referring to the chests. 'Yes.'

'We'll take 'em down.'

'No, I can save you the trouble.' Dannyl turned and focussed his will. As each chest drifted down toward the ground, a pair of the young men came forward and caught it, apparently accustomed to the use of magic for such purposes. They started down the pier, the rest of the men following.

'Sixth ship along, my lord,' the Piermaster said as the carriage pulled away.

Dannyl nodded. 'Thank you.'

As he reached the pier his footsteps began echoing hollowly on the wooden planking. Looking down, he saw glimpses of water through the cracks between the wide timbers. He followed the carriers around a great stack of boxes that were being loaded onto one ship, then a pile of what looked like well-wrapped carpets waiting beside another. Men were everywhere: hurrying up and down planks with loads on their shoulders, lounging on deck playing tiles, or striding about shouting orders.

Over the noise, Dannyl noted the subtler sounds of the Marina: the constant creak of boards and ropes, and the splash of water against hull and pier. He noticed small details: the decoration on masts and sails, the names painted carefully on hull and cabin, the water pouring from a hole in a ship's side. He frowned at that last detail.

Water was supposed to remain on the *outside* of a boat, wasn't it?

Upon reaching the sixth ship, the carriers clomped up a narrow gangplank. Looking up, Dannyl saw a pair of men watching him from the ship. He started up the plank cautiously, then with more confidence when he found it sturdy enough despite the flexing of the wood. As he stepped onto the deck the two men greeted him with bows.

They looked remarkably alike. Their brown skin and small stature were typical Vindo characteristics. They both wore tough, colourless clothing. One, however, stood a little straighter than the other, and it was he who spoke.

'Welcome to the *Fin-da*, my lord. I am Captain Numo.'

'Thank you, captain. I am Lord Dannyl.'

The captain gestured to the chests, which were resting on the deck a few strides away, the carriers standing nearby. 'No room for boxes in your room, my lord. We stow them below. You want anything, you ask my brother, Jano.'

Dannyl nodded. 'Very well. There is one item I will collect before they take them away.'

The captain nodded once. 'Jano show your room. We leaving soon.'

As the captain walked away, Dannyl touched the lid of the smaller chest. The lock snapped open. He removed a leather bag filled with necessities for the journey. Closing the lid again, he looked up at the carriers.

'This is all I'll need – I hope.'

They bent and carried the trunks away. Turning, Dannyl looked at Jano expectantly. The man nodded and gestured for Dannyl to follow.

Passing through a narrow door, they descended a short stairway into a wide room. The ceiling was so low even

Jano needed to stoop to duck under the beams. Roughly woven sheets were slung between hooks on the ceiling. These, he guessed, were the hanging beds he had heard about in stories and travellers' accounts.

Jano led him into a narrow corridor and, after a few steps, opened a door. Dannyl stared at the tiny room in dismay. A low bed as wide as his shoulders filled the entire interior. A small cupboard had been built into one end, and good quality reber-wool blankets lay neatly folded at the other.

'Small, yai?'

Dannyl looked across at Jano to find the man grinning. He smiled wryly, knowing his dismay must have been obvious.

'Yes,' Dannyl agreed. 'Small.'

'Captain has room twice as big. When we own big boat, we get big room, too, yai?'

Dannyl nodded. 'Sounds fair.' He dropped his bag on the bed, then turned around so that he could sit down, his legs extending into the corridor. 'It's all I need.'

Jano tapped the opposite door. 'My room. We keep each other company, yai? You sing?'

Before Dannyl could think of an answer a bell rang out somewhere above, and Jano looked up. 'Must go. We leaving now.' He turned, then paused. 'You stay here. Not get in way.' Without waiting for a reply, he hurried off.

Dannyl looked around the tiny room that would be his space for the next two weeks, and chuckled. Now he understood why so many magicians hated travelling by sea.

Stopping in the doorway of the classroom, Sonea felt her heart sink.

She had left Rothen's rooms early, hoping to get to the classroom ahead of the other novices so that she'd have time to gain some control over her fluttering stomach before meeting them. But several seats were already occupied. As she hesitated, faces turned toward her, and her stomach shrank into a tight knot. She quickly looked away to the magician who sat at the front of the classroom.

He was younger than she had expected, probably only in his twenties. An angular nose gave his face a disdainful expression. As she bowed, he looked up, his eyes fixing on her face, travelling to her new boots, then rising back up to her face again. Satisfied, he looked down at a sheet of paper and made a small tick against the list written there.

'Choose a seat, Sonea,' he said dismissively.

The room contained twelve perfectly aligned tables and chairs. Six novices, all perched on the edge of their seats, watched her consider the arrangement.

Don't sit too far from the other novices, she told herself. *You don't want them thinking you're unfriendly – or scared of them.* A few empty seats remained in the centre of the room, but she didn't like the idea of sitting in the middle, either. A chair against the far wall was vacant, flanked by three novices in the next row. That would do.

She was conscious of eyes following her as she moved to the chair. As she sat down she forced herself to look up at them.

At once the novices found something else to interest them. Sonea sighed with relief. She had been expecting more sneers. Perhaps only the boy she had encountered yesterday – Regin – was going to be openly unfriendly.

One by one the rest of the novices arrived at the door of the classroom, bowed to the teacher and took a seat.

The shy Kyralian girl hastily took the first chair she came to. Another almost forgot to bow to the magician, then stumbled over to the seat in front of Sonea. He didn't see her until he had reached the chair, and he stared at her in dismay before reluctantly sitting down.

The last novice to arrive was the unfriendly boy, Regin. He scanned the room with narrowed eyes before deliberately placing himself in the centre of the group.

A distant gong sounded, and the magician rose from his chair. Several novices, including herself, jumped visibly at the movement. Before their teacher could speak, however, a familiar face appeared in the doorway.

'Are they all here, Lord Elben?'

'Yes, Director Jerrik,' the teacher replied.

The University Director hooked his thumbs in the brown sash about his waist and regarded the class.

'Welcome,' he said, his voice more stern than welcoming, 'and congratulations. I offer this congratulation not because each of you has had the good fortune of being born with the rare and much envied ability to use magic. I offer it because each of you has been accepted into the university of the Magicians' Guild. Some of you have come from countries far from here, and will not return to your homes for many years. Some of you may decide to stay here for most of your life. You are all, however, stuck here for the next five years.

'Why? To become a magician. What is a magician, then?' He smiled grimly. 'There are many attributes that make up a magician. Some you already have, some you will develop, some you will learn. Some are more important than others.'

He stopped and swept his eyes over the class.

'What is the most important attribute of a magician?'

In the corner of her eye Sonea saw several of the novices straighten in their seats. Jerrik moved around the desk and strolled to her side of the room. He stared down at the boy in front of her.

'Vallon?'

Sonea saw the boy's back hunch as if he wanted to slide under his table.

'H-how well he does something, my lord.' The boy's weak voice was only just audible. 'How much he has practised.'

'No.' Jerrik turned on his heel and stalked to the other side of the class. He fixed one of the eager boys with his cold stare.

'Gennyl?'

'Strength, my lord,' the boy answered.

'Definitely not!' the University Director barked. He stepped forward, down between the rows of novices, and stopped by the timid Kyralian girl.

'Bina?'

The girl blinked prettily, then raised her head to gaze at the magician. His eyes bore into hers and she dropped her head quickly.

'Uh . . .' She paused, then brightened suddenly. 'Goodness, my lord. How he or she uses magic.'

'No.' His tone was gentler. 'Though a very important attribute and one we expect from all our magicians.'

Jerrik continued down the aisle. Sonea turned her head to watch him, but noticed that the other novices were staring rigidly at the front of the room. Feeling uneasy, she copied them, listening for the magician's footsteps as he moved closer.

'Elayk?'

'Talent, my lord?' The boy's Lonmar accent was strong.

'No.'

The footsteps grew closer. Sonea felt a tingling at the top of her spine. What would she say if he asked her? Surely all the possible answers had been offered already. She drew in a quiet breath and let it out slowly. He wouldn't ask her anyway. She was the unimportant girl from the . . .

'Sonea?'

Her stomach lurched. Looking up, she saw Jerrik standing over her, his eyes growing chillier as she hesitated.

Then she knew the answer. It was easy. After all, she should know this better than any of the novices since she had nearly died when her own powers had grown uncontrollable. Jerrik knew this, which was probably why he had asked her.

'Control, my lord.'

'No.'

The magician sighed and moved to the front of the room. She stared at the grain of the wooden table before her, her face hot.

The University Director stopped in front of the desk and crossed his arms. He looked around the room again. The class waited, expectant and ashamed.

'The most important attribute of a magician is knowledge.' He paused, then looked at each of the novices who had spoken in turn. 'Without it his strength is useless, he has nothing to be skilled or talented in, despite his best intentions.' The magician's eyes flickered to Sonea. 'Even if his powers surface of their own accord, he will soon be dead if he does not gain the *knowledge* of how to control them.'

As one, the class let out a breath. A few faces turned toward Sonea briefly. Frozen by self-consciousness, she kept her eyes on her desk.

'The Guild is the largest and most comprehensive store of knowledge in the world,' Jerrik continued, a note of pride rising in his voice. 'During the years that you spend here that knowledge, or at least some part of it, will be given to you. If you pay attention, listen to what your teachers tell you, and make use of the sources here such as the extensive library, you will excel. However,' his tone darkened, 'if you do not pay attention, pay your elders respect or take advantage of the centuries of knowledge gathered by your predecessors, you will shame only yourselves. The years ahead of you will not be easy,' he warned. 'You must be dedicated, disciplined and dutiful,' he paused and scanned the faces before him, 'if you are to reach your full potential as magicians of the Guild.'

The atmosphere in the room had changed from relief to a new kind of tension. The novices were so quiet that Sonea could hear them breathing. Jerrik straightened and put his hands behind his back.

'You are probably aware,' he said in a milder tone, 'of the Three Levels of Control that are the foundation of your university education. The First, unlocking your power, you will achieve today. The Second, the ability to access, draw, and contain your power, will be your aim for the rest of this morning, and every morning, until you can achieve all three without thinking. The Third, grasping the many ways that power can be used, will be taught to you in the years between now and your graduation – though, regardless of which discipline you choose to specialise in after graduation, there will be no point at which you will have completed the Third Level. Once you have graduated, it will be up to you to expand upon the knowledge we have given you, but you will, of course, never know all there is to know.' He smiled thinly.

'The Guild holds more knowledge than you could absorb in a lifetime, probably more than you could learn in five lifetimes. We have the three disciplines of Healing, Alchemy and Warrior Skills. So that you may learn enough of one to become a useful and accomplished magician, your teachers, and those before them, have gleaned what information is most relevant and important to give to you.' He lifted his chin slightly. 'Use this knowledge well, novices of the Magicians' Guild of Kyralia.'

He cast his eyes over the classroom once more, then turned and, with a nod to Lord Elben, left the room.

The class was still and quiet. The teacher remained motionless, noting the expressions on the faces of his charges with a smile of satisfaction. Then he stepped around to the front of the large table and addressed them.

'Your first lesson in Control begins now. Each of you has been designated a teacher for this lesson. You will find them waiting for you next door. Rise and make your way to this room now.'

Chairs scraped on the wooden floor as the novices got eagerly to their feet. Sonea rose slowly. The teacher's head turned and he regarded her coldly.

'Except you, Sonea,' he added, belatedly. 'You will remain here.'

This time all of the novices turned to stare at her. She

blinked from one face to another, feeling strangely guilty as understanding dawned in their eyes.

'Go on,' urged the teacher. The novices turned away. Sonea lowered herself back into her chair and watched the class file out. Only one turned to glance at her again before he stepped through the door. His lips curled up in a sneer. Regin.

'Sonea.'

She jumped and turned to stare at the teacher, surprised that he was still there.

'Yes, my lord.'

His eyes lost a little of their chilliness and he moved across the room to stand beside her seat. 'As you have already achieved the First and Second Levels of Control, I have brought you the first book the class will study.' Sonea lowered her eyes to a small paper-covered book he held in his hand. 'There will be practical exercises to go with the book, but they will involve all of the class. You will still gain much from studying the information in this.'

He placed the book on the table and turned away.

'Thank you, Lord Elben,' she said to his back.

He paused and turned to regard her with mild surprise, then continued to the door.

The room was empty and silent after he had gone. Sonea looked around at the other desks and chairs. She counted nine crooked seats.

She looked at the book on her desk and read: *Six Lessons for New Novices*, by Lord Liden, and a date. The book was over a century old. How many novices had worked their way through these exercises? She flicked through the pages. The script, she saw with relief, was clear and easy to read.

Magic is a useful art, but not without limitations. A

magician's natural area of influence lies within his or her body, the skin being the boundary of this area. Minimal effort is required to influence magic within this space. No other magician may influence this space, unless he or she is Healing, which requires skin to skin contact.

To influence what lies beyond the body, more effort is required. The further away the object to be influenced is from the body, the more effort is required. The same limitation is true of mental communication, though it is not as taxing as most magical tasks.

Rothen had told her as much, but she continued reading. Some time later, after she had read three of the lessons and was beginning on the fourth, two novices returned to the room. The first she recognised as Gennyl, the half-Lonmar boy who had gained a guardian during the ceremony. His companion was the other tall Lonmar boy. They glanced at her once as they moved to seats halfway down the classroom. She could sense a difference about them, as if their presence was amplified. She guessed this meant their powers had been released. They would soon learn to hide it, as she had. It appeared that achieving the First Level wasn't difficult or slow. The Second Level, she knew, was harder.

A murmuring conversation began, in the liquid language of their homeland. Another novice entered the room – a Kyralian boy with dark circles under his eyes. Sitting down, he remained silent, rigidly staring at his desk.

There was something strange about this one. She could sense an aura of magic about him, too, but it pulsed erratically, sometimes strong, sometimes fading beyond detection. Not wanting to upset him any further by her staring, she looked away. Until the novices had achieved both First and Second Levels of Control, she might sense all kind of strange things from them.

A laugh outside the doorway caught her attention before she could start reading again. This time five novices filed into the room, leaving only Regin missing. Without a figure of authority to watch them, the novices lounged around, sitting on their desks and talking in little groups. Her senses buzzed with their magical presences.

No-one approached Sonea. She was both relieved and disappointed. They didn't know what to expect from her, she reasoned, so they avoided her. She would have to make the first attempt to be friendly. If she didn't, then they might decide she didn't want to mix with them.

The pretty Elyne girl sat nearby, rubbing her temples. Remembering how Control lessons had given Rothen headaches, Sonea wondered if this girl might appreciate a little sympathy. Slowly, trying to look confident, she rose and moved across the room to the girl's table.

'It isn't easy, is it?' Sonea ventured.

The girl's eyes lifted to hers in surprise, then she shrugged and looked back down at her table. When no reply came, Sonea began to suspect, with a growing sickness in her stomach, that the girl was ignoring her.

'I don't like her,' the girl said suddenly, in a strong Elyne accent.

Sonea blinked in puzzlement. 'Like who?'

'Lady Kinla,' the girl said irritably. She pronounced the name as 'Keenlar'.

'The one teaching you Control? Hmmm, that *would* make it hard.'

'It's not that Lady Kinla's a bad person,' the girl sighed.

'It's just that I don't want her in my mind. She's so . . .' The girl's red curls swayed as she shook her head.

The seat in front of the Elyne girl was empty. Sonea lowered herself into it and turned to face the girl.

'You don't want her to see some things in your mind?' Sonea prompted. 'Things that aren't wrong or bad, but things you don't want just any person seeing?'

'Yes, that's it,' the girl looked up, her eyes wide and haunted, 'but I have to let her see them, don't I?'

Sonea frowned. 'No, you don't have to . . . well, I don't know exactly what you want to keep from her, but . . . well . . . those things *can* be hidden.'

The girl was staring at Sonea now.

'*How?*'

'You imagine a kind of doorway and put them behind it,' Sonea explained. 'Lady Kinla will probably see what you've done but she won't try to get to them just as Rothen didn't try to get to mine.'

The girl's eyes widened further still. 'Lord Rothen taught you Control? He was in your *mind?*' she gasped.

'Yes.' Sonea nodded.

'But he's a *man*.'

'Well . . . he taught me. Is that why you have a lady teacher? Do you have to be taught by a woman?'

'Of *course*.' The girl was staring at her in horror.

Sonea shook her head slowly. 'I didn't know. I don't see how it would make any difference being taught by a male or female magician. Perhaps . . .' She frowned. 'If I couldn't have hidden away all my secret thoughts it would have been better to have a woman teach me.'

The girl had pulled away from Sonea a little. 'It would be wrong for a girl of our age to share her mind with a man.'

40

Sonea shrugged. 'It's just minds. It's like talking, but quicker. There's nothing wrong with *talking* to a man is there?'

'No . . .'

'You just don't talk about certain things.' Sonea gave her a meaningful look.

A slow smile spread across the girl's face. 'No . . . except on special occasions, I suppose.'

'Issle.' A sharp voice cut across the noise in the room. Sonea looked up to see a middle-aged woman in green robes standing in the doorway.

'You've rested long enough. Come with me.'

'Yes, my lady,' the girl sighed.

'Good luck,' Sonea offered as the girl hurried away. She wasn't sure if Issle had heard, as the girl disappeared through the door without a backward glance.

Sonea looked down at the book in her hands and allowed herself a small smile. It was a start. Perhaps, later, she would talk to Issle again.

Returning to her desk, she continued reading.

Projection:

Moving an object is quicker and easier if in sight. Moving an object outside of view may be done by extending the mind sense to locate it first. This takes more effort and time, however, and . . .

Bored, Sonea began to watch the novices coming and going. She listened for their names, and tried to guess what they were like. Shern, the Kyralian boy with the dark circles under his eyes, had winced when his teacher returned and called his name. He had looked up at the magician with haunted eyes, and reluctance had been expressed in every movement as he had pushed back his chair and shuffled over to the door.

Regin had befriended two boys, Kano and Vallon. The shy Kyralian girl listened to their conversation attentively, and the Elyne boy drew little pictures in a paper-covered book. When Issle returned she collapsed in her seat and buried her head in her arms. Sonea had heard the others complaining of headaches and decided to leave the girl alone.

When the gong chimed at midbreak, Sonea let out a quiet sigh of relief. All she had done was read lessons she already knew, constantly distracted by the coming and going of the other novices. It hadn't been a particularly interesting first lesson.

Lord Elben strode into the room, causing the novices to scuttle hastily to their seats. He waited until they had settled, then cleared his throat.

'We will resume Control lessons at the same time tomorrow,' he told them. 'Your next class will be Guild history, held in the second history room upstairs. You may leave now.'

Several sighs of relief could be heard around the class. The novices rose, bowed to the teacher and started for the door. Hanging back, Sonea noted that the Elyne boy had joined Regin's group of new friends. She followed quietly, handing the teacher back his book as she passed, then lengthened her stride to catch up with Issle.

'Was it better the second time?'

The girl looked at Sonea, then nodded. 'I did what you said. It didn't work, but I think it might next time.'

'That's good. Everything gets easier after that.'

They walked in silence for several paces. Sonea searched for something to say.

'You're Issle of Fonden, aren't you?' a voice observed.

Issle turned and stopped as Regin and the other two novices approached.

'Yes,' she said, smiling prettily.

'Whose father is adviser to King Marend?' Regin asked, his brows rising.

'That's right.'

'I am Regin of Winar,' he bowed with exaggerated politeness, 'of House Paren. Can I escort you to the Foodhall?'

Her smile broadened. 'I'd be honoured.'

'No.' Regin smiled silkily. 'It is I who will be honoured.'

He stepped forward between Sonea and Issle, forcing Sonea to move backward to avoid him, and took the girl's arm. Regin's companions fell in behind the pair as they continued down the corridor. None looked at Sonea, and she found herself at the back of the group. When they had descended the stairs of the University she stopped and watched them walk away without a backward glance.

Issle hadn't even thanked her. *I shouldn't be surprised*, she told herself. *They're rich brats with no manners.*

No, she scolded herself. *Don't be unfair to them. If I'd been asked to accept one of them in Harrin's gang, it wouldn't have been easy. Eventually they'll forget that I'm different. Just give them time.*

CHAPTER 3

TELLING TALES

As Rothen's servant, Tania, set out the morning meal on the table, Sonea dropped into a seat with a sigh. Rothen looked up and, seeing the resigned and unhappy expression on her face, wished that he had been able to return straight after class yesterday, instead of spending hours discussing lessons with Lord Peakin.

'How did it go yesterday?' he asked.

Sonea hesitated before answering. 'None of the novices can use magic yet. They're all still learning Control. Lord Elben gave me a book to read.'

'All novices are unable to use magic when they begin with us. We don't develop their power until they have spoken the vow. I thought you would have realised this.' He smiled. 'There are some advantages in having your power develop naturally.'

'But it will take weeks until they can start lessons. All I did was read the same book – and it was about things I already know.' She looked up, her eyes bright with hope. 'Why don't I stay here until they've caught up?'

Rothen suppressed a laugh. 'We don't hold a novice back if he or she is a faster learner than the others. You should make the most of the opportunity. Ask for another book to read, or see if your teacher is willing to go through some exercises with you.'

She grimaced. 'I don't think the other novices will like that.'

He pursed his lips. She was right, of course, but he also knew if he asked Jerrik to keep her out of classes until the others were ready, the Director would refuse.

'Novices are expected to compete with each other,' he told her. 'Your classmates will always try to outdo you. It will make no difference if you hold yourself back for them. In fact, you will lose their respect if you sacrifice your learning for fear of upsetting them.'

Sonea nodded and looked down at the table. He felt a pang of sympathy for her. No matter how much he counselled her, it had to be confusing and frustrating to be suddenly confined to the small, petty world of the novices.

'You really haven't had that much of a head start,' he told her. 'It took me weeks to teach you Control because you had to learn to trust me. The fastest learners will be ready by the end of the week, the rest will take up to two. They'll catch up sooner than you expect, Sonea.'

She nodded. Taking a spoonful of powder from a jar, she mixed it with hot water from a jug. The pungent smell of raka reached Rothen's nose. He grimaced as she drank it, wondering how she could stomach the stimulant. He had persuaded her to try sumi, the drink popular in the Houses, but she had not acquired a taste for it.

Sonea drummed her fingernails against the side of the cup. 'Issle said something strange, too. She said male teachers shouldn't teach female novices.'

'Is this Issle an Elyne girl?'

'Yes.'

'Ah,' he sighed. 'The Elynes. They're fussier than Kyralians about the interaction of young girls with boys.

45

They insist that their daughters are taught by women, and are so shocked if they see a girl of any race taught by a man, that we've adopted this "rule" for all female novices. Ironically, they're quite open-minded about the activities of adults.'

'Shocked.' Sonea nodded. 'Yes, that's how she seemed.'

Rothen frowned. 'It might have been wiser to let her assume I'd brought in a female teacher for you. Elynes can be very judgmental about things like that.'

'I wish you'd told me that before. She was friendly at first but . . .' Sonea shook her head.

'She'll forget about it,' he assured her. 'Give it time, Sonea. In a few weeks you'll have a few companions, and you'll be wondering why you were so worried.'

She looked down at her cup of raka. 'I'd settle for just one.'

In the large, dimly lit office of the Guild Administrator a globe of magical light floated back and forth, sending shadows marching across the walls. As Lorlen reached the end of the letter he stopped pacing and muttered a curse.

'Twenty gold a bottle!'

Striding back to his chair, he sat down, opened a box and lifted out a sheet of thick paper. The decisive scratching of his pen filled the room as he wrote. He paused now and then, narrowing his eyes as he considered his words. Signing the letter with a flourish, he sat back and regarded his work.

Then, with a sigh, he dropped it into the waste box under his desk.

Suppliers of the Guild had been taking advantage of the King's money for centuries. Any item was two or three times the usual price when the buyer was the Guild. It was one of the reasons the Guild grew its own medicinal plants.

Placing his elbows on the table, Lorlen rested his chin on his palm and reconsidered the price list in the letter from the wine maker. He could simply neglect to order any of the wine. It would have political consequences of course, but none that couldn't be avoided if he purchased other goods from the same House.

But the wine was Akkarin's favourite. Made from the tiniest variety of vare berries, it was sweet and rich in flavour. The High Lord always kept a flask in his guestroom, and he would not be pleased if supplies of it ran out.

Lorlen grimaced and reached for a new sheet of paper. Then he paused. He should not be pandering to Akkarin's whims like this. It had never been his habit in the past. Akkarin might notice the change. He might wonder why Lorlen was acting so out of character.

But Akkarin must surely have noticed that Lorlen rarely dropped by for an evening chat these days. Lorlen frowned as he considered how long it had been since he had gathered the courage to visit the High Lord. Too long.

Sighing, he rested his forehead in his hands and closed his eyes. *Ah, Sonea. Why did you have to reveal his secret to me?* The memory ran through his mind. Sonea's memory, not his own, but the details were still vivid . . .

'It is done,' Akkarin said, then removed his cloak to reveal bloodstained clothes. He looked down at himself. *'Did you bring my robes?'*

At the servant's mumbled answer, Akkarin pulled off his beggar's shirt. Beneath it was a leather belt strapped to his waist

47

from which a dagger sheath hung. He scrubbed himself down, then moved out of sight and returned wearing his black robes. Reaching for the sheath, he removed a glittering dagger and began to wipe it on a towel. As he finished, he looked up at the servant.

'The fight has weakened me. I need your strength.'

The servant dropped to one knee and offered his arm. Akkarin ran the blade over the man's skin, then placed a hand over the wound . . .

Lorlen shuddered. Opening his eyes, he drew in a deep breath and shook his head.

He wished he could dismiss Sonea's memory as a misinterpretation of something innocent by someone who had believed magicians were bad and cruel, but memories that clear could not be false – and how could she have made it all up when she had not understood what she had seen? He almost smiled at her assumption that the blackrobed magician was a secret Guild assassin. The truth was far worse and, no matter how much Lorlen wanted to, he could not ignore it.

Akkarin, his closest friend and High Lord of the Guild, was practising black magic.

Lorlen had always felt a quiet pride that he belonged to, and now managed, the largest united alliance of magicians that had ever existed. Part of him was outraged that the High Lord, who should represent all that was respectable and good in the Guild, was dabbling in forbidden, evil magic. That part of him wanted to reveal the crime, to remove this potentially dangerous man from such a position of influence and authority.

But another part also recognised the danger of attempting to face the High Lord. It urged caution. Lorlen shuddered again as he recalled a day, many years before, when the trials had been held to select a new High Lord. In a test of strength, Akkarin had not only bested the most powerful magicians in the Guild but, in an exercise designed to find his limits, had easily withstood the combined strength of over twenty of the most powerful magicians.

Akkarin had not always been so strong. Lorlen, of all magicians, knew this well. They had been friends since their first day at the University. Over the years of their training they had fought many times in the Arena, and found their limits were similar. Akkarin's powers had continued to grow, however, so that by the time he returned from his travels he had far surpassed any other magician.

Now Lorlen wondered if this growth had been natural. Akkarin's journey had been a search for knowledge about magic from ancient times. He had spent five years travelling the Allied Lands, but when he returned, thin and despondent, he claimed the knowledge he had gathered had been lost during the final stage of the journey.

What if he *had* discovered something? What if he'd discovered black magic?

And then there was Takan, the man Sonea had seen assisting Akkarin in his underground room. Akkarin had adopted Takan as his servant during his travels, and had kept the man's services after his homecoming. What was Takan's role in this? Was he Akkarin's victim or accomplice?

The thought that the servant might be an unwilling victim was distressing, but Lorlen could not question the man without revealing his own knowledge of Akkarin's crime. It was too great a risk.

Lorlen massaged his temples. For months he had been

thinking around in circles, trying to decide what to do. It was possible that Akkarin had simply dabbled in black magic out of curiosity. Little was known about it, and there were obviously ways of using it that did not involve killing. Takan was still alive and going about his duties. It would be a terrible betrayal of their friendship if Lorlen revealed Akkarin's crime and caused him to be removed, or even executed, for what might be merely an experiment.

Then why had Akkarin been wearing bloodstained clothes when Sonea had seen him?

Lorlen grimaced. Something ugly had happened that night. '*It is done,*' Akkarin had said. A task fulfilled. But what – and why?

Perhaps there was a reasonable explanation. Lorlen sighed. *Perhaps I just wish there was.* Was his hesitation to act simply a reluctance to discover that his friend was guilty of terrible crimes, or a reluctance to see the man he had admired and trusted for so many years transform into a bloodthirsty monster?

In any case, he could not ask Akkarin. He had to find another way.

In the last few months he had compiled a mental list of information he needed. Why was Akkarin practising black magic? How long had this been going on? What could Akkarin do with this black magic? How strong was he and how could he be defeated? Though Lorlen would be breaking a law by seeking information about black magic, the Guild needed to know the answers to these questions if it was to confront Akkarin.

He'd had little success finding information in the Magicians' Library, but that came as no surprise. The Higher Magicians were taught enough about black magic to be able to recognise it; the rest of the Guild knew only that it was forbidden. Further information should not be easily found.

He needed to look further afield. Lorlen had immediately thought of the Great Library in Elyne, a store of knowledge even larger than that of the Guild's. Then he remembered that the Great Library had been Akkarin's first stop on his journey, and he began to wonder if he might find some answers by retracing his friend's steps.

But he could not leave the Guild. His position as Administrator demanded constant attention and any such journey would surely attract Akkarin's curiosity. Which meant that another must go in his place.

Lorlen had carefully considered who might be trusted with such a task. It had to be someone sensible enough to hide the truth if necessary. It also needed to be someone adept at digging out secrets.

His choice had been surprisingly easy to make.

Lord Dannyl.

As the novices entered the Foodhall, Sonea trailed behind. Regin, Gennyl and Shern hadn't returned to class at the end of the morning lesson, so Sonea had followed the rest. The hall was a large room containing several sets of tables and chairs. Servants constantly entered from a kitchen next to it, bringing trays laden with food for the novices to select from.

None of the other novices protested as Sonea dared to join them again. A few eyed her dubiously as she picked up her cutlery, but the rest ignored her.

As on the previous day, the conversation between the novices was awkward at first. Most were shy and unsure of each other. Then Alend told Kano that he had lived in Vin for a year and the others began asking questions about the country. The questions soon included other novices' homes and families, then Alend looked at Sonea.

'So you grew up in the slums?'

All of the faces turned toward Sonea. She finished chewing and swallowed, conscious of their sudden attention.

'For about ten years,' she told them. 'I lived with my aunt and uncle. We had a room in the North Quarter after that.'

'What about your parents?'

'Mother died when I was a child. Father . . .' she shrugged. 'He went away.'

'And left you all alone in the slums? That's awful!' Bina exclaimed.

'My aunt and uncle looked after me.' Sonea managed a smile. 'And I had a lot of friends.'

'Do you see your friends now?' Issle asked.

Sonea shook her head. 'Not much.'

'What about your thief-friend, the one Lord Fergun locked up under the University? Hasn't he been back a few times?'

Sonea nodded. 'Yes.'

'He's one of the Thieves, isn't he?' Issle asked.

Sonea hesitated. She could deny it, but would they believe her?

'I can't say for sure. A lot can change in six months.'

'Were you a thief, too?'

'Me?' Sonea gave a soft laugh. 'Not everyone who lives in the slums works for the Thieves.'

The others seemed to have relaxed a little. A few even nodded. Issle glanced around at them, then scowled.

'But you stole things, didn't you?' she said. 'You were one of those pickpockets at the Market.'

Sonea felt her face warm and knew her reaction had betrayed her. They would assume she was lying if she denied it. Perhaps the truth would gain their sympathy . . .

'Yes, I stole food and money when I was a child,' she admitted, forcing herself to lift her head and stare defiantly at Issle. 'But only when I was starving, or when winter was coming and I needed shoes and warm clothes.'

Issle's eyes brightened in triumph. 'So you *are* a thief.'

'But she was a child, Issle,' Alend protested weakly. 'You would steal, too, if you had nothing to eat.'

The others turned to frown at Issle, but she tossed her head dismissively, then leaned toward Sonea and fixed her with a cold stare.

'Tell me truthfully,' she challenged. 'Have you ever killed anyone?'

Sonea returned Issle's stare and felt anger growing. Perhaps if Issle knew the truth, the girl would hesitate before hassling her again.

'I don't know.'

The others turned to stare at Sonea.

'What do you mean?' Issle sneered. 'You either have or you haven't.'

Sonea looked down at the table, then narrowed her eyes at the girl. 'All right, since you just *have* to know. One night, about two years ago, I was grabbed by a man and pulled into an alley. He was . . . well, you can be sure he wasn't about to ask for directions. When I got a hand free I stuck my knife into him and ran. I didn't hang around, so I don't know if he lived or not.'

They were silent for several minutes.

'You could have screamed,' Issle suggested.

'Do you really think anyone is going to risk their life to save some poor girl?' Sonea asked coldly. 'The man might have cut my throat to shut me up, or I might have attracted more thugs.'

Bina shivered. 'That's awful.'

Sonea felt a spark of hope at the girl's sympathy, but it fled at the next question.

'You carry a *knife*?'

Hearing the Lonmar accent, Sonea turned to meet Elayk's green eyes. 'Everyone does. For opening parcels, slicing fruit—'

'Cutting purse strings,' Issle injected.

Sonea gave the girl a level look. Issle stared back coldly. *Obviously I wasted my time helping this one*, Sonea thought.

'Sonea,' a voice suddenly called. 'Look what I saved for you.'

The novices turned as a familiar figure strolled up to the table holding a plate. Regin grinned, then thrust the plate in front of Sonea. She flushed as she saw it was covered with bread crusts and food scraps.

'You're such a generous, well-mannered boy, Regin.' She pushed the plate away. 'Thank you, but I've eaten already.'

'But you must be hungry still,' he said in mock sympathy. 'Look at you. You're so small and skinny. You really look like you could do with a good meal or three. Didn't your parents feed you properly?' He pushed the plate in front of her again.

Sonea pushed it back. 'No, actually, they didn't.'

'They're dead,' someone offered.

'Well, why don't you take it with you in case you get hungry later?' With a quick shove he pushed the plate over the edge of the table into her lap. Several titters escaped the novices as soggy food splashed over her robes and onto the floor, covering both with thick, brown sauce. Sonea cursed, forgetting Rothen's careful instructions, and Issle made a small sound of disgust.

Looking up, she opened her mouth to speak, but at that instant the University gong began to ring.

'Oh, dear!' Regin exclaimed. 'Time for class. Sorry we can't stay to watch you eat, Sonea.' He turned to the others. 'Come on, everybody. We don't want to be late, do we?'

Regin swaggered away, the others following. Soon Sonea was the only novice left in the Foodhall. Sighing, she stood up, cradling the mess, and carefully pushed the food back onto the table. Looking down at the sticky brown sauce covering her robe, she cursed again, softly.

What was she going to do now? She couldn't go to her next lesson with food stains all over her. The teacher would only send her back to her room to change, which would give Regin even more to gloat over. No, she would have to dash back to Rothen's apartments first, and think of a more mundane excuse for her late arrival.

Hoping that she wouldn't encounter too many people on the way, she set off in the direction of the Magicians' Quarters.

As Dannyl heard sailors gathering in the common room at the end of the corridor, he smothered a groan. It was going to be another long night. Once again, Jano fetched Dannyl and the crew cheered as he joined them. A bottle appeared from somewhere, and they began taking mouthfuls of the potent-smelling Vindo liquor, siyo. As it reached him, Dannyl passed it straight to Jano, earning mocking disappointment from the sailors.

Once all had taken a drink, the sailors began to argue good-naturedly in their clipped native tongue. When they finally came to an agreement, they began to sing, urging Dannyl to join in. He had given in previously, but this time he fixed Jano with a stern stare.

'You promised to translate for me.'

The man grinned. 'You not like song.'

'Let me decide that.'

Jano hesitated as he listened to the singing. 'In Capia my lover has red, red hair . . . and breasts like sacks of tenn. In Tol-Gan my lover has strong, strong legs . . . and she wraps them both around me. In Kiko my lover has . . . ah,' Jano shrugged. 'I do not know your word for that.'

'I can guess,' Dannyl replied, shaking his head sadly. 'Enough translation. I don't think I want to know what I'm singing.'

Jano laughed. 'Now you tell me why you not drink siyo, yai?'

'Siyo smells strong. Potent.'

'Siyo *is* potent!' Jano said proudly.

'It's not a good idea to get a magician very drunk,' Dannyl told him.

'Why not?'

Dannyl pursed his lips, trying to think how to explain it in terms the Vindo would understand.

'When you are drunk – very drunk – you say and do things badly, or without meaning to, yai?'

Jano shrugged and patted Dannyl's shoulder. 'No worry. We not tell anybody.'

Dannyl smiled and shook his head. 'It's not a good thing

to do magic badly, or without meaning to. It can be dangerous.'

Jano frowned, then his eyes widened slightly. 'We give you little bit of siyo, then.'

Dannyl laughed. 'Very well.'

Waving his hands, Jano signalled for the sailors to pass the bottle to him. He wiped the mouth of it with his sleeve, then offered it to Dannyl.

Finding himself being watched intently by the others, Dannyl brought the bottle to his lips and sipped. A pleasantly nutty flavour filled his mouth, then a warmth seared his throat as he swallowed. He sucked in a breath, then exhaled slowly, appreciating the spread of warmth through his body. The sailors cheered as he smiled and nodded approvingly.

Jano handed the bottle back to the others, then patted Dannyl on the shoulder. 'Me glad I not magician. To like drink but not be able to.' He shook his head. 'Very sad.'

Dannyl shrugged. 'I like magic, too.'

The sailors broke into a new song and, without Dannyl asking, Jano translated. Dannyl found himself laughing at the absurd crudity of the lyrics.

'What does *eyoma* mean?'

'Sea leech,' Jano replied. 'Bad, bad thing. I tell you story.'

At once the others quietened, all watching Jano and Dannyl with bright eyes.

'Sea leech is about size of arm from hand to bend.' Jano lifted his arm to demonstrate, pointing at his elbow. 'It swims in small groups most of time, but when breeding many sea leech come together, and very, very dangerous. Climb side of ship thinking it is rock, and sailors must kill, kill, kill or eyoma stick on them and suck out blood.'

Dannyl looked at the other sailors, and they nodded eagerly. At once he began to suspect that this tale might be false or an exaggeration – a scary story that seamen told travellers. He narrowed his eyes at Jano, but the man was too engrossed in his tale to notice.

'Sea leech suck blood from all big fish in water. If ship sinks, men try to swim to shore, but if sea leech find them, they quick be tired and die. If men fall in water while breeding season, they drown from heaviness of many sea leeches.' He looked at Dannyl, his eyes wide. 'Nasty way to die.'

Despite his scepticism, Dannyl felt a chill at the man's description. Jano patted his arm again.

'You no worry. Sea leech live in warm water. Up north. Have little more siyo. Forget story.'

Dannyl accepted the bottle and sipped modestly. One of the sailors began to hum, and soon all were singing heartily. Dannyl let them bully him into singing along, but stopped as the door to the deck opened and the captain stepped inside.

As the captain descended, the crew sang a little more quietly, but did not stop. Numo nodded to Dannyl. 'I have something to give you, my lord.'

He gestured for Dannyl to follow him, then started down the corridor toward his room. Rising, Dannyl braced himself against the swaying of the boat with a hand on either wall. As he reached Numo's door he found himself entering a room that was, contrary to Jano's claim, at least four times the size of Dannyl's.

Charts were spread across a table in the centre of the

room. Numo had opened a small cupboard and was holding a box. Drawing a key out from under his shirt, he opened the lid and took out a folded piece of paper.

'Asked to give this to you before we arrive in Capia.'

Numo handed Dannyl the paper, then gestured to a chair. Sitting down, Dannyl examined the seal. It was stamped with the Guild symbol, and the paper was of the finest quality.

Breaking the seal, he unfolded the paper and instantly recognised Administrator Lorlen's handwriting.

> *To Second Guild Ambassador to Elyne, Dannyl, of family Vorin, House Tellen.*
>
> *You must forgive me for arranging for the delivery of this letter to take place after your journey had begun. I have a task I wish you to complete for me, in addition to your duties as Ambassador. This task must remain confidential, at least for now, and this method of delivery is a small precaution to that effect.*
>
> *As you know, High Lord Akkarin left Kyralia over ten years ago to gather knowledge of ancient magic, a quest that was not completed. Your task is to retrace his steps, to revisit all the places he visited and find out who helped him in his search as well as to collect information on the subject.*
>
> *Please forward all information to me by courier. Do not communicate with me directly. I look forward to hearing from you.*
>
> *With thanks, Administrator Lorlen.*

Dannyl read the letter several times, then folded it again. What was Lorlen up to? Retracing Akkarin's journey? Communication only by courier?

He opened the letter once more and scanned it quickly. Lorlen might be asking for secrecy simply because he didn't want it known that he was taking advantage of Dannyl's ambassadorial position to deal with a private matter.

That private matter, however, was Akkarin's quest. Did the High Lord know that Lorlen was reviving the search for ancient knowledge?

He considered the possible answers to that question. If Akkarin knew, then presumably he approved. If he didn't know? Dannyl smiled wryly. Perhaps there was something akin to a sea leech in Akkarin's stories, and Lorlen wanted to know if it was true.

Or perhaps Lorlen wanted to succeed where his friend had failed. The pair had competed with each other as novices. Lorlen obviously could not resume the search himself, so he had recruited another magician to act on his behalf. Dannyl smiled. *And he has chosen me.*

Folding the letter again, he rose and braced himself against the rocking of the ship. No doubt Lorlen would reveal his reasons for secrecy eventually. In the meantime, Dannyl knew he would enjoy having permission to snoop into someone's past, particularly someone as mysterious as the High Lord.

Nodding to Numo, he left the room, stowed the letter among his belongings, and returned to Jano and the singing crew.

CHAPTER 4

ATTENDING TO DUTY

As Sonea wandered slowly down the corridor of the University, she felt a wry relief. Tomorrow was Freeday, which meant she had no lessons to attend, and for a whole day she would be free of Regin and the other novices.

She was surprised at how tired she felt, considering how little she'd done in the past week. For most of the lessons she read books or watched the novices coming and going from their Control lessons. Not much had happened, yet she felt as though weeks – no, *months* – had passed.

Issle no longer acknowledged Sonea's presence at all, and, while this was better than open hostility, it seemed all of the novices had decided this was the best way to treat her, too. None of them would speak to her, even if she asked a sensible question about their lessons.

She considered each of the novices. Elayk was everything she had been told to expect of a typical Lonmar male. Brought up in a world where women were hidden away, living a life of luxury but little freedom, he was unused to talking to them, and treated Bina and Issle with the same cold indifference. Faren, the Thief who had hidden her from the Guild last year, had been nothing like this, but then Faren was definitely not a typical Lonmar!

While Gennyl's father was Lonmar, his mother was

Kyralian and he appeared to be comfortable around Bina and Issle. He ignored Sonea, but a few times she had noticed him watching her with narrowed eyes.

Shern rarely spoke to any of the other novices, spending most of his time staring into the distance. She was still conscious of his strange magical presence, but it no longer pulsed erratically.

Bina was quiet, and Sonea suspected the girl was simply too shy and awkward to join in any conversations. When Sonea had tried to approach her, the girl had recoiled, saying: 'I'm not allowed to talk to you.' Remembering the comments the girl's mother had made before the Acceptance Ceremony, Sonea was not surprised.

Kano, Alend and Vallon behaved like boys half their age, finding the most childish things amusing and boasting about their possessions and luck with girls. Having heard this sort of banter among the boys of Harrin's gang, Sonea knew the stories about the latter had to be invented. What kept her amused was that the boys she had known would have had enough experience by this age to have stopped bragging about it years ago.

Regin dominated all social activity. Sonea noted how he controlled the others with compliments, jokes, and an authoritative-sounding comment here and there; how they would all nod whenever he expressed an opinion. This had been amusing until he had started making snide comments about Sonea's past at every opportunity. Even Alend, who had shown some sympathy for Sonea at first, laughed at these jibes. And after she had made her failed attempt to engage Bina in conversation, Regin had been at the girl's side a moment later, all charm and friendliness.

'Sonea!'

The breathless voice came from behind her. She turned to find Alend hurrying toward her.

'Yes?'

'It's your turn tonight,' he panted.

'My turn?' She frowned. 'For what?'

'Kitchen duty.' He stared at her. 'Didn't they tell you?'

'No . . .'

He grimaced. 'Of course. Regin has the roster. We all have to do kitchen duty one night a week. It's your turn.'

'Oh.'

'You'd better hurry,' he warned. 'You don't want to be late.'

'Thanks,' Sonea offered. He shrugged and strode away.

Kitchen duty. Sonea sighed. It had been stiflingly hot all day, and she had been looking forward to a cool bath before the evening meal. Chores given to novices weren't likely to be distasteful or time-consuming, however, so she might still have time.

Hurrying down the spiral stairs to the ground floor, she let the smell of cooking guide her to the Foodhall. Inside, the room was busy and seats were filling quickly as more novices arrived. She followed one of the tray-carrying servants into the kitchen and found herself in a large room lined with long benches. Steam curled up from boiling tubs, meat sizzled on grills, and the air was filled with the clatter of metal on metal. Servants hurried about, calling to each other over the noise.

Sonea stopped inside the door, overwhelmed by the chaos and the aromas. A young woman looked up from stirring a pot. She stared at Sonea, then turned and called out to another, older woman wearing a large white shirt.

As the older woman saw Sonea, she left her pot, approached Sonea and bowed.

'How may I help you, my lady?'

'Kitchen duty,' Sonea shrugged. 'They tell me I have to help out.'

The woman stared at her. '*Kitchen* duty?'

'Yes.' Sonea smiled. 'Well, here I am. Where do I start?'

'Novices never come in here,' the woman told her. 'There's no kitchen duty.'

'But—' The words died in Sonea's throat. She scowled as she realised she'd been tricked. As if the sons and daughters of the Houses would ever be expected to work in a kitchen! The woman eyed Sonea warily.

'I'm sorry to have bothered you,' Sonea sighed. 'I think I've just fallen for a joke.'

An explosive giggle broke through the noise. The woman looked around Sonea's shoulder and her eyebrows rose. Sonea turned, a sick feeling growing inside. Filling the doorway were five familiar faces, their mouths stretched into ugly grins. As Sonea looked at them, the novices burst into uncontrolled laughter.

The noise in the kitchen subsided, and she realised that several of the servants had paused to see what was happening. Heat rushed to her face. She gritted her teeth and stepped toward the door.

'Oh, no. You're not leaving,' Regin declared. 'You can stay in here with the servants, where you belong. But, now I consider it, that's not right. Even servants are better than slum dwellers.' He turned to the kitchen woman. 'I'd watch out if I were you. She's a thief – and she'll admit it if you ask. I'd watch she doesn't sneak off with one of your knives, then stab you in the back when you're not looking.'

With that he reached for the door handle and pulled it closed. Sonea strode over and twisted the handle, but while it turned easily, the door would not open. A faint vibration stirred the air about her hand.

Magic? How could they be using magic? None of them had passed the Second Level yet.

Behind the door she could hear giggles and muffled comments. She recognised Alend's voice, and Issle's laugh was unmistakable. As she noted Vallon and Kano's laughter, she realised that the only voice she wasn't hearing was Regin's.

Which was probably because he was concentrating hard on holding the door closed with magic. Her heart sank as she realised what this meant. Regin had already mastered the Second Level and more. He could not only access and draw on his power, but had learned how to use it. Rothen had warned her that some novices might achieve this quickly, but why did it have to be Regin?

Remembering the months she had spent playing and practising magic, she smiled grimly. He still had a long way to go. She stepped back and regarded the door. Could she combat his magic? Probably, but she might destroy the door. She turned to the kitchen woman.

'There must be another way out of here. Would you show me out?'

The woman hesitated. Her expression held no sympathy any more, just suspicion. The sick feeling inside Sonea turned into anger.

'Well?' she snapped.

The woman's eyes widened, then her gaze dropped to the floor.

'Yes, my lady. Follow me.'

Gesturing for Sonea to follow, the woman wove her way through the benches. The kitchen servants stared at Sonea as she passed, but she kept her eyes on the woman's back. They entered a storeroom even larger than the kitchen, filled with shelves stacked high with food and utensils. At the far end of the storeroom, the woman stopped at another door, opened it and gestured wordlessly at the corridor beyond.

'Thank you,' Sonea said, then stepped out of the room. The door closed firmly behind her. She looked up and down the corridor. It was unfamiliar, but it had to lead somewhere. She sighed, shook her head and started walking.

Evenings in the Night Room were not as interesting as they used to be, Rothen mused. Where once he had half dreaded attending the weekly social gathering for the rush of questions he was subjected to about the mysterious slum girl, now he found himself ignored.

'That Elyne girl will need watching,' a female voice said from across the room. 'From what Lady Kinla said, it won't be long before *she* needs a private talk with a Healer.'

The reply was inaudible.

'Bina? Perhaps. Or do you mean . . .? No. Who would want to? Leave it to Rothen.'

Hearing his name, Rothen searched for the speakers. He found two young Healer women standing by a window nearby. One glanced up and, seeing him watching, blushed and looked away.

'There's something strange about her. It's something . . .'

Recognising this new voice, Rothen felt a thrill of triumph. The speaker was Lord Elben, one of Sonea's teachers. Louder, closer conversations in the room threatened to overwhelm the voice, but Rothen closed his eyes and concentrated as Dannyl had taught him to.

'She doesn't fit in,' a wavering voice replied. 'But who really expected her to?'

Rothen frowned. The second speaker was the history teacher for the First Year novices.

'It's more than that, Skoran,' Elben insisted. 'She's too quiet. She doesn't even talk to the other novices.'

'They don't like her much, either, do they?'

A wry laugh. 'No, who can blame them?'

'Think of Lord Rothen,' Skoran said. 'The poor man. Do you think he knew what he was getting into? I wouldn't want her coming back to my rooms every night. Garrel was telling me that she spun some tale about knifing a man when she lived in the slums. I wouldn't want a little murderess lurking around *my* rooms while I was asleep.'

'Charming! I hope Rothen keeps his door locked during the night, in that case.'

The voices faded as the pair moved away. Rothen opened his eyes again and looked down at his glass of wine. Dannyl had been right. This chair was in a good position for listening to other magicians' conversations. Dannyl had always said that the regular Night Room attendees were too eager to express their opinions to check who might be listening, and much could be learned from them.

Unlike Dannyl, however, Rothen felt uncomfortable spying on his fellow magicians. He rose and located Skoran and Elben. Forcing a polite smile, he approached the pair.

'Good evening, Lord Elben,' he said, inclining his head in greeting. 'Lord Skoran.'

'Lord Rothen,' they replied, nodding politely in return.

'I just came to ask how my little thief is going?'

The two teachers paused, their faces blank with surprise, then Elben laughed nervously.

'She's doing well,' he said. 'In fact she's doing rather better than I expected. She learns fast and her control over her powers is quite . . . advanced.'

'She had many months in which to practice, and we haven't really tested her strength yet,' Skoran added.

Rothen smiled. Few had believed him when he had described how strong Sonea was, despite knowing that a magician had to be strong for their powers to surface of their own accord.

'I look forward to hearing your opinion when you do test her,' he said, stepping away.

'Before you go,' Skoran lifted a wrinkled hand, 'I'd like to know how well my grandson, Urlan, is progressing in chemistry.'

'Well enough.' Rothen turned back to face the magician. As he was drawn into a discussion about the boy, he made a mental note to ask Sonea how well the teachers had been treating her. Not liking a novice was never a good excuse for neglecting their training.

Pausing at the bottom of the University stairs, Administrator Lorlen regarded the night-shrouded Guild. To his right lay the Healers' Quarters, a round two-storey building standing behind tall trees within the gardens. Before it ran the road to the Servants' Quarters, winding into a dark arm of the forest that surrounded the grounds. Directly before him lay a wide, circular road that curved between the University and the gates. Stables lay to the left of this, and then another arm of the forest.

Lurking between the edge of this forest and the other side of the gardens was the High Lord's Residence. The grey stone building did not glow in the moonlight like the other, white Guild structures, but was a ghostly presence at the forest edge. It was the only building other than the Guildhall that had survived from the beginnings of the Guild's formation. For over seven centuries it had accommodated the most powerful magician of each generation. Lorlen had no doubt that the man living there now was one of the strongest magicians it had ever housed.

Taking a deep breath, he started down the path to its door.

For now, forget all that, he told himself. *He is your old friend, the Akkarin you know well. We will talk about politics, our families, and Guild matters. You'll try to persuade him to visit the Night Room, and he'll decline.*

Lorlen straightened his shoulders as he reached the residence. As always, the door opened at his knock. Stepping inside, Lorlen felt a twinge of relief as neither Akkarin nor his servant stepped forward to greet him.

He sat down and considered the guestroom. Originally, it had been an entry hall with two well-worn staircases on either side. Guestrooms had become a common feature of homes centuries after the time of the residence's construction, so previous High Lords had entertained in one of the inner rooms instead. Akkarin had modernised the building by arranging for walls to be constructed to conceal the two staircases. By filling the space between them with comfortable furniture and warm carpets, he'd created a pleasant, if narrow, guestroom.

'What's this?' a familiar voice said. 'An unexpected visitor.'

Turning, Lorlen managed to smile at the black-robed man standing in the doorway to the stairs.

'Good evening, Akkarin.'

The High Lord smiled and, after closing the door behind him, moved to a narrow cabinet holding a store of wine and a selection of glasses and silverware. He opened a bottle and filled two glasses, choosing the very wine that Lorlen had decided not to buy the previous day.

'I almost didn't recognise you, Lorlen. It has been a while.'

Lorlen lifted his shoulders. 'Our little family has been a handful of late.'

Akkarin chuckled at Lorlen's use of their pet name for the Guild. He handed Lorlen a wine glass, then sat down. 'Ah, but they keep you occupied, and you get to reward them for good behaviour now and then. Lord Dannyl was an interesting choice for the Second Guild Ambassador for Elyne.'

Lorlen felt his heart skip a beat. He masked his alarm with a frown of concern. 'Not one you would have made?'

'He is an excellent man for the role. He showed initiative and boldness by seeking and negotiating with the Thieves.'

Lorlen lifted an eyebrow. 'He should have consulted us first, however.'

Akkarin waved a hand dismissively. 'The Higher Magicians would have argued about it for weeks, then made the safest decision – and they would have made the wrong one. That Dannyl could see that, and risked the disapproval of his peers for the sake of finding her, shows that he is not easily cowed by authority when its methods are contrary to the good of others. He will need that confidence when dealing with the Elyne court. I was surprised you didn't ask my opinion, but I'm sure you knew that I'd approve of your decision.'

'What news do you have for me?' Lorlen asked.

'Nothing exciting. The King asked me if the "little rogue", as he calls Sonea, had been included in the summer intake. I told him she had, and he was pleased. That reminds me of another amusing incident: Nefin of House Maron asked if Fergun could come back to Imardin now.'

'Again?'

'This is the first time Nefin has asked. The last one to ask was Ganen, about three weeks ago. It seems every man and woman in House Maron intends to approach me about this. I've even had children ask me when they'll see uncle Fergun again.'

'So what did you tell him?'

'That uncle Fegun had done a bad, bad thing, but not to worry, as the nice men at the Fort would make sure he was well looked after for all the years he stayed there.'

Lorlen laughed. 'I meant, what did you tell Nefin?'

'Precisely the same. Well, not in exactly the same words, of course.' Akkarin sighed and smoothed his hair. 'Not only do they give me the satisfaction of refusing, but I've had no marriage proposals from House Maron since Fergun departed. That is an even better reason to keep the man tucked away in the Fort.'

Lorlen took a sip of wine. He had always assumed Akkarin was uninterested in the frivolous women of the Houses, and would eventually find a wife among the women of the Guild. But now he wondered if Akkarin had resolved to remain a bachelor to protect his dark secret.

'Both House Arran and House Korin have asked if we can spare Healers to tend their racehorses,' Akkarin said.

Lorlen gave a sigh of exasperation. 'You told them we can't, of course?'

Akkarin shrugged. 'I told them I'd think about it. There may be a way we can turn such a request to our advantage.'

'But we need every Healer we have.'

'True, but both Houses are inclined to hoard their daughters, as if they, too, were more valuable for breeding than anything else. If they could be persuaded to let the girls who have talent join us, we would eventually have more than enough Healers to replace those who leave to tend the horses.'

'In the meantime, we have fewer Healers and must expend more of our existing Healers' time training the new girls,' Lorlen argued. 'And those girls might not choose to become Healers when they graduate.'

Akkarin nodded. 'Then it is a question of balance. We must gain enough girls to ensure we eventually make up for the Healers we send to tend the horses. Ultimately, we'll have more Healers to call upon if there should be a disaster, such as a fire or riot.' Akkarin tapped the arm of his chair with his long fingers. 'There is another advantage. Lord Tepo spoke to me a few months ago about wishing to expand our knowledge of animal healing. He spoke quite persuasively. This might be a means for him to start his studies in the field.'

Lorlen shook his head. 'It sounds like a waste of Healers' time to me.'

Akkarin frowned. 'I will discuss both ideas with Lady Vinara.' He looked up at Lorlen. 'Do you have any news for me?'

'I do,' Lorlen said. He leaned back in his chair and sighed. 'Terrible news. News that will disturb many in the Guild, but will affect you personally most of all.'

'Oh?' Akkarin's gaze sharpened.

'Do you have any more of that wine you're drinking?'

'It is the last bottle.'

'Oh dear.' Lorlen shook his head. 'Then the situation is worse than I thought. I'm afraid that's the last of it. I chose not to renew our supplies. After today, no more Anuren dark for the High Lord.'

'*That's* your news?'

'Terrible, isn't it?' Lorlen turned to regard his friend. 'Are you displeased?'

Akkarin snorted. 'Of course! Why didn't you order any more?'

'They wanted twenty gold a bottle.'

'A *bottle*!' Akkarin leaned back in his chair and whistled. 'Another good decision, though this time you should have mentioned it to me first. I could have said a few words here and there in court . . . well, I still can.'

'So I'll expect a more reasonable offer to arrive on my desk in the next few weeks?'

Akkarin smiled. 'I'll see what I can do.'

They sat in silence for a moment, then Lorlen drained his glass and rose. 'I should move on to the Night Room. Are you coming?'

Akkarin's expression darkened. 'No, I have someone to meet in the city.' He looked up at Lorlen. 'It was good to see you again. Come by more often. I don't want to have to arrange meetings with you just to find out Guild gossip.'

'I'll try.' Lorlen managed a smile. 'Perhaps you should

visit the Night Room more often. You might hear some gossip yourself.'

The High Lord shook his head. 'They're all too careful when I am around. Besides, my interests lie outside the confines of the Guild. I'll leave our family scandals to you.'

Placing his wineglass on the table, Lorlen moved to the door, which opened silently. He glanced back to see Akkarin sipping wine contentedly.

'Good night,' he said.

Akkarin lifted his glass in reply. 'Enjoy yourself.'

As the door closed behind him, Lorlen drew in a deep breath, then started walking. Thinking back, he reviewed what had been said. Akkarin had expressed only approval of Dannyl's appointment – which was ironic, considering. The rest of the conversation had been relaxed and unremarkable; it was easy to forget the truth at those times. But Lorlen was always amazed how Akkarin managed to allude to his secret activities during their conversations. *'My interests lie outside the confines of the Guild.'* That was putting it mildly.

Lorlen snorted softly. No doubt Akkarin was referring to attending court and the King. *I just can't help interpreting what he says in light of what I know.*

Visiting Akkarin had never been a trial before Sonea's Hearing. Now he left the High Lord's Residence tired and relieved the ordeal was over. He thought of his bed and shook his head. He still had to sit through endless requests and questions in the Night Room before he could slip away to his rooms. Sighing, he lenghtened his stride and started through the gardens.

CHAPTER 5

USEFUL SKILLS

As Sonea waited for the class to begin, she opened her book of notes and started to read. A shadow crossed her desk, and she jumped as a hand flashed in front of her and grabbed one of the sheets of paper. She made a desperate grab for it, but was too slow. The paper was whisked away.

'Well, what do we have here?' Regin strolled to the front of the class and leaned back on the teacher's desk. 'Sonea's notes.'

She stared at him coldly. The other novices were watching him with interest. Regin scanned the page and laughed with delight.

'Look at this *writing*!' he exclaimed, holding it up. 'She writes like a *child*. Oh, and the *spelling*!'

Sonea stifled a groan as he started to read, and made a great show of his 'struggle' to decipher words. After a few sentences, he stopped and puzzled aloud over their meaning. She heard several half-smothered laughs and felt her face beginning to burn. Regin grinned and began exaggerating the spelling mistakes on the page by pronouncing each word literally, and the room began to echo with unrestrained laughter.

Placing an elbow on the table before her, Sonea rested her chin in her hand and tried to look unconcerned, while her entire body turned hot, then cold, over and over, as anger and humiliation overtook each other.

Regin straightened suddenly and hurried back to his seat. As the laughter faded, the sound of footsteps could be heard. A purple-robed figure appeared in the doorway. Lord Elben peered down his long nose at the class, then moved to his seat and placed a wooden box on the table.

'Fire,' he began, 'is like a living creature and, like a living creature, it has needs.'

He opened the box and lifted out a candle and a small dish. With a quick stab, he speared the candle onto a spike in the centre of the dish.

'Fire needs air and food, just as all creatures do. Don't assume that it *is* a creature.' He chuckled. 'That is foolish, but do keep in mind that it often behaves as though it has a mind of its own.'

Behind her someone choked back a laugh. Sonea turned her head. In the corner of her eye she saw Kano pass something to Vallon, and her stomach turned. Unseen by Lord Elben, her handwriting was entertaining the entire class.

Slowly, she drew in a deep breath and sighed quietly. The second week of lessons showed no improvement on the first. All of the novices – except Shern, who had disappeared completely after a strange outburst in which he claimed to have been seeing sunlight coming through the ceiling – now gathered around Regin at every opportunity. It was clear that she was not welcome in this little gang, and that Regin intended to make her the butt of all his jokes and pranks.

She was the outcast. But unlike the boys who had tried and failed to be accepted in Harrin's gang, she could not find somewhere else to go. She was stuck with them.

So she had adopted the only defence she could think of: ignoring them. If she didn't entertain Regin and the others by reacting to their jibes, they would eventually grow bored and leave her alone.

'Sonea.'

She jumped and found Lord Elben frowning at her in disapproval. Her heart began to pound. Had he spoken to her? Had she been so engrossed in self-pity that she hadn't heard him? Would he chastise her in front of the class?

'Yes, Lord Elben?' she said, bracing herself for further humiliation.

'You will make the first attempt to light this candle,' he said. 'Now, I'll remind you that the production of heat is easier when . . .'

Relieved, Sonea focussed her will on the candle. She could almost hear Rothen's voice as his instructions repeated in her mind. *Draw a little magic, extend your will, focus your mind on the wick, shape the magic and release it . . .* She felt a sliver of her power jump to the wick and a flame spluttered into life.

Lord Elben blinked at it, his mouth still open. '. . . thank you, Sonea,' he finished. He looked around the rest of the class. 'I have candles for you all. Your task this morning is to learn how to light them, then practice lighting them quickly, with as little thought as possible.'

He gathered candles from the box and set them in front of each novice. At once they began to stare at the wicks. Sonea watched, her amusement growing as she saw that no candle, not even Regin's, began to burn.

Elben returned to his desk and took out a sphere of glass filled with blue liquid. He brought it to Sonea's table and set it down.

'This is an exercise that will teach you subtlety,' he told her. 'The substance in this container is sensitive to temperature. If you heat it slowly and evenly, it will change to red. If you do not, bubbles will form, and it will take several minutes for them to dissipate. I want to see red, not bubbles. Call me when you have achieved that.'

Nodding, Sonea waited until he had moved back to his desk, then concentrated on the sphere. Unlike lighting a candle, this needed only a warming energy. Drawing in a deep breath, she shaped some magic into a gentle mist so that it would heat the glass evenly. As she released it, the liquid darkened to a deep red.

Satisfied, she looked up and found Elben in discussion with Regin.

'I don't understand,' the boy was saying.

'Try again,' Elben said.

Regin stared at the candle in his hand, his eyes narrowing to slits.

'Lord Elben?' Sonea ventured. The teacher straightened and began to turn toward her.

'So it's like focussing magic into the wick?' Regin asked, drawing Elben's attention back to him.

'Yes,' Elben said, a note of impatience entering his voice. As Regin stared at his candle again, the teacher turned to look at Sonea's sphere. He shook his head.

'Not hot enough.'

Looking down at the sphere, Sonea saw that the liquid was cooling to a purple. Frowning, she focussed her will on it again, and the purple brightened to red again.

Regin jumped in his seat, and uttered a bark of surprise and pain. His candle was gone, and his hands were coated with molten wax, which he was frantically trying to peel off. Sonea felt a smile pulling at her lips, and covered her mouth with her hand.

'Are you scalded?' Elben asked, concerned. 'You can go to the Healers if you wish.'

'No,' Regin said quickly. 'I'm fine.'

Elben's brows rose. He shrugged, then collected another candle and set it on Regin's desk. 'Back to work,' he snapped at the rest of the class, who were staring at Regin's reddened hands.

Elben moved to Sonea's desk, then looked down at the sphere and nodded.

'Go on,' he said. 'Show me.'

Once again, Sonea concentrated on the sphere, and the liquid warmed. Elben nodded, satisfied. 'Good. I have another exercise for you.' As he returned to the box, she saw Regin watching her. A smile pulled at her lips again, and she saw his hands clench. Then Elben rapped on the boy's table as he passed.

'Back to work, *all* of you.'

Leaning on the deck railing, Dannyl breathed in the salty air with relish.

'Sick belly not so bad outside, yai?'

He turned to find Jano approaching, the little man walking along the rocking deck with ease. As Jano reached the railing, he turned and braced his back against it.

'Magicians not get sick on boats,' Jano observed.

'We do,' Dannyl admitted. 'But we can Heal it away. It takes concentration, though, and we can't keep our minds on it all the time.'

'So . . . you not feel sick when you think about not

feeling sick, but you not be able to think about not feeling sick always?'

Dannyl smiled. 'Yes, that's right.'

Jano nodded. From high on the mast, one of the crew rang a bell and called out a few words in the Vindo tongue.

'Did he say Capia?' Dannyl asked, turning to look up.

'Capia, yai!' Jano swung around and stared into the distance, then pointed. 'See?'

Dannyl gazed in the direction his companion was pointing, but could see nothing but a spray-clouded line of nondescript coast. He shook his head.

'You have better eyes than me,' he said.

'Vindo have good eyes,' Jano agreed proudly. 'Why we are sea-riders.'

'Jano!' a stern voice bellowed.

'Must go.'

Dannyl watched the Vindo sailor hurry away, then turned to regard the coast again. Still unable to see the capital of Elyne, he looked down and watched the bow cutting through the waves, then let his gaze wander over the surface of the water. Throughout the voyage he had found the constant ripple of the water soothing and quite hypnotic, and had been fascinated by the way it changed colour depending on the time of day, and the weather.

When he looked up again the land was closer, and he could see rows of tiny pale squares above the shore – distant buildings. A shiver ran over his skin, and he felt his heartbeat quicken. He drummed his fingers on the railing as he watched the coast drawing closer.

A large gap between the buildings proved to be the entrance to a bay, well protected from the pounding waves of the sea. The houses were sprawling mansions, surrounded by walled gardens that descended in levels to a white beach. All were constructed of a pale yellow stone that glowed warmly in the morning light. As the ship drew level with the bay entrance, Dannyl caught his breath. The houses on either side formed the arms of a city that embraced the entire bay. Within, he could see grander buildings rising above a high sea wall. Domes swelled behind them and towers rose toward the sky, some linked by great stone archways.

'The captain want you to stand by him, my lord.'

Dannyl nodded at the crewman who had addressed him, then made his way along the deck, to where the captain was standing by a large wheel. The sailors were hurrying about, checking ropes and tossing Vindo words to each other.

'You asked for me, captain?'

The man nodded. 'Just want you to stand here, out of way, my lord.'

Positioning himself where Numo had pointed, Dannyl watched as the man stared alternately at the coast, then the sea. Then Numo bellowed an order in his native tongue and began turning the wheel. At once the crew leapt into action. Ropes were pulled. The sails swung about, falling limp as they no longer caught the wind. The ship rocked and tilted as it turned toward the coast.

Then the sails billowed and snapped, filling with wind again. The crew bound ropes into new positions, called confirmations to each other, and settled down to wait.

When they had sailed considerably closer to the coast, the scene was repeated again. This time the ship took them through the entrance of the bay. The captain turned to regard Dannyl.

'You been to Capia before, my lord?'

Dannyl shook his head. 'No.'

Numo turned and nodded at the city. 'Pretty.'

Simple facades of arches and columns were visible now. Unlike the mansions of Kyralia, few of the buildings bore elaborate decoration, though some towers and domes were sculpted into subtle spiral or fan-like patterns.

'Better when sun sets,' Numo told him. 'You hire boat one night and see it.'

'I will,' Dannyl replied quietly. 'I definitely will.'

The captain's mouth twitched into the closest expression of a smile that Dannyl had seen so far. It vanished quickly as the man began shouting orders again. Sails were rolled at their base to make them smaller. The ship slowed, drifting toward a gap between the thousands of watercraft that were anchored in the bay. Ahead, several ships were moored at the high sea wall.

'You get things from room now,' Numo said, glancing over his shoulder at Dannyl. 'We arrive soon, my lord. Send man to tell your people you here. They come get you.'

'Thank you, captain.' Dannyl walked down the deck and below to his cabin. As he tidied his room and checked his bag he felt the ship slow and swing about. Muffled orders reached him through the roof, then everything shuddered as the hull met the wall of the wharf.

When he climbed out onto the deck again, the crew were lashing the ship to heavy iron rings on the wall. Large, bulging sacks hung from the side of the ship, protecting it from the wharf. A narrow walkway ran along the side of the wall with stairs at either end leading up to the top.

The captain and Jano stood together beside the rail.

'You can be on your way now, my lord,' Numo said, bowing. 'It was honour to transport you.'

'Thank you,' Dannyl replied. 'It was an honour riding with you, Captain Numo,' he added in Vindo. 'Sail well.'

Numo's eyes widened slightly in surprise. He bowed stiffly, then strode away.

Jano grinned. 'He like you. Magicians not try be polite our way.'

Dannyl nodded. That didn't surprise him. As four sailors appeared with Dannyl's chests, Jano gestured for Dannyl to follow, then they walked across the plank down to the walkway. Dannyl stopped after a few steps, disconcerted by the way the wall seemed to sway and rock under his feet. He stepped aside so that the crewmen carrying the chests could pass. Jano looked back and, noticing Dannyl's puzzled expression, laughed.

'You must get your legs used to land again,' he called. 'Not take long.'

With a hand to the wall, Dannyl followed the sailors along the walkway and up the stairs. At the top he found himself beside a wide, busy road running along the edge of the wharf. The sailors set down the chests then perched themselves on the wall, apparently pleased to be doing nothing but watching the traffic.

'We had good journey,' Jano said. 'Good wind. No storm.'

'No sea leeches,' Dannyl added.

Jano laughed and shook his head. 'No eyoma. They swim in north seas.' He paused. 'You good man to practice speaking this language with. Learn many new words.'

'I've learned a few Vindo words, too,' Dannyl replied. 'Not many I could speak in the Elyne court, but they will come in handy if I should ever visit a Vindo drinking house.'

The little man grinned. 'If you come to Vin, you welcome to stay with Jano's family.'

Dannyl turned to regard the man, surprised. 'Thank you,' he said.

Pointing to the traffic, Jano narrowed his eyes. 'Your people coming, I think.'

Following his gesture, Dannyl searched for a black carriage with Guild symbols painted on the sides, but saw none. Jano took a step toward the stairs.

'I will go now. Sail well, my lord.'

Dannyl turned to smile at the man. 'Sail well, Jano.'

The sailor grinned, then hurried down the stairs. Turning back to the street, Dannyl frowned as a carriage of polished red wood stopped in front of him, blocking his view. Then realisation dawned as a sailor from the ship leapt down from the driver's seat and began helping the other crewmen load the chests onto a shelf at the back of the vehicle.

The carriage door opened and a richly dressed man climbed out. For a moment Dannyl was taken aback. He had seen Elyne courtiers before, and had been relieved that he would not have to adopt the ridiculous finery that was fashionable in the Elyne court. Yet he had to admit that the elaborate, close-fitting garb suited this handsome young man. *With such a face as that*, Dannyl mused, *this one must be a favourite among the ladies*.

The man took a hesitant step forward. 'Ambassador Dannyl?'

'Yes.'

'I am Tayend of Tremmelin.' The man bent into a graceful bow.

'I'm honoured to meet you,' Dannyl replied.

'I am *most* honoured to meet you, Ambassador Dannyl,' Tayend replied. 'You must be tired after your journey. I will take you directly to your house.'

'Thank you.' Dannyl wondered why this man had been sent in place of servants, and looked at Tayend closely. 'Are you from the Guild House?'

'No,' Tayend smiled. 'I am from the Great Library. It was arranged by your Administrator that I meet you here.'

'I see.'

Tayend gestured to the door of the carriage. 'After you, my lord.'

Climbing aboard, Dannyl breathed a little sigh of appreciation for the luxurious interior. After so many days living in a tiny cabin, with little privacy or comforts, he was looking forward to a bath and something more sophisticated than soup and bread.

Tayend settled on the opposite seat, then knocked on the roof to signal the driver. As the carriage pulled away from the wharf, Tayend's gaze slid to Dannyl's robes, then flitted away. He looked out of the window, swallowed audibly, then rubbed his hands on his trousers.

Suppressing a smile at the man's nervousness, Dannyl considered all he had learned of the Elyne court. He hadn't heard of Tayend of Tremmelin, though he had read of others from the family.

'What is your position in court, Tayend?'

The young man made a dismissive gesture. 'Only a minor one. I avoid it, mostly, and it avoids me.' He glanced at Dannyl, then smiled self-consciously. 'I am a scholar. The Great Library is where I spend most of my time.'

'The Great Library,' Dannyl repeated. 'I have always wanted to see it.'

Tayend's face lit with a wide smile. 'It is a marvellous place. I will take you there tomorrow, if you wish. I've found that magicians appreciate books in a way that most courtiers never do. Your High Lord spent many weeks there once – long before he became High Lord, of course.'

Dannyl looked at the young man, his pulse quickening. 'Did he really? What could have interested him so much?'

'All sorts of things,' Tayend replied, his eyes bright. 'I was his assistant for some days. Irand – the head librarian – couldn't keep me out of the library when I was a boy, so he employed me to fetch and carry. Lord Akkarin read all the oldest books. He was looking for something, but I never found out exactly what it was. It was such a mystery. One day he didn't arrive at his usual time, or the next day, so we asked after him. He had packed up and left all of a sudden.'

'How interesting,' Dannyl mused. 'I wonder if he had found what he was looking for.'

Tayend glanced out of the window. 'Ah! We're almost at your house. Would you like me to collect you tomorrow – oh, you'll want to go to court first, won't you?'

Dannyl smiled. 'I will take you up on your offer, Tayend, but I cannot say when. Shall I send a message when I know?'

'Of course.' As the carriage rolled to a halt, Tayend unlatched the door and pushed it open. 'Just send a note to the Great Library – or just come. I'm always there during the day.'

'Very well,' Dannyl said. 'Thank you for collecting me from the wharf, Tayend of Tremmelin.'

'It was an honour, my lord,' the young man replied.

Dannyl climbed out of the carriage and found himself standing in front of a wide, three-storey house. Columns, bridged by arches, supported a deep verandah. The space between the middle columns was wider than the rest, and the verandah there curved upward to form an arch reminiscent of the University entrance. Beyond was a replica of the University doors.

Four servants had removed the chests from the carriage. Another stepped forward and bowed.

'Ambassador Dannyl. Welcome to the Guild House of Capia. Please follow me.'

From behind, Dannyl heard a cultured voice repeat the title in a whisper. He resisted turning to look at Tayend; instead he smiled to himself and followed the servant into the house. The young scholar was obviously more than a little awed by magicians.

Then he sobered. Tayend had met and assisted Akkarin ten years before. Lorlen had arranged for the scholar to meet him. Coincidence? He doubted it. Lorlen obviously intended for Dannyl to enlist Tayend's help for his research into ancient magic.

In the little garden the scent of flowers was almost unbearably sweet. A tiny fountain pattered somewhere in the background, hidden by the night shadows. Lorlen brushed away the petals that had fallen onto his robes.

The couple sitting on the opposite bench were distant relations and members of the same House as Lorlen. He had grown up with their eldest son, Walin, before entering the Guild. Though Walin lived in Elyne now, Lorlen liked to visit his old friend's parents now and then, especially when Derril's garden was at its best.

'Barran is doing well,' Velia said, her eyes shining in the torchlight. 'He's sure he'll be promoted to captain next year.'

'Already?' Lorlen replied. 'He has accomplished a lot in the last five years.'

Derril smiled. 'He certainly has. It's good to see our youngest has become such a responsible man – despite Velia spoiling him so much.'

'I don't spoil him any more,' she protested. Then she sobered. 'I'll be relieved when he no longer has to patrol the streets, though,' she added, her smile suddenly gone.

'Hmmm.' Derril looked at his wife and frowned. 'I must agree with Velia. Every year the city becomes more dangerous. These recent murders are enough to make even the bravest man lock his doors at night.'

Lorlen frowned. 'Murders?'

'You haven't heard?' Derril's eyebrows rose. 'Why, the whole city's in a stir about them.'

Lorlen shook his head. 'I might have been told, but events in the Guild have occupied my mind lately. I haven't paid much attention to city matters.'

'You should poke your head out of that place more often,' Derril said disapprovingly. 'I'm surprised you haven't taken an interest in this. They say it's the worst set of murders seen in the city for over a hundred years. Velia and I know more about them, of course, because of Barran.'

Lorlen smothered a smile. Not only did Derril relish telling people the 'secret' information that his son passed on, but he enjoyed being the first to know anything. It must have been satisfying indeed for him to be the first to inform the Administrator of the Magicians' Guild of these crimes.

'You had better tell me about them then – before anyone else realises my ignorance,' Lorlen prompted.

Derril leaned forward and placed his elbows on his knees. 'What is chilling about this murderer is that he performs some kind of ritual as he kills his victims. A woman witnessed one of the murders two nights ago. She had been packing clothes away when she heard her employer struggling with a stranger. When she realised the pair were coming into the room, she hid inside a cupboard.

'She said that the stranger tied up her employer, then took out a knife and cut off his shirt. He made small cuts on the man's body, five on each shoulder.' Derril splayed his fingers over his shoulder. 'Those cuts are how the Guard knows it's the same man doing the murders. The woman said the murderer placed his fingers over the cuts and started chanting under his breath. When he was finished whatever he was saying, he cut the man's throat.'

Velia made a noise of disgust, then rose. 'Excuse me, but this gives me the chills.' She hurried inside.

'The servant said something else,' Derril added. 'She said she thought the man was dead before his throat was cut. Barran says the cuts on the man's shoulders weren't enough to kill anybody, and there was no sign of poison. I think he has decided that the man passed out. I'd be half dead with fright, myself . . . are you all right, Lorlen?'

Lorlen forced his rigid facial muscles into a smile. 'Yes,' he lied. 'I just can't believe I haven't heard about this yet. Did the woman give a description of the murderer?'

'Nothing useful. She said it was difficult to see because it was dark and she was watching through a keyhole, but that the man had dark hair and was dressed in shabby clothes.'

Lorlen drew in a deep breath and let it out slowly. 'And chanting, you said. How strange.'

Derril grunted in agreement. 'Until Barran joined the Guard, I had no idea the world held such crooked and disturbed people. The things some people do!'

Thinking of Akkarin, Lorlen nodded. 'I'd like to know more about this. Will you tell me if you hear anything?'

Derril grinned. 'I've caught your interest, haven't I? Of course I will.'

CHAPTER 6

AN UNEXPECTED PROPOSAL

Rothen looked up in surprise as Sonea entered the room. 'Back already?' His eyes slid to her robes. 'Oh. What happened?'

'Regin.'

'Again?'

'All the time.' Sonea dropped her book of notepaper on the table. It made a squelching noise and a small puddle of water began to form around it. Opening it, she found that all her notes were saturated, the ink running and mixing with the water. She groaned as she realised she would have to write them all out again. Turning away, she walked into her bedroom to change.

At the entrance to the University, Kano had leapt out and thrown a handful of food in her face. She had approached the fountain in the centre of the courtyard, planning to wash it off, but as she leaned over the pool the water had surged up over her, drenching her to the skin.

Sighing, she opened her clothes cupboard and pulled out an old shirt and a pair of trousers and changed into them. Picking up the saturated robes, she returned to the guestroom.

'Lord Elben said something interesting yesterday.'

Rothen frowned. 'Oh?'

'He said that I'm several months ahead of the class – almost as good as the winter intake of novices are.'

He smiled. 'You did have months of practice before you started.' Then his smile faded as he saw her clothes. 'You must wear your robes all the time, Sonea. You can't go to class like that.'

'I know, but I don't have any clean ones left. Tania will bring some back tonight.' She held out the dripping robes. 'Unless you could dry these for me?'

'You should be able to do that yourself by now.'

'I can, but I'm not supposed to do any magic unless—'

'—instructed by a magician,' Rothen finished. He chuckled. 'That rule is a flexible one, Sonea. Generally it's understood that, if a teacher instructs you to practice what he has taught you, you're free to do it outside of class unless he says otherwise.'

She grinned, then looked down at the robes. Steam began to mist from the material as she sent heat flowing through it. When the robes were dry, she set them aside and helped herself to a leftover sweet cake from the morning meal.

'You said once that an exceptional novice can be moved to a higher class. What would it take for me to do that?'

Rothen's eyebrows rose. 'A lot of work. You may be well practised at using magic, but your knowledge and understanding of it would need much improvement.'

'So is it possible?'

'Yes,' he said slowly. 'If we work every night and Freeday you might pass the half-year tests in a month or so, but the hard work wouldn't stop there. Once you had advanced, you would need to catch up with the winter novices. If you fail the First Year tests, you'll drop back down to the summer class again. That means you'd have to work very hard for two or three months.'

'I understand.' Sonea bit her lip. 'I want to try it.'

Rothen considered her closely, then moved to the chairs and sat down. 'So you've changed your mind, then.'

Sonea frowned, puzzled. 'Changed my mind?'

'You wanted to wait until the others had caught up.'

She waved a hand dismissively. 'Forget them. They're not worth it. Do you have the time to teach me? I don't want to take you away from your classes.'

'That won't be a problem. I'll do my preparation work while you study.' Rothen leaned forward. 'I know you're doing this to get away from Regin. I have to point out that the next class mightn't be any better.'

Sonea nodded. She dropped into a chair beside him and began to carefully separate her notes. 'I've thought about that. I don't expect them to *like* me, just to leave me alone. I've watched them when I could, and there doesn't seem to be someone like Regin among them. They have no single novice who rules them.' She shrugged. 'I can live with being ignored.'

Rothen nodded. 'You've thought about this carefully, I see. Very well. We'll do it.'

A new feeling of hope swept over Sonea. This was a second chance. She grinned at him. 'Thank you, Rothen!'

His shoulders lifted. 'I am your guardian, after all. Giving you special treatment is my role.'

Holding up the wet sheets of paper, she started drying them. The sheets curled as they dried, the ink setting the letters into grotesque smudges. She sighed again at the thought of rewriting them.

'Although Warrior Skills is not my area of expertise,'

Rothen said, 'I think you'll find it useful to know how to raise and hold a basic shield. That ought to protect you from pranks like this.'

'Whatever you say,' Sonea replied.

'And since you've already missed the start of class, you may as well stay here and learn it now. I'll tell your teacher . . . well, I'll think of a good excuse.'

Surprised and pleased, Sonea set the dried notes aside. Rothen rose and pushed the table out of the way.

'Stand up.'

Sonea obeyed.

'Now, you know that everyone, magicians and nonmagicians, has a natural boundary protecting the area contained by our body. No other magician can influence anything within that area without first exhausting us. Otherwise a magician could kill another simply by reaching inside and crushing the heart.'

Sonea nodded. 'The skin is the boundary. The barrier. Healing gets past it, but only by skin to skin contact.'

'Yes. Now, so far you've extended your influence like an arm, reaching out to, say, light a candle or lift a ball. A shield is like extending all of your skin outward, like inflating a bubble around yourself. Watch, and I'll make a shield that is visible.'

Rothen's gaze became distracted. His skin began to glow, then was as if a layer of it pushed outwards, smoothing and losing the contours of the body. It expanded and formed a translucent globe of light around him, then fell back inward and disappeared.

'That was a shield of light only,' he said. 'It would not have repelled anything. But it's useful to start with because it's visible. Now, I want you to make the same sort of shield, but just around your hand.'

Sonea lifted a hand and concentrated on it. Making it glow was easy – Rothen had already taught her how to create a light cool enough that it wouldn't burn anything. Focussing on her skin, she sought a sense of it as a border to the influence of her magic, then pushed outward.

At first the glow expanded in erratic bursts, but after several minutes she managed to control its growth so it spread in all directions at once. Eventually a glowing sphere surrounded her hand.

'Good,' Rothen said. 'Now try it for your whole arm.'

Slowly, with a few hesitations, the globe elongated to her shoulder, then bloated to a larger sphere.

'Now your upper body.'

It was the strangest feeling. She felt as if she had spread herself out to fill a bigger space. As she enlarged the sphere to include her head her scalp tingled.

'Very good. Now all of you.'

Bits of the sphere collapsed inward as she concentrated on her legs, but after attending to them she found herself surrounded entirely within a glowing ball. Looking down, she realised that it extended below her feet, into the floor.

'Excellent!' Rothen said. 'Now draw it back inward from all directions at once.'

Slowly, and not without a few parts collapsing sooner than others, she pulled the sphere back inward until it sat against her skin. Rothen nodded thoughtfully.

'You've got the idea,' he said. 'You just need some practice. Once you have it right, we'll work on changing the shield to basic repelling and containing ones. Now, let's see that again.'

*   *   *

As the door closed behind Sonea, Rothen gathered his books and papers. From what he had heard, Garrel's novice was a natural leader. It was unfortunate, but not unexpected, that the boy chose to strengthen his hold on the class by turning them against another novice. Sonea had been the obvious victim. Unfortunately, it had dashed all hopes of her being accepted by the rest.

He sighed and shook his head. Had he worked at stamping out her slum vocabulary and schooling her habits and mannerisms for nothing? He had assured Sonea so many times that she had only to make a friend or two and her past would be forgotten. But he had been wrong. Her classmates had not only rejected her, but had turned on her.

The teachers had not taken a liking to her, either, despite her exceptional abilities. Tales of knifings and childhood thieving were circulating, according to Rothen's elderly friend, Yaldin. The teachers could not neglect her education, however. He could make sure of that.

—*Rothen!*

Stopping, Rothen concentrated on the voice in his mind.

—*Dannyl?*

—*Hello, old friend.*

As Rothen focussed his mind on the voice it became clearer and a sense of its personality grew. He also perceived the presence of other magicians, their attention drawn by the call, fading away as they turned their minds from the conversation.

—*I was expecting a communication sooner than this. Was your ship delayed?*

—*No, I arrived two weeks ago. I haven't had a moment to spare since. The First Ambassador had arranged so many introductions and briefings I can hardly keep up. I think he's disappointed that I actually need to sleep.*

Rothen restrained himself from asking if the First Guild Ambassador to Elyne had become as portly as was rumoured. Mental communication was not completely private, and it was always possible that another magician might hear.

—Have you seen much of Capia?

—A little. It is as beautiful as they say. An image of a grand city of yellow stone, blue water and boats, came to Rothen.

—Have you been to court yet?

—No, the King's aunt died a few weeks ago and he has been in mourning. I'm visiting today. Should be interesting.

A sense of smugness followed the words, and Rothen knew his friend was thinking of all the scandal, rumour and gossip he had dug up about the people of the Elyne court before leaving Kyralia.

—How is Sonea going?

—Her teachers praise her abilities, but there is a troublemaker in her class. He has gathered the rest of the novices to his side.

—Can you do anything? There was sympathy and understanding behind Dannyl's words.

—She just proposed moving to the next class.

—Poor Rothen! That will be hard work – for both of you.

—I can manage. I only hope she doesn't find the winter novices as unfriendly.

—Give her my sympathies. Dannyl's attention wavered. *I must go now. Farewell.*

—Farewell.

Rothen gathered his books and started for the guestroom door. Remembering the unpopular, sullen novice that

Dannyl had been, he felt a little better. The situation might be tough for Sonea now, but it would work itself out in the end.

'Tayend of Tremmelin, eh?' Errend, the First Guild Ambassador to Elyne shifted in his seat, his impressive stomach cinched by the sash over his robes. 'He's the youngest son of Dem Tremmelin. A scholar of the Great Library, I believe. Don't see him in court much – though I have seen him with Dem Agerralin. Now *there's* a man of dubious associations.'

Dubious associations? Dannyl opened his mouth to ask the Ambassador to elaborate, but the big man was distracted as the carriage swung about.

'The Palace!' he exclaimed, gesturing to the window. 'I will introduce you to the King, then it is up to you to socialise as you please. I have an appointment that will fill most of the afternoon, so feel free to take the carriage back when you've had enough. Just remind the driver to return at dusk for me.'

The carriage door opened and Dannyl followed Errend out. They stood at one side of a large courtyard. Before them was the Palace, a sprawling structure of domes and balconies standing at the top of a long, wide staircase. Grandly dressed people were making their way up the stairs, or resting on stone seats placed at intervals for this purpose.

Turning back to his companion, Dannyl found Errend floating just above the ground beside him. The First Ambassador smiled at Dannyl's expression of astonishment.

'No sense in walking if you don't have to!'

As the man floated up the stairs, Dannyl examined the faces of the courtiers and servants about him. They did not appear surprised by this use of magic, though some glanced at the Ambassador and smiled. While a man of bulk and cheerful character, Errend was obviously also a strong and skilled magician. Impressed, yet reluctant to draw attention to himself in such a flamboyant manner, Dannyl decided to use his legs instead.

He found Errend waiting at the top. The man gestured expansively away from the Palace.

'Look at that view! Isn't it wonderful?'

Still breathing deeply from the climb, Dannyl turned around. The entire bay spread before him. The pale yellow buildings shone in the sunlight, and the water was a lustrous blue.

'"A necklace for a King", the poet Lorend once said.'

'It is a beautiful city,' Dannyl agreed.

'Full of beautiful people,' Errend added. 'Come inside. I will introduce them to you.'

Another arched facade stood before them, the grandest Dannyl had yet seen. The arches were several times the height of a man, low at each side, and soaring high at the centre. Behind the tallest arch a doorless entrance offered access to the Palace.

Six stiff-backed guards eyed Dannyl as he followed Errend into a cavernous room. The interior was vast and airy. Fountains and stone sculptures had been placed at intervals along either side, and arched doorways between them led to further rooms and corridors. Plants draped from alcoves in the walls or sprouted from huge pots standing on the stone floor.

Errend started down the centre of the room. Groups of

men and women stood or strolled about, some with children. All were dressed in sumptuous clothing. As Dannyl passed they examined him with curiosity, the closest bowing gracefully.

He glimpsed Guild robes here and there: women in green, men in red or purple. To the magicians who looked his way and nodded, he inclined his head politely in return. Guards dressed in uniform stood at every doorway, watching all attentively. Individual musicians wandered about, playing stringed instruments and singing quietly. A messenger raced by, his face shining with sweat.

At the end of the hall, Errend passed through another arch into a smaller room. Opposite the arch stood a pair of doors decorated with the Elyne King's mark: a fish leaping over a bunch of grapes. A guard bearing the same mark on his breastplate stepped forward to ask for Dannyl's name.

'Lord Dannyl, Second Guild Ambassador for Elyne,' Errend replied.

It does sound grand, Dannyl thought. He felt a stirring of excitement as he followed Errend across the room. Two courtiers were shooed off a large cushioned bench, and the guard indicated the magicians should sit. Errend settled down with a sigh.

'This is where we wait,' he said.

'How long?'

'As long as it takes. Our names will be whispered to the King as soon as he finishes with his current audience. If he wishes to see us straightaway, we will be called. If he doesn't,' Errend shrugged and waved at the people in the room, 'we wait our turn, or we go home.'

Feminine voices and laughter filled the room. A group of women sitting on a bench opposite Dannyl's were listening to the murmuring of a brightly dressed musician sitting cross-legged on the floor at their feet. An instrument lay across the man's knees, and he was running his fingers across the strings to produce an idle trickle of notes. As Dannyl watched, the man turned to croon something to one of the women, and she put a hand to her mouth to cover her smile.

As if sensing that he was being watched, the man looked up and met Dannyl's gaze. He rose in one graceful movement and began plucking at the strings, coaxing out a melody. To Dannyl's amusement, what he'd assumed was a shirt was actually a strange belted costume with a short skirt, and the musician's legs were covered in brightly painted yellow and green stockings.

'*A man in a robe. A man in a robe.*
The man in the robe, is in our abode.'

The musician danced across the room, stopping in front of the bench. Bending slightly, the musician crossed his eyes at Dannyl.

'*A man in a dress. A man in a dress.*
The man in the dress, will cause him distress.'

Unsure how to react to this, Dannyl looked questioningly at Errend. The Ambassador was watching with bored tolerance. The musician spun about and struck a dramatic pose.

'*A man with a belly. A man with a belly . . .*'

The musician paused and sniffed the air.

'*. . . the man with the belly, has a nice smelly.*'

Errend's mouth twitched into a half-smile as a scattering of laughter came from around them. The musician bowed, then spun on his heel and raced back across the room to the women.

'In Capia my lover has red, red hair, and eyes like the deepest sea,' he sang in a sweet, rich voice. *'In Tol-Gan my lover has strong, strong arms and she winds them both around me.'*

Dannyl chuckled. 'I've heard another version of this song sung by Vindo sailors, but it would not be at all acceptable to the ears of those young ladies.'

'No doubt the song you heard was the original, sweetened here for the court,' Errend replied.

The musician presented his instrument to one of the ladies with great ceremony, then began performing backflips. 'What a strange man,' Dannyl said.

'He practises the art of flattery with the aim to insult.' Errend waved a hand dismissively. 'Just ignore him. Unless, of course, you do find him entertaining.'

'I do, though I'm not sure why.'

'You'll get over it. He once—'

'The Guild Ambassadors for Elyne,' boomed the voice of the King's guard.

Errend rose and strode across the room, Dannyl following a step behind. The guard gestured for them to wait, then disappeared behind the door.

Dannyl heard Errend's title called, then his own. There was a pause, then the guard returned and ushered them through.

The audience chamber was smaller than the previous room. Two tables stood on either side, and at them sat several men of middle to late years – the King's advisers. In the centre was another table, with documents, books, and a plate of sweets arranged on it. Behind this central table, in a large cushioned chair, sat the King. Two magicians stood behind him, their watchful eyes noting every movement in the room.

Following Errend's example, Dannyl stopped and dropped to one knee. It had been many years since he had knelt before a King – and he had been only a child, brought to the Kyralian court with his father as a rare treat. As a magician, he took it for granted that all but other magicians would bow to him. Though he did not feel a great desire to have people make such an obeisance to him, if they didn't he felt oddly slighted, as if common courtesy had been breached. Gestures of respect were important even if just for the sake of good manners.

But to kneel before another was humbling, and that was an emotion he was unused to experiencing. He could not help thinking how satisfying it must be for a King at these moments, to be one of only a few people in the Allied Lands who magicians would genuflect to.

'Rise.'

Standing again, Dannyl looked up to find the King examining him with interest. At over fifty years of age, Marend's reddish-brown hair was streaked with white. His gaze, however, was alert and intelligent.

'Welcome to Elyne, Ambassador Dannyl.'

'Thank you, Your Highness.'

'How was your journey?'

Dannyl considered. 'Good winds. No storms. Pleasantly uneventful.'

The man chuckled. 'You sound like a sailor, Ambassador Dannyl.'

'It was an educational voyage.'

'And how do you plan to spend your time in Elyne?'

'When I am not dealing with the issues and requests

that come my way, I shall explore the city and surrounds. I am particularly looking forward to seeing the Great Library.'

'Of course,' the King smiled. 'Magicians seem to have a limitless hunger for knowledge. Well, it is a pleasure to meet you, Ambassador Dannyl. I'm sure we will encounter each other again. You may go.'

Dannyl inclined his head respectfully, then followed Errend to a door on one side. They entered a smaller room, where several guards stood, talking quietly. Another man in uniform ushered them through a second door into a corridor, which led to one of the side doors of the large room they had first entered.

'Well,' Errend said. 'That was quick and not very exciting, but he's had a good look at you now, and that was the point of this little trip. Now, I'm going to leave you here. Don't worry. I've arranged for somebody to – ah, here they come.'

Two women approached. They bowed with dignity as Errend introduced them. Dannyl nodded in reply, smiling as he remembered some particularly interesting gossip he had unearthed about these sisters.

As the elder sister hooked her hand under Dannyl's arm, Errend smiled and excused himself. The sisters then led Dannyl about the room, introducing him to several famous Elyne courtiers. Soon Dannyl had put faces to many of the names he'd memorised.

All of these courtiers seemed genuinely eager to meet him, and he found himself feeling almost uneasy about their interest. Finally, as the sun began to send long beams of light into the room and he saw others leaving, Dannyl decided he could excuse himself without appearing rude.

Once he had extracted himself from the sisters, he started toward the Palace entrance but before he reached it a man stepped out and addressed him.

'Ambassador Dannyl?' The man was thin, his hair cut very short, and his clothes were a dark green that was sombre compared to the colours of the rest of the Elyne court.

Dannyl nodded. 'Yes?'

'I am Dem Agerralin.' The man bowed. 'How was your first day at court?'

The man's name was familiar, but Dannyl could not remember why. 'Pleasant and entertaining, Dem. I have made many new acquaintances.'

'But I see you are on your way home.' Dem Agerralin took a step back. 'I will make you late.'

Suddenly Dannyl recalled where he'd heard the name before. Dem Agerralin was the man of 'dubious associations' that Errend had spoken of. Dannyl looked closer. The Dem was a man in his middle years he guessed. There was nothing obviously remarkable about him.

'I am in no hurry,' Dannyl said.

Dem Agerralin smiled. 'Ah, that is good. There is a question I wish to ask you, if you will allow me.'

'Of course.'

'It is a private matter.'

Intrigued, Dannyl indicated that the man should continue. The Dem seemed to consider his words, then made an apologetic gesture.

'There is little that escapes the notice of the Elyne court and, as you might have guessed already, we have a fascination for the Guild and magicians. We are all very curious about you.'

'I have noticed.'

'So it should not surprise you that certain rumours have reached us about you.'

A chill prickled Dannyl's skin. He carefully schooled his expression to one of surprise and puzzlement.

'Rumours?'

'Yes. Old ones, but ones that I and a few others have had cause to recall and reconsider since we learned you were coming to live in Capia. Do not be alarmed, my friend. Such matters are not considered as, ah, taboo here as they are in Kyralia, though it is not always wise to be too public about it. We are all very curious about you, so may I be so bold as to ask if those rumours had any truth to them?'

The man's tone was hopeful. Dannyl realised that he was staring at the man in disbelief, and forced himself to look away. If a courtier asked such a question in Kyralia, it might start a scandal that could ruin a man's honour and lower the standing of his House. In response, Dannyl ought to be outraged, and let the Dem know that such questions were inappropriate.

But the anger and bitterness he'd once felt toward Fergun for circulating such rumours had faded since the Warrior had been punished for blackmailing Sonea. And besides, though he had not found himself a wife to forever dispel those lingering suspicions, the Higher Magicians had still chosen him to be a Guild Ambassador.

Dannyl considered how he should reply. He was wary of offending the man. The Elynes must be less reserved than Kyralians, but how much? Ambassador Errend *had* called Dem Agerralin a man of 'dubious associations'. In any case, it would be foolish to make an enemy on his first day at court.

'I see,' Dannyl said slowly. 'I think I know the rumour you refer to. It seems I will never shake that one, though it's been ten – no, fifteen – years since it started. The Guild, as you must know, is a very conservative place, which is why the novice who circulated that rumour knew it would cause me great difficulties with my peers. He was prone to making up all manner of stories about me.'

The man nodded, his shoulders dropping. 'I see. Well, please forgive me for bringing up a painful subject. I had noted that the former novice you speak of is now living in the mountains – a fort, I believe. We had wondered about that one as well, since the one who denounces loudest is often most likely . . .'

Dem Agerralin let his sentence hang as the man drew near. Looking up, Dannyl was surprised to see Tayend approaching. Once again, he was impressed by the scholar's striking appearance. Dressed in dark blue, his red-blond hair tied back, Tayend looked very much at place in the court. The scholar bowed gracefully, then smiled at them both.

'Ambassador Dannyl, Dem Agerralin.' Tayend inclined his head to both of them. 'How are you, Dem?'

'Well,' the man replied. 'And you? We haven't seen you at court for a while, young Tremmelin.'

'Regrettably, my duties at the Great Library keep me away.' Tayend did not sound at all regretful. 'I'm afraid I must steal Ambassador Dannyl from you, Dem. There is a matter I need to discuss with him.'

Dem Agerralin glanced at Dannyl, his expression unreadable. 'I see. Then I must bid you goodbye, Ambassador.' He bowed, then strolled away.

Tayend waited until the man was out of hearing, then

narrowed his eyes at Dannyl. 'There's something you should know about Dem Agerralin.'

Dannyl smiled wryly. 'Yes, I think he made it clear what that is.'

'Ah.' Tayend nodded. 'And did he bring up the matter of rumours concerning yourself?' As Dannyl frowned in dismay, the scholar nodded. 'I thought he would.'

'Is *everybody* discussing this?'

'No, only a few people in certain circles.'

Dannyl wasn't sure if he should be relieved at that news. 'It's been years since those accusations were made. I'm surprised they reached the Elyne court at all.'

'You shouldn't be. The idea that a Kyralian magician might be a lad – which is the polite term here for men like Agerralin – is amusing. But don't worry. It does sound like the usual name-calling between boys. If I may say so, you're surprisingly calm, for a Kyralian. I was half afraid you'd blast poor old Agerralin to ashes.'

'I wouldn't remain Guild Ambassador for long if I did.'

'No, but you don't even seem angry.'

Again, Dannyl considered how to answer. 'When you've spent half of your life denying such rumours, you come to sympathise with the kind of person you're claimed to be. To have inclinations that are unacceptable, and to have to either deny them or undertake elaborate measures to hide them, would be a terrible way to live.'

'That is how it is in Kyralia, but not here,' Tayend said, smiling. 'The Elyne court is both awful in its decadence, and wonderful for its freedom. We expect everyone to have a few interesting or eccentric habits. We love gossip, yet we don't place too much faith in rumours. In fact, we have a saying here: "There's always a bit of truth in each rumour;

108

the trouble is finding out which bit." So, when are you coming to the library?'

'Soon,' Dannyl replied.

'I look forward to seeing you there.' Tayend took a step away. 'But for now, I have another matter to attend to. Until then, Ambassador Dannyl.' He bowed.

'Until then,' Dannyl replied.

Watching the scholar stride away, Dannyl shook his head. He had gathered rumours and speculation about the Elyne courtiers like little prizes, never thinking that they would be doing the same regarding him. Did the entire court know of the rumour that Fergun had started so many years ago? Knowing that it was still discussed made Dannyl uneasy, but he could only trust that Tayend was right, and the court would not take such stories seriously.

With a sigh, he stepped through the Palace entrance and started down the long staircase to the Guild carriage.

CHAPTER 7

THE GREAT LIBRARY

Sonea hugged her books closer to her chest. It had been yet another day of constant pranks and insults. The week loomed before her like an endless trial. Only the fifth *week*, she reminded herself. Five long *years* stood between now and graduation.

Each day was exhausting. When she wasn't enduring Regin and the other novices, she was going out of her way to avoid them. If the teacher left the classroom, even for a minute, Regin used the time to harass her. She had learned to keep her notes out of reach and to take extreme care whenever she walked across the room or sat in her chair.

For a little while she had managed to escape him for an hour each day by returning to Rothen's rooms at midbreak to eat with Tania, but Regin began ambushing her on the way to and from the University. She had tried staying in the classroom for the hour a few times, but once Regin realised what she was doing, he waited until the teacher had left and returned to harass her.

Eventually she had arranged with Rothen that she would meet him in his classroom during the midbreak. She helped him set up or dismantle the contraptions of glass vials and pipes for his lessons. Tania brought little lacquered boxes filled with savouries for them to eat.

Her stomach always sank when the gong called novices to afternoon classes. Rothen and Tania had both offered to escort her to and from classrooms, but she knew that this would only confirm to Regin and his friends that they were getting to her. At all times, she endeavoured to ignore the pranks and snide comments, knowing that reacting to them would only encourage more.

The final gong always brought relief. Whatever social games the novices indulged in after lessons must have been more interesting than taunting her, because the entire class always hurried away as soon as the teacher dismissed them. Sonea would wait until they were gone and then make her way in peace to the Magicians' Quarters. But just in case they changed their minds, she always took the long route through the gardens, choosing a different path every time and keeping close to other magicians and novices.

Today, like every day, as she neared the end of the corridor she felt her shoulders relax and the knot in her stomach begin to unwind. Silently she thanked Rothen for letting her stay in his rooms. It made her shudder to think of the torments Regin would have devised for her if she had to return to the Novices' Quarters each day.

'There she is!'

Recognising the voice, she felt cold rush over her. The corridor was full of novices from higher classes, but that had never been a deterrent. She lengthened her stride, hoping to reach the busy Entrance Hall of the University where there was sure to be a magician or two, before Regin and his friends could catch up.

The sound of running feet filled the corridor behind her.

'Sonea! Soooooneeeeeaaaa!'

The older novices about her turned at the noise. Sonea knew by their stares that Regin and his gang were right behind her now. She drew in a deep breath, resolving to face Regin without flinching.

A hand grabbed her arm and pulled her around roughly. She shook it off and glared at Kano.

'Were you ignoring us, slum girl?' Regin asked. 'That's very rude, but I guess we can't expect you to have any manners, can we?'

They encircled her. She glanced around at the grinning faces. Hugging her books closer to her body, she stepped forward and pushed her shoulder between Issle and Alend to break free from the ring of bodies. Hands reached out, grabbed her shoulders and yanked her back into the middle. Surprised, she felt a growing dread. They hadn't tried to physically abuse her before, other than giving her arm a yank to make her trip over, or fall into something unpleasant.

'Where are you going, Sonea?' Kano asked. Someone gave her another shove in the back. 'We want to talk to you.'

'Well, I don't want to talk to you,' she growled. Turning, she tried to push her way through again, but was shoved and pulled back into the circle. She felt a flash of fear. 'Let me through.'

'Why don't you beg us to, slum girl?' Regin jeered.

'Yeah, go on and beg. You must be good at it.'

'You had plenty of practice in the slums.' Alend laughed. 'Surely you haven't forgotten so quickly. I bet you were one of those snivelling brats that hang around the back of our fathers' houses begging for food.'

'Please give me some food. Pleeese!' Vallon whined. 'I'm staaaarving!' The others laughed and joined in.

'Or perhaps she had something to sell,' Issle suggested. 'Good evening, my lord.' Her voice became a suggestive wheedle. 'Need some company?'

Vallon choked back a laugh. 'Just think how many men she's had.'

Sniggers filled the corridor, and then Alend recoiled from her. 'She's probably diseased.'

'Not any more.' Regin sent Alend a knowing look. 'They told us the Healers checked her when she was found, remember? They'd have fixed her up.' He turned to Sonea and looked her up and down, his lips pursed.

'So . . . Sonea.' His voice became silky, 'How much did you *charge?*' He moved closer, and as Sonea shrank away hands pressed into her back to push her toward him again. 'You know,' he drawled. 'Perhaps I was wrong. Perhaps I *could* get to like you. You're a bit skinny, but I can overlook that. Tell me, did you specialise in any certain, ah, *favours?*'

Sonea tried to shrug away the hands on her shoulders, but the novices tightened their gip. Regin shook his head in mock sympathy. 'I suppose the magicians said you had to give it up. How frustrating for you. But they don't have to know. We won't tell them.' He tilted his head to one side. 'You could make a lot of money around here. Lots of rich customers.'

Sonea stared at him. She couldn't believe he would even pretend to be interested in bedding her. For a moment she was tempted to call his bluff, but knew if she did, he'd claim she'd taken him seriously. Over his shoulders she could see that the other novices in the corridor had stopped to watch the scene with interest.

Regin leaned closer. She could feel his breath on her

face. 'We'll just call it a business arrangement,' he crooned. He was just trying to intimidate her, and to see how much she would endure. Well, she had dealt with this kind of bullying before.

'You're right, Regin,' she said. His eyes widened in surprise. 'I have met many men like you before. And I do know exactly what to do with them.' She snaked a hand up and wrapped it tightly around his throat. His hands flew to his neck, but before he could grab her wrist she slipped a leg around his and shoved with all her strength. She felt his knee buckle and enjoyed a surge of triumph as he fell backward, arms flailing the air, and crashed onto the floor.

Silence filled the corridor as all novices, young and old, stared at him. Sonea sniffed with disdain.

'What a fine example you are, Regin. If this is how the men of House Paren behave, then they have no better manners than the average bolhouse lout.'

Regin stiffened and his eyes narrowed to slits. She turned her back at him and glared at the other novices, daring any to touch her again. They backed away and, as the circle broke, she strode through.

She had taken only a few steps when Regin's voice echoed loudly in the corridor.

'You're obviously well qualified to make such comparisons,' he called. 'How does Rothen compare? He must be a very happy man, having you living in his rooms. Ah, it all makes sense now. I always wondered how you managed to convince him to be your guardian.'

Sonea felt herself go cold, then hot anger flooded her body. She clenched her fists, resisting the urge to turn back. What could she do? Hit him? Even if she dared

114

strike the son of a House, he would see it coming, and shield. And then he would know how much he had got to her.

The quiet muttering of the older novices followed her down the corridor. She forced herself to keep her eyes on the stairs ahead, not wanting to see the speculation in their faces. They wouldn't believe what Regin had suggested. They *couldn't*. Even if they believed the worst of her because of her origins, nobody would think something like that of Rothen.

Would they?

'Administrator!'

Lorlen stopped at the University entrance and turned to face Director Jerrik. 'Yes?'

The Director approached Lorlen and handed him a piece of paper. 'I received this request from Lord Rothen yesterday. He wants to move Sonea to the winter intake of First Year novices.'

'Really?' Lorlen scanned the page, skimming through Rothen's explanations and assurances. 'Do you think she's capable?'

Jerrik pursed his lips thoughtfully. 'Possibly. I've asked the First Year teachers, and they all believe she could do it if she studied hard.'

'And Sonea?'

'She certainly seems willing to do the work.'

'Then you will allow it?'

Jerrik frowned and lowered his voice. 'Probably. What I don't like about this is the true motivation behind the change.'

'Oh? What is that?' Lorlen resisted smiling. Jerrik had

always maintained that novices never worked harder purely for the sake of learning. They were motivated by the need to impress, be the best, please their parents, or to be in the company of friends or someone they admired.

'As we expected, she hasn't mixed with the other novices well. In such circumstances, the rejected novice often becomes an object of derision for others. I believe she wants only to get away from them.' Jerrik sighed. 'While I admire her determination, my concern is that the winter class will be no more accepting. She will have worked hard for nothing.'

'I see.' Lorlen nodded as he considered Jerrik's words. 'Sonea is a few years older than the others in her class, and she is mature for her age – by our standards at least. Most novices are little more than children when they come here, but they lose most of their childish habits during the first year. The winter novices may be less troublesome.'

'True, they are a sensible group,' Jerrik agreed. 'Training in magic can't be hurried along, however. She can fill her mind with knowledge, but if she hasn't gained the skill to use her powers well, she may make dangerous mistakes later.'

'She has been using her powers for over six months,' Lorlen reminded him. 'Though Rothen spent that time teaching her the basic education she needed to enter the university, her powers would have become familiar to her – and it must be frustrating to watch the other novices fumbling with theirs.'

'So I take it you are in favour of allowing this?' He gestured to Rothen's request.

'I am.' Lorlen handed back the request. 'Give her the opportunity. I think you'll find her more resourceful than you expect.'

Jerrik shrugged. 'Then I will allow it. She will be tested in five weeks. Thank you, Administrator.'

Lorlen smiled. 'I will be interested to hear how well she does. Will you keep me informed?'

The old man nodded. 'If you wish.'

'Thank you, Director.' Lorlen turned away and started down the University stairs to the waiting carriage. He entered, tapped on the roof to signal the driver, and leaned back as the vehicle jerked into motion. It passed through the Guild Gates and rolled on into the city, but Lorlen was already too deep in thought to notice.

The invitation to dinner at Derril's house had come the day before. While Lorlen often had to decline such invitations, he had reorganised his work to allow this visit. If Derril had more news of the murders, Lorlen wanted to hear it.

Derril's story of the murderer had chilled Lorlen. The cuts on the victim, the strange ritual, the witness's belief that the victim was dead before his throat was slashed . . . perhaps it was only because the idea of black magic was in his mind already that these murders sounded so suspicious.

But if they were the work of a black magician, that would mean one of two things: either a rogue magician capable of black magic was preying on people in the city, or this murderer was Akkarin. Lorlen shivered as he considered the implications of these two possibilities.

When the carriage stopped he looked up in surprise to find they had arrived. The driver climbed down and opened the door, revealing an elegant mansion fronted with balconies.

Lorlen stepped out and was greeted at the door by one

of Derril's servants. The man took Lorlen through the house to an internal balcony overlooking the garden. Lorlen placed his hands on the balcony rail and gazed down at the drooping little oasis of vegetation; the plants looked sad and scorched around the edges now.

'I'm afraid this summer has been a little too much for most of my plants,' Derril said mournfully as he walked out of the house to join the Administrator. 'My gan-gan bushes won't survive. I'll have to arrange for new ones to be sent from the mountains of Lan.'

'You should have them pulled out now before the roots spoil,' Lorlen suggested. 'Ground gan-gan root has remarkable antiseptic properties and, if added to sumi, is a good treatment for digestive disorders.'

Derril chuckled. 'You still haven't forgotten all the Healer training, have you?'

'No.' Lorlen smiled. 'I may grow into a grumpy old Administrator, but I'll be a healthy one. I've got to put all that knowledge of medicine to use somehow.'

'Hmmm.' Derril's eyes narrowed. 'I wish the Guard had someone with your knowledge in their ranks. Barran has another mystery on his hands.'

'Another murder?'

'Yes and no,' Derril sighed. 'They think this one is a suicide. At least that's what it looks like.'

'Does he believe it was made to look like one?'

'Perhaps.' Derril lifted an eyebrow. 'Barran has come for dinner. Why don't we go in and ask him to tell you more about it?'

Lorlen nodded and followed the old man into the house. They entered a large guestroom, its windows covered by paper screens decorated with paintings of flowers and

118

plants. A young man in his mid-twenties sat in one of the luxurious chairs. His wide shoulders and slightly hooked nose reminded Lorlen instantly of the man's brother, Walin.

Barran looked up at the Administrator, then rose hastily and bowed.

'Greetings, Administrator Lorlen,' he offered. 'How are you?'

'Good, thank you,' Lorlen replied.

'Barran,' Derril said, waving Lorlen into a seat, 'Lorlen is interested in this suicide you've been investigating. Can you tell him the details?'

Barran shrugged. 'It's no secret – just a mystery.' He turned to look at Lorlen, his blue eyes troubled. 'A woman approached a guard in her street and told him that she'd discovered her neighbour dead. He investigated and found a woman with her wrists cut.' Barran paused and his eyes narrowed. 'The mystery is that she hadn't lost a great deal of blood yet and she was still warm. In fact the wounds were quite shallow. She should have been alive.'

Lorlen absorbed this. 'The blade might have been poisoned.'

'We've been considering the possibility, but if that's the case, then it must be a subtle poison we've never heard of. All poisons leave signs, even if the damage is only visible in the internal organs. We found no weapon, which might have retained some residue, and that is strange in itself. If someone slashes their wrists, the implement they used is usually close by. We searched the house and found nothing but a few kitchen knives, which were clean and still in their box. She wasn't strangled, either, from what we can tell. But there are other details which make me suspicious.

'I found footprints that didn't match the shoes of any servants, friends or family. The intruder's shoes were old and strangely shaped, so they left some distinctive markings. In the room where the woman was discovered, the window was unlocked and not quite closed. I found fingerprints and smudges on the sill that looked like dried blood, so I had another look at the body and discovered the same fingerprints on her wrists.'

'Hers?'

'No, the fingerprints were large. A man's.'

'Someone tried to stop the bleeding, perhaps, then fled through the window when he heard others approaching?'

'Perhaps. But the window is three storeys up and the wall is smooth and has few handholds. I don't think even an experienced thief could have climbed down.'

'Were there any footprints below?'

The young man hesitated before answering. 'When I went outside to inspect the ground I found the strangest thing.' Barran traced an arc in the air. 'It was as though someone had flattened the dirt into a perfect circle. In the centre were two footprints, the same as those in the room above, and others, leading away. I followed them, but they led onto pavement.'

Lorlen's heart skipped a beat, then began to race. A perfect circle on the ground and a drop of three storeys? To levitate, a magician must create a disk of power below his feet. It could leave a circular impression in soft soil or sand.

'Perhaps this imprint was already there,' Lorlen suggested.

Barran shrugged. 'Or he used some kind of ladder with a circular base. It is a strange case. There were, however, no cuts on the woman's shoulders so I don't believe she was a victim of the serial murderer we've been looking for. No, that one hasn't struck for a while, unless we simply haven't heard—'

The chime of a gong interrupted them. Velia appeared in the doorway, holding a tiny gong and striker.

'Dinner is ready,' she announced. Rising, Lorlen and Barran started toward the dining room. She gave her son a hard look. 'And there'll be no talking about murders or suicides at my table! It'll put the Administrator off his meal.'

Dannyl watched from the carriage windows, as the grand yellow stone buildings of Capia moved in and out of view. The sun was low in the sky, and the whole city seemed to glow with warm light. The streets were full of people and other carriages.

Each day and most evenings of the last three weeks he had been occupied with visiting or entertaining influential people, or helping Errend deal with ambassadorial business. He had met most of the Dems and Bels that frequented court. He had learned the personal history of every Guild magician living in Elyne. He had recorded the names of Elyne children with magical potential, answered or forwarded questions to the Guild from courtiers, negotiated the purchase of Elyne wines, and Healed a servant who had burned himself in the Guild House kitchen.

That so much time had passed without a chance to begin Lorlen's research worried him, so he resolved that the next time he had a few hours free he would visit the Great Library. A messenger sent to Tayend to ask if an evening visit was possible had returned with the assurance that he could explore the library at any time he wished, so when Dannyl learned that he would have this evening free, he had ordered an early meal and a carriage.

Unlike Imardin, Capia's streets wound about in a haphazard way. The carriage zigzagged back and forth, occasionally rolling around the side of a steep hill. Mansions gave way to large houses, which were replaced by rows of small, neat buildings. A turn over a rise took Dannyl along the edge of a shabbier area. Wood and other, cruder, materials replaced yellow stone, and the men and women roaming the street wore coarser clothing. Though he saw nothing as confronting as the sights he had seen in the slums of Imardin while searching for Sonea, Dannyl was mildly dismayed. The face of Elyne's capital city was so beautiful it was disappointing to find that it, too, had its poor area.

Leaving the houses behind, the carriage set out into rolling hills. Fields of tenn swayed in the slight breeze. Vare berry vines, planted in rows, hung full of fruit waiting to be harvested and then stored ready to make wine. Orchards of heavily laden pachi and piorre trees appeared here and there, some of the fruit being picked by teams of Vindo who travelled to Elyne each year for the work.

As the last rays of sunlight deepened from yellow to orange, and the carriage continued to roll further away from the city, Dannyl grew concerned. Had the driver misunderstood his instruction? He lifted a hand to knock on the roof, then paused as the carriage turned around the foot of a hill.

Ahead, the dark ribbon that was the road curved to meet the base of a tall cliff. In the light of the setting sun, the yellow stone glowed as if a fire burned within. Shadows stood out starkly, marking straight edges, windows and arches of a towering facade that he recognised from sketches in books.

'The Great Library,' Dannyl murmured in wonder.

A huge doorway had been carved out of the cliff face, filled with a massive wooden door. As the carriage drew closer, Dannyl saw that a small square of darkness at the bottom edge was actually a man-sized doorway built within the larger door. A figure waited beside it.

Dannyl smiled as he saw the man's bright clothing. He drummed his fingers on the window frame impatiently as the carriage slowly closed the distance to the library. As it pulled up before the facade, Tayend strode forward to open the carriage door.

'Welcome to the Great Library, Ambassador Dannyl,' he declared, bowing gracefully.

Dannyl looked up and shook his head in wonder. 'I can remember seeing pictures of this in books when I was a novice. They don't come close to showing what it's really like. How old is it?'

'Older than the Guild,' Tayend replied, a little smugly. 'About eight or nine centuries, we think. Parts of it are older, and the best is still to come – so follow me, my lord.'

They stepped through the small door, Tayend closing and bolting it behind them, and entered a long corridor with a curved roof. This extended into darkness, but before Dannyl could create a globe light, Tayend directed him to a steep, torch-lit stairway at one side.

At the top of this Dannyl found himself in a long, narrow room. On one side were the windows he had seen from the carriage. They were huge, and filled with small squares of glass fixed within an iron framework. The wall opposite was patterned by squares of golden light. Chairs were positioned in groups of three or four at intervals, and standing beside the closest was an elderly man.

'Good evening, Ambassador Dannyl.' The man bowed with the cautious stiffness of the very old. 'I am Irand, the librarian.'

Irand had a deep, startlingly strong voice that suited the inhuman size of the library. Short white hair covered his scalp thinly, and he wore a simple shirt and trousers made from a dusty grey fabric.

'Good evening, Librarian Irand,' Dannyl replied.

A smile creased the librarian's face. 'Administrator Lorlen informed me that you had a task to perform for him here. He said you would want to see all the sources that the High Lord checked during his research.'

'Do you know what those sources were?'

The old man shook his head. 'No, but Tayend has some recollection of them. He was Akkarin's assistant, and has agreed to help you in your search.' The old man nodded to the scholar. 'You will find his knowledge of ancient languages useful. He will also send for food and drink if you need it.' Tayend nodded eagerly, and the old man smiled.

'Thank you,' Dannyl replied.

'Well then, don't let me keep you waiting.' Irand's eyes seemed to gleam for a moment. 'The library awaits.'

'This way, my lord,' Tayend said, moving back to the stairs.

Dannyl followed the scholar down to the dark passage again. Lamps stood in a row on a shelf to one side. Tayend reached for one.

'Don't trouble yourself,' Dannyl said. He focussed his will and a globe light swelled into existence beside his head, sending their shadows down the passage. Tayend glanced at the globe light and winced.

'They always leave spots in front of my eyes.' He reached up and took down a lamp. 'I might need to leave you on your own at some point, so I'll take one with me anyway.'

With the lamp swinging at his side, Tayend started down the passage. 'This place has always been a store of knowledge. We have some crumbling bits of paper from eight centuries ago in one of our rooms, which contain references to a library of sorts that was old even then. Only a few rooms were used as a library originally. The rest of this place once housed a few thousand people. We've filled almost every room with books and scrolls, tablets and paintings – and we've carved more rooms out of the rock ourselves.'

As they walked Dannyl watched the darkness retreat like some kind of magic-fearing mist. Abruptly, they came to a blank wall, the darkness fleeing to either side. Tayend turned and started down the passage to his right.

'So which languages do you know?' Dannyl asked.

'All of the ancient dialects of Elyne and Kyralia,' Tayend replied. 'Our old languages are very similar, but the further back you look, the more differences there are. I can speak modern Vindo – I learned it from some servants at home – and a bit of Lans. I can translate the ancient Vindo and Tentur glyphs, given access to my books.'

Dannyl glanced at his companion, impressed. 'That's a lot of languages.'

The scholar shrugged. 'Once you know a few, the rest come easily. One day I'll get around to learning modern

Lonmar, and a few of their old languages. I just haven't had reason to yet. After that, well, perhaps I'll start on Sachakan languages. Their old tongues are also quite similar to ours.'

After several more turns and a few stairways, Tayend paused at a doorway. With an unusually sober expression, he indicated that Dannyl should enter before him. Stepping through, Dannyl drew in a breath of amazement.

Uncountable rows of shelves extended into the distance, divided by a wide aisle directly in front of him. Though the ceiling of the room before him was low, the far wall was so far away he could not see it. Massive columns of stone filled the gap between roof and floor every hundred paces. All was sparsely lit by lamps set on top of heavy iron bases.

The enormous room emanated a feeling of incomprehensible age. Compared to the solid weight of the stone columns and ceiling, the books seemed like such fragile, temporary things. Humbled, Dannyl felt a melancholy descend upon him. He could remain for a year in this place and still make no more imprint on it than a moth wing brushing against the cold stone walls.

'Compared to this, everything else in the library is recent,' Tayend said in a hushed voice. 'This is the oldest room. Perhaps thousands of years old.'

'Who made it?' Dannyl breathed.

'Nobody knows.'

Dannyl started down the aisle, gazing at the endless shelves of books.

'How am I going to find what I need?' he asked despairingly.

'Oh, that's not a problem.' Tayend's voice was suddenly

bright – a sound that cut through the heavy silence of the room. 'I have everything waiting for you in the same study room that Akkarin used. Follow me.'

Tayend started down the aisle, his steps light and springy. After passing several shelves, he turned and walked between them, then reached a large stone stairway that rose into a gap in the ceiling. Taking the steps two at a time, he led Dannyl up to the beginning of a wide corridor. Again, the ceiling was disturbingly low. Doors stood open on either side, and Tayend stopped beside one and gestured for Dannyl to enter.

Dannyl found himself in a small room. A large stone table stood in the middle, and piled on top of it were several stacks of books.

'Here we are,' Tayend said. 'And these are the books Akkarin read.'

The volumes ranged from tiny, palm-sized books to a huge tome that would have been a challenge to carry. Dannyl examined them, unstacking and restacking as he read the titles.

'Where do I start?' he asked aloud.

Tayend pulled a dusty volume from the middle of a stack. 'This was the first one Akkarin read.'

Dannyl looked at Tayend, impressed. The young man's eyes were bright with enthusiasm.

'You remember *that* well?'

The scholar grinned. 'You need a good memory to use the library. How else do you find a book again after you've read it?'

Dannyl looked down at the tome in his hands. *Magical Practices of the Grey Mountains Tribes*. The date below the title indicated that the book was at least five centuries old, and he knew there hadn't been tribes living in the mountains between Elyne and Kyralia for at least that long. Intrigued, he opened it and started reading.

CHAPTER 8

JUST WHAT HE INTENDED

'So we just sit and listen?' Yaldin's brow furrowed, and his eyes roved about as he concentrated on the voices in the Night Room. Rothen suppressed a chuckle. The elderly magician's face was too expressive. Anyone who saw him would know that he was trying hard to listen to something.

But with Dannyl gone, Rothen needed someone else to 'spy' on the other magicians. Everybody was being cautious now that a scandalous rumour was circulating. Since the rumour involved Rothen, the gossips always checked if he was nearby before talking freely, so he had decided to train his elderly friend, Yaldin, in Dannyl's techniques.

'You're being too obvious, Yaldin.'

The old man frowned. 'Obvious? What do you mean?'

'When you—'

'Lord Rothen?'

Startled, Rothen looked up to find Administrator Lorlen standing beside his chair.

'Yes, Administrator?'

'I would like to speak to you in private.'

Glancing about, Rothen noted that several magicians standing nearby were eyeing Lorlen expectantly. Yaldin frowned, but said nothing.

'Of course,' Rothen replied. He rose and followed Lorlen

across the room to a small door. It swung open at Lorlen's approach, and they stepped through into the Banquet Room.

The room was dark. A globe light flared above the Administrator's head and floated up to illuminate a large table. Lorlen moved to one of the chairs. Taking a seat next to the Administrator, Rothen braced himself for the conversation he had been dreading.

Lorlen glanced at Rothen, then let his eyes slide to the table. He sighed and his expression became grim.

'Are you aware of the rumours circulating about you and Sonea?'

Rothen nodded. 'I am.'

'No doubt Yaldin has told you.'

'And Sonea.'

'Sonea?' Lorlen's eyebrows rose.

'Yes,' Rothen said. 'She told me four weeks ago that one of her fellow novices had invented the rumour, and she was concerned people would believe it. I told her not to worry. Gossip has a lifespan, that speculation eventually becomes old news, and is forgotten.'

'Hmmm.' Lorlen frowned. 'Rumours like this are not dismissed as lightly as you may hope. Several magicians have come to me to express their concerns. They feel it is not proper for any magician to have a young woman living in their rooms.'

'Moving her will do nothing to disprove the rumour.'

Lorlen nodded. 'That is true. Nevertheless, it would prevent further speculation that could be quite harmful to you both. In retrospect, Sonea should have moved to the Novices' Quarters when she began classes.' He looked at Rothen directly. 'Not to prevent what the rumours suggest, but to prevent rumours beginning at all. Nobody believes anything untoward has occurred between you and Sonea.'

'Then why move her at all?' Rothen spread his hands. 'She will still spend time with me in my rooms, in study or simply for the evening meal. If we give in now, how long will it be before others question the intent behind every moment we spend together?' He shook his head. 'Leave things as they are, and those who are foolish enough to give this gossip credence will be assured that no evidence of improper conduct has been found.'

A wry smile curled Lorlen's mouth. 'You are confident, Rothen. What does Sonea think?'

'This rumour has upset her, of course, but she believes that it will be forgotten when she is no longer the target of Garrel's favourite.'

'When – if – she reaches the winter intake?'

'Yes.'

'Do you think she will reach the higher class and manage to stay there?'

'Easily.' Rothen smiled, not bothering to conceal his pride. 'She is a fast learner, and quite determined. The last thing she'll want to do is slip back down to Regin's class.'

Lorlen nodded, then looked at Rothen closely. 'I don't share your optimism about this rumour, Rothen. Your arguments against moving her have some merit, but if you are wrong, the situation could grow much worse. I believe she should be moved, for her own sake.'

Rothen frowned at the Administrator. Surely Lorlen did not think that Rothen would bed a novice, particularly a girl less than a third his age? Lorlen's gaze was level and hard, however, and Rothen realised with a shock that the magician had actually considered the possibility.

131

Lorlen *couldn't* believe this of him! How could he even think about it? When had Rothen given Lorlen cause to doubt him?

Then, in a flash, the reason came to him. *It is because of Akkarin,* he thought. *If I had learned that my closest and oldest friend was practising the evilest of magic, I would be reassessing my presumptions about everyone I knew.* Taking a deep breath, Rothen considered his next words carefully.

'Only you can understand why I want to keep her close by my side, Lorlen,' he said in a low voice. 'She has enough to fear here already without being sent to live among those who would do her harm, where she might be vulnerable to more than just the other novices.'

Lorlen frowned, then his eyes widened slightly and he looked away. He straightened and nodded slowly. 'I understand your concern. It must be frightening for her. But if I make a decision that goes against the opinion of the majority, it will draw attention. I do not feel she will be in any greater danger living in the Novices' Quarters . . . but I will try to defer the decision as long as possible in the hope that this will blow over, as you believe it will.'

Rothen nodded. 'Thank you.'

'And,' Lorlen added as an afterthought, 'I shall keep a closer eye on this novice, Regin. Troublemakers are a problem that should be addressed long before graduation.'

'That would be appreciated,' Rothen replied.

Lorlen rose, and Rothen followed suit. For a moment their eyes met, and Rothen saw a raw, harassed look in Lorlen's gaze that sent a shiver down his spine. Then Lorlen turned away and started toward the door to the Night Room.

Once there, they parted, Lorlen moving to his customary

chair. As Rothen crossed to his own seat he caught several glances cast in his direction. He kept his expression sober and unconcerned. Yaldin looked up at him questioningly.

'Nothing of great concern,' Rothen said, dropping into his chair. 'Now, where were we? Oh, yes. Being obvious. This is what you looked like . . .'

At the sound of the knock on her door, Sonea sighed. She stopped writing and, without turning, called out, 'Come in.'

The door clicked open.

'There's someone to see you, Lady Sonea,' Tania said in a strained voice.

Glancing over her shoulder, Sonea saw that a woman in green robes stood in the doorway of her bedroom. A black sash circled the woman's waist. Sonea leapt to her feet and bowed quickly.

'Lady Vinara.'

Sonea looked at the Head of Healers carefully. It was hard to gauge the Healer's mood, since Vinara's expression always seemed to be stern and cold. The woman's grey eyes seemed steelier than usual.

'It's a little late to be studying,' Vinara noted.

Sonea glanced at her desk. 'I'm working to catch up with the winter class.'

'So I've heard.' Vinara gestured at the door, which swung shut. Before it closed, Sonea caught a glimpse of Tania watching anxiously. 'I wish to talk to you privately.'

Sonea indicated that Vinara could take her chair, then perched on the edge of the bed. She watched, her stomach tight with dread, as Vinara sat down and arranged her robes.

'Are you aware of certain rumours regarding Lord Rothen and yourself?'

Sonea nodded.

'I have come here to question you about them. You must be honest with me, Sonea. These are serious matters. Is there any truth in them?'

'No.'

'Lord Rothen has not made any improper suggestions?'

'No.'

'He's not . . . touched you in any way?'

Sonea felt her face warming. 'No. Never. It's just a stupid rumour. Rothen has never touched me, or me him. It makes me sick to hear them say it.'

Vinara nodded slowly.

'I am glad to hear it. Remember, if you have any cause to be afraid, or if you have been coerced in any way, you do not have to stay here. We will help you.'

Sonea swallowed her anger. 'Thank you, but there's nothing going on here.'

Vinara's eyes narrowed. 'I must also tell you that, if these rumours were proven to be true, and you were a willing participant, your standing in the Guild would be damaged. At the least, you would lose Rothen's guardianship.'

Of course. Regin would love that. It might be what he was aiming for all along. Sonea gritted her teeth. 'If it comes to that, Lorlen can truth-read me again.'

Vinara straightened and looked away. 'Let's hope it does not come to that.' She sniffed. 'Well, I am sorry I had to raise these delicate issues with you. You must understand that it is my duty to investigate. If you have anything you wish to discuss, please come and see me.' She rose and regarded Sonea critically. 'You are exhausted, young woman. Too much study will make you sick. Get some sleep.'

Sonea nodded. She watched as Lady Vinara opened the door and glided out, then waited until she heard Tania close the main door to the apartments. Then, she turned and pounded her pillow with her fists.

'I want to kill him!' she growled. 'I want to sink him in the Tarali River with rocks tied to his feet so nobody ever finds his body.'

'Lady Sonea?'

Hearing the timid voice, Sonea looked up and tossed strands of her messed-up hair out of her eyes. 'Yes, Tania?'

'Wh-who do you want to kill?'

Sonea threw the pillow back into place. 'Regin, of course.'

'Ah.' Tania sat on the edge of the bed. 'You had me worried for a moment. They've been questioning me, too. I didn't believe it, of course, but they told me all these things to watch out for and . . . well . . . I . . .'

'Don't worry, Tania,' Sonea sighed. 'There's only one person in the Guild who has ever tried something like that on me.'

The servant's eyes widened. 'Who?'

'Regin, of course.'

Tania scowled. 'What did you do?'

Remembering, Sonea smiled. 'Just a little trick I learned from Cery.' Standing up, she began to explain.

It was late when Lorlen returned to his office in the University. Earlier in the day Lord Osen, his assistant, had brought in a small box of mail. Rifling through, Lorlen had seen a small package from Elyne among the rest of the letters. He had set it aside to read later.

Brightening his globe light, Lorlen now retrieved the package. He opened it and regarded Dannyl's elegant writing appreciatively. The young magician's script was confident and neat. Lorlen settled back in his chair and started reading.

To Administrator Lorlen.

I first visited the Great Library a week ago, and have returned each night to continue my research. The Librarian Irand has assigned to me the same scholar who helped the High Lord in his search: Tayend of Tremmelin. This man has an extraordinarily good memory of the High Lord's visits, and I have made considerable progress.

According to Tayend, the High Lord carried a journal in which he made notes, copied passages from books, and drew maps. Guided by the scholar, I have read through half of the sources the High Lord consulted, and copied out much that is useful, including everything Tayend remembers the High Lord showing interest in.

There are several subjects that I could pursue from here, which is how it was for the High Lord as well. Most require a journey to a tomb, temple or library in the Allied Lands. When I have finished reading, I should know all the possibilities the High Lord considered. From there I must choose which one I will pursue.

To aid in my decision, Tayend visited the wharf, where records have been kept of all arrivals and departures for many years. He found mention of a Lord Akkarin who arrived here over ten years ago, then left some months later for Lonmar, then returned to Capia to take another ship to the Vin Islands, returning again to Capia a month later. There were no further entries.

Considering the information I have gathered, it is likely that the High Lord visited the Splendid Temple in Lonmar. I have copied out my notes, and included them with this letter.

Second Guild Ambassador for Elyne, Dannyl.

Putting the letter down, Lorlen leafed through the notes that followed. They were clear and well-written, describing and piecing together scraps of information from ages before the formation of the Guild. Finally, on the last page, Dannyl had included a small note.

Found a book describing the Sachakan War written soon after the event. It is remarkable in that it portrays the Guild as the enemy – and it paints an unflattering image indeed! After completing this task I will return to the library to read it through.

Lorlen smiled. If he'd known Dannyl was this good at research, he would have made use of him earlier. Though Dannyl had not yet unearthed anything that could be used against Akkarin, he had gathered a lot of information in a short time. Lorlen's hopes that something useful would be found had grown stronger.

No awkward questions had been asked, either. As he'd hoped, Dannyl was sensible enough to keep the matter confidential even though he didn't know the reason for the secrecy. If Dannyl did discover something that caused him to suspect that Akkarin had learned black magic, Lorlen was sure the young magician would inform him in secret.

What then? Lorlen pursed his lips, considering. He would probably have to tell Dannyl the truth. But he was confident that the young magician would see the wisdom of avoiding a confrontation with Akkarin until it could be done without risk. Knowing that Rothen and Sonea had agreed to this plan would also help to convince Dannyl to stay silent.

But it would be better to avoid telling Dannyl the truth for as long as possible. For now, Lorlen would help Dannyl gather as much information as he could. Pulling out a sheet of paper, Lorlen wrote a letter to the First Guild Ambassador. He sealed it carefully, marked the address of the Guild House in Elyne, then placed it in another box on his desk. Lord Osen would arrange for a courier to send it tomorrow.

Rising, Lorlen stowed Dannyl's letter and notes in a box that he kept for important documents. He strengthened the magical barrier that prevented others from reaching the contents, then stowed it in a cupboard behind his desk. As he left the room he allowed himself a small smile.

Akkarin was right when he said I chose the right man for the position of Second Guild Ambassador to Elyne.

CHAPTER 9

CONSIDERING THE FUTURE

'Could you get me a plainer one of these?' Sonea asked, holding up the silver hairbrush.

'Oh, not that, too?' Tania sighed. 'Aren't you going to take anything nice?'

'No. Nothing valuable and nothing that I like.'

'But you're leaving so much behind – what about a pretty vase? I'll bring you some flowers now and then. It'll make the room so much nicer.'

'I'm used to much worse, Tania. When I work out a way to hide or protect things, I might come and get some books.' Sonea regarded the contents of a box lying on her bed. 'That's it.'

Tania sighed. She picked up the box and carried it out of the room. Following her, Sonea found Rothen pacing in the guestroom. His brow was furrowed and when he saw her he hurried over and took her hands.

'I'm sorry about this, Sonea,' he began. 'I—'

'Don't apologise, Rothen,' she told him. 'I know you did what you could. It's better that I go.'

'But it's nonsense. I could—'

'No.' She gave him a level look. 'I *have* to go. If I don't, Regin will make sure they find proof. And he still might try, if his aim is to have your guardianship of me removed.

Then the teachers can ignore me and I won't be able to do anything about it.'

His frown returned. 'I hadn't thought of that,' he growled. 'It's not right that a mere novice should cause us this much trouble.'

She smiled. 'No, but he won't stop me from getting ahead of him, will he? We'll keep working.'

Rothen nodded. 'We will.'

'Then I'll meet you outside the Magicians' Library in an hour?'

'Yes.'

She squeezed his hands and let them go, then nodded to Tania. The servant lifted the box and carried it to the door. As Sonea stepped into the doorway she looked back and smiled at Rothen.

'I'll be fine, Rothen.'

He managed a thin smile in reply. Turning away, Sonea started down the corridor, Tania at her side.

The Magicians' Quarters were unusually busy for a Freeday morning. Sonea ignored the stares of the magicians who passed, knowing the anger she felt would be too hard to hide if she met their gaze. She half heard Tania mutter something about fairness as they started down the stairs, but didn't ask her to repeat it. She'd had enough of such talk in the last few days.

She had sounded much braver than she felt, back in Rothen's rooms. Once in the Novices' Quarters there would be no escape from Regin. She could lock her room door with magic – Rothen had shown her how – but she was sure Regin would find some way to get at her. And she couldn't stay in there all the time.

This was his revenge for her slandering of his House.

140

She should have thrown him on the floor and left it at that. But she'd opened her mouth and insulted him and he wasn't going to let her get away with it. So much for ignoring him in the hope he'd get bored and leave her alone.

Now it wasn't just the novices muttering her name in the corridors. She'd heard enough whispers from magicians to know their opinion of her. None really cared who had started the rumour or why. 'Rumours like these should never start in the first place,' as one teacher had put it. Living with Rothen looked suspicious, especially when her past was taken into consideration. As if every woman of the slums was a whore!

And she'd heard many people asking why she should be treated any differently than the other novices. They had to live in the Novices' Quarters. So should she.

Reaching the doors to the Magicians' Quarters, Sonea started across the courtyard. The stifling heat of midsummer was well past, and the day was pleasantly warm. She could feel a faint heat radiating from the paving stones.

She had never entered the Novices' Quarters before. Only once, during the night she and Cery had snuck around the Guild so long ago, had she peeked through the windows and seen the rooms inside. They had been small, plain and undecorated.

Several groups of novices stood around the entrance. They stopped their conversations to stare at her, some leaning closer together to whisper. She gave them a mild glance as she passed, then stepped through the open doors.

More novices roamed along the corridor inside, and Sonea resisted the urge to scan for familiar faces. Tania moved to the right of the entrance and knocked on a door.

As they waited, Sonea watched the novices in the corridor from the corner of her eye. She wondered where Regin was. Surely he'd be present for this little moment of victory.

The door opened and a thin, sharp-featured Warrior looked down at Sonea. She bowed and considered the mutterings and complaints she'd heard about the Director of the Novices' Quarters. Ahrind wasn't liked.

'So. You're here,' he said coldly. 'Follow me.'

He strode down the corridor, novices carefully veering out of his path, and stopped at a door not far along. It clicked open to reveal a room as plain and small as the ones she remembered.

'No changes to the room,' Ahrind said. 'No visitors after the evening gong. If you are to be absent for any number of nights, please inform me two days prior to the first evening. The room is to be kept clean and tidy. Make arrangements with the servants as necessary. Am I clear?'

Sonea nodded. 'Yes, my lord.'

He turned and strode away. Exchanging a glance with Tania, Sonea entered the room and looked around.

It was slightly bigger than her bedroom had been, containing a bed, a cupboard for her clothes, a desk and some shelves. Moving to the window, she looked out at the Arena and the gardens. Tania set the box down on the bed and began unpacking.

'I didn't see that boy,' Tania noted.

'No. That doesn't mean he wasn't watching, or one of his followers.'

'It's good that you're so close to the entrance.'

142

Nodding, Sonea took her notebooks, pens and paper out of the box and stowed them in the drawers of the desk. 'Ahrind probably wants to keep an eye on me. Make sure I'm not a bad influence.'

Tania made a rude noise. 'The servants don't like him much. I'd give him no reason to notice me, if I were you. What are you going to do about meals?'

Sonea shrugged. 'I'll have dinner with Rothen. Otherwise . . . the Foodhall, I expect. I might be able to slip in, take something, and slip away again before Regin finishes.'

'I'll bring you something to eat here, if you like.'

'You shouldn't,' Sonea sighed. 'You'll just make yourself a target.'

'I'll come with one of the other servants, or get one to drop something off for you. I'm not going to let that boy deprive you of food.'

'He won't, Tania,' Sonea assured her. 'Now, everything's unpacked.' She rested her palm over the cupboard door, then over the drawer of the desk. 'Everything's locked. Let's meet Rothen at the Magicians' Library.'

Smiling, Sonea shooed the servant out of the room, locked the door, and set off for the University.

'What's this in my pocket?' Drawing a slip of paper out of his coat, Tayend examined it. 'Ah, my notes from my visit to the wharf.' He read them and frowned. 'Akkarin was gone for six years, wasn't he?'

'Yes,' Dannyl replied.

'That meant he spent five of them here, after he returned from the Vin Islands.'

'Unless he travelled overland to somewhere else,' Dannyl pointed out.

'Where to?' Tayend frowned. 'I wish we could ask the family he stayed with, but they're likely to let Akkarin know someone was asking about him and you seem to want to avoid that.' He drummed his fingers on the railing of the ship.

Dannyl smiled and turned his face into the wind. He had come to like the scholar since they had begun working together. Tayend had a quick mind and a good memory, and was companionable as well as a good assistant. When Tayend had offered to accompany Dannyl on his journey to Lonmar, Dannyl had been surprised and pleased. He'd asked if Irand would allow it.

'Oh, I only work here because I want to,' Tayend had replied, clearly amused. 'In fact, I don't *work* as such. I get the run of the library in exchange for making myself useful to visitors and researchers.'

When Dannyl had expressed his desire to visit Lonmar and Vin he had been sure that the First Ambassador would disapprove. After all, he'd only been in Elyne a few months. But Errend had been delighted. It seemed that Lorlen had asked him to visit these countries to deal with some ambassadorial matters, and Errend was not at all fond of ship travel. He'd promptly decided that Dannyl would go in his place.

This was all suspiciously convenient . . .

'How did he get back to the Guild?'

Dannyl started, then turned to regard Tayend. 'Who?'

'Akkarin.'

'They say he just walked up to the Guild Gates, all dirty and dressed in ordinary clothes, and nobody recognised him at first.'

Tayend's eyes widened. 'Really? Did he say why?'

Dannyl shrugged. 'Possibly. I have to admit, I didn't pay much attention at the time.'

'Wish we could ask him.'

'If we're looking for ancient magic, the reason Akkarin turned up looking shabby at the end of his search is probably not going to tell us anything. Lorlen said his quest wasn't completed, remember.'

'I'd still like to know,' Tayend insisted.

The ship rocked as it passed through the arms of the bay. Looking back, Dannyl sighed with appreciation at the shining city. He was lucky, indeed, to have been assigned the role of Guild Ambassador in such a place. Tayend stowed the slip of paper away.

'Goodbye, Capia,' he said wistfully. 'It's like leaving the arms of a beautiful lover you've shamelessly taken for granted. Only in the leaving do you realise what you have.'

'The Splendid Temple is said to be a magnificent place.'

Tayend looked around the ship's deck. 'Yes, and we will be seeing it for ourselves. What an adventure awaits us! What fine sights and memorable experiences – and what a fantastic way to travel.'

'You might want to wait until you see your room before you come up with any more grand descriptions of our journey – though I must say you will find sleeping in it a memorable experience.'

Tayend swayed as the ship rolled through the waves. 'It will stop this soon, won't it? When it gets further out?'

'Stop what?' Dannyl asked slyly.

The scholar looked at him in horror, then flung himself at the railing and vomited. Dannyl immediately felt ashamed of his teasing remark.

'Here.' He took Tayend's hand and placed his palm on

the man's wrist. Closing his eyes, he sent his awareness into the scholar's body, but the sense of it vanished as the scholar snatched his hand away.

'No. Don't.' Tayend bad flushed a bright red. 'I'll be fine. It's seasickness, right? I'll get used to it.'

'You don't have to be ill,' Dannyl said, puzzled by the scholar's reaction.

'Yes, I do.' Tayend leaned over the railing again. After a moment, he slumped against the rail and wiped his mouth on a nosecloth. 'It's all part of the experience, you see,' he told the waves. 'If you stop me feeling it, I won't have any good stories to tell.'

Dannyl shrugged. 'Well, if you change your mind . . .'

Tayend coughed. 'I'll let you know.'

As the last rays of light left all but the highest leaves within the forest, Lorlen stepped out of the University and made his way toward the High Lord's Residence.

Once again, he must endeavour to store all he knew in some dark part of his mind. Once more he would make friendly conversation, tell a few jokes, and drink the best wine in the Allied Lands.

He would have trusted his life to Akkarin, once. They had been close as novices, confiding in each other, defending each other. Akkarin had been the one most likely to break Guild rules and propose mischief. Lorlen frowned. Had that led to this interest in black magic? Was Akkarin just bending the rules for the sake of his own entertainment?

He sighed. He didn't like fearing Akkarin. It was easier, on nights like this, to invent a good reason for Akkarin to be using black magic. But doubts always remained.

'*The fight has weakened me. I need your strength.*'

What fight? Who had Akkarin battled? Remembering the blood that had covered Akkarin in Sonea's memory, Lorlen could only conclude that the adversary had been badly hurt. Or murdered.

Lorlen shook his head. The stories Derril and his son had told were strange and disturbing. Both involved victims that appeared to be dead despite wounds that weren't severe. This wasn't enough to prove a black magician had been at work, however. He could not help thinking that, if he wasn't worried about Akkarin, he might have been more inclined to bring the deaths to Vinara's attention. The Healer might know a way to detect if a person had been killed with black magic.

But if the Guild started looking for a black magician, would it all lead to a premature confrontation with Akkarin?

Stopping at the door of the High Lord's Residence, Lorlen sighed. He must push these things from his mind. Some of the magicians actually suspected that the High Lord could read thoughts from a distance. While he didn't believe this, Akkarin did have an uncanny ability to discover secrets before anyone else.

As always, the door swung inward as soon as he knocked. Stepping inside, he found Akkarin standing a few steps away, holding out a glass of wine.

Lorlen smiled and accepted the glass. 'Thank you.'

Taking another glass from a nearby table, Akkarin lifted it to his lips. He regarded Lorlen over the brim. 'You look tired.'

Lorlen nodded. 'I'm not surprised.' He shook his head and turned away, starting toward a chair.

'Takan says dinner will be ready in ten minutes,' Akkarin said. 'Come upstairs.'

Moving to the left side of the room, Akkarin opened the door to the stairs and waved Lorlen through. As he climbed, Lorlen felt an uneasiness steal over him, and he was suddenly acutely aware of the black-robed magician following behind him. He pushed the feeling away and stepped into the long corridor at the top of the stairs.

Halfway along, a pair of doors stood open, inviting Lorlen into the dining room. Takan stood within. As the servant bowed, Lorlen resisted looking too closely at the man, though he'd had few opportunities to examine Takan since learning of Akkarin's activities.

Takan moved to a chair and drew it out. Settling into it, Lorlen watched the man perform the same service for the High Lord, then hasten away.

'So what is bothering you, Lorlen?'

Lorlen looked at Akkarin in surprise. 'Bothering me?'

Akkarin smiled. 'You seem distracted. What is on your mind?'

Rubbing the bridge of his nose, Lorlen sighed. 'I had to make an unpleasant decision this week.'

'Oh? Is Lord Davin trying to purchase more materials for his weather experiments?'

'No – well, that too. I had to move Sonea to the Novices' Quarters. It seemed cruel when she's obviously not getting along well with her classmates.'

Akkarin shrugged. 'She was fortunate to spend as long with Rothen as she did. Someone was bound to protest eventually. I'm surprised the issue wasn't raised earlier.'

Nodding, Lorlen waved a hand. 'It is done. I can only try to keep an eye on the situation between her and her classmates, and urge Lord Garrel to curb Regin's antics.'

'You can try, but even if you asked Garrel to follow his novice about it wouldn't stop the boy doing whatever he's doing. She will have to learn to fend for herself if she's to gain the other novices' respect.'

Takan arrived with a tray, and set down small bowls of soup. Cupping the bowl in one long-fingered hand, Akkarin sipped experimentally, then smiled.

'You always mention Sonea when you come here,' he remarked. 'It's not like you to show an interest in a particular novice.'

His mouth full of the salty soup, Lorlen swallowed carefully. 'I'm curious to see how well she fits in – to see how much her background hampers her progress. It is in all our interests to see she adapts to our ways, and fulfils her potential, so I take note of her progress from time to time.'

'Thinking of recruiting more from the lower classes, perhaps?'

Lorlen grimaced. 'No. Are you?'

Looking away, Akkarin lifted his shoulders slightly. 'Sometimes. There must be a lot of potential we miss by ignoring so much of the population. Sonea is proof of that.'

Lorlen chuckled. 'Not even *you* could persuade the Guild to try it.'

Returning with a large platter, Takan set it down between Lorlen and Akkarin. He removed the empty bowls and replaced them with plates. As the servant disappeared again, Akkarin began selecting from the many dishes arranged on the platter.

As he followed suit, Lorlen allowed himself a little sigh of contentment. It was good to be eating a proper formal dinner again. The rushed meals he ate in his office were never as good as freshly prepared food.

'What news do *you* have?' he asked.

Between mouthfuls, Akkarin described the antics of the King and his court. 'I've heard good reports of our new Ambassador in Elyne,' he added. 'Seems that more than a few young unmarried women have been presented to him, but he has been politely disinterested in all of them.'

Lorlen smiled. 'I'm sure he's enjoying himself.' Pausing, he decided this was a good opportunity to pose a question about Akkarin's travels. 'I envy him. Unlike you, I never had the opportunity to travel, and I don't know if I will ever get the time now. I don't suppose you kept a diary? I know you used to when we were novices.'

Akkarin regarded Lorlen speculatively. 'I remember a certain novice who used to try to read my diary at every opportunity.'

Chuckling, Lorlen looked down at his plate. 'Not any more. I'm just looking for a travel story to read late at night.'

'I can't help you,' Akkarin said. He sighed and shook his head. 'My journal and all the notes I made were destroyed during the last part of my journey. I have often wished that I had made a copy, and sometimes I have a fancy to return and collect all the information again. Like you, I have responsibilities that keep me in Kyralia. Perhaps when I'm an old man I'll slip away again.'

Lorlen nodded. 'Then I'll have to look elsewhere for travel stories.'

As Takan returned for the platter, Akkarin began to suggest books. Lorlen nodded and tried to look attentive, but a part of his mind was racing ahead. Knowing Akkarin, there probably was a diary. Had it contained references to black magic? Was it really destroyed, or was Akkarin lying? It might be in the High Lord's Residence somewhere. Could he sneak in and search for it?

But as Takan served bowls of stewed piorres laced with wine Lorlen knew that such a search would be risky. If Akkarin found even the slightest evidence of an intruder, he would be alerted to the possibility of someone knowing his secret. Better to wait and see if Dannyl discovered anything before trying something that dangerous.

CHAPTER 10

HARD WORK PAYS OFF

'Sonea has succeeded in completing the half-year tests, Lord Kiano,' Jerrik announced. 'I have moved her to this class.'

Eight pairs of eyes fell on Sonea. The novices were arranged in a half-circle around the teacher's desk. She looked at each face, trying to read their expressions. None sneered at her, but she saw no welcoming smiles, either.

The teacher was a short, stocky Vindo with sleepy eyes. He nodded to the University Director and Rothen, then regarded Sonea. 'Take a seat from the back of the room and join the others.'

Sonea bowed and went to the stack of chairs near the far wall. Picking up a seat, she considered the novices. With their backs to her she could not see their faces and know which might care if she sat near them. Then, as she headed back to the front of the room, a boy looked across at her and smiled faintly. She moved toward him and was gratified to see him slide his chair aside a little to make room.

Rothen and Jerrik had retreated from the doorway. Their echoing footsteps in the corridor quickly faded away. Lord Kiano cleared his throat, looked around the class and resumed his lecture.

The other novices bent over their notebooks, writing

rapidly. As the Healer rattled out a rapid string of illnesses and the medicines that should be used to treat them, Sonea quickly pulled out a sheet of paper and began scribbling down everything she heard. She had no idea what she should be taking down, so she wrote every word in a messy scrawl that she suspected she'd have trouble deciphering later. When Lord Kiano finally paused to draw a diagram on a board she was able to cautiously look around at the other novices.

One girl and six boys. Aside from a tall Lan youth, an Elyne and a Vindo boy, the rest were Kyralian – though the boy beside her was unusually short and might be half Vindo. His skin was blotchy and his hair hung in limp strands.

Sensing her gaze he smiled uncertainly, then grinned as she returned the smile. Then his eyes dropped to the page in her hand and he frowned. He turned his notes so she could read them and wrote on the corner of a page.

Did you get everything?

Sonea shrugged and wrote on the corner of her page: *I hope so – he talks so fast.*

The boy started to write something else, but Lord Kiano then began a detailed explanation of the drawing and both Sonea and her companion realised with a shock that they should have been copying it. For several minutes she scribbled and sketched as fast as she could. Before she had managed to finish, the familiar sound of the midbreak gong echoed through the University.

Lord Kiano moved to stand in front of the class. 'Before the next class I want you to study and memorise the names and potency of the plants with mucolytic qualities as detailed in chapter five. You may go.'

As one, the novices rose and bowed to the teacher. The teacher turned to the board and waved his hand. To Sonea's dismay, the diagram disappeared from its surface.

'How much did you copy?'

She turned. The boy stood next to her, craning his neck to see her notes. Sonea turned the page to show him. 'Not all, but it looks like you caught a few things I missed. Can I . . . can we compare notes?'

'Yes. If . . . if you don't mind.'

The other novices had packed away their belongings and were filing out of the class. A few glanced back at her, perhaps curious about their new classmate. She looked at the boy.

'Are you going to the Foodhall?'

His smile faded a little. 'Yes.'

'I'll come with you, then.'

He nodded. They followed the rest of the class into the corridor. The novices walked in pairs, but stayed close enough to suggest they would all keep together. A few glanced at her, but none moved away or made any obvious attempt to snub her.

'What's your name?' she asked the boy.

'Poril. Family Vindel, House Heril.'

'I'm Sonea.' She searched for something else to ask. 'You've all been here since last winter?'

'Oh, everyone except me.' Poril shrugged. 'I started the summer before last.'

A slow learner. She wondered what was holding him back. He could be strong magically but still have trouble understanding the lessons, or he might simply be too weak to complete the tasks he was given.

Poril started to talk about his family, his brothers and sisters – of which there were six – and numerous other details about himself. She nodded and encouraged him, dreading the inevitable questions about herself.

The class descended to the ground floor of the University, then entered the Foodhall. As they moved to a table Sonea hesitated, but Poril stepped forward and quietly slipped into one of the seats. She sat down beside him, and was relieved that the others accepted this with no protest.

Servants brought trays of food, and all began to eat and talk. She listened carefully as they discussed people she didn't know, and the lesson. They seemed distracted by her presence, though, and eventually one of the boys looked at her directly.

'You're from Regin's class, aren't you?' he asked, waving a hand toward one side of the room.

Sonea's stomach turned. So her old class was known as 'Regin's class'.

'Yes,' she admitted.

He gestured with his cutlery. 'They gave you a rough time from what I hear.'

'At times.'

The boy nodded, then shrugged. 'Well, you won't get that from us. There's no time for playing around now. You'll have to work hard. This isn't Control exercises any more.' The other novices nodded.

She held back a laugh. Control lessons? He obviously didn't know much about her history . . . or he did and this was just a more subtle kind of jibe than what she was used to.

The talk turned to other subjects. Remembering the boy's gesture when he spoke of Regin, she glanced to her right. Familiar faces watched her from a few tables away.

She wondered what they had thought when she hadn't appeared for lessons that morning. They had probably expected her to fail the mid-year tests.

It had been hard work. Three months had passed since she had started at the University, and in that time she had completed six months' work. Next, she had to catch up on the work the winter class had covered, which meant squeezing another six months' work into three. It was not going to be easy.

Sensing her gaze, Regin looked up from his plate and stared at her. She met his gaze levelly. His eyes narrowed and he pushed his chair back.

A stab of apprehension chased away her satisfaction and she quickly looked away. What did he plan to do? Out of the corner of her eye she saw Kano lay a hand on Regin's arm. They spoke for several minutes. Regin drew his chair back to the table and Sonea let out the breath she had been holding.

She looked up as a servant offered a platter of food, then waved the woman away, her appetite gone. Regin may not be in her class any longer, but that would not stop him harassing her in the Foodhall, or on the way to and from the Novices' Quarters. In the corner of her eye she could see him turn to stare at her again. No, she wasn't rid of him completely.

But she had a chance to make a friend now. Looking at the faces around her, she felt a stirring of hope. She might even become friends with all of them.

Rothen felt a presence at his side and looked up.

'Forgive me for interrupting,' Lord Jullen said stiffly, 'but I would like to close the library now.'

'Of course.' Rothen nodded, rising. 'We'll be out as soon as we've packed up.'

As the librarian moved back to his desk near the door of the Magicians' Library, Sonea sighed and closed the large book she had been reading. 'I never knew people's bodies were so complicated.'

Rothen chuckled. 'This is just the beginning.'

They packed everything away efficiently. Books were snapped shut, paper was slipped into boxes, pens and ink bottles safely stowed. Rothen returned a few volumes to the library shelves, then ushered Sonea out of the library.

The University was dark and quiet, and Sonea was silent as she walked beside him. Unable to work in his rooms for fear of raising suspicions again, he had suggested they use hers instead. She had shaken her head, pointing out that Regin could easily persuade another novice to come up with a story of suspicious noises or overheard conversations.

Her suggestion of working in the Magicians' Library was brilliant. The lessons were observed by the librarian, Lord Jullen, and she had access to books other novices needed special permission to use. Regin, like her, could only enter the library under the supervision of his guardian.

Rothen smiled. He had to admire her ability to turn a bad situation to her advantage. As they stepped outside, he surrounded them both with a shield of magic and warmed the air within. Nights were growing increasingly chilly. Fallen leaves skittered over the courtyard, making quiet scraping noises as they touched the pavement. Winter was only a month away.

Reaching the Novices' Quarters, they walked inside. The corridor was empty and silent. Rothen escorted her to her door, then murmured a farewell. He turned away and heard the door click behind him.

He had taken only a few steps when a figure entered the corridor. Recognising the boy, Rothen slowed and narrowed his eyes.

Their gaze locked. As Rothen passed, Regin turned his head to maintain the contact, his gaze unflinching despite the disapproval Rothen knew must show in his expression. The boy's mouth curled upward slightly before he finally turned away.

Snorting softly, Rothen continued out of the Novices' Quarters. Regin had only harassed Sonea once or twice since she had moved to her new room, and not at all since she had changed classes. He had hoped the boy was losing interest in her. But as Rothen considered the confidence and malevolence in the boy's gaze he felt a growing certainty that his hopes were in vain.

—Rothen!

Recognising the sender immediately, he froze in mid-step and almost tripped over.

—Dorrien! he replied.

—I have good news, Father. Lady Vinara has decided it's time I reported to her again. I will be visiting the Guild soon — probably in a month or so.

Behind Dorrien's sending were complex feelings. Rothen knew that travelling to Imardin for the sake of formality irked his son. Dorrien could not help worrying how the village he lived in would cope without a Healer for several weeks. There was also a reassuring eagerness in Dorrien's sending. They hadn't seen each other in over two years.

But it wasn't just that. Every time Rothen had

communicated with his son lately he had detected a reluctant curiosity. Dorrien wanted to meet Sonea.

—*That is good news.* Rothen smiled and continued out of the Novices' Quarters. *It's been too long since you visited me. I've been wishing there was some way I could order you home.*

—*Father!* Dorrien's sending was tinged with half-serious suspicion. *You didn't arrange this, did you?*

—*No.* Rothen chuckled. *But I might keep it in mind for the future. I shall have your old room readied for you.*

—*I'll be staying for two weeks, so be sure to stock up on that good wine from the Lake District of Elyne. I'm heartily tired of the local bol.*

—*Done. And bring some raka with you. I've heard that the raka from the Eastern District is the best. Sonea is very fond of it.*

—*It is the best,* Dorrien said proudly. *All right, raka in exchange for wine. I'll contact you again when I leave. I must go now.*

– *Take care, my son.*

Rothen felt the familiar presence fade from his mind. He smiled as he reached the Magicians' Quarters. Dorrien may be curious to meet Sonea, but what would she make of him? Chuckling, he started up the stairs to his room.

'I feel better tonight,' Tayend told the ceiling of his cabin. 'I told you I'd get used to it eventually.'

Looking over the narrow passage to where his friend lay, Dannyl smiled. Tayend had dozed most of the day. It had been stiflingly hot, and the evening's humidity made sleep impossible.

'You didn't have to suffer so long. Surely a day of seasickness would have been enough adventure for you.'

159

Tayend glanced at Dannyl, his expression shameful. 'Yes I did.'

'You're afraid of being Healed, aren't you?'

The scholar gave a quick nod, more like a shiver.

'I've never encountered anyone who was, but I've heard of it happening before.' Dannyl frowned. 'Can I ask why?'

'I'd rather not talk about it.'

Dannyl nodded. Rising, he stretched as best he could. It seemed that all merchant ships had cramped living spaces – which was probably due to the small stature of their makers. Most ships that roamed the seas around the Allied Lands were built and sailed by the Vindo.

It had taken two weeks to sail to Capia, and he had been heartily thankful to greet dry land again when he arrived. Lonmar's capital city, Jebem, was four weeks' journey from Capia, and Dannyl was already tired of his surroundings. To make things worse, there had been little wind in the last few days and the captain had informed him that the ship would be delayed as a result.

'I'm going up for some air.'

Tayend grunted a reply. Leaving the scholar, Dannyl started down the passage and entered the common room. Unlike the previous crew, this one kept quiet at night. They sat in pairs or on their own, some huddled in the bag-like beds they used. Walking past, Dannyl climbed the stairs to the door and pushed through to the deck.

Heavy air greeted him. Though it was autumn in Kyralia, the weather had grown warmer as they travelled north. Walking along the deck, Dannyl nodded at the sailors on watch. They barely bothered to respond, some ignoring him completely.

He missed the company of Jano. None of these sailors

were at all interested in trying out their conversational or singing skills on him. He even missed the occasional mouthful of potent siyo.

Lanterns kept the ship brightly lit. At night, from time to time, a sailor hung one from a pole and leaned out over the railing to inspect the hull of the ship. Once, Dannyl had asked what the man was looking for, but by the blank look he received he guessed the sailor was not familiar with his language.

All was still tonight, and Dannyl was undisturbed as he leaned on the stern railing, watching the water ripple in the light. It was easy, at night, to imagine the shadow of a wave was a creature's back sliding through the water. Occasionally over the last two weeks he had glimpsed fish leaping through the waves. A few days ago he had been exhilarated to see anyi swimming with the bow wave, some as large as a human. The spiny creatures had lifted their whiskered noses and uttered strange, haunting cries.

Turning away, he started along the rail then stopped as he saw that several short lengths of thick black rope were strewn across his path. He frowned, thinking how easily he could have tripped.

Then one of the ropes moved.

Taking a step back, he stared at the thing. It was too smooth to be rope. And why would a rope be cut into short pieces, anyway? Each length of blackness glimmered slimily in the lantern light.

One turned and started creeping toward him.

'Eyoma!'

The warning cry echoed in the night, and was repeated all around. Dannyl looked around at the sailors in disbelief.

'I thought they were a joke,' he muttered as he backed away from the creatures. 'They were supposed to be a joke.'

'Eyoma!' A sailor hurried toward him, a large pan in one hand, a paddle in the other. 'Sea leech. You be away from rail!'

Turning around, Dannyl realised that more of the creatures were behind him. They were climbing onto the deck from all sides. He started toward the middle of the ship, then dodged as one of them made a small leap toward him. Another raised its front half up as if sniffing the air, but he could see no nose – just a pale, round mouth ringed by sharp-looking teeth.

Stepping past him, the sailor swung the pan he was carrying. Liquid spilled out, splashing over the creatures and the deck. A familiar, nutty odour reached Dannyl's nostrils, and he looked at the sailor questioningly.

'Siyo?'

The creatures seemed as appalled by their dousing as Dannyl would have been. As they began to writhe, the sailor pushed them over the edge of the ship with a paddle. Small splashes followed.

Two more sailors joined the first. They took it in turns to refill their pans from an open barrel lashed to the ship, splash the leeches and sweep them from the deck. It was done with such matter-of-fact efficiency that Dannyl began to relax. When one of the crew accidentally doused another with the liquor, he choked back a laugh.

But the black creatures kept coming, flowing over the deck in greater numbers until it seemed like the night was eating away at the edge of the ship. One of the sailors swore and glanced down. A leech had attached itself to his ankle. It wrapped its body about the sailor's leg with alarming speed. Still swearing, he splashed it with siyo, then, as it let go and began to writhe, he kicked it off the deck.

Sobering, Dannyl moved forward, determined to help. As one of the sailors stepped forward to push the creatures away, Dannyl caught his arm and halted him. Gesturing toward the leeches, Dannyl focussed his will and pushed. The leeches scattered off the deck and splashed into the sea.

He met the sailor's eyes, and the man nodded once.

'Why the siyo?' Dannyl asked as the man brought another pan. 'Why not just push them off?'

'Not siyo,' the man said discarding the paddle. 'Yomi. Left from making siyo. Burns eyoma and stop coming back.'

The sailor continued to splash the liquid down and Dannyl kept pushing the creatures off. Then the ship shifted strangely in the water, listing slightly to one side, and the sailor cursed.

'What's happening?'

The man looked pale. 'Too many eyoma. If big swarm, ship be made heavy. If swarm on one side mostly, ship turn over.'

Glancing around, Dannyl saw that the captain and more than half of the crew had gathered on the low side of the ship, where the deck was black with the leeches. Thinking of Jano's story, he realised the danger the crew faced. If the ship capsized and they fell into the water, they would not survive long.

'How do you stop them?' he asked, shoving more of the creatures back into the sea.

'Not easy.' The sailor hurried away to draw more liquid

from the barrel, then returned to Dannyl's side. 'Hard to get yomi on hull.'

The ship listed further. Dannyl picked up the paddle the man had discarded and handed it back. 'I'm going to see if I can help.'

The sailor nodded. Striding down the deck, Dannyl found his way blocked by scattered sea leeches that had evaded the sailors. He saw black shadows wriggling along ropes, in corners and on the railing. Raising a magical barrier about himself, he walked past them, flinching as they leapt at him. A slight sizzle followed as they met the barrier and fell away. Satisfied, he continued on.

Before he had reached the captain, a familiar voice called from the door to the common room.

'What's happening?'

Seeing Tayend peering out, Dannyl felt a stab of alarm. 'Stay downstairs.'

A leech dropped from a rope and landed near the door. Tayend stared at it in horrified fascination. 'Another one.'

'Close the door!' Dannyl focussed his will and the door slammed shut. At once it flew open again. Tayend leapt out.

'They're in here, too!' he cried. Dodging the leech near the door, he hurried to Dannyl's side. 'What are they?'

'Eyoma. Sea leeches.'

'But . . . you said they were a joke!'

'Obviously, they're not.'

'What's the captain doing?' Tayend asked, his eyes widening further.

Looking up, Dannyl caught his breath as the captain strode into the thick blanket of leeches covering the port deck. The man ignored the creatures that wound up his legs. He held the end of a hose in one hand. The other end was attached to a barrel. Leaning over the railing, the captain aimed the hose at the hull and barked an order. A crewman began turning a handle set into the barrel. Soon liquid was spurting out of the hose in the captain's hands.

Though crewmen splashed yomi at the captain's legs, more leeches quickly replaced those that fell away. Within a few minutes the captain's legs were streaked with blood from the eyoma bites. Dannyl started toward the scene, Tayend following.

'Stay here,' he told the scholar.

Looking at the leeches covering the deck between him and the captain, Dannyl hesitated. He took a deep breath, then waded into the slimy blackness. Sizzling surrounded him as they met his shield. He felt the creatures burst as they were crushed beneath his boots.

Reaching the captain's side, Dannyl touched a leech that had climbed to the man's shoulders. It fell away, leaving a circle of small puncture marks. The man turned to stare at Dannyl, then nodded gratefully.

'Go back,' Dannyl ordered.

The man shook his head, but not in refusal. 'No kill too many or ship go over other way.'

'I understand,' Dannyl replied.

The ship was listing alarmingly now. Leaning over the railing, Dannyl considered the hull. It was almost invisible, only the occasional ripple of light showing in the darkness. Creating a globe light, he sent it down to illuminate the creatures. He caught his breath. The hull was a wriggling mass of leeches.

Gathering power, he released it in a spray of stunstrikes. A shower of leeches fell back into the sea. They would probably survive the stunstrike, but he did not want to risk using forcestrike or firestrike on the hull. As more leeches fell away the ship slowly righted itself, then began to tilt toward the other side.

Crossing the deck, Dannyl leaned over the railing on the other side. Once more he forced the leeches to loose their hold, and the ship straightened again. As he made his way back to the port side, Dannyl noted that the sailors had turned their efforts to cleaning leeches off the deck. One man was roaming about dealing with the ones that had curled around ropes or slipped into cracks or corners.

The sense of danger had passed, but the grim work continued endlessly as the leeches kept climbing onto the ship. Soon Dannyl lost count of the times he had crossed the deck. He refreshed himself with Healing magic, but as the hours passed his head began to ache from the constant mental exertion.

At last the onslaught lessened and dwindled, and only a few sluggish leeches remained. Hearing his name called, he straightened and turned to see that all was lit by the faint light of dawn. A small crowd had gathered around him. The captain raised his arm, then a cheer rose among the sailors.

Surprised, Dannyl smiled, then joined in the cheering. He felt exhaused, but also elated.

From somewhere a small barrel was produced, and a mug was passed from sailor to sailor. As Dannyl accepted the mug, he smelled the familiar tang of real siyo. The mouthful sent warmth spreading through him. He looked around for Tayend, but the scholar was nowhere in sight.

'Your friend sleeps,' one of the sailors said.

Relieved, Dannyl accepted another mouthful of siyo. 'Do you encounter eyoma often?'

'Now and then,' the captain said, nodding. 'Not like this.'

'Never seen swarm so big,' another sailor agreed. 'Good that you passenger. If not with us, we be fish bait today.'

The captain looked up suddenly and said something in Vindo. As the crew moved to the ropes, Dannyl realised that a mild wind had risen. The captain looked exhausted, but pleased.

'You get sleep now,' he suggested to Dannyl. 'Helped us good. May need help tonight.'

Nodding, Dannyl made his way to his cabin. He found Tayend asleep, a frown creasing the scholar's forehead. He paused, concerned to see dark circles under the young man's eyes. He wished that he could heal his friend, then considered administering a little Healing power while Tayend was asleep.

But to do so would be a betrayal of trust, and Dannyl did not want to risk ruining this new friendship. Sighing, he lay down on his own bed, closed his eyes and gave in to exhaustion.

CHAPTER 11

UNWELCOME ARRIVALS

Sweet juice filled Sonea's mouth as her teeth broke through the skin of the pachi. She held the yellow fruit between her teeth and turned the pages of Poril's book until she found the right diagram.

'There it is,' she said after taking the fruit out of her mouth again. 'The blood system. Lady Kinla said we had to memorise all the different parts.'

Poril looked down at the page and groaned.

'Don't worry,' she assured him. 'We'll work out some way to help you remember. Rothen has shown me some really useful exercises for remembering lists.'

Seeing his doubtful expression, Sonea smothered a sigh. She had quickly discovered why Poril was having trouble with his studies. He was neither smart nor strong, and tests sent him into fits of terror. Worst of all, he was so demoralised by this that he had given up trying.

But he was also hungry for companionship. Though she had not seen the other novices being deliberately cruel to the boy, they obviously didn't like him. He was from House Heril, which was out of favour in court for reasons she had not yet discovered. She didn't think that was why he was avoided, however. He had several irritating habits, the worst being a ridiculous, high-pitched laugh that set her teeth on edge.

The rest of the class ignored her, too. She had quickly realised they were not purposefully avoiding her though, and that they did not dislike her in the way they disliked Poril. It was simply that each had formed a close friendship with another classmate, and had no wish to include a third.

Trassia and Narron were clearly more than just friends. Sonea had seen them holding hands a few times, and noted that Lord Ahrind kept a close watch on the pair. Narron was already determined to become a Healer, and his results in that subject were the best in the class. Trassia was also most interested in Healing, but in a passive way that suggested her interest was due only to Narron's enthusiasm – or the expectation that women were most suited to Healing.

The only Elyne in the class, Yalend, spent his time with the talkative Vindo boy, Seno. Hal, the stiff-faced Lan boy, and his Kyralian friend, Benon, formed the other pair. Though quieter than the boys in Regin's class, these four still talked endlessly about the horse races, told unlikely stories about girls in court, and fooled about as if they hadn't reached the end of their childhood.

Which they hadn't, she was coming to understand. The children of the slums grew up fast because they had to. These novices had lived their lives in the midst of luxury, and had less reason to mature quickly than their brothers and sisters outside the Guild.

Until they graduated, they were free from family responsibilities, such as presenting themselves at court, marriage, and managing whatever income-producing 'interests' in farming or manufacturing their family was involved in. Joining the Guild extended their childhood for an extra five years.

Though Poril was a year older, he was sometimes the most childish of all the novices. His friendliness seemed genuine, but she suspected he was pleased that he wasn't the novice from the lowest social background any more.

Regin, to her surprise and relief, had ignored her since she had left his class. She glimpsed him in the Foodhall each day, and occasionally saw his gang gathering in the corridors before classes, but he didn't attempt to harass her. Even the rumour that had circulated concerning her relationship with Rothen had been forgotten. Teachers no longer eyed her with suspicion, and she rarely heard Rothen's name whispered as she walked down the corridor.

'If only we knew which parts she'll ask us to name,' Poril sighed. 'The big ones, I suppose – and a couple of small ones.'

Sonea shrugged. 'Don't waste your time trying to guess what she'll ask. It will take as much effort as memorising them all.'

A gong rang out. Through the trees, Sonea could see other novices reluctantly gathering their belongings and hurrying toward the University. Like them, Sonea and Poril had spent the midbreak outside enjoying the rare warmth of a sunny autumn day. She stood and stretched.

'After class, let's go to the library and study.'

Poril nodded. 'If you want.'

Walking quickly, they hurried out of the gardens and into the University. The rest of the novices were already seated in the classroom. As Sonea took her seat, Lord Skoran entered the room.

Putting down a small pile of books, the magician cleared his throat and faced the novices. Then a movement in the doorway drew his attention away. All of the class turned to watch as three figures stepped into the room. Seeing Regin among them, Sonea felt a chill of foreboding.

University Director Jerrik looked around the room. His eyes skipped over the other novices' faces. As they met hers he frowned, then he glanced at the novice at his side.

'Regin has succeeded in completing the half-year tests.' Jerrik's usually stern voice held a hint of reluctance. 'I have moved him to your class.'

Sonea's stomach turned over. The magicians were still talking, but she could not bring herself to focus on the words. She felt her chest tighten, as if an invisible hand had wrapped itself around her and was squeezing. Her heartbeat grew louder until it roared in her ears.

Then she remembered to breathe.

Suddenly dizzy, she closed her eyes. When she opened them again, Regin was wearing his most charming smile. His gaze moved from the other novices to her. Though his mouth remained fixed in the same wide smile, and not a muscle of his face appeared to move, somehow his expression changed completely.

She tore her eyes away. *This is impossible. How could he have caught up? He must have cheated.*

Yet she couldn't see how he could deceive the teachers and still pass their tests. That left only one possibility. He must have started extra studies not long after she had – probably as soon as he had learned what she intended to do. And he had done it in secret, most likely with the help of his guardian.

But *why?* All his friends were in the other class. Perhaps he thought he would gather another gang of admirers here. She felt a trickle of hope. It was unlikely that even *he* could break up the pairing that this class was firmly set into. Unless . . .

Knowing Regin, once he had decided to go to the effort of rising to the next class he would have made friendly overtures to all the novices in it. He would have made sure he was welcome.

Looking around the class, Sonea was surprised to see Narron regarding Regin with a frown. The boy looked displeased. Then she remembered how she had been told firmly that this class had no time for 'playing around'.

So perhaps Regin hadn't befriended her new classmates. Yet he had gone to a lot of effort to rise a level.

Maybe he just couldn't stand seeing a slum girl do better than him. Fergun had been willing to take great risks to have her expelled from the Guild because he didn't want lower-class entrants joining. Her success or failure to learn and be accepted would be taken into account if the Guild ever considered taking in members from outside the Houses again. What if Regin was trying to hamper her learning, to ensure she failed and lower-class entrants were never welcomed again.

Then I had better make sure he doesn't succeed!

She had escaped him once, she could do it again by studying harder and reaching the next class.

Even as the idea occurred to her, she knew it wasn't possible. It had taken her every night and Freeday to finish a half year's learning three months early, and she still had to catch up on what this class had covered already in the months before she had joined it. She didn't have any time left to learn what the Second Years had studied as well.

Perhaps it would be better to let him think he'd won. He'd leave her alone if he thought she wasn't doing as well as him. She didn't have to be the best novice in her class to prove that entrants from outside the Houses could succeed as magicians.

If she fell back to the first class she was sure Regin's pride wouldn't allow him to follow her. She dismissed that idea faster than the first. The summer class was still under Regin's sway, even if he had left it. At least her current class wasn't united against her . . .

She blinked, suddenly realising that Lord Skoran's thin, wavering voice had been the only sound in the room for some time.

'. . . and in continuing our assessment of the Sachakan War, I want you to find out all you can about the five Higher Magicians who joined the battle at the second stage. They were from countries outside Kyralia, and their aid was gathered by a certain young magician named Genfel. Choose one of these magicians and write a four-thousand word description of his life before he became involved in the war.'

Picking up her pen, Sonea began writing. Regin may have reached the higher class, but he still had much work to do before he caught up with them. For a few weeks he would be too busy to harass her, and by then she would know if he was going to have any influence over the rest of the class. Without them to support him, it would not be so easy for him to make her the target of his pranks.

'Jebem, halai!'

At the cry, Dannyl looked up eagerly.

'What is it?' Tayend asked.

Dannyl set aside his plate with a grimace. Though dried

marin paste was a delicacy, nothing could make stale ship bread appetising.

'Jebem has been sighted,' he said, rising. Hunching over so he did not knock his head on the roof, Dannyl moved toward the door. As he stepped outside, light dazzled him. The sun hung low over the sea, setting the waves glittering brightly. The heat of the day lingered in the air and radiated from the deck.

Looking to the north, Dannyl caught his breath, then ducked inside the doorway and beckoned to Tayend. Straightening, he moved down the deck to the bow, and gazed at the distant city.

Low houses built of flat, grey stones spread endlessly along the coast. From among them rose thousands of obelisks.

Tayend had appeared at his side. 'Big, isn't it?' the scholar breathed.

Dannyl nodded. The small coastal villages they had passed in the last few days had been made up of houses in the same simple style, with a handful of obelisks rising above them. The houses of Jebem were no grander, but the sheer size of the city was astounding. The obelisks among them were like a forest of needles, and the low sun painted all with a vivid red-orange light.

They watched silently as the ship continued along the coast. A row of rocky outcrops appeared, running parallel to the city like guards. The ship sailed into the gap between. When they drew level to the part of the city where the obelisks were thickest, the ship slowed and turned into a narrow channel. On either side, dark-skinned men hurried to the stone banks. They tossed ropes to the sailors, which were then looped around stout posts on the ship. The other ends were already fastened to teams of gorin. The large beasts began hauling the ship down the channel.

For the next hour the Lonmar wharf-labourers guided the ship along the channel until it reached an artificial marina. Several other ships, some twice the size of their own, rocked gently in the water. As the ship was lashed to posts along the wharf, Dannyl and Tayend returned to their rooms to gather their belongings.

After a brief and formal exchange with the captain, they walked down the gangplank to dry land. Their trunks were handed to four men. A fifth stepped forward and bowed.

'Greetings, Ambassador Dannyl, young Tremmelin. I am Loryk, your translator. I will take you to the Guild House. Please follow me.'

He made a quick, imperious gesture at the carriers and started into the city. Following, Dannyl and Tayend walked along several wharves and onto a wide street.

Dust filled the air, muting the colours around them. The sea breeze was replaced by a stifling heat and a mixture of perfume, spice and dust. Men filled the streets, all well covered in simple Lonmar clothing. Voices surrounded them, but the liquid-sounding words were incomprehensible. Those men they passed stared at Dannyl openly, then at Tayend, their gaze neither welcoming nor disapproving. Occasionally one narrowed his eyes at Tayend, who had put on his fanciest court costume and looked very out of place.

The scholar was unusually quiet. Looking at his companion, Dannyl recognised the now-familiar signs of unease: a small crease had appeared between Tayend's brows and he walked a half-step behind. As the scholar met his gaze, Dannyl gave him a reassuring smile.

'Don't worry. It's unsettling at first, being in a strange city.'

Tayend's frown disappeared, and he drew level with Dannyl as they followed the translator through a narrow alley. Emerging in a large square, Dannyl checked his stride and looked around in dismay.

Wooden stages had been built all around. On the closest a woman stood, hands bound. Beside her was a man dressed in white, his head shaved and covered with tattoos and holding a whip in his left hand. Another man was striding among the crowd that had gathered around the stage, reciting something from a piece of paper.

Dannyl lengthened his stride to catch up with the translator.

'What is he saying?'

Loryk listened. 'The woman has shamed her husband and family by inviting another man into her bedroom.' He waved a hand. 'This is Judgment Square.'

Shouts rang out, drowning out the rest of the proclamation. A crowd had gathered around several of the stages. As Dannyl followed the carriers away from the woman, he noticed a young man standing nearby, watching her. The man's dark eyes glittered with moisture, but his face was set and rigid.

Husband or lover? Dannyl wondered.

The centre of the square was less crowded. The carriers crossed and made their way between two stages. The whitedressed men standing on the stages held swords. Dannyl kept his eyes on the translator's back, but a voice rose above the jeering of the crowd and Loryk slowed.

'Ah . . . he says: this man has shamed his family with his unnatural . . . what is your word? Lusts? He has earned

176

the ultimate punishment for corrupting the souls and bodies of men. Just as the sun sets and darkness purges the world of sin, only his death may cleanse those souls he has soiled.'

Despite the heat, Dannyl felt cold spread through his body. The condemned man was slumped against a pole, his expression resigned. The crowd began to shout, their faces twisted in hatred. Dannyl looked away, struggling to hold back a tide of horror and anger. The man was going to be executed for a crime that in Kyralia earned only dishonour and shame, and in Elyne – according to Tayend – was no crime at all.

Dannyl could not help thinking back to the scandal and rumour that had caused him so much trouble as a novice. He had been accused of the same 'crime' as this man. Proof hadn't mattered; once the rumour had started, he had been treated as an outcast by both novices and teachers. He shivered as the crowd roared again behind them. *If I'd been unlucky enough to be born in Lonmar, this might have been how the matter ended.*

Loryk entered another alley and the jeering faded behind them. Dannyl glanced at Tayend. The scholar's face was white.

'It's one thing to hear or read of the strict laws of another land, quite another to see them being enacted,' the scholar murmured. 'I swear that I will never complain about the excesses of the Elyne court again.'

The translator continued along another street, then stopped as the carriers entered a low building.

'The Guild House in Jebem,' he announced as they reached the door. 'I will leave you here.'

The man bowed and walked away. Examining the

building, Dannyl noted a plaque bearing the Guild symbol set into the wall. Otherwise, the building was the same as any other they had seen. Stepping through the open door, they entered a room with a low ceiling. An Elyne magician stood nearby.

'Greetings,' he said. 'I am Vaulen, First Guild Ambassador for Lonmar.'

The man was grey-haired and thin. Dannyl inclined his head. 'Second Guild Ambassador for Elyne, Dannyl.' He gestured to Tayend, who bowed gracefully. 'Tayend of Tremmelin, scholar of the Great Library and my assistant.'

Vaulen nodded to Tayend politely. His eyes dropped to Tayend's violet shirt. 'Welcome to Jebem. I feel I must warn you, Tayend of Tremmelin, that the Lonmar people value humility and simplicity and disapprove of bright clothing, no matter how fashionable. I can recommend a good tailor who can provide you with quality attire in a simpler style for your stay.'

Dannyl expected to see a glint of rebellion in the scholar's eyes, but Tayend bowed his head graciously. 'Thank you for the warning, my lord. I will see this tailor tomorrow if he is available.'

'I have had rooms prepared for you,' Vaulen continued. 'I'm sure you want to rest after your journey. We have separate baths here – the servants will show you where. Afterwards, you are welcome to join me for the evening meal.'

They followed a servant down a short corridor. The man gestured to two open doors, bowed, then strode away. Tayend stepped inside one of the rooms, then stopped and gazed around, looking lost.

Dannyl hesitated, then stepped inside. 'Are you all right?'

Tayend shuddered. 'They're going to execute him, aren't they? They probably already have.'

Realising Tayend was talking about the condemned man in Judgment Square, he nodded. 'Probably.'

'Nothing we could do. Another country, different laws, and all that.'

'Unfortunately.'

Tayend sighed and sat down on a chair. 'I don't want to spoil the adventure for you, Dannyl, but I already dislike Lonmar.'

Dannyl nodded. 'Judgment Square wasn't exactly an encouraging introduction to the country,' he agreed. 'But I don't want to judge Lonmar too quickly. There must be more to this place. If you saw the slums of Imardin first, you might not think much of Kyralia. Hopefully we've seen the worst, and the rest can only be better.'

Tayend sighed, then moved to his trunk and opened it. 'You're probably right. I'll try to find some plainer clothes.'

Dannyl smiled tiredly. 'Sometimes this uniform has advantages,' he said, tugging the sleeve of his robe. 'Same old purple robes every day, but at least I can wear them anywhere throughout the Allied Lands.' He moved to the doorway. 'If I don't see you in the baths, then I'll meet you at dinner.'

Without looking up, Tayend lifted a hand to wave. Dannyl left the scholar to rifle through the bright clothes in his trunk and entered the other room.

He sobered as he considered the next few weeks. After he had dealt with his ambassadorial duties in the city, they would visit the Splendid Temple as part of their research. It was said to be a serenely beautiful place, yet it was the centre of the strict Mahga religion that set out the punishments that he had encountered today. Suddenly he wasn't looking forward to the visit.

Yet they might find information about ancient magic there. After a month stuck in the confines of a ship, he was looking forward to stretching his legs and mind again. Hopefully he was right that the rest of Lonmar could only be more welcoming than Judgment Square.

It was late when Lorlen returned to his office. Taking Dannyl's latest report from his secure box, he sat down at the desk and read it through again. As he finished he leaned back in his chair and sighed.

He had been thinking about Akkarin's diary for weeks now. If it existed, it would be in the High Lord's Residence somewhere. Considering what the diary might contain, Lorlen doubted it was kept in Akkarin's library with ordinary books. It was probably stowed in the cellar beneath the building, and Lorlen was sure that place was securely locked.

A chill breeze touched his skin. He shivered, then cursed under his breath. His office had always been draughty, something that the previous Administrator had complained of constantly. Rising, he hunted for the source of the breeze as he had often done in the past but, as always, the chill disappeared as suddenly as it had come.

Shaking his head, he started pacing. Dannyl and his scholar companion should arrive in Lonmar soon and they would visit the Splendid Temple. Lorlen hoped they would find nothing – the idea that information about black magic might exist in such a place was appalling to consider.

He stopped pacing at a knock on the door. Striding over, he pulled it open, expecting to receive a gentle lecture about getting enough sleep from Lord Osen. Instead, a dark silhouette filled the doorway.

'Good evening, Lorlen,' Akkarin said, smiling.

Lorlen stared at the High Lord in surprise.

'Are you going to let me in?'

'Of course!' Shaking his head as if to clear it, Lorlen stepped back. Akkarin strolled inside and folded himself into one of the large cushioned chairs. The High Lord's gaze strayed to Lorlen's desk.

Following his friend's gaze, Lorlen caught his breath as he saw Dannyl's letter lying open. It took all his will to stop himself rushing over and stuffing the pages back into the box. Instead, he crossed the room casually, stopping to straighten a chair, then dropped into his seat with a sigh.

'As always, you find me in a mess,' he muttered. Picking up Dannyl's letter, he dropped it back in the secure box. After tidying a few more items on the desk, he slipped the box into a drawer. 'What brings you here at this late hour?'

Akkarin shrugged. 'Nothing in particular. You're always visiting me, so I thought it was time I dropped in to see you. I knew better than to try your rooms first, though this is a late hour even for you.'

'It is.' Lorlen nodded. 'I was just reading some mail, then I was going to finish for the night.'

'Anything interesting? How is Lord Dannyl?'

Lorlen's heart skipped. Had Akkarin been able to see Dannyl's signature, or had he recognised the writing? He frowned as he tried to remember what had been written on the exposed page.

'He's on his way to Lonmar to settle the council's

argument about Greater Clan Koyhmar. I asked Errend to see to it, since he now has a Second Ambassador to deal with Elyne matters while he's away, but Errend decided to send Dannyl in his place.'

Akkarin smiled. 'Lonmar. A place that will either whet the appetite for travel, or kill it.'

Lorlen leaned forward. 'What did it do for you?'

'Hmmm,' Akkarin considered the question carefully. 'It did give me a hunger to see more of the world, but it also hardened me as a traveller. Lonmars may be the most civilised people of the Allied Lands, but there is much that is harsh and cruel about them. You learn to tolerate their sense of justice, perhaps understand it as well, but by doing so your own beliefs and ideals are strengthened. The same could be said of Elyne frivolity, or the Vindo obsession with trade. There is more to life than fashion and money.'

Akkarin paused, his gaze distant, then shifted in his seat. 'And you discover that, just as not every Elyne is frivolous, or every Vindo is greedy, not every Lonmar is unbending. Most are kind and forgiving, preferring to resolve disputes privately. I did learn much about them, and though the whole journey there proved to be a waste of time as regards my research, the experience has proven to be valuable to my role here.'

Lorlen closed his eyes and massaged them. A waste of time? Was Dannyl also wasting his time?

'You are tired, my friend,' Akkarin said, his voice softening. 'I am keeping you from your bed with my tales.'

Blinking, Lorlen looked up at the High Lord. 'No – don't mind me. Please go on.'

'No.' Akkarin rose, his black robes rustling. 'I was putting you to sleep. We'll catch up another time.'

Disappointment and relief mingled as Lorlen followed Akkarin to the door. Stepping into the corridor, Akkarin turned back to regard Lorlen, and smiled crookedly.

'Good night, Lorlen. You will get some rest, won't you? You look exhausted.'

'Yes. Good night, Akkarin.'

Closing the door, Lorlen sighed. He had just learned something useful – or had he? Akkarin might be saying he had found nothing in Lonmar to hide something he *had* discovered. It was odd that he should suddenly talk of the journey when he had avoided the subject in the past.

Lorlen winced as a cold draught chilled his neck. Distracted from his thoughts, he yawned, then returned to his desk and moved the secure box to its proper place in the cupboard. Feeling better, he left the office and started for his rooms.

He must be patient. Dannyl would find out soon enough whether his journey to Lonmar was a waste of time.

CHAPTER 12

NOT WHAT THEY HAD IN MIND

How had he done it?

Sonea walked slowly down the corridor. In her arms was the box in which she kept her pen, inkwell and unbound folder of notes and fresh paper.

The folder was empty.

Once more she searched her memory. When had she given Regin an opportunity to get to her belongings? She was always cautious, never leaving her notes unattended for a moment.

But in the classroom, during Lady Kinla's lesson, the novices were often called from their seats to observe some demonstration. It was possible Regin had slipped her notes out of their cover as he passed her table. She had believed such nimble-fingeredness was beyond the pampered children of the Houses. Obviously she was wrong.

She had checked her room thoroughly, and even slipped back into the University to check the classroom late in the night. All the time she had searched, she had known she wouldn't find the notes, at least not in one piece or before today's tests.

As she entered the classroom her suspicions were confirmed by Regin's smug expression. Refusing to show any drop in her composure, she bowed to Lady Kinla and moved to her usual seat beside Poril.

Lady Kinla was a tall, middle-aged Healer. Women Healers always wore their hair bound back in a knot at the nape of their neck, and on Lady Kinla this fashion gave her thin face a permanently severe expression. As Sonea sat down the Healer cleared her throat and looked at each of the novices intently.

'Today I will test you on the lessons we have covered in the last three months. You may consult your notes.' She lifted a few sheets of paper, her eyes flitting across the page. 'Firstly, Benon . . .'

Sonea felt her heart skip as the testing began. Lady Kinla wandered up and down the classroom, threading her way past the novices as she threw questions at them. When Sonea heard her name she felt her heart skip, but, to her relief, the question was easy and she could answer it from memory.

Slowly, however, the questions became more difficult. As other novices began to hesitate and consult their notes before answering, Sonea grew anxious. The air stirred beside her as Kinla walked past her chair.

Then the Healer stopped and turned to stare at Sonea. She took a few steps forward until she towered over Sonea's desk.

'Sonea,' she placed a fingertip on the table. 'Where are your notes?'

Sonea swallowed. For a second she considered pretending that she had forgotten them. But making up such a story would give Regin even more satisfaction, and another excuse came to mind . . .

'You said this lesson would be a test, my lady,' she said. 'I didn't think I would need to take any notes.'

Lady Kinla's eyebrows rose, and she regarded Sonea

speculatively. From somewhere behind them came a smothered chuckle of anticipation.

'I see.' The teacher's tone was dangerous. 'Name twenty bones of the body, starting from the smallest.'

Sonea cursed silently. Her answer had angered the Healer, who obviously didn't expect Sonea to be able to remember so much.

But she had to try. Slowly, then with more confidence, Sonea drew the names from memory, counting them on her fingers as she spoke. When she had finished Lady Kinla stared at her in silence, lips pressed into a thin line.

'You are correct,' the Healer said grudgingly.

With a quiet sigh of relief, Sonea watched the teacher turn and continue her meandering among the novices' desks. Glancing at the class, she found Regin staring at her, his eyes narrowed to slits.

She looked away. Thankfully, she had helped Poril with his notes and could copy them out again for herself. She doubted she'd see her own again now.

A few days after their arrival, the Splendid Temple priests replied to Dannyl's request to see the collection of scrolls. He was relieved at this break from his ambassadorial duties. Already, the squabbling of the Lonmar Council of Elders was trying his patience.

Lorlen's reasons for sending a foreign Guild Ambassador to Lonmar were annoyingly valid. One of the Greater Clans had fallen out of favour and fortune. No longer able to support its novices and magicians, the other clans were required to take on the responsibility.

Studying the agreements between the Guild and other lands had been part of Dannyl's preparations for his role.

While the Kyralian King apportioned part of his tax revenue to pay for the needs of Kyralian magicians, and left the selection of entrants to chance, other lands had different approaches. The Elyne King offered a number of places each year and chose applicants with a mind to future political implications. The Vindo sent as many entrants as they could find and afford, which was not many since they had little magical ability in their bloodlines.

The Lonmars were ruled by a Council of Elders made up of representatives from the Greater Clans. Each Clan funded the training of its own magicians. The centuries-old agreement made between the Lonmars and the Kyralian King stated that, if a clan should be unable to finance its magicians, the other clans must equally share the cost of supporting them. The Guild did not want magicians falling on hard times, and turning to unethical uses of magic to survive.

Not surprisingly, several clans were protesting. From what Ambassador Vaulen had told Dannyl, however, they only needed to be gently and firmly reminded of the disadvantages of having the agreement annulled, their magicians sent home and access to Guild training withheld, and they would co-operate. Vaulen played the role of gentle Elyne persuader, Dannyl was to be the firm, immovable Kyralian.

But not today.

Hearing that Dannyl's request to the Temple had been successful, Ambassador Vaulen had immediately ordered servants to prepare the Guild carriage.

'Today is a day of rest,' he said. 'Which means the Elders will be visiting each other and debating what to do. You may as well do some sightseeing.' He offered them dried fruit softened with honeyed water as they waited.

'Is there anything I should know about the priests before I go?' Dannyl asked.

Vaulen considered. 'According to Mahga doctrine, all men find a balance between joy and pain in their lives. While magicians are considered to have been gifted with magic, they are barred from the priesthood. Only a few exceptions have been made.'

'Really?' Dannyl straightened. 'In what circumstances?'

'In the past, a few were judged to have suffered greatly and could seek balance by joining the priesthood, but only if they gave up their powers – though they were still barred from the higher ranks.'

'I hope this doesn't mean that they'll cause me pain to balance my own gifts.'

Vaulen smiled. 'You are an unbeliever. That is balance enough.'

'What can you tell me of High Priest Kassyk?'

'He respects the Guild, and speaks highly of the High Lord.'

'Why Akkarin in particular?'

'Akkarin visited the Temple over ten years ago, and it seems he impressed the High Priest greatly.'

'He has a way of doing that.' Dannyl looked at Tayend, but the scholar was absorbed in eating. Tayend, to his surprise, had returned from the tailor the day after their arrival dressed in typically colourless Lonmar clothes. 'They're very comfortable,' the scholar had explained. 'And I fancied owning some as a souvenir of our visit.' Shaking his head, Dannyl had replied: 'Only you could turn a statement of humility into an object of indulgence.'

'Your carriage is here,' Vaulen said, rising.

Hearing hoofbeats and the creak of springs outside,

Dannyl moved to the door. Tayend followed, wiping the sticky residue from the dried fruit off his fingers with a damp cloth.

'Give my regards to the High Priest,' Vaulen said.

'I will.' Dannyl stepped out of the building. At once he was bathed in the heat radiating from a sunlit wall on the other side of the street. Dust raised by the carriage tickled his throat.

A servant opened the carriage door. Climbing in, Dannyl winced as he entered the suffocatingly hot cabin. Tayend followed, settling onto the opposite seat with a grimace. The servant handed them two bottles of water, then signalled the driver to leave.

Opening the carriage windows in the hope of catching a breeze, Dannyl endured the dust that billowed in, washing it from his throat with mouthfuls of water. The streets were narrow, which kept them as shaded as possible, but the clutter of pedestrians slowed the carriage. Some streets were covered by wooden roofs, forming dark tunnels.

After a few brief conversations, they fell silent. Talking only filled their mouths with dust. The carriage moved slowly, plodding through the endless city. It was not long before Dannyl tired of seeing people and houses that all looked the same. He slumped against the side of the carriage and dozed.

The new sound of pavement under the horses' hooves roused him. Looking out of the window, he saw smooth walls passing on either side. After a hundred paces or so the corridor ended and the carriage entered a wide court-yard. At last the Splendid Temple came into view.

As with all Lonmar architecture, the building was

single-storeyed and undecorated. The walls were marble, however, the blocks fitting together so accurately it was difficult to make out their edges. Obelisks were set into the face of the building at intervals, each as wide at the base as the building was high, and rising higher than the carriage window allowed him to see.

The carriage stopped and Dannyl climbed out, too eager to leave the stifling heat of the interior to wait for the driver to open the door. Looking up, he drew in a breath as he saw how tall the obelisks were. Placed every fifty paces or so in all directions, they filled the sky.

'Look at them all,' Dannyl said to Tayend quietly. 'It's like a forest of gigantic trees.'

'Or a thousand swords.'

'Or masts of ships waiting to take souls away.'

'Or an enormous bed of nails.'

'You're in a good mood today,' Dannyl remarked dryly.

Tayend smiled crookedly. 'I am, aren't I?'

As they approached the door to the Temple, a man in a simple white robe stepped out to greet them. His hair was white, contrasting with the rich black of his skin. Bending only slightly, he clasped his hands together, then opened them in the ritual gesture of the Mahga followers.

'Welcome, Ambassador Dannyl. I am High Priest Kassyk.'

'Thank you for allowing us to visit,' Dannyl replied. 'This is my assistant and friend, Tayend of Tremmelin, scholar of the Great Library of Capia.'

The High Priest repeated the gesture. 'Welcome, Tayend of Tremmelin. Would you both like to see some of the Splendid Temple before viewing the scrolls?'

'We would be honoured,' Dannyl replied.

190

'Follow me.'

The High Priest turned and led them into the coolness of the temple building. They wandered down a long corridor, the priest gesturing as he explained the history or religious significance of features. Long corridors crossed the one they followed. Light filtered through small, narrow windows set just below the arched roof. Occasionally they passed a tiny courtyard filled with wide-leafed plants, surprising the visitors with their unexpected lushness. At other times they stopped at fountains set into the walls to drink a palmful of water.

The High Priest showed them the small rooms where the priests lived and spent their time in study or contemplation. He guided them through large, cavernous halls where prayers and rituals were held each day. Finally he guided them into a complex of small rooms where scrolls and books were displayed.

'Which texts would you like to see?' Kassyk asked.

'I would like to see the Dorgon scrolls.'

The priest regarded Dannyl quietly before he replied.

'We do not allow non-believers to read those texts.'

'Oh.' Dannyl frowned, disappointed. 'This is not good news. I have been led to believe these scrolls were available for viewing, and have travelled far to see them.'

'That is unfortunate indeed.' The High Priest looked genuinely sympathetic.

'Forgive me if I am wrong, but you have allowed them to be read before, haven't you?'

Kassyk blinked in surprise. He nodded slowly. 'Your High Lord, when he visited ten years ago, did persuade me to read them to him. He assured me that no-one would seek this information again.'

Dannyl exchanged a glance with Tayend. 'Akkarin was not High Lord then, but even if he had been, how could he have guaranteed this?'

'He made a vow never to repeat what he had heard.' The priest's frown deepened. 'Or refer to the scrolls to any other. He also said that the information was of no interest to the Guild. Nor was it of interest to him, as he was seeking ancient magic, not religious lore. Are you looking for the same truths?'

'I can't say, as I don't know exactly what Akkarin was looking for. These scrolls may be relevant to my research despite being of no use to the High Lord.' Dannyl held the priest's gaze. 'If I make the same vow, will you read them to me?'

The priest considered Dannyl. After a long pause, he nodded. 'Very well, but your friend must stay here.'

Tayend's shoulders slumped, but as he dropped into a nearby chair he let out a sigh of relief. Leaving the scholar fanning himself, Dannyl followed the High Priest through the rooms of scrolls. After a labyrinthine journey, they stepped into a small, square room.

All around were shelves covered in squares of flawless, clear glass. Drawing closer, Dannyl saw that fragmented pieces of paper were pressed under the glass.

'The Dorgon scrolls.' The High Priest moved to the first. 'I will translate for you if you will vow on the honour of your family and the Guild to never divulge their contents to anyone.'

Dannyl straightened and turned to face Kassyk. 'I swear on the honour of my family and House, and the Magicians' Guild of Kyralia, that I will never communicate what I learn from these scrolls to any man or woman, old or young, unless my silence will bring harm of the greatest kind upon the Allied Lands.' He paused. 'Is that acceptable? I cannot swear otherwise.'

The wrinkles around the old man's mouth had deepened with amusement, but he answered solemnly. 'It is acceptable.'

Relieved, Dannyl followed the High Priest to the first of the scrolls, and listened as the man began to read. They slowly made their way around the room, Kassyk pointing to and explaining diagrams and pictures in the text. When the last scroll had been read, Dannyl sat down on a bench in the centre of the room.

'Who would have guessed?' he said aloud.

'No-one at the time,' Kassyk replied.

'I can see why you don't want them read.'

Kassyk chuckled and sat beside Dannyl. 'It is no secret to those who enter the Priesthood that Dorgon was a trickster who used his meagre powers to convince thousands of his holiness. It was what happened later that has deep significance. He began to see there were miracles within his tricks, and that miracles were in fact tricks of the Great Power. But anyone who read these scrolls would not know that.'

'Why do you keep these scrolls, then?'

'They are all we have of Dorgon. His later works were copied, but this is the only original text that has survived. They were kept and preserved by a family who resisted the Mahga religion for centuries.'

Dannyl looked around the room and nodded. 'There is certainly nothing harmful here, or useful, either. I have come to Lonmar for nothing.'

'So said your High Lord, before he was High Lord.'

Kassyk smiled. 'I remember his visit well. You were polite, Ambassador Dannyl. The young Akkarin laughed out loud when he heard what you learned today. Perhaps the truths you are seeking are more alike than you first thought.'

Dannyl nodded. 'Perhaps.' He looked at the High Priest. 'Thank you for allowing me to know this, High Priest. I apologise for not believing you when you said they contained nothing of ancient power.'

The man rose. 'I knew that you would always remain curious if I denied you. Now you know, and I trust you to keep your word. I will return you to your friend.'

Rising, they started back through the labyrinth of passages.

'*All* of the books on the Sachakan War are taken?' Sonea asked.

Lord Jullen looked up. 'That *is* what I said.'

Sonea turned away and mouthed a curse that would have earned a stern lecture from Rothen.

When the class was set an exercise that involved taking books from the library, an elaborate dance ensued in which they competed politely for the best books. Not wanting to join them, Sonea had tried Rothen's library, but found he had nothing on the subject. By the time she had returned to the Novices' Library, there was nothing useful left. That had left the Magicians' Library, which had apparently been raided, too.

'They're all gone,' she told Rothen as she reached his side.

His eyebrows rose. '*All* of them? How can that be? There's a restriction on the number of books each novice or magician can borrow.'

'I don't know. He probably persuaded Gennyl to borrow some, too.'

'You don't know it was Regin's doing, Sonea.'

She snorted softly.

'Why don't you have a copy made?'

'That would be expensive, wouldn't it?'

'It's what your allowance is for, remember.'

She winced and looked away. 'How long would it take?'

'That depends on the book. A few days for printed ones, a few weeks for handwritten. Your teacher will know which volumes are best.' He chuckled and lowered his voice. 'Don't tell him your reasons, and he'll be impressed by your apparent interest in the subject.'

She picked up her folder of notes. 'I may as well go. I'll see you tomorrow.'

He nodded. 'Do you want me to come with you?'

She hesitated, then shook her head. 'Lord Ahrind keeps a close eye on everyone.'

'Good night, then.'

'Good night.'

Lord Jullen eyed her suspiciously as she left the Magicians' Library. It was chilly outside, and she hurried across to the Novices' Quarters. Stepping through the door, she saw the small crowd of novices in the corridor and stopped. As they saw her their faces split with wide grins. Looking beyond them, she saw the words someone had written on her door with smeared ink. Gritting her teeth, she took a step forward.

As she did, Regin emerged from the crowd. She braced herself for his mocking words, but he suddenly retreated again as quickly as he had appeared.

'Hai! Sonea!'

Recognising the voice, she spun about. Two figures had entered the corridor, one tall, one short. Lord Ahrind's eyes narrowed as he saw the writing on the door. He stepped past her, and she heard the denials of the novices behind her.

'I don't care who did it. *You* will clean it off. *Now!*'

But Sonea ignored it all. Her attention had been captured by a familiar, friendly face.

'Cery!' she breathed.

Cery's grin faded as he took in everything behind her. 'They're giving you a hard time, aren't they.' It was not a question.

She shrugged. 'They're just children. I—'

'Sonea.' Lord Ahrind returned to their side. 'You have a visitor, as you can no doubt see for yourself. You may speak to him in the corridor, or outside. *Not* in your room.'

Sonea nodded. 'Yes, my lord.'

Satisfied, he stalked to his door and disappeared. Looking around, she saw that all of the novices but one had disappeared. She watched the remaining boy wipe the ink off her door. By the sullen look he gave her before he hurried away and disappeared into his room, she guessed he had been merely one of the audience, not the one who had written the message.

Though the corridor was empty, Sonea could imagine ears pressed against doors, listening to her conversation with Cery.

'Let's go outside. Wait here. I'll just get something.'

Slipping inside her room, she collected a small package, then returned to the corridor and led Cery out to the gardens. They found a sheltered bench. As she created a barrier of warmth around them both, Cery's eyebrows rose and he gave her an approving look.

'You've picked up a few useful tricks.'

'Just a few,' she agreed.

His eyes darted around, constantly watching the shadows. 'Remember when we were in this garden last,' he said. 'Creeping through those trees. That's nearly a year ago now.'

She grinned. 'How could I forget?'

Her grin faded as she remembered what she had witnessed beneath the High Lord's Residence. At the time she had been too eager to get away to tell Cery what she had seen. Later, she had told him she'd watched a magician performing magic, but she hadn't known it was forbidden black magic. Now, of course, she had promised the Administrator that she would keep the truth hidden from all but Rothen.

'That boy is the leader isn't he? The one who hid when he saw that magician – Lord Ahrind, isn't it?'

She nodded.

'What's this boy's name?'

'Regin.'

'He been bothering you much?'

She sighed. 'All the time.' As she told him of the pranks and jibes, she felt both embarrassed and relieved. It felt good to be talking to her old friend, and satisfying to see the anger on Cery's face.

He swore colourfully. 'That boy needs a good lesson, if you ask me. Would you like me to teach him?'

Sonea chuckled. 'You'd never get close to him.'

'Oh?' He smiled slyly. 'Magicians aren't supposed to hurt people, are they?'

'No.'

'So he can't use his powers in a fight with a non-magician, can he?'

197

'He won't fight you, Cery. He'd consider it beneath himself to fight a dwell.'

He made a rude noise. 'Is he a coward, then?'

'No.'

'He's got nothing against giving you some rub, though. You were a dwell.'

'He's not fighting me. He's just making sure everyone remembers where I'm from.'

Cery considered this for a while, then shrugged. 'Then we'll just have to kill him.'

Surprised at the absurdity of the suggestion, she laughed. 'How?'

His eyes flashed. 'We could . . . lure him into a passage, then cave it in.'

'That's all? He'd only have to shield himself, then push the rubble away.'

'Not without using up his magic. How about we cover him with a lot of rubble? A whole house.'

'It would take a lot more than that.'

He pursed his lips, thinking. 'We could trip him into a vat of sewage and seal him in.'

'He'd blast his way out.'

'Then we'll trick him into boarding a ship, then sink it far out in the sea.'

'He'd make a bubble of air around himself and float.'

'Ah, but he couldn't hold it forever. He'll get tired, then drown.'

'We can hold a basic shield for a long time,' she told him. 'All he has to do is communicate with Lord Garrel by mind and the Guild would send out another boat to rescue him.'

'If we sank the ship a long way from any magicians, he might die of thirst.'

'He might,' she conceded, 'but I doubt it. Magic makes us robust. We survive longer than ordinary people – and besides, we've learned how to extract salt from water. He wouldn't go thirsty, and he could catch and cook fish to eat.'

Cery uttered a small gasp of impatience. 'Stop it! You're making me jealous. Can't you wear him out for me first? Then I'll give him a good softening.'

Sonea laughed. 'No, Cery.'

'Why not? Is he stronger than you?'

'I don't know.'

'What then?'

She looked away. 'It's not worth it. Whatever you do, he'd get me back.'

Cery sobered. 'Seems he gets enough fun out of you already. It's not like you to just put up with something like this. Fight him, Sonea. Sounds like you've got nothing to lose.' His eyes narrowed. 'I could do it the Thieves' way.'

She looked at him sharply. 'No.'

He rubbed his hands together. 'He hurts my kin, I hurt his.'

'No, Cery.'

His expression had grown distant, and he didn't appear to be listening. 'Don't worry, I wouldn't kill them or harm the weaker ones, just scare some of the men in the family. Regin will work it out eventually, 'cause he'll twig that one of his kin always gets visited by a messenger just after he does something to you.'

Sonea shuddered. 'Don't joke about it, Cery. It's not funny.'

'I wasn't joking. He wouldn't dare touch you.'

She grabbed his arm and turned him to face her. 'This

isn't the slums, Cery. If you think Regin will keep silent because he'd have to admit what he's doing, you're wrong. You'd be playing right into his hands. Harming his family is a far greater offence than giving another novice a hard time. I'd have used connections with the Thieves to harm another novice's family. They might throw me out of the Guild for that.'

'Connections with the Thieves.' Cery's nose twitched. 'I see.'

'Oh, Cery.' Sonea grimaced. 'I appreciate that you want to help. I really do.'

He scowled into the trees. 'I can't do anything to stop him, can I?'

'No.' She smiled. 'But it is fun thinking about dunking Regin in the sea or dropping a house on him.'

His lips curled into a smile. 'Sure is.'

'And I'm glad you dropped by. I haven't seen you since before I started at the University.'

'Work's kept me busy,' he said. 'You heard about the murders?'

Sonea frowned. 'No.'

'Been lots of them lately. Strange ones. The Guard are out for the killer, causing everybody a lot of rub, so the Thieves want him got.' He shrugged.

'Have you seen Jonna and Ranel?'

'They're well. Your little cousin is strong and healthy. You going to drop in soon? They say it's been a while.'

'I'll try. I'm so busy. There's so much studying to do.' She reached into her pocket and pulled out the packet. 'I want you to give this to them.' She pressed it into his hand.

He tested its weight, then looked at her in surprise. 'Coins?'

'Part of my allowance. Tell them it's a little of their taxes going to a better cause – and if Jonna still won't take it, give it to Ranel. He's not so stubborn.'

'But why give it to me to deliver?'

'Because I don't want anyone here to know. Not even Rothen. He'd approve but . . .' She shrugged. 'I like to keep some things to myself.'

'And me?'

She smiled and shook a finger at him. 'I know exactly how much is in there.'

He pushed out his bottom lip. 'As if I'd steal from a friend.'

She laughed. 'No, you wouldn't. Just everybody else.'

'Sonea!' a voice called.

They looked up. Lord Ahrind stood outside the Novices' Quarters, his head turning to and fro as he searched for her. Sonea stood up and the magician located her. He gestured imperiously for her to come inside.

'I'd better go,' she said.

Cery shook his head. 'It's strange hearing you call them "my lord" and jumping at their orders.'

She pulled a face at him. 'Like you didn't for Faren. At least I know that, in five years, I'll be ordering everyone else around.'

An odd look crossed Cery's face. He smiled and shooed her away. 'Go on. Get back to your studies. I'll try to drop by soon.'

'I'll hold you to that.'

She started toward the Novices' Quarters reluctantly. Lord Ahrind watched her, his arms crossed.

'And tell that boy I'll break his arms if he doesn't leave you alone,' Cery called, just loud enough for her to hear.

She turned to grin at him. 'I'll do it myself if he pushes me far enough. By mistake, of course.'

He nodded approvingly, then waved her on. When she reached the Novices' Quarters she looked back. He was still standing by the bench. As she waved he gave a quick signal in the street sign language. She smiled, then let Lord Ahrind usher her inside.

CHAPTER 13

THIEF!

As she left the Novices' Quarters, Sonea caught her breath with surprise and pleasure. The sky was a luminous pale blue, streaked with glowing orange clouds. Somewhere behind Sarika's Hill, the sun was rising.

She had discovered that she enjoyed these early hours, when everything was still and peaceful. As winter approached, dawn had come later each day, and today she was finally seeing it for herself.

Yawning servants blinked at her as she entered the Foodhall, and one wordlessly wrapped up a savoury bread bun for her to take away. They were used to her unpredictable appearances now. From there she headed to the Baths. Of all places in the Guild, they had turned out to be one of the safest. Women and men were strictly separated and, to ensure this, a section had been built for each, divided by a thick wall. Neither Issle nor Bina had ever attempted to bother her there. There was nearly always another female magician using the Baths, so the chances for harassment were less.

Regin had discovered quickly that any insult or insinuation he directed at her did not impress his new classmates. As she had hoped, he hadn't managed to charm them into following him about, either, and his attempt to befriend Poril had been almost comically unsuccessful, as the boy recoiled in fear and disbelief.

At midbreak, when the novices visited the Foodhall, Regin always rejoined his former class. She guessed he was not about to abandon his old gang when his new classmates were not interested in starting a new one. And now that their harassment had begun again, they needed time to plan their moves.

They had only the hours before the first class and after the last to find and torment her. She made sure she was hard to find until the last moments before the first gong. After class, however, the gang usually lay in wait for her and she could do little to avoid them.

Though her classmates did not join in, they never stepped forward to help her, either. And Poril was no deterrent. He stood back, pale and trembling, as she endured Regin's taunting.

Sometimes she managed to avoid the gang by offering to carry something for the teacher, or asking a question that took most of the walk out of the University to answer. The presence of almost any magician in the corridor gave her an opportunity to escape them. Rothen met her after class sometimes, but she always endured sneering remarks about it the next day.

In the Novices' Quarters, the gang left her alone. They had pushed through the door of her room one day and started messing up her belongings. A quick mental query to Lord Ahrind asking how to deal with uninvited guests had brought him storming in to demand what was going on. They hadn't attempted to enter her room again – as far as she could tell.

She had bought a sturdy box with a carry handle to tote her belongings in, tired of having her books knocked out of her hands, her notes set on fire, and her pens and inkwell shattered. And protecting this box with magic kept her shield-holding skills well honed.

As she left the Baths, Sonea noted the identities of the novices around the courtyard. She tightened her grip around the handle of her box as she entered the University and started up the stairs. Stepping into the second-floor corridor, she quickly scanned the faces. A huddle of brown robes had gathered outside her classroom, heads close together. Her stomach sank.

Glancing about, she saw a magician talking to a novice a hundred paces away. Was he close enough to deter any mischief? Possibly.

Walking as quietly as she could, Sonea approached the novices. When she was only a few paces away from the room, the magician suddenly turned and strode away down the stairs. At the same time, Issle looked up and saw Sonea.

'Ugh!' Issle's clear voice filled the corridor. 'What's that *smell*?'

Regin looked up and smiled.

'It's the smell of the slums. Look, it gets stronger the closer you get.'

He stepped in front of Sonea and his attention dropped to her side.

'Perhaps there's something smelly in her new box, eh?'

Sonea backed away as Regin reached out toward her box. Then a tall, black-robed figure stepped out of the passage beside them and Regin froze in place, his arms still extended.

As Sonea's momentum brought her out of Regin's reach and into the path of the magician, she realised she was the only one still moving. All of the other novices in the corridor had stopped, their attention fixed on the magician.

The black-robed magician. The High Lord.

In the back of her mind a voice shrieked: *It's him! Run! Get away!* She took a few hurried steps backward out of his path. No, she thought, *don't draw attention to yourself. Behave as he'd expect you to.* Regaining her balance, she bowed respectfully.

He continued past without looking at her. Taking her lead, the other novices bowed hastily. She decided to take advantage of the distraction and slipped past Regin into the classroom.

At once she felt the effect of the High Lord's presence vanish. The novices in the room lounged about in their seats. Lord Vorel was so engrossed in whatever he was writing he did not notice her bow. Taking her place beside Poril, she closed her eyes and let out a long sigh.

In those few moments, with everyone else near-frozen with surprise, it had felt as if only she and the dark figure of her nightmares existed. And she had *bowed* to him. She looked down at her hands, still gripping the handle of her box. She bowed so much now that she thought nothing of it. But this was different. It angered her. Knowing what he was, and was capable of doing . . .

Suddenly the room filled with the scraping of chairs as all the novices around her rose to their feet. Sonea followed suit, realising that the last of the novices had arrived and she hadn't heard Lord Vorel addressing the class. The Warrior gestured at the door, and the novices began to file out. Puzzled, Sonea followed Poril.

'Leave your books here, Sonea,' Vorel said.

Sonea looked down at her box, then glanced at the rest of the tables to see that the other novices had also left their belongings behind. Reluctantly she returned to her desk and set the box on top of it, then hurried away to catch up with the class.

The novices were talking excitedly among themselves. Poril, however, looked ill.

'Where are we going?' she whispered to him.

'Th-the Arena,' he replied, his voice shaking.

Sonea felt her heart skip a beat. The Arena. So far the Warrior Skills lessons had consisted of history classes, and endless instruction on creating barriers. All were performed in the University classrooms. They had been told they would eventually be taken to the Arena to learn the offensive side of the discipline.

A strange feeling – not quite dread – settled upon her as the class descended the stairs and walked out of the University. She hadn't been close to the Arena since the day, almost a year ago, when Rothen had taken her to see a demonstration of Warrior Skills as part of his attempt to persuade her to stay and join the Guild. Watching the novices throwing magic at each other had been disturbing. It had brought back unpleasant memories of the day she had thrown the stone at the magicians and first used magic, and how they had unintentionally killed the boy they thought had attacked them.

It had been a simple error, but it had turned an innocent boy into a charred corpse. The lectures on safety, that the other novices seemed to dismiss so easily, always chilled her. She could not help wondering how often mistakes did happen.

Ahead, Regin, Hal and Benon were striding along the garden path eagerly. Even Narron and Trassia's faces were flushed with excitement. Perhaps the thought of accidentally killing someone from the Houses, or the nobility of another land, might sober them. But would the prospect of killing a former slum girl cause them to pause?

As they reached the wide flat space outside the Arena, Sonea looked up at the eight curved spires spaced around it. She could feel a faint vibration in the air from the magical barrier the spires supported. Making herself walk to the edge, she looked down at the structure. The base was a sunken stone circle covered with white sand. The spires were spaced evenly around it. From their bases, stone steps rose to the level of the garden. To one side was a square portal that allowed access to the inside of the Arena via a short underground staircase.

'Follow me,' Lord Vorel ordered. He started down the staircase, leading the novices through the portal and into the Arena. 'Form a line.'

The novices obeyed, Poril taking the last place. Lord Vorel waited until they had fallen silent, then cleared his throat.

'This will be your first lesson in the basic strikes. It will also be the first time you use magic in full strength. Heed this warning: what you do today is dangerous.' He stared at them all, in turn, as he spoke. 'We must all use the utmost caution during these exercises. Even at your level you are quite capable of killing. Remember this well. I will not tolerate any foolery. Carelessness will be punished *severely*.'

A chill ran down Sonea's spine. *I hope the punishment is severe enough to convince Regin that an 'accident' isn't an easy way to get rid of me.*

Vorel suddenly smiled and rubbed his palms together eagerly. 'I will be teaching you the three basic strikes at this level. Firstly, we'll see what each of you uses instinctively. Regin.'

Regin stepped forward.

Lord Vorel walked backward until he was almost at the edge of the Arena, then raised his hands and made a spreading motion. A glowing disc of half-visible energy appeared in front of him. Stepping aside, he nodded to Regin.

'Gather your power and send it toward this shield.'

Regin lifted a hand and extended it toward the target. A frown crossed his face, then a brilliant bolt of light shot from his hand and struck the disc.

'Good,' Lord Vorel said. 'A forcestrike, but with a great deal of wasted energy spent on light and heat. Hal.'

Sonea stared at the glowing disc of magic. Vorel was probably using the shield to detect what kind of energies the novices were throwing at it . . . but she kept seeing a memory of something else, something that made her stomach twist with dread and nausea.

Again a bolt of energy struck the disc, this time tinged blue. A memory of light and screams flashed through her mind.

'A heatstrike,' Vorel said, then went on to explain the differences between forcestrikes and heatstrikes. A part of her mind was slotting this information away, yet she could not drag herself from the memories . . .

The crowd running . . . a blackened corpse . . . the smell of burned flesh . . .

'Benon.'

The Kyralian boy stepped forward. The beam that sprang forth from his hand was almost transparent.

'Forcestrike.' Vorel sounded pleased. 'Narron . . .'

Another bolt of power seared the air.

'Forcestrike mostly, but a great deal of heat. Trassia . . .'

A streak of flames dazzled Sonea's eyes.

'Firestrike.' Vorel sounded bemused. 'Seno . . .'

The Vindo boy frowned for a long time before a pulse of light leapt from his hand. It went awry and missed the disc. As it struck the barrier of the Arena the air filled with a muted tinkling, like distant shattering glass. Fine threads of energy rippled outward. Sonea swallowed hard. Soon it would be her turn. Soon . . .

'Yalend.'

The boy beside her stepped forward and struck at the disc without hesitation.

'Sonea . . .'

She stared at the disc, but all she could see was a boy staring back at her. Fearful, yet not comprehending . . .

'Sonea?'

She took a deep breath and pushed the nightmare image away. *When I decided I would join the Guild, I knew I would have to learn this. These fights are just a game.* A dangerous game created so that fighting skills were kept alive in case the Allied Lands were attacked.

Lord Vorel took a step toward her, then stopped as she lifted a hand. For the first time since her Control lessons she consciously reached to the energy inside her. The other novices shifted impatiently.

The image of the boy returned. She needed to replace it with something else, or her nerve *would* break. As Regin muttered something about being afraid, another figure appeared in her mind's eye and she smiled. She focussed her will and sent out a blast of anger.

What passed for a curse among the magicians could be heard over the clear sound of shattering glass. Sonea felt her stomach turn over. Had she missed the disc?

Ripples of light curved to the top of the Arena's spires and disappeared. The disc was gone. Puzzled, she looked to Lord Vorel, who was rubbing his temples.

'I did not say you should throw *all* your strength into it *yet*, Sonea,' he said. 'That was a . . . combination of . . . firestrike and forcestrike – I think.' He turned to Poril, who went instantly rigid. 'I shall restore the target in a moment. Do not strike until I tell you to.'

He remained silent for several minutes, his eyes closed. Then he drew in a deep breath and set up the disc again.

'Go on, Poril.'

The boy sighed. Lifting a hand, he sent an almost invisible strike at the shield.

'Good,' Vorel said, nodding. 'A forcestrike, with no wasted magic. Now, you will all strike again, but this time in full strength. After that, you will all learn to shape your strikes to a purpose. Regin.'

Sonea watched as the novices attacked the barrier. It was difficult to know if the strikes were more powerful, but Vorel seemed satisfied. As it came to Sonea's turn he hesitated, then shrugged.

'Go on. Let's see if you can do it again.'

Amused, she drew on her power and let it loose. The disc seemed to hold, then it wavered and disappeared. White light arced up and over the Arena barrier, causing the novices to duck involuntarily. The air shivered with the sound of it, then all fell silent.

Vorel regarded her speculatively. 'No doubt your age has given you an advantage,' he said, almost to himself. 'Just as Poril's experience has given him control.' He set up the barrier again. 'Poril, show us a forcestrike.'

The boy's strike was almost invisible. Vorel gestured to the barrier.

'As you could see – or *not* see – Poril's strike was economical. There was no excess light or heat. Its potency was directed forward, and in no other direction. You will now try to shape your power into forcestrikes. Regin, you will begin.'

As the class continued, Sonea realised she was enjoying herself. Shaping her strikes was challenging, but easy once she had the 'feel' of each type. When Vorel directed them back to the classroom she was almost disappointed that the lesson had ended.

Looking around, she noted the smiles and excited exchanges between the other novices. They hurried up the stairs and filled the corridor with chatter. Entering the classroom, they quietened as they returned to their seats.

Lord Vorel waited until the room was silent, then crossed his arms.

'In the next lesson we will return to the refinement of barriers.' The novices slumped with disappointment. 'What you have seen today should show clearly why it is so important for you to learn to shield yourself well,' he said sternly. 'For the remaining time before midbreak I would like you to write down what you have learned today.'

A low moan escaped the lips of several novices. As they began to open their notebooks, Sonea reached for the latches of her box. Touching them, she realised she had forgotten to set the magical lock.

Opening it, she breathed a sigh of relief as she found her belongings intact. She lifted out her folder of notes, but as she did something slipped from the pages and fell to the floor with a metallic sound.

'That's my pen!'

Sonea looked up to see Narron glaring at her. Frowning, she looked down and saw a sliver of gold lying on the floor at her feet. She bent down and picked it up.

A hand plucked the pen from her fingers. She looked up to see Lord Vorel staring down at her. He turned to Narron.

'Is this the pen you said was missing?'

'Yes.' Narron turned to stare at Sonea. 'Sonea had it in her box.'

Vorel's jaw tightened as he turned his eyes back to Sonea.

'Where did you get this from?'

Sonea looked down at the box in her hands.

'It was in here,' she said.

'She stole my pen!' Narron declared indignantly.

'I did not!' she protested.

'Sonea.' Vorel's fingers curled around the pen. 'Come with me.'

He turned on his heel and strode to the front of the class. Sonea stared at him in disbelief, until he turned and scowled at her.

'*Now!*' he barked.

Closing the box, Sonea rose and followed him to the door, conscious of the eyes that followed her. She glanced at the novices. Surely they didn't believe she had stolen Narron's pen – not when it was so clear that Regin had played a trick on her again?

They stared back at her, their eyes narrowed in suspicion. Poril looked down and avoided her eyes. She felt a stab of hurt and turned away.

She was the slum girl. The girl who had admitted to stealing as a child. The outsider. A friend of Thieves. They had seen Regin taunting her, but they had never known about the notes and books he had stolen, or the numerous other tricks he had played on her. They didn't know how cunning and determined he was.

She couldn't accuse Regin. Even if she dared to, and risked a truth-read, she couldn't prove that he had actually done it. She had only her own innocence to prove, and she dared not risk a truth-read for that, for if she did, and the University Director didn't allow her to choose the truth-reader, someone might learn about the High Lord's crime.

Vorel paused at the door. 'Narron, you had better come too,' he said. 'The rest of you finish your notes. I will not return before midbreak.'

As he entered the University Director's office, Rothen noted the posture of the occupants. Jerrik sat at his desk, his arms crossed and a grim expression darkening his face. Sonea was slumped in a chair, her eyes focussed elsewhere. Another novice perched on a stool nearby, sitting very straight. Behind him stood the Warrior, Lord Vorel, whose gaze burned with anger.

'What is this about?' Rothen asked.

Jerrik's frown deepened. 'Your novice has been found to be in possession of a pen belonging to her classmate, Narron.'

Rothen looked at Sonea, but she didn't raise her head to meet his eyes.

'Is this true, Sonea?'

'Yes.'

'Details?'

'I opened my box and picked up my notes, and the pen fell out.'

'How did it get in there?'

She shrugged. 'I don't know.'

Jerrik stepped forward. 'You didn't put it there?'

'I don't know.'

'What do you mean?'

'I don't know if I put it there.'

He frowned. 'How can you not know? You either put it there, or you didn't.'

She spread her hands. 'It's possible it was in with my notes when I put them away last night.'

Jerrik shook his head in exasperation, then drew in a deep breath.

'Did you steal Narron's pen?'

Sonea frowned. 'Not deliberately.'

Having had similar conversations with Sonea himself, Rothen almost smiled. This was no time for wordplay, however. 'So you're saying you might have stolen it accidentally?' he asked.

'How can you steal something accidentally?' Jerrik exclaimed. 'Stealing is a deliberate act.'

Vorel gave a snort of disgust. 'Sonea, if you don't deny it, we can only assume you're guilty.'

She looked up at the teacher, and her eyes suddenly narrowed. 'What does it matter? You've already made up your minds. Nothing I say will make any difference.'

The room was silent for several heartbeats, then, as Rothen saw Vorel's face begin to colour, he stepped forward and placed a hand on Sonea's shoulder.

'Wait for me outside, Sonea.'

She walked out of the room and closed the door.

'What am I to make of that?' Jerrik exclaimed. 'If she is innocent, why wind us about with these evasive answers?'

Rothen looked pointedly at the novice, Narron. Jerrik followed his gaze, then nodded. 'You may return to class, Narron.'

The boy stood. 'May I have my pen back, Director?'

'Certainly.' Jerrik nodded to Vorel. Seeing the expensive-looking gold pen that the teacher handed over, Rothen winced. It probably had been a gift to mark the boy's acceptance into the Guild.

When Narron had left the room, Jerrik looked at Rothen expectantly. 'You were saying, Lord Rothen?'

Rothen clasped his hands behind his back. 'Are you aware of the harassment Sonea has been receiving from other novices?'

Jerrik nodded. 'Yes, I am.'

'Have you identified the leader of these troublemakers?'

The University Director's mouth twitched. 'Are you saying this leader arranged this apparent theft?'

'I'm only suggesting you consider the possibility.'

'You would need proof. As it is, all we have is a missing pen found among Sonea's belongings. She refuses to deny taking it, and has not accused Regin of planting it there. What am I to believe?'

Rothen nodded in acknowledgment. 'I'm sure Sonea would like to have evidence to the contrary, but if she isn't accusing anyone, then she probably hasn't. In this situation, is there any point in protesting her innocence?'

'That doesn't prove she didn't do it,' Vorel said.

'No, but I was asked to explain her behaviour, not prove that she is innocent. I can only vouch for her character. I don't believe she did this.'

Vorel made a small noise, but remained silent. Jerrik regarded them both, then waved dismissively. 'I will consider your words. Thank you. You may go.'

Sonea was leaning against the wall outside, staring at her boots sullenly. Vorel narrowed his eyes at her, but strode past without speaking. Moving to her side, Rothen leaned on the wall and sighed.

'It doesn't look good.'

'I know.' Her tone was resigned.

'You said nothing of Regin?'

'How can I?' She looked up and met his gaze. 'I can't accuse him, even if I did have proof.'

'Why n—' The answer came to him in a flash. Guild rules. An accuser must submit to a truth-read. She couldn't risk one. Secrets entrusted to them might be revealed before their time. Disturbed, frustrated, he frowned at the floor in silence.

'Do you believe them?'

He looked up. 'Of course not.'

'Not even the slightest doubt?'

'Not the slightest.'

'Perhaps you should,' she said bitterly. 'Everyone else was waiting for it to happen. It doesn't matter what I say or do. It doesn't make a difference. They know I've done it before, so they think I'll do it again whether I have a reason to or not.'

'Sonea,' he said softly. 'What you say and do *does* make a difference. You know that. Just because you stole out of need a long time ago, it doesn't mean you'll do so now. If you had some kind of irresistible stealing habit, we'd have seen evidence of it before now. You should deny it, clearly and forcefully, even if you think no-one will believe you.'

She nodded, though he wasn't sure she was convinced.

They both looked up as the midbreak gong rang out. Rothen pushed himself away from the wall.

'Come and eat with me. We haven't had midbreak meal together in weeks.'

She smiled grimly. 'I don't think I'll be welcome in the Foodhall for a while.'

CHAPTER 14

BAD NEWS

One by one the novices filed past Lord Elben's table, each picking up a glass jar. Knowing that she would receive hostile stares if she joined them, Sonea waited. To her dismay, Regin was the last to approach the table. Looking at her, he hesitated, then stepped forward and picked up the last two jars. Lord Elben frowned as Regin examined both, but as the teacher's mouth opened, Regin thrust one of the jars at Sonea.

'Here.'

She reached out to take it, but just before her fingers touched the jar it dropped from his hand, struck the floor and shattered.

'Oh, *sorry* about that,' Regin exclaimed. He backed away from the glass fragments. 'So clumsy of me.'

Lord Elben looked down his long nose at Regin, then Sonea. 'Regin, find a servant to clean this up. Sonea, you'll have to observe this lesson.'

Sonea returned to her seat, unsurprised. The 'theft' of Narron's pen had changed more than just the novices' opinion of her. Before the 'theft', Elben would have told Regin to give her the last jar, or sent him off to get a new one.

The 'theft' had only confirmed what the novices and teachers already suspected. Her official punishment had been to spend an hour shelving books in the Novices' Library every evening, which had proven to be quite enjoyable – when Regin wasn't hanging about making the task difficult. The punishment had ended last Fourday, but both novices and teachers still treated her with suspicion and contempt.

Most of the time, she was ignored in class. But when she came too close to another novice, or dared to speak to one, she received cold stares. She hadn't tried to rejoin them in the Foodhall. Instead she returned to her old habit of skipping the midbreak meal or eating with Rothen.

Not everything had changed for the worse, however. Now that she knew her powers were so much stronger than the other novices, she had discovered a new confidence. She didn't need to conserve her strength for the class activities, as the novices had been advised to do, so she kept a strong shield up to protect herself from missiles, shoves or other pranks. This meant she could easily push past Regin and his followers if they surrounded her in the corridors.

Her room door was protected by a shield of its own, as was her window and her box. She was using magic all day and night, yet she never felt tired or drained. Not even after a particularly strenuous Warrior Skills class.

But she was alone. Looking at the empty seat in front of her, she sighed. Poril had injured himself a week before, having burned his hands while studying. She missed him, particularly since he hadn't seemed to care that she had apparently been proven to be a thief.

'Lord Elben?'

Sonea looked up. In the doorway stood a woman in green robes. She stepped aside and propelled a short novice into the room with a gentle push. Sonea felt her heart lighten.

'I have decided that Poril is well enough now to attend classes. He still won't be able to do anything with his hands, but he can watch.'

Poril's gaze went straight to Regin. Looking away quickly, he bowed to Lord Elben, then hurried to his seat. The Healer nodded to the teacher, then retreated from the room.

As Elben began to instruct the class, Sonea's attention slipped to her friend's back from time to time. Poril didn't seem to be paying attention to the lesson. He sat stiffly, occasionally looking down at his hands, which were reddened with fresh scars. When the midbreak gong rang out hours later, he waited until the rest of the novices had left, then rose quickly and hurried toward the door.

'Poril,' she called after him. Bowing hastily toward Elben, she caught up with the boy in a few paces.

'Welcome back, Poril.' As he looked at her she smiled. 'Need some help catching up?'

'No.' He frowned and lengthened his stride

'Poril?' Sonea reached out to grab his arm. 'What's wrong?'

Poril looked at her, then glanced at the rest of the class walking further down the corridor. Regin was hovering at the back of the group, glancing at them over his shoulder and smiling in a way that sent a chill over Sonea's skin.

Poril shivered. 'I can't talk to you. I can't.' He shook her hand off.

'But—'

'No, leave me alone.' He turned away, but she caught his arm again and held it firmly.

221

'I'm not going to leave you alone until you tell me what's going on,' she said between gritted teeth.

He hesitated before answering. 'It's Regin.'

Looking at Poril's pale face, she felt her stomach turn over. He kept looking at the other novices, and she knew he didn't want to tell her any more. He just wanted to get away from her. 'What did he say?' she pressed.

Poril swallowed. 'He says I can't talk to you any more. I'm sorry . . .'

'And you're just going to do what he says?' It was unfair, she knew, but she was burning with anger now. 'Why didn't you tell him to go and drown himself in the Tarali River?'

He lifted his scarred hands. 'I did.'

Sonea's anger turned to ice. She stared at Poril. 'He did *that?*'

Poril's nod was so slight she almost missed it. She looked down the corridor, but the class had reached the stairs and descended out of view.

'That's . . . Why didn't you tell anyone?'

'I can't prove it.'

A truth-read would prove it. Did Poril have a secret to hide, like she did? Or was he simply so frightened by the thought of a magician reading his mind he would do anything to avoid it?

'He can't get away with burning your hands just because you're my friend,' she growled. 'If he threatens you again, tell me. I'll . . . I'll . . .'

'What? You can't do anything, Sonea.' His face was flushed now. 'I'm sorry, but I can't. I just can't.' He turned away and ran down the corridor.

Shaking her head, Sonea followed at a distance. Reaching

the stairs, she descended slowly. As she reached the ground floor she heard a low rumbling sound. Looking down the corridor toward the Great Hall, she blinked in surprise.

The hall was full of magicians. They stood in pairs or larger groups, talking. Sonea paused, wondering what had brought so many together. It was not a Meet day, so there must be another reason.

'I wouldn't draw attention to myself, if I were you,' a voice said at her ear.

Recoiling, she turned to stare at Regin.

'They might decide they missed one,' he said, his eyes bright with glee.

She stepped away from him, puzzled but sure she didn't want to know what he was talking about. His eyes flashed with delight as he saw her incomprehension, and he drew closer.

'Oh, you don't get it, do you?' His grin was ugly. 'Had you forgotten? Today is that most festive day of the year for slum trash like you. The day of the Purge.'

Realisation struck her like a blow. The Purge. Every year, since the first Purge over thirty years before, the King sent the Guard and the Guild out to clear the city streets of 'vagrants and miscreants'. The purpose, or so the King claimed, was to make the streets safer by removing petty thieves. In truth, the Thieves were barely inconvenienced by the event; they had their own ways in and out of the city. Only the poor, homeless people were herded into the slums. And, in the case of her own family a year ago, those people who rented rooms in 'overcrowded and unsafe' stay-houses. She had been so angry that day, she had joined a gang of youths throwing stones at the magicians, and had loosed her power for the first time.

223

Regin laughed with delight. Feeling anger rising, she forced herself to turn and walk away. Regin stepped forward to block her path. His face was twisted with triumph and cruel satisfaction, and she felt grateful that novices did not join in the Purge. Then she thought to the future and shuddered. Clearly Regin was looking forward to the day he could use his powers to chase helpless beggars and poor families out of the city.

'Don't go now,' Regin said, nodding toward the hall. 'Don't you want to ask your guardian how much fun he had?'

Rothen? He wouldn't . . . Sure that he was simply baiting her, she turned around. Scanning the faces, she found a familiar one in a nearby group. Rothen.

She went cold. How *could* he have gone when he knew how she felt about the Purge? But he couldn't refuse the King's orders . . .

Yes, he could! Not all magicians go. He could have refused and let another go in his place!

As if sensing her gaze, Rothen looked up and met her eyes. His attention slid to Regin, and he frowned.

Regin chuckled. Suddenly all she wanted to do was get away. Turning, she strode past Regin out of the University. Regin followed, taunting her all the way to the Magicians' Quarters where he finally stopped and let her enter alone. Entering Rothen's rooms, she was relieved to find them empty. She did not want Tania about right now in case she snapped at the servant out of frustration.

She was pacing when the door opened a short time later. 'Sonea.'

Rothen's expression was apologetic. She didn't answer him, but stopped at the window and stared outside.

'I'm sorry, I know this feels like a betrayal,' he said. 'I wanted to tell you I was going. I kept putting it off, and I didn't hear we were to be called out today until early this morning.'

'You didn't have to go,' she said. Her voice sounded like that of a stranger's, dark with anger.

'I did,' he said.

'No, you didn't. Someone else could have gone instead.'

'True,' he agreed. 'But that's not why I had to go.' He drew closer, his voice low and gentle. 'Sonea, I had to be there, to do whatever I could to ensure no mistakes were made. If I hadn't gone, and something did happen . . .' He sighed. 'Everyone was uneasy this time. It may be hard to perceive, but the Guild's confidence in itself was shaken by what happened last year. Whether that came from a fear of making mistakes, or,' he chuckled, 'another magic-wielding dwell, it doesn't matter. The Guild needed someone to keep an eye on it.'

Sonea looked down. It made sense. She felt her anger fading. Sighing, she looked at him and managed a nod. He smiled hopefully.

'Forgive me?'

'I suppose,' she said grudgingly. Looking down at the table, she saw that Tania had left a meal of savoury breads and other cold dishes. Clearly a meal prepared by someone who wasn't sure when anyone would return to eat it.

'Come and eat,' Rothen said.

Accepting the invitation, she moved to a chair and sat down.

The Guild carriage pulled up beside a plain two-storey building. Stepping out, Lorlen ignored the curious and startled looks from the people walking along the street. He strode to the entrance of the First City Guard House and, as a servant opened the door for him, walked through into a narrow hall.

The room was tastefully but not expensively decorated. Comfortable chairs were arranged in groups around the room. It reminded Lorlen of the Night Room in the Guild. A corridor off the hall gave access to the rest of the building.

'Administrator.'

Lorlen turned to see Derril's son rising from one of the chairs.

'Captain Barran. Congratulations on your new position.'

The young man smiled. 'Thank you, Administrator.' He gestured toward the corridor. 'Come to my office, and I'll tell you the latest news.'

Barran guided Lorlen to a door near the end of the corridor. A small, yet comfortable room lay beyond. One wall was lined with drawers, and a desk divided the space evenly in two. Barran gestured to one of two chairs, then, as Lorlen sat down, he took the other.

'Your father said that you've changed your mind about the woman we talked about,' Lorlen prompted. 'That you now think it was a murder.'

'Yes,' Barran replied. 'There have been several more apparent suicides too similar to that one. In each case, the weapon has been missing and there were signs of an intruder. Each victim had hand or fingerprints on the wounds. It is too strange a coincidence.' He paused. 'These suicides began a month or so after the ritual murders stopped, almost as if the murderer realised he was attracting attention and decided to change his methods in the hope people would assume suicide.'

Lorlen nodded. 'Or perhaps it is a new murderer.'

'Perhaps.' Barran hesitated. 'There is something else, though it may not be related. I asked my predecessor if he'd ever seen something as strange as this. He told me that a series of murders have been happening, on and off, for the last four or five years.' He chuckled. 'He said this was just the price we pay for living in cities.'

A chill ran down Lorlen's spine. Akkarin had returned from his journey just over five years ago. 'Nothing like this happened before then?'

'I don't think so. He would have said so, if something had.'

'So the murders were the same?'

'Only in that they followed a pattern for a while, then changed to another. My predecessor suspected that one of the Thieves was targeting a rival group at first. They might be marking their victims in a certain way so their rivals knew who had done the killing. But the victims didn't appear to have any connections to each other, or the Thieves.

'Then he considered the possibility of an assassin who was building his reputation with recognisable kills. Few of the victims had bad debts or any other obvious reason for their assassination, however. My predecessor could find no common reason for the deaths, just as I cannot find one now.'

'Not even simple robbery?'

Barran shook his head. 'A few victims were robbed, but not all.'

'Witnesses?'

'From time to time. Their descriptions vary. One detail was common, however.' Barran's eyes brightened. 'The murderer wears a ring with a large red gem.'

'Really?' Lorlen frowned. Had he ever seen Akkarin

227

wearing a ring? No. Akkarin never wore jewellery. That did not mean he couldn't be slipping a ring on his finger when out of sight. But why would he do that?

Lorlen sighed and shook his head. 'Was there any sign these victims were killed with magic?'

Barran smiled. 'Father would find that very exciting, but no. There are some strange aspects to some of the murders, but no sign of strike burns, or anything that we haven't found an ordinary explanation for.'

Of course, a death through black magic wouldn't leave any signs that Barran would recognise. Lorlen wasn't even sure there were signs any magician could recognise. He should, however, get as many details as possible.

'What else can you tell me?'

'Do you want the details of each murder?'

'Yes.'

Barran gestured to the wall of drawers. 'I've had all the records of strange serial murders moved into here. There are a lot to cover.'

Lorlen regarded the drawers with dismay. So many . . .

'The most recent ones, then?'

Barran nodded. He moved to the wall and drew out a large folder from one of the drawers.

'It is good to know the Guild is willing to take an interest in matters like these,' he said.

Lorlen smiled. 'My interest is mainly personal, but if there is anything the Guild can do, let me know. Otherwise, I'm sure the investigation is in the hands of those most qualified to tackle it.'

Barran smiled wryly. 'I hope so, Administrator. I certainly hope so.'

*   *   *

Above the curving barrier of the Arena dark grey clouds slowly rolled toward the North Quarter. The trees in the gardens lashed back and forth as the wind caught their branches. The limbs had darkened as the cold season approached, but the last few leaves that clung to them were bright red and yellow.

Inside the Arena, the air was still. The barrier protected it from the wind, but not the cold. Sonea resisted the desire to wrap her arms around herself and press the layers of woollen underclothes closer to her body. Lord Vorel had ordered them to drop any existing shields, including any shield for warmth.

'Remember these laws of magic,' he called. 'One: a shield under attack takes more effort to hold against a strike, than the strike used against it. Two: a curved or altered strike path takes more effort than a straight one. Three: light and heat travel faster and easier than force, so a forcestrike takes more effort than a firestrike.'

Lord Vorel stood in front of the class with his legs braced and his arms akimbo. He looked at Sonea.

'Strikes are easy. That's why it's so common for magicians to overdo them. That's also why shields are the most important skill of a Warrior, and why novices spend most of their time practising them. Remember the rules of the Arena. Once your outer shield has fallen you have lost the battle. We don't need any more proof than that.'

Sonea shivered, and knew it was not entirely from the cold. This would be the first lesson in which the novices would fight each other. All the warnings Vorel had issued ran through her mind. She looked at the faces of the other novices.

Most looked flushed and excited, but Poril was as white as snow. Since she and Poril always paired off for class exercises, Lord Vorel would probably put them against each other. She resolved to be careful and to take it easy on her former friend.

'You will be paired off initially according to strength,' Vorel told them. 'Regin, you will be fighting Sonea. Benon, you will be fighting Yalend. Narron will fight Trassia. Hal, Seno and Poril will take turns.'

Sonea felt her blood turn to ice. *He paired me with Regin!*

But it made sense. They were the two strongest novices in the class. Suddenly she wished she had seen this coming and had pretended to be weaker than she really was.

No, I must not think this way. Vorel had told them many times that a battle was already lost if a magician began it convinced of defeat. *I will defeat Regin*, she told herself. *I am stronger. It will be my revenge for Poril's injuries.*

It wasn't easy to hold onto that determination as Lord Vorel called her forward to stand next to Regin. He placed a hand on her shoulder and she felt his magic surround her as he created an inner shield. A second Warrior, Lord Makin, shielded Regin.

'The rest of you move outside,' he ordered. As the novices obediently filed through the passage, Sonea forced herself to meet Regin's gaze. His eyes were bright and the edge of his lips curled up into a sly smile.

'Now,' Vorel said as the novices sat down on the stairs outside the Arena. 'Take your positions.'

Swallowing hard, Sonea moved to one side of the Arena. Regin strolled to the other and turned to face her. Vorel and Makin backed away to the edge and Sonea sensed them creating shields around themselves. Her heart was beating quickly.

Vorel looked from her to Regin, then made a quick gesture.

'Begin.'

Sonea threw up a strong shield and braced herself, but the barrage of strikes she expected didn't come. Regin stood with his weight resting on one leg and his arms crossed. Waiting.

Sonea narrowed her eyes. There was supposed to be some significance to the first strike, and what it revealed of the character of the combatant. Looking closer, she realised that Regin didn't even have a shield raised. He shifted his weight, drummed the fingers of one hand against his arm, tapped his foot, then looked at the teacher questioningly.

Sonea risked a glance at Lord Vorel. The Warrior was watching intently, apparently unperturbed by the lack of fighting.

Regin sighed loud enough that even the novices outside the Arena could hear it. Then he yawned. Sonea smothered a smile. This wasn't a battle of magic, it was a battle to see who lost patience first.

She placed her hands on her hips, then looked up at the novices, no longer concerned about keeping her attention on Regin. Some were watching intently, others looked puzzled or bored. She looked at the teacher again. Lord Vorel met her gaze with a cold stare.

Perhaps she could lure Regin into striking first. *Perhaps if I drop my shield . . .*

Cautiously, she let her protective outer barrier dissolve. Immediately the world was ablaze with white fire. The hasty shield she threw up to repel the strikes held for a few seconds, then wavered and collapsed. Heat prickled her skin where Regin's magic met Vorel's inner shield.

'Halt!'

The strikes vanished, leaving dark spots in Sonea's vision. She blinked at Lord Vorel as he strode forward to stand in the centre of the Arena.

'Regin is victor,' he announced. A weak cheer came from the other novices. Sonea felt her face warming as Regin bowed graciously.

'Sonea.' Lord Vorel turned to her. 'Dropping your shield is inadvisable unless you are skilled at raising it again quickly. If you intend to use this strategy again you should practice your defence more. You may both leave. Benon and Yalend will be next.'

Sonea bowed, then strode toward the portal as quickly as she could. As she entered the passage a gloom settled over her. *It's only the first battle*, she told herself. She couldn't expect to win all the time, especially not against Regin whose guardian was, after all, a Warrior.

If they were always paired by strength, she would have to fight Regin in every lesson. It was clear already that Regin preferred the Warrior Skills discipline, and she'd heard Hal saying something about Regin having private lessons. Since she had no real desire to become a Warrior or have extra lessons, she was sure he was always going to be better at it than her.

Vorel had said they'd be paired off by strength *initially*, however. If pairings changed according to skill and talent, and she proved less skilled than Regin, Vorel would match her against one of the other novices.

That meant she had two choices: try to do well and eventually end up fighting Regin all the time, or let herself fail so she could avoid him.

Sighing, Sonea clomped up the stairs and joined the

novices sitting on the steps surrounding the Arena. Either way, she was probably going to suffer many more humiliating defeats. Wistfully, she thought of the Dome, the old ball-like stone structure next to the Novices' Quarters. Before the Arena was constructed, novices had been trained within it. The thick walls had protected outsiders from stray strikes loosed by the combatants within, yet had restricted the view of the battle to teacher and student. While it was an airless, oppressive room, at least it had been private.

Watching Benon and Yalend start their bout, Sonea quickly grew bored. She couldn't see how these lessons, with all their rules, could prepare magicians for real war. No, these Warriors spent their entire lives indulging in a dangerous game when their magic could be put to better uses – like Healing.

She shook her head. When the time came to choose a discipline, she knew she would not be taking the red robes.

CHAPTER 15

A SURPRISE ATTACK

As soon as Sonea stepped into the classroom she felt a difference, like a strange current of magic in the air. She hesitated in the doorway, her relief at having evaded Regin's gang evaporating.

Lord Kiano looked up, his attention snapping to her with a peculiar eagerness as if she was a welcome distraction.

'There will be no classes today, Sonea.'

She stared at the teacher in surprise.

'No classes, my lord?'

Kiano hesitated. A hiss brought her attention to the centre of the room. Only four novices had arrived before her. Benon was holding his head in his hands. Trassia and Narron had moved their chairs beside him. Regin sat quietly behind them, his eyes flat and expressionless for once. Trassia was staring at Sonea with accusing eyes.

'A novice has died,' Kiano explained. 'Shern.'

Sonea frowned, remembering the novice from the summer class whose powers had felt so strange. *Died?* Questions sprang into her mind. How? When?

'Oh, just go away,' Trassia growled. Startled by the girl's outburst, Sonea stared at her.

'He was Benon's cousin,' Kiano told her in a low voice.

Trassia glared back. Slowly, understanding came. By

234

asking why the class had been cancelled, Lord Kiano had been forced to speak of Shern's death in front of Benon. Sonea felt her face heating. As Narron looked up at her and scowled, she backed out of the room and fled.

She stopped running after only a few steps as anger and frustration caught up with her. How could she possibly have known that Shern was dead, or that Benon was his cousin? Asking why the class had been cancelled was a perfectly reasonable question.

Wasn't it?

Her thoughts returned to Shern. When she searched her feelings she could find no more than a mild sadness. Shern had never even spoken to her, or anyone. In fact, the entire summer class had ignored him during the few weeks he had attended the University.

As she reached the end of the staircase she saw that Rothen was climbing toward her, and felt a surge of relief.

'There you are,' he said. 'You've heard?'

'They cancelled classes.'

'Yes.' He nodded. 'They always do when this happens. I went to find you in your room, but you weren't there. Come and have a hot drink with me.'

Walking beside him, Sonea remained silent. It seemed remarkable that the Guild would close the University because of the death of a novice who had barely spent more than a few weeks there. But since all of the novices, apart from her, were from the Houses, the boy had probably been related to several novices and magicians.

'Shern was in your first class, wasn't he?' Rothen asked as they entered his guestroom.

'Yes.' Sonea hesitated. 'Can I ask what happened to him?'

'Of course.' Rothen collected a pot and cups from a side

235

table, then brought out two jars from a cupboard. 'Do you remember what I told you about Control failing when a magician dies?'

'Any unused magic is let loose, and consumes the body.'

Rothen nodded. He set down the crockery and jars. 'Shern lost Control of his magic.'

Sonea felt a chill run down her spine. 'But he passed the Second Level.'

'He did, but not well or completely. His mind was never stable enough.' Rothen shook his head. 'Such a state is rare, but it does sometimes occur. You see, when children are found to have the potential for magic we also test them for problems like this. Sometimes they simply don't have the mental strength or stability to Control magic.'

'I see,' Sonea said, nodding. Rothen poured water from a jug into the pot, and added sumi leaves from one of the jars. Reaching for the other jar, Sonea mixed raka powder with water and heated the mix with a little magic.

'Unfortunately, some people develop mental instability when they grow older,' Rothen continued, 'or when their magic is released. By then it is too late. Sooner or later they lose the Control they have been taught – usually in their first few years. Shern started to show signs of insta-bility months ago. The Guild took him away from the city to a place we had built for such novices. We try to keep them calm and happy, and they are treated by Healers who are well versed in the problem. But no-one has ever found a cure, and any binding we place on their powers doesn't seem to hold for long.'

Sonea shivered. 'When I first saw him I thought his presence was strange.'

Rothen frowned. 'You sensed the instability that early? No-one else did. I must tell this to—'

'No!' Sonea's heart lurched. If Rothen told anyone that she had sensed something wrong with Shern, the other novices would have something else to blame her for. 'Don't. Please.'

Rothen regarded her speculatively. 'Nobody is going to look on you badly for not saying anything. You couldn't possibly have understood what you were sensing.'

She held his eyes. Rothen sighed. 'All right. I suppose it doesn't matter now.' He placed his hands around the pot. At once steam began to drift from the funnel. 'How do you feel about all of this, Sonea?'

She shrugged. 'I didn't know him.' She then told him what had happened when she walked into the classroom. 'It's as if it was all my fault.'

Rothen frowned as he poured himself a cup of the brewed sumi. 'They probably snapped at you because you interrupted at a bad time. Don't worry about what they said. By tomorrow they will have forgotten about it.'

'So what am I going to do today?' she wondered aloud.

Rothen paused to sip his drink, then smiled. 'I thought we might make a few plans for Dorrien's visit.'

The captain of the *Anyi* had been delighted when Dannyl asked if he was headed for the Vin Islands. At first Dannyl had assumed the man was eager to see his homeland, but grew suspicious when the captain insisted that Dannyl and Tayend move into his own cabin. From what he knew of Vindo sailors, it should take more than homesickness or respect for the Guild to motivate a captain to give up his own space.

The evening after they left, Dannyl had discovered the true reason for the captain's enthusiasm.

'Most ships to Kiko Town go to Capia first,' the captain told them, over a generous meal. 'This way much faster.'

'Why don't they sail straight to Kiko Town?' Tayend asked.

'Bad men live on Upper Islands of Vin.' The captain scowled. 'They rob ships, kill crew. Dangerous people.'

'Oh.' Tayend looked at Dannyl. 'And we're going to sail past these islands?'

'No danger this time.' The captain smiled at Dannyl. 'We have magician on board. Show Guild flag. They no dare rob us!'

Remembering the conversation, Dannyl smiled to himself. He suspected that merchants occasionally risked this route anyway, protecting themselves by displaying the Guild flag even when they didn't have a magician on board. The pirates might have worked this out, too, and he wouldn't have been surprised if a Guild uniform, real or copied, was kept in a chest somewhere for the days when a flag wasn't enough to keep pirates away.

He had been too relieved to be leaving Lonmar to care. The dispute with the Council of Elders had taken over a month of fussing and arguing to settle. While the duties he would attend to in Vin were minor, he wondered if they, too, would turn out to be more trying than they appeared.

As the distance from Lonmar lengthened and the crew had grown increasingly tense and watchful, Dannyl had realised the threat of pirates was real. From the overheard conversations that Tayend translated, Dannyl guessed that an encounter with pirates was not a risk, but a certainty.

It was a little disconcerting to know that these men believed their lives depended on his presence on the ship.

He looked at Tayend, lying on the second narrow bed. The scholar was pale and thin. Bouts of seasickness had taken their toll on his health. Despite weakness and obvious discomfort, Tayend still refused to let Dannyl heal him.

So far, their journey had not been the pleasant adventure Tayend had hoped for. Dannyl knew the scholar had been relieved to leave Lonmar, too. When they reached Kiko Town, he decided, they would spend a week or two resting. The Vindo were known for their warmth and hospitality. Hopefully they would make up for the heat and strangeness of Lonmar, and Tayend would regain his strength and enthusiasm for travelling.

Two small windows offered a glimpse of the sea on either side. The sky was a dusky late-afternoon blue, clear of clouds. Moving closer, Dannyl saw the distant shadow of islands dotting the horizon on one side – and two large boats.

Hearing a yawn, he glanced at Tayend. The scholar was sitting up, stretching.

'How are you feeling?' Dannyl asked.

'Better. What's it like outside?'

'Quite pleasant, from the looks.' The boats were smaller than the *Anyi*. They skimmed over the waves, coming closer rapidly. 'I think we'll have some company before dinner.'

Tayend braced himself against the cabin wall and made his way to Dannyl's side. He peered through the window.

'Pirates?'

Hasty footsteps approached the door of the cabin, followed by several rapid knocks.

'I see them,' Dannyl called.

Tayend slapped him on the shoulder. 'Time to be the hero, my magician friend.'

Dannyl gave Tayend a withering look before opening the door and stepping into the corridor beyond. The youngest of the sailors, a boy of perhaps fourteen years, beckoned wildly.

'Come out! Be quick!' he said, his eyes wide.

Following the boy, Dannyl made his way through the common room and stepped out onto the deck. Locating the captain at the stern of the ship, he made his way across ropes and up a short flight of stairs to join the man.

'Bad men,' the captain said, pointing.

The boats were less than two hundred paces away. Dannyl glanced up at the *Anyi*'s mast to see the Guild flag snapping in the wind. Looking around the deck, he saw that all of the crew, even the boy, carried knives or short, crudely made swords. A few held bows, all loaded and already aimed at the approaching ships.

Tayend made a small noise of disgust. 'The crew don't seem to have much confidence in you,' he murmured.

'They're not taking any chances,' Dannyl replied. 'Would you?'

'You're our hero and protector. I know you'll save us.'

'Must you keep saying that?'

Tayend chuckled. 'I only want you to feel needed and appreciated.'

The lead boat did not slow as it neared the *Anyi*. Concerned that the pirates intended to ram the ship, Dannyl moved to the railing, ready to turn the boat's bow. It swung about at the last moment, sails suddenly turning so that the boat was sailing alongside the *Anyi*.

Stocky, muscular men crowded these smaller vessels. Large shields were held up toward the ship, ready for a rain of missiles. Between them, Dannyl caught the glint of sunlight on blades. Two men held coiled ropes, weighted at one end with grappling hooks.

The men he could see were darker and taller than the average Vindo, suggesting a mix of Vindo and Lonmar blood. All were staring at him, their expressions guarded. One or two glanced at a man at the prow of the boat. This, Dannyl guessed, must be their leader.

As the second boat drew up next to the ship, the man raised a hand and called out in the Vindo language. Tayend made a small, strangled noise, but the crew of the *Anyi* remained silent. Dannyl glanced at the captain.

'What did he say?'

The captain cleared his throat. 'He ask how much you sell your pretty friend for. Say he make profit selling as slave in the West.'

'Really?' Dannyl glanced at Tayend. 'What do you think? Fifty gold?'

Tayend turned to glare at Dannyl.

The captain chuckled. 'I not know right price for man slaves.'

Grinning, Dannyl shook his head. 'Neither do I. Tell the pirate my friend is not for sale. Tell him,' Dannyl turned to regard the pirate, 'that he cannot afford the cargo on this ship.'

The captain repeated the words in Vindo. The pirate smiled, then raised a hand to signal to the other boat. Men hurried to ropes and pulleys, and soon the vessels had pulled away from the ship and were moving away rapidly.

The captain took a step toward Dannyl. 'You kill now,'

he said urgently. 'Before they get away.'

Dannyl shook his head. 'No.'

'But pirate bad people. Always rob ships. They kill. They take slaves.'

'They didn't attack us,' Dannyl replied.

'You kill them, you make sea safer.'

Dannyl turned to face the captain. 'Killing the men on one or two boats won't make any difference. Others will replace them. If the Vindo people want magicians to remove the pirates from these islands, they must arrange it with the Guild. By law, I can only use my powers in defence unless under direct command from my King.'

The captain lowered his eyes and moved away. Dannyl heard the man muttering in his own language before ordering the crew back to their duties. Several of the sailors looked displeased, but returned to their work without complaint.

'They're not the only ones disappointed by your performance,' Tayend said.

Dannyl regarded his friend speculatively. 'You also think I should have killed them?'

Tayend narrowed his eyes at the retreating pirates. 'I wouldn't have protested.' Then he shrugged. 'But mostly I was hoping for a little display of magic. Nothing too fancy. Just some sparks and fire.'

'Sparks and fire?'

'Yes. Maybe a little waterspout.'

'Sorry to disappoint you,' Dannyl replied dryly.

'And what was all that about selling me to slavers – and for only *fifty* gold! How insulting!'

'I'm sorry. Would a hundred gold have been more appropriate?'

'No! And you don't sound particularly sorry.'

'Then I apologise for failing to be convincing in my apology.'

Tayend rolled his eyes. 'Enough! I'm going inside.'

Sonea hugged her box of notes to her chest and sighed. It was growing dark rapidly. The sunlight had streaked the forest with long shadows when she had set out, but only a misty half-light remained now, making it difficult to distinguish the edges of things. She resisted an urge to create a light, knowing that it would make her all too easy to find.

A twig snapped nearby.

She stopped and stared through the trees. In the distance the lights of the Healers' Quarters could be seen flickering through the trunks. She saw no movement, heard no sound.

Releasing the breath she had been holding, she started walking again.

A few weeks earlier, Lord Kiano had taken the class to the fields and glass-roofed houses beyond the Healers' Quarters, where medicinal plants were grown. He had shown them several species, telling them how to identify each plant. Afterwards, he had told them that, each week, he would select a novice to accompany him to the fields after the class, where he would test them on their knowledge.

That afternoon had been her turn. After the test, he had dismissed her, leaving her to return to the Novices' Quarters on her own. Knowing that Regin wouldn't miss an opportunity to waylay her out of the sight of the magicians, she had lingered, pretending to be interested in examining the plants, in the hope that she could follow

Kiano back. But when the teacher had begun a lazy conversation with a gardener she realised she would be waiting a long time.

So she decided to try her other plan. Guessing that Regin would be waiting for her on the usual path, she had cut through the forest, hoping to circle around the Healers' Quarters to the path that led to the front of the University.

A crunch to her left brought her to a stop again. She felt her blood turn cold as she heard a smothered laugh and knew her plan had failed.

'Good evening, Sonea.'

Spinning around, she saw a familiar silhouette among the trees. She willed a globe light into existence, and the darkness shrank back. Regin stopped, a smile spreading across his face as two more figures appeared beside him: Issle and Alend. Hearing sounds all around, Sonea saw Gennyl, Vallon and Kano emerging from the shadows.

'Nice night for a walk in the forest,' Regin observed, looking around. 'So quiet. Peaceful. No-one to interrupt us.' He stepped closer. 'The teachers aren't giving you special treatment any more, are they? Such a shame. It really isn't fair that we get extra attention and you don't. So I thought I'd give you some lessons myself.'

The sound of snow crunching under boots told Sonea that the novices behind her were drawing close. She strengthened her shield but, to her surprise, they moved around her to stand behind Regin.

'Hmmm,' Regin continued. 'Perhaps I could teach you some of what Lord Balkan has shown me.' He glanced at the others and nodded. 'Yes, I think you'd find that interesting.'

Sonea's mouth went dry. She had known Regin was

taking extra classes in Warrior Skills, but not that he was learning under Balkan, the Head of that discipline. As Regin raised his palms, the other novices moved closer to their leader and placed their hands on his shoulders.

'Defend yourself,' Regin said, mimicking Lord Vorel's commanding tone.

Throwing more magic into her shield, she blocked the flow of energy that flashed from each of Regin's palms. The strikes were weak, but rapidly grew in force until they were stronger than anything she had faced in the Arena. Surprised, she poured more and more magic into her shield.

How was this possible? She had fought Regin enough times to know his strength. He had always been much weaker than her. Had he been holding back, just waiting for a moment to surprise her with his real strength?

Regin's face stretched into an ugly grin, and he took a step toward her. Abruptly, the attack weakened, then stopped as he paused to glare at the others. They hurriedly stretched forward to regain their hold on his shoulder.

As they touched Regin again, he resumed his attack. She considered what this meant. Obviously the others were lending him their power. She hadn't heard that it was possible, but there was plenty about the Warrior Skills she didn't know – or might have missed during Vorel's long and boring lectures.

Her senses rang with the magic that filled the air. The snow between them had melted into sizzling puddles. So much power . . . the thought of what was being directed at her was appalling, and set her heart racing. If she failed to hold her shield, the consequences would be brief – and fatal. He was taking such a risk . . . or was he?

What if he means to kill me?

Surely not. He would be expelled from the Guild.

Yet when she pictured Regin facing the assembled magicians in the Guildhall, she could easily hear what they'd say. An unfortunate accident. He wasn't to blame for her poor skills. Four weeks' work in the library, and don't let it happen again.

Anger replaced her fear. As she regarded the novices, she saw that they were glancing at each other doubtfully. Regin was no longer grinning, but frowning with concentration. He growled something, and the others protested in reply. Whatever they were doing, it wasn't having the effect they'd expected.

Was this, then, as strong as they could be when combined? She smiled. She was holding them off easily. He had underestimated her – and if the globe light floating above them was any indication, she still had strength to spare.

How, then, would this end? She was sure striking back would break their attack. But if they could not defend themselves *she* might be the one facing the Higher Magicians and exile.

And if they did manage to shield, they would still continue to hound her all of the way back to the Novices' Quarters. How could she get away from them? She glanced up at the globe light. If she extinguished it, it would take a few minutes for their eyes to grow used to the dark. She could slip away. Unfortunately, she would suffer the same night-blindness . . .

Blindness . . .?

She smiled. Closing her eyes tightly, she exerted her will. Light flashed brightly behind her eyelids, and she felt the attack falter. When she opened her eyes again the novices were blinking or rubbing their faces.

'I can't see!' Kano exclaimed.

It worked! She grinned as Alend swore vehemently and spread his arms out, having nearly lost his balance on the uneven ground. Issle groped about until she found a tree, then grasped it as if she was afraid it would run away.

Sonea took a step backward. Hearing the crunch of snow, Regin reached out and took a step toward her. His boot landed in the mud created by the melted snow, then slipped sideways. He landed face first in the mire. An exclamation of disgust and frustration burst from him as he struggled to his feet.

Sonea choked back laughter. A murderous look crossed Regin's face and he leapt up from the ground. Evading his groping hands, Sonea backed away from the novices.

'Thanks for the lesson, Regin. I never knew you were a man of such *vision*!'

Chuckling, she turned away and started toward the lights of the University.

CHAPTER 16

THE RULE ABOUT ACCUSATIONS

Rothen was dismantling a delicate construction of tubes, valves and glass baubles when a voice spoke his name. He looked up to find a young man in servant's clothes, wearing the green sash that marked him as a Healers' messenger, standing in the doorway of the classroom.

'Yes?' Rothen said.

'Lady Vinara requests your presence in the Healers' Quarters.'

Rothen's heart skipped. What could Vinara want? Had something happened to Sonea? Had one of Regin's pranks gone too far? Or was it someone else? His old friend, Yaldin? Or Ezrille, his wife?

'I will be there shortly,' he replied.

The messenger bowed and hurried away. Rothen looked at the novice who had stayed back to assist him. Farind smiled.

'I'll finish if you want, my lord.'

Rothen nodded. 'Very well. Just make sure you dispose of the acid carefully.'

'Of course.'

Hurrying down the corridor, Rothen tried to stop himself guessing the reason for Vinara's summons. He would know soon enough. The night air was icy cold outside the University, so he surrounded himself with a shield and warmed the air within. Reaching the Healers' Quarters he found Lady Vinara waiting for him in the entrance.

'You sent for me?' Rothen asked breathlessly.

Her lips twitched into a faint smile. 'There was no need to hurry, Lord Rothen,' Vinara told him. 'The novices here who claim to be victims of your favourite are not about to expire. Do you know where Sonea is?'

Victims? What had she done? 'Studying in her room, most likely.'

'You haven't seen her this evening?'

'No.' Rothen frowned. 'What is this about?'

'Six novices found their way here an hour ago. They claim that Sonea ambushed them in the forest and blinded them.'

'Blinded them? How?'

'With a bright light.'

'Oh.' Rothen relaxed, but seeing the Healer's grim expression, he grew worried again. 'Not permanently?'

She shook her head. 'No. None of their injuries are serious – certainly not bad enough to waste Healers' time on. They will recover.'

'Any injuries other than blindness?'

'Cuts and bruises from finding their way out of the forest.'

'I see.' Rothen nodded slowly. 'Would one of these novices be Garrel's favourite, Regin?'

'Yes.' Her lips thinned. 'I have heard Sonea has a particular dislike for this boy.'

Rothen gave a short, bitter laugh. 'The feeling is mutual, I assure you. May I speak to Regin?'

'Of course. I will take you to him.' Vinara turned and began to walk along the main corridor of the building.

As Rothen followed, he considered all that Vinara had told him. He didn't believe for a minute that Sonea had ambushed Regin and his friends. More likely they had ambushed her. Something had gone wrong, however.

They might have blinded themselves so they could blame her for it, but he doubted that had been the case. If they had intended to do so, they would have arranged for others to find and guide them back to the Healers' Quarters. That they hadn't even called for assistance mentally suggested they had hesitated to call attention to their situation.

Vinara stopped by a door and gestured inside. Looking into the room, Rothen saw a familiar young man in mud-stained robes sitting on the edge of a bed. Regin's face was flushed. His fists clenched and unclenched and his eyes burned fiercely at a point far beyond the shoulder of his guardian, Lord Garrel.

The magician turned to regard Rothen and his expression darkened. Ignoring him, Rothen listened instead to Regin, who was just at the end of a long, angry whine.

'I swear, she was trying to kill us! I know the Guild law. She should be expelled!'

Rothen glanced at Vinara, then back at the boy, and felt a smile pulling at his lips. If Regin wanted to raise Guild law, then so be it.

'That's a very serious accusation, Regin,' he said quietly. 'And it would be most inappropriate for your guardian to confirm the truth of it.' He turned to look at the woman beside him. 'Perhaps Lady Vinara would suggest someone.'

Vinara blinked, then her eyes twinkled as she realised what Rothen meant.

'I will perform the truth-read,' she said.

Regin drew in a sharp breath. Looking back to the novice, Rothen was gratified to see the boy had turned white. 'No, I didn't mean . . .' he spluttered. 'I'm not—'

'Are you withdrawing your accusation, then?' Rothen said.

'Yes,' Regin gasped. 'I withdraw my accusation.'

'So what *did* happen tonight?'

'Yes,' Vinara said, her voice darkening. 'Why did Sonea attack you, as you claim?'

'Clearly she intended to ensure they could not attend classes for a few days,' Garrel replied.

'I see,' Rothen said. 'What is going to occur in the next few days that she might want you to be absent from?'

'I don't know . . . I guess she just wanted to hurt us.'

'And so she followed six novices into the forest,' Rothen gave Vinara a meaningful look, 'certain that she would be able to overcome your combined strength? She must be better at Warrior Skills than her marks indicate.'

Regin's sightless eyes sought his guardian.

'What were the six of you doing in the forest in the first place?' Vinara asked.

'We were just . . . exploring. For fun.'

'Hmmm,' she said. 'That's not what your friends say.'

Regin opened his mouth, then closed it again. Garrel rose. 'My novice has suffered an injury and needs rest. Surely this questioning can wait until he is recovered.'

Rothen hesitated, then decided it was worth the risk. He turned to Vinara. 'He's right. We don't need to hear

Regin's answers. I'm sure Sonea will submit to a truth-read to prove her innocence.'

'No!' Regin exclaimed.

Vinara's eyes narrowed. 'If she is willing, you cannot prevent it, Regin.'

The novice grimaced, as if tasting something bad. 'All right. I'll tell you. We followed her into the forest and played a trick on her. It was nothing dangerous. We were just . . . practising what we'd learned in class.'

'I see.' Vinara's voice was chilly. 'Then you had better tell us what this trick was – and bear in mind that Sonea's memory will confirm or deny everything you say.'

Sighing, Sonea marked the page of the book with a slip of paper, then rose to answer the door. She opened it carefully, bracing it with magic in case Regin tried to force his way in. To her surprise, Lord Osen stood in the corridor outside.

'Forgive the intrusion,' Lord Osen said. 'Administrator Lorlen wishes you to meet him in his office.'

Sonea stared at him, the warmth draining from her face. A cold dread entered her stomach. The Administrator . . . she hadn't spoken to him in months. What did he want? Was it anything to do with the High Lord? Had Akkarin discovered that she knew his secret?

'Don't be concerned,' Osen told her, smiling. 'He just wants to ask a few questions.'

Stepping out of her room, she followed him out of the Novices' Quarters, across the courtyard and through the back entrance of the University. Their footsteps echoed in the empty corridor. As he opened the door to the Administrator's office, Sonea drew in a breath. The room was filled with magicians. Some sat in chairs, others were standing. As she stepped inside she realised that most of the Higher Magicans were present.

Seeing Rothen, she let her breath out in relief. Then she saw Lord Garrel and her heart sank. So this was about her encounter with Regin, then. He must have told a fine tale to stir up the Higher Magicians.

Rothen smiled and beckoned to her. Feeling ill, she moved to his side.

'Sonea.'

She turned to face Lorlen, who was sitting behind a large desk. The blue-robed magician's expression was sober.

'An incident that happened between you and six novices earlier this evening has been brought to our attention. We want you to tell us what happened.'

She looked around the room, then swallowed hard.

'Lord Kiano took me to the fields for a test. I came back the long way, around the Healers' Quarters. Regin and his friends stopped me in the forest.' She hesitated, wondering how she was to avoid saying anything that could be taken as an accusation.

'Go on,' Lorlen said. 'Tell us what happened.'

Taking a deep breath, Sonea continued. 'Regin said he wanted to show me something he'd learned from Lord Balkan,' she glanced toward the red-robed magician, 'and then the others put their hands on his shoulders. His strike was stronger than usual and I realised the others were giving him extra power somehow.'

'What did you do?'

'Shielded.'

'That's all?'

'I didn't want to strike back. They might not protect themselves well enough.'

'Wise. What happened then?'

'I still had my globe light so I knew I had power left.'

A sharp intake of breath to her left made her jump. She turned to see Lady Vinara looking at her appraisingly.

'Go on,' Lorlen said.

'I knew that they wouldn't give up, and I had to get away before they decided to do something else. So to stop them following me I dazzled them with light.'

She could hear many low voices murmuring behind her. Lorlen made a small gesture and they fell silent.

'A few questions come to mind,' he said. 'Why did you take the long way back from the fields?'

'I knew they would be waiting for me,' Sonea replied.

'Who?'

'Regin and the others.'

'Why would they do that?'

'They always . . .' She shook her head. 'I wish I knew, Administrator.'

Lorlen nodded. He looked to Vinara.

'Her story matches Regin's.'

Sonea stared at the Healer. 'Regin *told* you that!'

'Regin accused you of trying to kill them,' Rothen explained quietly. 'When he realised this meant he must submit to a truth-read, he withdrew his accusation. So I said you would submit to one to prove your innocence. After that, the truth came out.'

She looked at him in surprise. He had suggested someone *truth-read* her? What if Regin hadn't confessed? Rothen must have been sure Regin would tell the truth once he knew it would be revealed anyway. 'So what's this meeting about, then? Why are all the Higher Magicians here?'

Rothen did not have a chance to reply.

'Does anybody have questions for Sonea?' Lorlen asked.

'Yes.'

Lord Sarrin straightened and stepped forward.

'After this confrontation did you feel tired? Exhausted?'

Sonea shook her head. 'No, my lord.'

'Did you perform any other magic tonight?'

'No – actually, yes. I put a binding on my door.'

Lord Sarrin pursed his lips and looked at Lord Balkan. The Warrior regarded her speculatively.

'Have you been practising Warrior Skills in your own time?' he asked.

'No, my lord.'

'Have you had any other encounters with novices using this method of combining power before?'

'No, I'd never heard of it.'

Lord Balkan leaned back into his chair and nodded to the Administrator. Lorlen looked around the room.

'Any more questions?'

The magicians looked at each other, then shook their heads.

'Then you may go, Sonea.'

She rose and bowed to the magicians. They watched silently as she passed. Only after the door had swung closed did she hear voices in the room, too muffled to be understood.

She stared at the door, then slowly began to smile. In trying to cause her trouble, Regin had brought worse on himself. Turning, she made her way back to the Novices' Quarters sure that, for once, no-one would bother her on the way.

*   *   *

'So much power in one so young.' Lord Sarrin shook his head. 'Only a few have progressed so quickly.'

Lorlen nodded. His own powers had developed rapidly. As had Akkarin's. And they had both been elected to two of the highest positions in the Guild. He could see the dismay in the Higher Magicians' faces as this occurred to them.

Normally they would be pleased to find such promise in a novice. But Sonea was the slum girl, and she had recently demonstrated her questionable character by stealing a pen. Though Lorlen was prepared to believe this was an isolated incident, perhaps in reaction to the other novices' harassment, other magicians had not been so forgiving.

'We should not foster any high expectations yet,' he said, to reassure them. 'She might simply be an early developer, and this is as strong as she will get.'

'She is already stronger than most of her teachers and,' Sarrin gestured toward Rothen, 'perhaps her own guardian.'

'Is that a problem?' Rothen asked coolly.

'No.' Lorlen smiled. 'It has never been in the past. You just need to be cautious.'

'Do we need to raise her a class again?' Jerrik crossed his arms and frowned.

'It is only her strength that is advanced,' Vinara replied. 'Not her skills. She still has a great deal to learn.'

'All we need do is warn her teachers,' Lorlen said. 'They should not test her strength without taking the usual precautions.'

To Lorlen's satisfaction, all the magicians nodded. Regin's actions had revealed more than his own cruel nature. He had shown everyone just what Sonea was capable of. Lorlen suspected that Rothen, too, was surprised by just how strong she had proven to be.

Rothen's attention was on Lord Garrel, however. Regin's guardian had been silent for most of the discussion. Lorlen frowned. They must not forget the seriousness of the incident that had brought them together.

'What is to be done about Regin?' he asked in a tone that cut through the murmuring.

Balkan smiled. 'I think the young man has learned his lesson. He'd be a fool to provoke her now.'

The other magicians nodded and voiced their agreement.

'Some discipline is needed,' Lorlen insisted.

'He broke no rule,' Garrel protested. 'Balkan gave him permission to practice this strategy with his classmates.'

'Waylaying another novice is not what we call "practising",' Lorlen replied. 'It is dangerous and irresponsible.'

'I agree,' Vinara said firmly. 'And his punishment should reflect this.'

The magicians exchanged glances.

'Regin has been taking extra lessons in Warrior Skills,' Balkan said. 'Since they were the source of the trouble, I will stop them for a term of . . . three months.'

Lorlen pursed his lips. 'Extend that until the middle of the Second Year. I believe his class will have covered all the lessons on honour and fairness by then.'

Watching Rothen, Lorlen saw the magician raise a hand to scratch his nose and cover a smile. Garrel's expression darkened, but he remained silent. The corner of Balkan's mouth curled upward.

'Very well,' the Warrior agreed. 'Until the half-year tests of the Second Year have passed, then.'

Lorlen looked up at the other magicians. They nodded their approval.

'That's settled, then.'

Jerrik sighed, looked around at the others and stepped forward. 'If that is all, I will return to my work.'

Lorlen watched as Lord Sarrin and Lady Vinara also rose and followed the University Director out of the room. Lord Garrel followed. Balkan was regarding Rothen closely.

'It's a pity Sonea has no enthusiasm for the Warrior Skills discipline. We rarely find women warriors of her strength . . . or resourcefulness.'

Rothen turned to regard the Warrior. 'I can't pretend to be disappointed at her lack of enthusiasm,' he replied.

'Have you been discouraging her?' There was a note of warning in Balkan's voice.

'Not at all,' Rothen replied smoothly. 'It was a certain incident in the North Square that discouraged her, and I doubt I could rectify that if I tried. It took me long enough to persuade her that we weren't all battle-crazed villains.'

Balkan smiled crookedly. 'You have satisfied her that we are not, I hope.'

Rothen sighed and looked away. 'Sometimes, I think I'm the only one who is trying.'

'The enmity from other novices was inevitable and it will not stop after graduation. She must learn to deal with it. At least, this time, she used magic rather than less honourable skills.'

Rothen narrowed his eyes at the other magician. Balkan returned his stare levelly. Sensing the tension rising between the two magicians, Lorlen slapped the top of his desk lightly.

'Just make sure they keep their battles to the Arena,'

he said. 'Had it been summer they might have set the entire forest alight. I have enough to do without such disasters adding to my work. Now, if you please . . .' he waved to the door with both hands. 'I want my office back!'

The two magicians bowed their heads. Apologising, they walked to the door and stepped outside. As the door closed Lorlen breathed a sigh of relief and exasperation.

Magicians!

CHAPTER 17

A CAPABLE COMPANION

The paths through the gardens had been cleared of snow, but the trees still carried a coating of white along their bare branches. Rothen looked up at the University. Icicles hung from the windows, adding more decoration to the stone frames. As they reached the front of the building snow began to fall, so Rothen led Sonea up the stairs to the shelter of the Entrance Hall.

—Rothen?

—Dorrien.

—I hope you have a dozen heat globes set in your room. I can't believe this cold snap. It's worse than any I remember. I'm just coming in sight of the gates now.

Rothen glanced down at Sonea. Her eyes were narrowed at the street beyond the gates.

'Here he comes,' she murmured.

Looking up, Rothen saw a lone rider approaching. The rider waved a hand and one of the gates began to swing inward. Before it had fully opened, he urged his horse through and into a gallop.

The horse pounded around the circular road, its rider's green robes snapping in the wind. Dorrien was grinning, his face flushed.

'Father!' As the horse slid to a stop, Dorrien threw his leg over the saddle and leapt lightly to the ground.

'Very showy, Dorrien,' Rothen said dryly, starting back down the University stairs. 'One day you're going to fall flat on your face.'

'No doubt right in front of you,' Dorrien replied, drowning Rothen in green cloth as he embraced him, 'so you can say "I told you so".'

'Would *I* say that?' Rothen asked innocently.

'Yes, you would . . .' Dorrien's blue eyes flicked over Rothen's shoulder.

'So *this* is your new novice.'

'Sonea.' As Rothen beckoned, Sonea started down the stairs.

Dorrien pressed the horse's reins into Rothen's hand and stepped forward. As always, seeing his son's smile after a long absence brought an ache of sadness. It was when Dorrien was at his most charming that he reminded Rothen of his deceased wife. The boy had also inherited Yilara's almost obsessive dedication to Healing.

He's not a boy any longer, Rothen reminded himself. Dorrien had turned twenty-four a few months past. He was a grown man. *At that age*, Rothen mused, *I had a wife and son*.

'Greetings, Lady Sonea.'

'Greetings, Lord Dorrien,' Sonea replied, bowing gracefully.

A servant from the stables appeared while they were talking, and Rothen passed the horse's reins to the man.

'Where shall I take the bags, my lord?' the servant asked.

'My rooms,' Rothen told him. The man nodded and led the horse away.

'Let's get out of the cold,' Dorrien suggested.

Nodding, Rothen started up the University stairs. As they entered the warmth of the interior, Dorrien sighed.

'It is good to be back,' he said. 'How are things here, Father?'

Rothen shrugged. 'As quiet as usual – at least, the only dramas in the last year seemed to have involved us.' He smiled at Sonea. 'And you know all about them.'

Dorrien chuckled. 'Yes. And how is *Ambassador* Dannyl?'

'He hasn't communicated with me directly for some months, but I have received a few letters, and a box of Elyne wine.'

'Any left?'

'Yes.'

'Now that's good news.' Dorrien rubbed his hands together.

'How are matters in the north-east?'

Dorrien shrugged. 'Nothing unusual. A bout of winter-fever was the most exciting event of the last year. As usual, a few of the farmers tried to continue with their work and got themselves a case of lungrot on top. A few accidents to deal with, a few old ones passing on, a few new babes taking their place. Oh, and one of the reber-herder boys came to me with burns. He claimed he was attacked by what the locals call the Sakan King.'

Rothen frowned. 'The Sakan King? Isn't that an old superstition about a ghost that lives on Mount Kanlor?'

'Yes, but I'd say from the injury that the boy had dropped some burning wood on himself.'

Rothen chuckled. 'Young boys can be amazingly creative when they don't want to admit they've done something wrong, or foolish.'

'This was a rather entertaining story,' Dorrien agreed. 'The boy invented quite a vivid picture of this Sakan King.'

Rothen smiled. Mind communication was too direct for

this kind of chatter. It was so much better to be talking face to face. In the corner of his eye he could see Sonea watching Dorrien. As his son turned away to peer into the Foodhall she gave him a more appraising look.

Dorrien noted the direction of Rothen's gaze and glanced back at her. She took this as an invitation to join the conversation.

'Did you have a difficult journey?'

Dorrien groaned. 'Awful. Blizzards in the mountains and endless snow for the rest. But when the Guild calls, one must come, even if it means spending every shred of your power carving a path through the snow and keeping yourself and your horse from freezing.'

'Could you have waited until spring?'

'Spring is the busiest time for the reber-herders. The reber start to drop their young, the farmers work too hard, have accidents.' He shook his head. 'Not a good time.'

'Summer, then?'

Dorrien shook his head again. 'Someone always comes down with heat exhaustion or sunburn. And summer-cough.'

'Autumn?'

'Harvest time.'

'So winter *is* the best time.'

'There's always someone who comes to me with frostrot, and living indoors for months can be a health problem, and—'

'There's no good time, is there?'

He grinned. 'No.'

Emerging from the back entrance of the University, they walked through falling snow to the Magicians' Quarters. Rothen saw Sonea's eyebrows rise as Dorrien stepped onto the tiled area in the stairwell and began to float upwards.

'Are you still using the stairs, Father?' Dorrien crossed his arms and shook his head. 'I suppose you're still preaching about exercise and laziness. What about keeping your skills in shape as well as your body?'

'I'm surprised you have any energy left to levitate after all the trials you went through on the way here,' Rothen replied.

Dorrien shrugged. Looking closely, Rothen noted signs of strain in the young man's expression. *So he's showing off*, Rothen mused. Yaldin had once commented that Dorrien could charm the wool off a reber if he set his mind to it. Rothen looked at Sonea. She was staring at Dorrien's feet, probably sensing the disc of energy beneath them.

They reached the top of the stairs, Dorrien stepping onto the landing with a quiet sigh of relief. He gave Sonea an appraising look.

'Has my father shown you how to levitate yet?'

She shook her head.

'Well, we'll have to do something about that.' Dorrien sent Rothen a reproachful look. 'It's a skill that can come in very handy at times.'

—For impressing young ladies?

Dorrien ignored that. Rothen smiled and led them to his door. They entered the warmth of the guestroom and were greeted by Tania.

'Warmed wine, my lords?'

'Please!' Dorrien exclaimed.

'None for me,' Sonea said, remaining in the doorway. 'I still have three chapters of medicine to study.'

Dorrien looked as if he might protest, then changed his

mind. 'It's close to the end of First Year for you, isn't it, Sonea?'

'Yes, two weeks until the First Year tests.'

'A lot of studying.'

Sonea nodded. 'Yes, so I must leave you two to catch up. I am honoured to meet you, Lord Dorrien.'

'Nice to meet you, too, Sonea.' Dorrien lifted his glass. 'I'll see you later, or at dinner.'

The door closed quietly behind her. Dorrien's eyes lingered.

'You didn't tell me she had short hair.'

'It was much shorter a year ago.'

'She's so fragile-looking.' Dorrien frowned. 'I expected something . . . rougher, I suppose.'

'You should have seen how thin she was when she first came here.'

'Ah,' Dorrien sobered. 'Raised in the slums. No wonder she's so small.'

'Small, perhaps,' Rothen agreed, 'but not weak. Not in the magical sense, anyway.' Rothen considered his son. 'I was hoping you might distract her a little. All she's thought about since summer is study and her problems with the other novices.'

The glint of humour flared into life again in Dorrien's eyes. 'Distract her? I think I can do that – if you think she won't find a country Healer horribly boring.'

The main street of Kiko Town wound around the island in an unbroken spiral, ending at the Vindo Emperor's home at the peak. The city had been built that way, according to Dannyl's guide, to confound and slow invaders. The road was also used as a route for parades during festivals, ensuring that all city dwellers had a view of the procession.

The harvest festival had been in full swing when Dannyl and Tayend arrived, and was still going three days later. The tasks Lorlen had asked Errend to take care of were minor, but numerous. Dannyl could not start to work on them until the festival was over, so he and Tayend had been relaxing in the Guild House since they had arrived, only slipping out to watch the street performances or buy wine and local delicacies.

Celebrants, singers, dancers and musicians filled the main road for most of each day, making it difficult to get anywhere quickly. The procession could be avoided, however, by using the steep stairways bridging each loop of the spiralling main road. It was not an easy journey when travelling upward, and Tayend was breathing hard when they finally reached their destination; a wine merchant's shop on the main road, several staircases uphill from the Guild House.

Stopping to lean against a building, Tayend waved Dannyl toward the shop. 'I'll rest,' he gasped. 'You go.'

At once a girl carrying bracelets of flowers stepped out of the procession, approached the scholar and tried to persuade him to buy some. Tayend had been more than a little overwhelmed by the boldness of Vindo women, but they had been told by their guide that the Vindo friendliness was simply local good manners.

Leaving Tayend occupied, Dannyl entered the shop and began selecting wine. Knowing that Tayend would appreciate something familiar, he chose several bottles of Elyne wine. Like most Vindo, the merchant spoke Dannyl's language well enough to make his price known, but not well enough to barter.

As the man began to pack the bottles into a box, Dannyl moved to the shop's bay window. The flower girl had moved on. Tayend leaned against the corner of the building, his arms crossed and his attention taken by a group of male acrobats.

Then a hand shot out, grasped Tayend's arm, and pulled the scholar into the shadows.

Dannyl stepped closer to the bay window, then froze. He could see Tayend now, pressed up against the wall of an alley beside the shop. A dirty-looking Vindo with straggly hair had one hand around the scholar's neck. The other held a blade to Tayend's side.

White with terror, Tayend stared at the mugger. The man's lips moved. A demand for money, Dannyl guessed. He took a step toward the door, then forced himself to stop. What would happen if the mugger was confronted by a magician?

Dannyl's imagination raced forward. He saw the mugger using Tayend as a hostage . . . taking the scholar with him as he escaped . . . stabbing Tayend when Dannyl was out of sight.

Whereas if Tayend gave up his money, the man would simply take it and go.

Tayend's eyes moved to the window and locked with Dannyl's. Nodding toward the mugger, Dannyl mouthed the words: 'Give it to him.' Tayend frowned.

Seeing the change in the scholar's expression, the mugger glanced toward the window. Ducking out of view, Dannyl cursed. Had the man seen him? He peered around the edge of the window.

Tayend was pulling his bag of coins out of his coat. The mugger grabbed it, then tested its weight. With a grin of triumph, he stowed it in his pocket.

Then, with a swift jab, he sunk the knife into Tayend's side.

Horrified, Dannyl leapt out of the shop. Tayend was doubled over, blood gushing from the wound. Seeing that the mugger was bracing himself to stab again, Dannyl reached out with magic. The mugger's expression changed to surprise and horror as he saw Dannyl. Then he was flying through the air. Thrown over the road, he slammed into the opposite building with a sickening crack and fell to the ground, the celebrants scattering as he landed among them.

For a moment Dannyl stared at the man in surprise and horror. He hadn't meant to react so strongly. Then Tayend gave a low moan and he put the mugger out of his mind. Dashing forward, he caught Tayend as the scholar crumpled, and lowered him to the ground. Tearing away the bloodied shirt, Dannyl pressed his hand to the wound.

Closing his eyes, he sent his mind inward. The knife had cut deep, severing veins, arteries and organs. Dannyl called on Healing power and focussed it on the damaged area. He diverted blood, persuaded tissue to knit together, and encouraged Tayend's body to draw away grime from the dirty knife. Healers usually worked only until a wound was sealed and safe, saving their power for other patients, but Dannyl poured his energy forth until only scar tissue remained. Then he listened to the body under his hand as he had been taught, checking that everything was working properly.

Other messages reached him. Tayend's heart raced. His muscles were stiff with tension. A feeling of relief and dread touched Dannyl's mind. He frowned. A lingering fear was to be expected, but there was something different about this feeling of dread. His senses shifted to the mental level and suddenly Tayend's thoughts spilled into his mind.

Perhaps he won't see . . . No, it's too late! he's probably seen already. Now he'll reject me. Kyralian magicians are like that. They think we're perverted. Unnatural. But no! He'll understand. He says he knows what it's like. But he's not a lad himself . . . or is he? He could be hiding it. No, he couldn't be. He's a Kyralian magician. Their Healers would have detected it, and thrown him out . . .

Surprised, Dannyl drew away from Tayend's mind, but kept his eyes closed and his hand on the scholar's side. So this was why Tayend refused Healing. He was afraid that Dannyl would sense that . . . that he was like Dem Agerralin. Tayend desired men.

Memories of the last few months flashed through Dannyl's mind. He recalled the day after the sea leech attack. Tayend had found a pair of leeches entwined around each other and a rope. A sailor had noticed Tayend's interest.

'They breed,' the man said.

'Which is the boy, and which is the girl?' Tayend asked.

'Not boy or girl. Same.'

Tayend's brows rose and he glanced at the sailor. 'Really?'

The man moved away to collect a pan of siyo. Tayend looked up at the leeches.

'Good for you,' he'd said.

Remembering his time in Elyne, Dannyl recalled his conversation with Errend. *'He's the youngest son of Tremmelin . . . scholar, I believe . . . Don't see him in court much – though I have seen him with Dem Agerralin . . . a man of dubious associations.'*

Then the Dem Agerralin: *'We are all very curious about you . . .'*

We?

Tayend himself, in the Palace: *'The Elyne court is both awful in its decadence, and wonderful for its freedom. We expect everyone to have a few interesting or eccentric habits.'*

Tayend had been uneasy for their whole stay in Lonmar. Dannyl knew what they had witnessed in Judgment Square had shocked Tayend, but he had expected the scholar would eventually forget the incident and enjoy the rest of the 'adventure'. But Tayend had remained fearful and quiet.

And now, of course, he's worried how I will react. We Kyralians aren't exactly known for our tolerance of men like Tayend. I know that only too well. No wonder he was afraid of being Healed. He believes that Healers can sense if a man desires other men, as if it's an illness.

Dannyl frowned. So what should he do now? Should he let Tayend know that he had discovered his secret, or would it be better to pretend that he hadn't noticed anything?

I don't know. I need more time to consider. For now . . . yes, I will pretend I don't know.

Opening his eyes, he found Tayend staring at him. Smiling, Dannyl drew away his hand. 'Are you—?'

'My lord?'

Looking up, Dannyl saw that a crowd had gathered around him. The man who had addressed him was a Vindo guard. Other guards were questioning people. One inspected the prone mugger, then extracted Tayend's money bag from the man's hand.

The guard standing over Dannyl nudged a bloodied knife on the ground by Tayend's foot with the toe of his

270

sandal. 'No trial,' he said, meeting Dannyl's eyes nervously. 'People say you kill bad man. You in right.'

Looking through the crowd, Dannyl saw the staring eyes of the mugger. Dead. A shiver ran down his spine. He had never killed before. That was something else he would have to think about later. As the guard moved away, Dannyl turned to Tayend and gave the scholar a questioning look.

'Are you recovered?'

Tayend nodded quickly. 'If you don't count the fact that I'm still shaking.'

The wine merchant stood in the doorway of his shop, looking uncertain and frightened. A younger man stood beside him with the box of wine in his arms. 'Come on, then. Let's get our wine. I don't know about you, but I just got a lot thirstier.'

Tayend took a few unsteady steps, then seemed to regain his confidence. A guard pressed the money bag into his hands. Dannyl smiled at the scholar's expression, then, indicating that the merchant's companion should follow, started toward the Guild House.

The words on the page before Sonea suddenly disappeared under fat black droplets. She looked over her shoulder, but no-one stood nearby. Hearing more drops hit the page, she looked up and saw an ornate ink bottle hovering high above her.

From behind the shelves of books to her left she heard giggles. The bottle moved, threatening to splash ink on Sonea's robes. Narrowing her eyes at it, she sent out a flash of power. At once the ink sizzled and dried, and the ink bottle began to glow red. It shot away toward the shelves, and she heard a yelp.

Smiling grimly, she looked down again, but her smile vanished as she saw the ink drying on the page. She drew out a nosecloth and dabbed at the spots. Then she muttered a curse as the ink spread.

'Bad idea. You're only making it worse,' said a voice at her shoulder.

She jumped and turned to find Dorrien standing behind her. Before she could stop herself, she snapped the book shut.

He shook his head. '*That* certainly won't help.'

Sonea frowned with annoyance and searched for a retort, but he reached out to take the book from her.

'Here, let me have a look.' He laughed. 'First Year Alchemy. This isn't even worth saving!'

'But it's from the library.'

Dorrien leafed through to the stained pages and grimaced. 'There's nothing you can do to fix this,' he said, shaking his head. 'But don't worry. Rothen can have another copy made.'

'But . . .'

Dorrien's brows rose. 'But?'

'It will cost—'

'Money?' Dorrien finished. 'That's hardly a problem, Sonea.'

Sonea opened her mouth to protest, but closed it again.

'You don't think it's fair for him to pay for it, do you?' Dorrien dropped into one of the chairs beside her. 'After all, you don't damage the book.'

Sonea chewed on her lip. 'You saw them?'

'I passed a novice nursing burned fingertips and another holding what looked like a melted ink bottle. When I saw you trying to rescue this book, I guessed the rest.' His lips twitched. 'Rothen has told me of your admirers.'

She regarded him silently. He laughed at her expression, but it was a laugh edged with bitterness.

'I wasn't very popular in my First Year of University, either. I understand a little of what you're going through. It's torture, but you can get yourself out of it.'

'How?'

He put the book down on the table and leaned back in the chair. 'Before I say anything, you had better tell me what they've done to you so far. I need to get an idea what these novices are like, particularly Regin, before I can help you.'

'Help me?' She regarded him dubiously. 'What can you do that Rothen can't?'

He smiled. 'Maybe nothing, but we won't know that if we don't try.'

Somewhat reluctantly, she told him about the first day, about Issle and how all the class turned from her. She related how she had worked until she could join the next class only to have Regin follow her, and how soon after he had put Narron's pen in her box so that everyone would think she was a thief. And then she described the ambush in the forest.

'I don't know why, but I left that meeting with the Higher Magicians with a feeling that something else was going on that I didn't know about,' she finished. 'They didn't ask the sort of questions I expected.'

'What were you expecting?'

Sonea shrugged. 'Questions about who started the whole thing. They only asked if I was tired.'

'You had just demonstrated how strong you were, Sonea,' Dorrien pointed out. 'They would have been more interested in that than some squabble between you and the novices.'

'But they banned Regin from Balkan's class until the middle of next year.'

'Oh, they had to punish him,' Dorrien waved a hand dismissively, 'but that's not why they questioned you. They wanted you to confirm his story, but mostly they wanted to gauge your limits.'

Sonea thought back to that interview and nodded slowly.

'From what I've heard, you're stronger than many of the lower-level teachers now,' he continued. 'Some believe your powers have developed young and won't grow much further, others think you'll continue at this rate and become as powerful as Lorlen. Who knows? It doesn't mean anything until you know *how* to use that power.'

Dorrien leaned forward and rubbed his palms together. 'But the magicians have to acknowledge that Regin and his friends are ganging up on you now. Unfortunately, they can only do something about it when there's proof. We have to give them that proof. I think we should convince them that he was the one who planted Narron's pen in your box.'

'How?'

'Hmmm.' Dorrien leaned back in his chair and drummed his fingers on the cover of the book. 'Ideally, it should involve him trying to set you up as a thief again. Then when he's caught, everyone will have to consider that you were set up before. Yet we'll have to make sure there's no possibility that they'll think *we* set *him* up . . .'

As they tossed ideas back and forth, Sonea felt her spirits lighten. Perhaps Dorrien *could* help her. He was certainly nothing like she had expected him to be. In fact, she decided, he was nothing like *any* magician she had met before.

I think I actually like him, she mused.

CHAPTER 18

FRIENDSHIP

Opening the door to her room, Sonea blinked in surprise.

'Enough studying,' Dorrien announced. 'You've been stuck in there every night this week. It's Freeday, and we're going out.'

'Out?' Sonea repeated.

'Out,' he affirmed.

'Where to?'

'That,' Dorrien's eyes twinkled, 'is a secret.'

Sonea opened her mouth to protest, but he put a finger to her lips. 'Shh,' he said. 'No more questions.'

Curious despite her annoyance, she pulled the door closed and followed him down the corridor of the Novices' Quarters. She caught a soft sound behind her and looked back over her shoulder. Regin was peering out from the open doorway of a room, his lips curled into a sly smile.

Turning away, she followed Dorrien outside. The sun was shining, though the grounds were still buried deep under snow. Dorrien walked fast, and she had to hurry to keep up with him.

'How far away is this secret place?'

'Not far.' Dorrien smiled.

Not far. Like most of Dorrien's answers, it told her

nothing. She pressed her lips together, determined to ask no more questions.

'Have you been out of the grounds many times since you came here?' he asked, slowing his stride as they entered the University.

'A few times. Not since I started at the University, though.'

'But that's nearly six months ago.' Dorrien shook his head. 'Rothen really should take you out more. It's not healthy spending all your time indoors.'

Amused by his disapproval, she smiled. She couldn't imagine him being comfortable indoors for long periods of time. A light tan coloured his face and hands, hinting at long hours spent under the sun. His strides were long and easy, and she had to walk fast to keep up.

She had expected a younger Rothen. While Dorrien's eyes were the same brilliant blue as his father's, his jaw was narrower and his frame was thinner. However, the main difference was in their personalities. Or was it? While Rothen was dedicated to teaching novices, Dorrien was commited to looking after the villages in his care. They just practised different disciplines and lived in vastly different surrounds.

'Where did you go?' Dorrien asked.

'I visited my aunt and uncle in the slums a few times,' she told him. 'Every time I did, I think a few magicians were worried I might try to run away.'

'Have you ever thought of running away, Sonea?'

Surprised by the question, she looked at him closely. His gaze was level, and his expression serious.

'Sometimes,' she admitted, lifting her chin.

Dorrien smiled. 'Don't think you're the only novice who

ever did,' he said quietly. 'Nearly all of us think about it at some time – usually just before testing time.'

'But you did get away in the end, didn't you?' Sonea pointed out.

He laughed. 'You could look at it that way.'

'How long have you been working in the country?'

'Five years.' Reaching the end of the corridor, they stepped into the Entrance Hall, and started up the stairs.

'Do you miss the Guild?'

He pursed his lips. 'Sometimes. I miss Father most, but I also miss having access to all the medicines and knowledge here. If I need to find out how to treat an illness I can communicate with Healers here, but it's a slower process and I often don't have the medicines in my store that I need.'

'Is there another Healers' Quarters where you live?'

'Oh, no,' Dorrien smiled. 'I live in a little house on a hillside, on my own. People come to me to have their illnesses treated, or I visit them. Sometimes I have to travel for several hours, and I have to take everything I might need with me.'

Sonea absorbed this as she followed him up the second flight of stairs. When they reached the top she noted that, while she was a little out of breath, Dorrien wasn't at all affected by the exertion.

'This way.' He beckoned and walked down the main corridor. They were on the third floor of the University. Mystified, Sonea wondered what could be so interesting up here.

Dorrien turned into a smaller passage. After taking several turns and passing through a small, unused room, he stopped before a door and waved a hand slowly over a panel set into the wood. Sonea heard a click, then the door swung inward. Gesturing for her to follow, Dorrien moved into an unlit staircase. As the door closed behind them a globe of light sparked into existence above Dorrien's head.

'Where are we?' Sonea breathed. They had taken so many turns that she was completely disorientated. She was sure they were somewhere near the front of the University. There were no floors above, yet the staircase continued upward.

'We're inside the University,' Dorrien told her with an innocent smile.

'I know *that*.'

He chuckled and turned toward the stairs. They climbed up to another door which responded to Dorrien's hand as the other had. As it swung open, a blast of icy wind rushed in to chill her skin.

'Now we're *outside* the University,' Dorrien said as they stepped through the door.

Finding herself on a wide pathway, Sonea caught her breath in surprise. They were standing on the University's roof.

It curved slightly to prevent rain and snow gathering. She could see the large glass ceiling of the Great Hall in the centre. A little snow had gathered around the frame of each panel of glass. The ornate edging that topped the two longer sides of the building formed a sturdy railing at waist height.

'I didn't know it was possible to get onto the roof,' she admitted.

'Only a few magicians are allowed to come here,' Dorrien told her. 'The locks respond to their touch. I was given access by Lady Vinara's predecessor, Lord Garen.' Dorrien's expression became wistful. 'After mother died, he and I became friends of sorts. He was like an additional grandfather, I suppose. One who was always around to talk to me. He taught me when I decided to b—'

A blast of wind whisked his words away and grabbed at their robes. Sonea's fringe whipped around her face, stinging her eyes. She reached behind her head and grabbed the clip that held her hair back. Turning to face the wind, she gathered the wayward strands together and fastened them tightly.

Then the wind abruptly stopped. Sensing the barrier Dorrien had created to shield them, she looked up to find him watching her, his eyes bright in the sunlight.

'Come down here,' he beckoned.

He strode down to the railing. Sonea followed, noting how the surface of the roof had been carved with grooves to prevent boots slipping when it was wet. Dorrien stopped halfway along the length of the building. Brushing snow off the railing, she leaned over to stare at the ground. It was a dizzingly long way down.

A group of servants hurried along the path, making their way through the gardens toward the Healers' Quarters. She could see the roof of the circular building over the treetops. Turning to her right, she saw the Novices' Quarters, the Dome, the Seven Arches building and the Baths. Behind was Sarika's Hill, the forest dusted with snow. At the top of the hill the disused, crumbling lookout was just visible, mostly hidden by trees.

Turning around completely, she looked at the city, then beyond. A ribbon of blue, the Tarali River, wound away from Imardin toward the horizon.

'Look,' Dorrien said, pointing. 'You can see barges on the river.'

Sonea shaded her eyes and saw a long line of flat craft floating on the river just beyond the city outskirts. On each stood tiny men with poles, with which they constantly prodded the riverbed. She frowned.

'Isn't the river deep?'

'It is closer to the city,' Dorrien told her, 'but up there it's still shallow enough for the bargemen. When they arrive in the city a boat will come out and guide them into the port. They're carrying produce from the north-west, most likely,' Dorrien noted. 'See the road on the other side of the river?'

Sonea nodded. A narrow brown line ran beside the blue line of the river.

'When they have delivered their load they will tie the barges to gorin, who will pull them back upstream. The gorin will be used to bring other trade downstream – they're slower and cheaper to hire.

'To get to my home, you follow that road.' Dorrien pointed. 'The Steelbelt Ranges appear on the horizon after a few days' riding.'

Sonea followed the direction of his finger. Dark clumps of trees grew along the distant road, and beyond them she could see fields stretching to the horizon.

She had studied maps of Kyralia, and knew that mountains marked the border between Kyralia and Sachaka, just as, in the north-west, the Grey Mountains formed the border of Elyne. As she stared out into the distance, a strange feeling stole over her. There were places out there she had never seen – never even thought to wonder about – but they were still a part of her country.

And beyond that there were other lands she had only recently begun to learn about.

'Have you ever been outside Kyralia?'

'No,' Dorrien shrugged. 'I might travel one day. Never had a good reason to go, and I don't like being away from my village too long.'

'What about Sachaka? You live right near one of the passes, don't you? Haven't you ever slipped through to have a look?'

He shook his head. 'A few of the herders have, probably to see if it was worth grazing there. There are no towns on the other side, not for many days' ride. Just wasteland.'

'The wasteland from the war?'

'Yes.' He nodded. 'You've been paying attention to your history lessons, I see.'

She shrugged. 'It's the only interesting part. Everything else – the Alliance and formation of the Guild – is mindlessly boring.'

He laughed, then moved away from the railing. They walked slowly back to the door and entered the little room again. Pausing at the top of the stairs, he placed a hand on her arm.

'So, did you like my surprise?'

She nodded. 'Yes.'

'Better than studying?'

'Of course.'

He grinned and stepped sideways. Sonea gasped as he dropped down the stairwell. A moment later he rose into sight again, floating on a disc of magic. She pressed a hand to her chest, feeling her heart pounding.

'You nearly stopped my heart, Dorrien!' she scolded.

He laughed. 'Want to learn how to levitate?'

She shook her head.

'Of course you do.'

'I have three more chapters to read.'

His eyes twinkled. 'You can read them tonight. Do you want to learn this when the other novices are watching? If I teach you now, nobody but me will see the mistakes you make.'

She chewed her lip. He had a point . . .

'Go on,' he urged. Throwing his arms out, he spun around in a circle. 'I won't let you out the door downstairs if you refuse.'

Sonea rolled her eyes. 'Oh, very well!'

The Guild House in Kiko Town was built on a steep slope. Numerous balconies allowed visitors a view of the sea, the beaches, and the long, spiral road – still filled with celebrants. The sound of rhythmic music drifted up to Dannyl's ears. In one hand he held a glass of Elyne wine, in the other was the bottle. Taking a sip, he moved from the balcony railing to a chair and sat down, setting the bottle beside him. Stretching his legs out, he let his mind wander.

As always, it wandered straight to Tayend.

The scholar had been awkward and nervous around Dannyl since the mugging. Though Dannyl had tried to behave as if he hadn't noticed anything unusual, it seemed this hadn't convinced Tayend that his secret had remained undiscovered. The scholar believed that a magician, when Healing, would find some physical sign to betray his inclinations, and the only way Dannyl could reassure him that this wasn't true was to tell Tayend he was wrong. That, of course, would reveal that Dannyl had learned the secret anyway.

Tayend feared that Dannyl would reject his friendship.

It was a reasonable fear. Though Kyralians didn't execute men for this 'unacceptable' behaviour as the Lonmar did, it was still considered wrong and unnatural. Men were punished by the removal of titles and by the man's family being treated as if they were all tainted by association. If a family discovered one of their own had such unnatural tendencies, they sent him away to manage small estates or family interests.

Dannyl had heard of Guild magicians in the past who had been punished in this way. Though they weren't expelled, they became outcasts in every other way. He had been told, during the troubles he faced as a novice, that if the rumours proved true he might not be allowed to graduate.

In all the years since, he had been careful to avoid drawing suspicion on himself again. In the past few days he had been struggling with the unsettling thought that, if Tayend's preferences were well known in Elyne, it was inevitable that the court would be speculating about his own. The rumour from his past would only add fire to the gossip, and while such gossip might not be dangerous in Elyne, once it reached the Guild . . .

Dannyl shook his head. After spending several months travelling with Tayend, any damage to his reputation had already been done. To regain his reputation he ought to disassociate himself from Tayend as soon as they returned to Elyne. He ought to make it clear he had been appalled to discover his assistant was, as the Elyne put it, a 'lad'.

Tayend will understand, a voice in the back of his mind said. *Or will he?* said another. *What if he grows angry and tells Akkarin about Lorlen's research?*

No, the first replied. *It would ruin his integrity as a scholar. And perhaps you can end this friendship kindly, without hurting his feelings.*

Dannyl scowled down at his wineglass. Why did it always come to this? Tayend was a good companion, a man he liked and valued. Thinking of ending their friendship for fear of gossip reaching the Guild made him feel ashamed and angry. Surely he could enjoy the scholar's company without endangering his reputation.

Let the gossips talk, he thought. *I'll not let them ruin another promising friendship.*

But if the Guild heard, and was outraged enough to order him home . . .

No, they wouldn't do something that dramatic on the strength of a mere rumour. They know what the Elyne court is like. They won't act unless they hear something really *damning.*

And they won't, Dannyl told himself. It was clear he would never escape this sort of speculation. So he would have to learn to live with it. Manage it. Perhaps even turn it to his advantage . . .

'You're not planning to drink that bottle all by yourself, are you?'

Startled, Dannyl looked up to see Tayend standing at the door to the balcony.

'Of course not,' he replied.

'Good,' Tayend said. 'Otherwise I'd look a fool carrying this around.' He held up an empty glass.

As Dannyl poured the wine Tayend stared at him, but looked quickly away as Dannyl met his eyes. The scholar moved to the railing and stared out over the sea.

It's time, Dannyl decided. *Time to tell him the truth, and that I'm not going to push him away.* He took a deep breath.

'We have to talk,' Tayend said suddenly.

'Yes,' Dannyl agreed. He considered his words carefully. 'I think I know why you wouldn't let me Heal you.'

Tayend winced. 'You said to me once that you understood how difficult was it for . . . for men like me.'

'But you said that men like you are accepted in Elyne.'

'They are, and they aren't.' Tayend looked down at his glass, then drained it. He turned to face Dannyl. 'At least we don't disown people for it,' he said accusingly.

Dannyl grimaced. 'As a nation, Kyralia isn't known for tolerance. You know I've experienced that for myself. We aren't all prejudiced, however.'

A frown creased Tayend's brow. 'I was going to be a magician, once. A cousin of mine tested me and found potential. They were going to send me to the Guild.' Tayend's eyes misted over, and Dannyl saw longing in the scholar's face, but then the scholar shook his head and sighed. 'Then I heard about you and I realised that it didn't matter whether the rumours were true or not. It was clear that I could never be a magician. The Guild would work out what I was and send me straight home.'

Dannyl suddenly felt a strange, dull anger. With his impressive memory and sharp intellect, Tayend would have been a fine magician. 'So how did you avoid joining the Guild?'

'I told father I didn't want to.' Tayend shrugged. 'He didn't suspect then. Later, when I began to associate with certain people, he decided he'd worked out my real reason. He believes I turned down the chance because I wanted to indulge myself in ways the Guild wouldn't allow. He never understood that I wouldn't be able to hide what I was.' Tayend looked down at his empty glass, then strode forward and picked up the bottle. Refilling his glass, he downed the wine quickly.

'Well,' he said, looking out over the ocean, 'if it's any consolation, I always knew the rumours about you couldn't be true.'

Dannyl winced. 'Why do you say that?'

'Well, if you were like me, and couldn't help what you felt, then the Healers would find out, wouldn't they?'

'Not necessarily.'

The scholar's eyes widened. 'Are you telling me . . .?'

'They sense the physical. That is all. If there is something in a man's body that causes him to desire men, the Healer's haven't found it yet.'

'But I was told . . . I was told Healers can tell if there's something wrong with someone.'

'They can.'

'So this . . . isn't a wrongness or . . .' Tayend frowned and looked at Dannyl. 'So how did *you* know about me?'

Dannyl smiled. 'Your mind was shouting it so loud I could hardly ignore it. People with magical potential who don't learn to use it often project their thoughts strongly.'

'Oh?' Tayend looked away, his face reddening. 'How much did you . . . read?'

'Not much,' Dannyl assured him. 'Mostly your fears. I didn't continue listening. That's not good manners.'

Tayend nodded. He thought for a moment, then his eyes widened. 'You mean I could have joined the Guild!' He frowned. 'But I'm not sure I would have liked it much.' Moving to the chair next to Dannyl's, Tayend sat down. 'Can I ask a personal question?'

'Yes.'

'What *really* happened between you and that novice?'

Dannyl sighed. 'Nothing.' He glanced at Tayend and found the scholar watching him expectantly. 'Very well. The whole story, then.

'I wasn't popular. New novices often seek older ones to help with their studies, but I had trouble finding someone who'd agree to help me. I'd heard tales about one of the older boys, and that other novices avoided him because of these stories, but he was one of the best in his year and I decided to ignore the rumours. When he agreed to help me I was rather pleased with myself.' He shook his head. 'But there was a novice in my class who hated me.'

'Lord Fergun?'

'Yes. We'd thrown insults and played tricks on each other since classes first started. He'd heard the tales about my helper, and they were all he needed to start new rumours. The next I knew I was being questioned by the Higher Magicians.'

'What happened?'

'I denied the rumours, of course. They decided the best way to stop the gossip was to keep us apart, so I was ordered to stay away from the boy. Of course, this was all the confirmation the novices needed.'

'What happened to him? Were the rumours about him true?'

'He graduated and returned to his country. That's all I can tell you.' Seeing Tayend's gaze sharpen with curiosity, Dannyl added: 'No, I'm not going to tell you his name.'

Looking disappointed, Tayend leaned back in his chair. 'So what happened then?'

Dannyl shrugged. 'I kept studying and made sure I didn't bring suspicion on myself again. Eventually everyone forgot about it, except Fergun – and the Elyne court, it seems.'

Tayend didn't smile. A crease appeared between his eyebrows. 'And what will you do now?'

Dannyl refilled his glass. 'Since the Tombs of White Tears are closed during the festival, there's not much to do except drink and relax.'

'And then?'

'I guess we visit the Tombs.'

'And then?'

'That depends on what we find. Either way, we'll return to Elyne.'

'That's not what I mean.' Tayend held Dannyl's eyes. 'If being seen with a novice that might or might not have been a lad was enough to cause you so much trouble, then associating with a man known to be a lad must be much, much worse. You said you must avoid bringing suspicion on yourself. I can still assist you from the library, but I'll send what I find to you by messenger.'

Dannyl felt something twist inside. He hadn't considered that Tayend might suggest this. Remembering his earlier thoughts of ending the friendship he felt a pang of guilt.

'Oh, no,' he replied. 'You won't get rid of me that easily.'

'But what could bring more suspicion upon you than associating with—'

'—a scholar of the Great Library,' Dannyl finished. 'A useful and valuable assistant. And a friend. If the gossips are going to talk, they'll have started already. They'll have more to talk about if they hear we're communicating in secret.'

Surprised, Tayend opened his mouth to speak, then

shook his head. Looking down at his glass, he lifted it to toast Dannyl.

'Here's to friendship, then.'

Smiling, Dannyl lifted his glass to meet the scholar's.

Rothen ran a finger along the spines of the books as he searched. He paused as the door of the Magicians' Library opened, and looked up to see Dorrien striding into the room followed by Sonea. He frowned. Sonea had asked him to get several books from the library, but here she was with Dorrien.

Lord Jullen scowled and told her to leave her box on the shelves near the door. She pulled a few sheets of paper out and left the box behind. Dorrien nodded politely to the librarian, then led Sonea into the long rows of shelving.

Deciding to find the books before pursuing the pair, Rothen continued his search, eventually finding the first book on his list several shelves from where it should have been. He silently cursed the magician who had misplaced it.

He was only vaguely aware of somebody approaching Lord Jullen and asking for help, but he did notice that Dorrien had begun a friendly conversation with Lord Galin in the next aisle. A loud coughing started behind him, and he glanced behind to see Lord Garrel holding a nose-cloth to his mouth. Then an exclamation drew his attention away.

'Regin!' Galin barked, striding out into the aisle. Looking through the shelves, Rothen could see Regin standing next to Jullen's desk.

'Yes, my lord?' His expression was all innocence and puzzlement.

'What did you just put in this box?'

'What box, my lord?'

Galin's eyes narrowed.

'What is the problem, Lord Galin?' Lord Garrel strode down the aisle and approached Jullen's desk.

'I just saw Regin take something from Jullen's desk and put it in this box.' Galin pulled Sonea's box off the shelf and placed it on the desk in front of Regin.

Hearing murmuring voices, Rothen looked around to see magicians gathered in twos and threes, watching this drama unfold. Lord Jullen strode out from behind the shelves. He looked from the magicians to the novice and then to the box. 'What is going on here? This is Sonea's box.'

Galin's brows rose. 'Is it? How *very* interesting.' He repeated what he'd seen. Lord Jullen's eyebrows dropped into a disapproving frown.

'Shall we see which of your possessions Regin has decided that Sonea would dearly like to own?'

Regin paled. Rothen felt a smile spread over his face. He nearly yelped in surprise as a hand touched his shoulder. Turning, he found Dorrien standing beside him, a familiar mischievous glint in his eyes.

'What have you done?' Rothen whispered accusingly.

'Nothing,' Dorrien replied, his eyes wide with feigned innocence. 'Regin did it all himself. I just made sure someone was watching.'

Hearing Sonea's box click open, Rothen watched as Jullen took out a black, shiny object. 'My two-hundred-year-old Elyne inkwell.' The librarian frowned. 'Valuable, but leaky. I must congratulate you, Regin. Even if Sonea had managed to return it herself, her notes would still be covered in ink.'

Regin looked at his guardian desperately.

'No doubt he wanted to ruin her notes,' Garrel said. 'Just a silly prank.'

'I don't believe so,' Galin interrupted. 'Or he would simply have poured the contents all over her papers and left the inkwell on Lord Jullen's desk.'

Garrel's expression darkened, but Galin's accusing stare remained steady. Lord Jullen looked from one magician to the other, then up at the shelves.

'Lord Dorrien,' he called.

Dorrien stepped into the aisle. 'Yes?'

'Please find Sonea and bring her here.'

Dorrien nodded and strode down the rows of shelving. Rothen watched Sonea's face as she came in sight of the magicians. At once her expression became wary. As Jullen explained what had happened her eyes widened, and she gave Regin a glare.

'I'm afraid your notes are ruined, Sonea,' Jullen said, tilting the box toward her. She looked inside and grimaced. 'If you'd like, I'll lock your box in my cupboard from now on.'

She looked up at him, surprised. 'Thank you, Lord Jullen,' she said in a quiet voice.

He closed the box and placed it in the cupboard behind his desk. Galin looked at Regin. 'You may return to your study, Sonea. Regin and I are going to have a chat with the University Director.'

She glanced at Regin once more, then turned away and walked back to the shelves. Dorrien hesitated, then followed.

Galin eyed Garrel. 'Are you coming?'

The Warrior nodded.

As the two magicians and the novice left the library, Dorrien and Sonea approached Rothen. They both wore a look of unconcealed smugness. Shaking his head, Rothen gave them both a stern look.

'That was risky. What if no-one had seen?'

Dorrien smiled. 'Ah, but I made sure someone did.' He looked down at Sonea. 'You managed to look convincingly surprised.'

She smiled slyly. 'I was just surprised it worked.'

'Hmph!' Dorrien said. 'Has nobody got any confidence in me?' He sobered and looked at Rothen. 'Did you notice who took Jullen away from his desk and distracted everyone while Regin was doing his evil deed?'

Rothen thought back. 'Garrel? No. Don't be ridiculous. Regin was taking advantage of the situation. Just because Garrel was the one who asked for help and coughed at the same moment Regin made his move doesn't mean he's involving himself in childish pranks.'

'You're probably right,' Dorrien said. 'But I would keep an eye on him if I were you.'

CHAPTER 19

THE TESTS BEGIN

The sky was just warming with the glow of dawn when Sonea left the Baths. The air was still cold, however, so she created a barrier about herself and heated the air within it. As she paused to straighten her robes, a green-robed figure stepped from the section of the Baths reserved for males.

Recognising Dorrien, she felt her mood lighten. Since he'd planned to leave early this morning, they'd said their farewells last night over dinner in Rothen's rooms. But now she had one more opportunity to speak to him before he left.

'I should have guessed you were an early riser,' she said.

Turning, he blinked in surprise. 'Sonea! What are you doing up at dawn?'

'I always start early. I can get a few things done without anyone bothering me.'

He smiled crookedly. 'A wise move, though maybe that won't be necessary now. Regin has been leaving you alone, hasn't he?'

'Yes.'

'Good.' Tilting his head slightly, he gave her an odd look. 'I was going to visit an old haunt of mine before I go. Want to come?'

'Where is it?'

'In the forest.'

She glanced up at the trees. 'Another one of your secret places?'

Dorrien smiled. 'Yes, but this time it really is a secret.'

'Oh? But if you show me, then it won't be a secret.'

He chuckled. 'I suppose not. It's just a place I used to visit when I was a boy. I hid there whenever I was in trouble.'

'Then I'm sure you hid there a lot.'

'Of course.' He grinned. 'So, are you coming?'

She looked down at her box. Her next stop was to be the Foodhall. 'It won't take long?'

He shook his head. 'I'll have you back in time for the tests.'

'Very well,' she said.

He started along the path that led up into the forest. Walking beside him, she thought back to the last time she had taken this route. It had been a cold night almost a year before, when she was still a 'prisoner' of the Guild. Rothen had decided she needed fresh air and some exercise. Not far into the forest there was an ancient cemetery, and Rothen had explained what happened to magicians when they died.

She shivered as she remembered. When a magician's life ended, his mind relinquished Control over his power. The remaining magic left in the body consumed it, turning flesh and bone to ash and dust. Since there was nothing to bury, magicians were never interred, so the existence of the ancient cemetery was a mystery.

Dorrien's strides were long, and she had to walk quickly to keep up. Thinking back to the conversation of the previous evening, she remembered how eager he was to return to his home, but she couldn't help wishing he could stay a little longer. She couldn't remember enjoying herself as much as she had in the last few weeks. Though Rothen was good company, Dorrien was energetic and was always looking for opportunities for fun. He had taught her to levitate, and to play several games. All these games involved magic, and he was obviously relishing having a partner to play them with.

'What's it like being the only magician among ordinary people?' she asked.

Dorrien considered the question. 'It's satisfying and challenging. People don't ever forget that you're different, no matter how close you get to them. They feel uncomfortable because you can do something they don't understand. Some of the farmers won't let me touch them, even though they're happy to let me Heal their animals.'

She nodded. 'People in the slums are like that. They're terrified of magicians.'

'Most of the farmers were afraid of me at first. It took quite a while before they trusted me.'

'Do you get lonely?'

'Sometimes. It's worth it, though.' They had reached the road now, and Dorrien turned to the left. 'There's something *right* about what I do. There are people in those mountains who would have died if I hadn't been around to help.'

'That must be wonderful, knowing you saved someone's life.'

Dorrien smiled. 'It's the best use magic can be put to. In comparison, the rest is just frivolous games. Father wouldn't agree, but I've always thought Alchemy a waste of power, and Warrior Skills . . . well, what can I say?'

'The Alchemists say that they have created and invented ways to make people's lives safer and more comfortable,' Sonea pointed out. 'The Warriors say they are essential to the defence of Kyralia.'

He nodded. 'The Alchemists *have* done some good work, and it *isn't* wise to let magicians forget how to defend themselves. I guess I have a grudge against those who spend their time indulging themselves when they could be helping others. The ones who waste all their time on glorified hobbies.'

Sonea smiled as she thought of Dannyl's experiments with transferring mind images to paper – abandoned now that he was a Guild Ambassador in Elyne. Dorrien probably wouldn't approve of Dannyl's 'hobby'.

'There are too many Alchemists and not enough Healers,' Dorrien continued. 'The Healers restrict their time to those with money and status because they don't have time to treat everyone. We all learn basic Healing. There's no reason why Alchemists and Warriors couldn't spend some of their time assisting Healers. Then we could help more people.

'I treat anyone who needs my help: herders, crafters, farmers, passing travellers. There's no good reason why Healers here shouldn't do the same. The crafters here pay taxes, and part of that tax goes toward maintaining the Guild. They should have access to the service that their money sustains.'

His voice had grown stronger. Obviously this was something he believed in passionately.

'And the people in the slums?' she prompted.

He checked his stride and turned to look at her. 'Yes,' he said, walking at a slower pace. 'Though I think we would have to be careful how we went about it.'

She frowned. 'Oh?'

'The slums are part of a much bigger problem, and we could easily waste a lot of time and effort. They're like, if you'll forgive me saying so, boils on the skin of the city, pointing to deeper troubles in the body. The boils won't go away until the deeper problems are addressed.'

'Deeper problems?'

'Well,' Dorrien glanced at her again, 'if I stick to my analogy I'd say that the city has grown into a fat, sweet-sucking old Warrior. He's either unaware or uncaring that his greedy habits are destroying the systems of his body or that his paunch is making him ugly. He is already far from fit, but as he doesn't have any more enemies to worry about, he's happy to sit back and indulge himself.'

Sonea stared at him, impressed. What he was saying, she realised, was that the King and the Houses were greedy and lazy, and the cost of this was felt by the rest of the city's citizens — like the dwells. He looked at her again, uncertainty in his eyes.

'That is,' he added quickly, 'I'm not saying we shouldn't do anything because it's too big a problem. We should be doing something.'

'Like what?'

He smiled. 'Ah, but I don't want to spoil our walk by ranting and raving. Here, we've reached the road.'

Stepping onto the road, Dorrien led her past the houses of the older, retired Guild residents. As they reached the end of the road he continued into the forest, his boots crunching through the snow. Sonea followed behind, walking in his footsteps.

Soon the ground became uneven. Her heavy box made negotiating the forest difficult, so she left it sitting on a log, protected by a barrier of magic. The steep slope soon had her breathing hard. Eventually Dorrien stopped and placed his hand on the trunk of an enormous tree.

'The first marker. Remember this tree, Sonea. Walk in the same direction that the road leads until you reach it, then turn east and climb until you find the wall.'

'The Outer Wall?'

He nodded. Sonea suppressed a groan. The Outer Wall had to be a long way into the forest. They tramped uphill through the snow for several minutes, until Sonea was gasping for breath.

'Stop!' she cried when it seemed her legs couldn't carry her any further.

Dorrien turned and grinned, and she was gratified to see he was breathing hard. He gestured at a pile of snow-covered rocks ahead.

'The wall.'

Sonea stared at the snow, then realised that the rocks underneath were actually huge slabs of stone, scattered through the forest. This rubble was all that was left of the Outer Wall.

'Now,' Dorrien said between breaths. 'We head north again.'

Before she could protest he was striding away. No longer climbing uphill, it was easier walking and she gradually caught her breath. Dorrien reached an outcrop of rocks, clambered over them and disappeared. Sonea followed his scrapings in the snow and found herself standing inside a small circle of boulders. From the profusion of trees she could see that this place would be well hidden when their leaves grew back. To one side water rippled down the rocks and gathered in an ice-edged pool before spilling away over more rocks.

Dorrien stood several paces away, smiling.

'This is it. The spring. The source of the Guild's water.'

Walking to his side, she saw water pouring out of a crack in the rocks.

'It's wonderful,' she said, looking up at Dorrien. 'It must be lovely in summer.'

'Don't wait for summer.' Dorrien's eyes shone. 'It's just as wonderful in spring. I used to start visiting as soon as the snow began to thaw.'

Sonea tried to picture Dorrien as a boy, scrambling up the slope and sitting here on his own. The boy who became a novice of the Guild, then a Healer. She would come back, she decided. It would be a place to go when she needed some time alone, away from Regin and the other novices. Perhaps that was what Dorrien had intended all along.

'What are you thinking, little Sonea?'

'I want to thank you.'

His eyebrows rose. 'Thank me?'

'For baiting Regin. For taking me up on the roof of the University.' She chuckled. 'For teaching me to levitate.'

'Ah,' he waved a hand dismissively. 'That was easy.'

'And for making me enjoy myself again. I think I almost believed that fun wasn't part of being a magician.' She smiled crookedly. 'I know you have to go back, but I wish you could stay longer.'

His expression grew serious. 'I'll miss you, too, little Sonea.' He took a step closer then opened his mouth as if to say something else, but no words came. Putting a finger under her chin, he tilted her head up, bent closer and pressed his lips to her mouth.

Surprised, Sonea pulled away a little. He was very

close, his eyes bright and questioning. Suddenly her face was too warm, and her heart was pounding very fast. She was smiling foolishly and, though she tried, she couldn't stop. Dorrien laughed quietly, then bent to kiss her again.

This time his lips lingered and she was conscious of their softness and warmth. She felt a shiver run down her spine, but she wasn't cold. When he moved away she swayed forward a little, prolonging the touch.

He stepped backward, his smile fading. 'I'm sorry, that wasn't fair of me.'

She swallowed. Found her voice. 'Not fair?'

He looked down at his feet, his expression serious. 'Because I'm going away. Because you might want or need someone else between now and who-knows-when and turn them away because of me.'

Sonea laughed, a little bitterly. 'I doubt it.'

Dorrien's gaze became wary. Sonea frowned. Did he now think that she welcomed his attention only because she thought nobody else would ever be romantically interested in her?

Was she? Until a moment ago she hadn't even considered the possibility that he could be more than just a friend. She shook her head and smiled.

'You've given me quite a surprise this time, Dorrien.'

The corners of his lips curled upward.

—*Dorrien?*

She recognised Rothen's mind-voice.

—*Father*, Dorrien replied.

—*Where are you?*

—*I went for a morning walk.*

—*The stablemaster is here.*

—I'll be there soon.

Dorrien grimaced apologetically. 'I'm afraid we took longer getting here than I thought we would.'

She felt a stab of apprehension. Was she late for the First Year tests?

'Come on.'

They scrambled over the rocks and started back. After several minutes hurrying through the forest, they reached the log she had left her box on. Not long after, they arrived at the road and were able to break into a jog.

From time to time she glanced at Dorrien, wondering what he was thinking. Other times she noticed him watching her, and he smiled as she looked up to meet his eyes. He reached out and took her hand. His fingers were warm, and she was disappointed when they came in sight of the Guild and he let his hand fall to his side.

As they approached the Magicians' Quarters, Rothen strode out of the doors to meet them.

'Your horse is waiting out front, Dorrien.' Rothen looked them both up and down, noting the snow on their shoes and robes with raised eyebrows. 'You had better dry yourselves.'

Steam wafted up from Dorrien's clothes as they started down the path alongside the University. Concentrating, Sonea heated the air around her robes to dry them. A servant met them before the University staircase, holding the reins of Dorrien's horse.

Dorrien enveloped first Rothen, then Sonea, in a firm hug.

'Take care of each other,' he said.

'Take care of yourself,' Rothen replied. 'Don't push yourself through blizzards just to get home sooner.'

Dorrien swung up onto the saddle. 'There's never been a blizzard that could keep me from home!'

'Then what have you been complaining about for these past four weeks?'

'Me? Complain?'

Laughing, Rothen crossed his arms. 'Get out of here, Dorrien.'

Dorrien grinned. 'Farewell, Father.'

'Farewell, Dorrien.'

Dorrien's eyes flickered to Sonea's. She felt a tentative touch at the edge of her mind.

—*Farewell, Sonea. Learn fast.*

Then Dorrien's horse galloped away, racing through the gates and out into the snow-covered streets of the city.

For a few minutes they remained staring at the gates. Rothen sighed and turned to look at Sonea. His eyes narrowed.

'Hmmm,' he said. 'Something's going on here.'

She kept her expression neutral. 'Like what?'

'Don't worry.' He smiled knowingly, and started up the University stairs. 'I approve. I don't think the age difference will matter. It's only a few years. You do realise you have to stay here until graduation, don't you?'

Sonea opened her mouth to protest, then closed it again as she saw a movement in the Entrance Hall. She caught Rothen's arm.

'I don't mind you speculating, Rothen,' she told him quietly. 'But I'd appreciate it if you did so privately.'

He frowned and looked at her in surprise. She kept her attention on the hall. As they stepped inside, the room echoed with the sound of rapid footsteps on the stairway treads. Looking up, Sonea glimpsed a familiar novice hurrying upward.

Her stomach turned. She'd had a clear look at the expression on Regin's face before he slipped out of sight. She might have gained a begrudging sympathy from the teachers now that Regin had been caught setting her up as a thief, but she doubted she was free of his taunting. Preparations for the First Year tests had kept the boy occupied, but she suspected he was planning a particularly nasty revenge.

'I'll see you tonight,' she told Rothen.

He nodded solemnly. 'Good luck, Sonea. I know you'll do well.'

She smiled, then started up the staircase. Reaching the top, she cautiously entered the corridor. The University was full of novices, their low voices and tense expressions creating an atmosphere of expectation and dread. Reaching her classroom, she stepped inside.

Regin sat in his usual place, watching her closely. Turning away, she bowed to the two teachers standing at the front of the room, and moved to her seat. She opened her box and took out the history project Lord Skoran had set. Flicking through the pages she was relieved to find them still in order, with no damage done. Though they had been intact when she had sealed the box before leaving her room, she had almost expected to find Regin had got at them somehow.

Skoran nodded approvingly as she handed the pages to him. To her satisfaction, he locked them in a box.

All the time, she was conscious of Regin watching her. Returning to her seat, she ignored the face she could see in the corner of her eye. She watched as the last novices entered the class and gave their work to the teacher. When all were present, Lord Vorel stepped forward and stood before them with his arms crossed.

'Today you will complete your First Year tests in Warrior Skills,' he informed them. 'You will be required to fight all other members of the class, and will be marked according to skill, Control and, of course, number of victories. Please follow me.'

Sonea rose with the rest of the class. As the first novices filed out of the room, Regin turned and met her eyes. He smiled sweetly.

She had grown practised at returning his looks with cold indifference. A chill dread now descended upon her. Though she was still far stronger than the other novices, the restrictions Vorel put on her kept her from using her powers to her advantage. Somehow the inner shield he held around novices to protect them as they fought told him if her strikes were more powerful than he thought appropriate. Regin was still better at Warrior Skills than she, and though the boy no longer had lessons with Lord Balkan, nothing had prevented him from having extra lessons with Lord Garrel.

As she stepped from the classroom, a servant in a messengers' uniform skidded to a halt beside her.

'Lady Sonea,' the man said. 'I have been sent to deliver an urgent request for you to return to Rothen's rooms immediately.'

Surprised, she looked up at Lord Vorel. The magician frowned.

'We cannot wait for you, Sonea. If you do not return within the hour we will have to arrange a testing early next year.'

Sonea nodded. Thanking the messenger, she started along the corridor.

Why had Rothen sent for her? He would have barely

had enough time to reach his rooms since they parted. Perhaps he'd discovered that Regin *did* have something planned, and had called her away to prevent it.

She shook her head. Rothen wouldn't do that. He would attempt to alert Vorel to Regin's plans rather than call her away from an important test.

Unless he wanted to simply tell her what to expect Regin to do. Perhaps he wanted to suggest a way she could turn whatever it was to her advantage. She could always still slip back to the Arena in time for the bouts.

But if that was so, why hadn't he simply met her outside the classroom?

And why wasn't he in *his* classroom, preparing to test his own class?

She frowned as she descended to the ground floor of the University. What if there was some other reason for the summons? The messenger hadn't said that the message had come *from* Rothen. In that case *Rothen* might be the reason she was summoned. He might be ill. He wasn't old, but he wasn't young, either. He might be—

Stop worrying! she told herself. It's probably nothing serious. Nevertheless she half ran across the courtyard to the Magicians' Quarters. Her heart raced as she hurried up the stairs, and down the corridor to Rothen's door.

The door swung open at her touch. Rothen stood by the window. He turned as she entered the room. She opened her mouth to ask the question hovering on her lips, but caught herself as she saw his warning expression.

She felt the presence first. It was tangible, unhidden. It filled the room like a thick, suffocating smoke. Terror sent her heart racing, but she managed to compose her expression to what she hoped was only surprise and respect.

You don't know why he's here, she told herself as she turned. *Don't let him see that you're frightened of him.* Keeping her eyes on the floor, she turned to face the visitor and bowed.

'Excuse me, High Lord.'

He didn't reply.

'Sonea.' Rothen's voice was low and tense. 'Come here.'

She looked at Rothen and felt her stomach twist. His face was pale, almost sickly. He beckoned, and his hand shook slightly. Disturbed by these signs of fear, she hurried to his side.

Rothen's voice was surprisingly calm as he addressed the High Lord. 'Sonea is here, as you requested, High Lord. How may we assist you?'

Akkarin fixed Rothen with a stare that would have turned her to ice.

'I am here to find the source of a certain . . . rumour. A rumour I drew from the Administrator concerning you and your novice.'

Rothen nodded. He seemed to choose his next words with great care.

'I thought that rumour about us had passed. Nobody appeared to give it credence and—'

The dark eyes flashed. 'Not *that* rumour. I am referring to a rumour about *my* nocturnal activities. A rumour that must be stopped.'

A hand seemed to close on Sonea's throat, making it hard to breathe. Rothen was frowning and shaking his head.

'You are mistaken, High Lord. I know nothing of your—'

'Do not lie to me, Rothen.' Akkarin's eyes narrowed. 'I would not have come here if I was not certain of it.' He took a step toward them. 'I have just read it from Lorlen's mind.'

All colour drained from Rothen's face. He stared at Akkarin in silence. *If Akkarin read Lorlen's mind,* she thought, *he knows everything!* She felt her knees weaken, and, afraid she would sink to the floor, gripped the window sill behind her.

The High Lord smiled thinly. 'I saw much that impressed me: how Sonea visited the Guild while she was still a renegade, what she witnessed that night, how Lorlen discovered this while truth-reading her during the guardianship Hearing, and that he ordered you both to keep the discovery a secret so that he could work out how he could possibly enforce the Guild's law. A sensible decision. And fortunate for you all.'

Rothen straightened and raised his head to face Akkarin again. 'We have not spoken a word of it to anyone.'

'So you say.' The High Lord's voice softened, but lost none of its chill. 'I would know that for certain.'

Sonea heard Rothen's sharp intake of breath. The two magicians stared at each other.

'And if I refuse?'

'I will take whatever measures you force me to take, Rothen. You cannot prevent me reading your mind.'

Rothen looked away. Abruptly, Sonea recalled Cery's description of Akkarin's mind-reading. Cery had told her that, when Akkarin had discovered him imprisoned in a room under the University by Fergun, he had allowed the High Lord to read his mind to confirm the truth. It had been an easy thing, completely unlike Rothen's mind-sharing or Lorlen's truth-read, and she had concluded that the legend about Akkarin being able to read minds, whether they be willing or not, must have some truth in it.

Stiffly, as though his bones were those of a man twenty years older, Rothen moved toward the High Lord. Sonea stared at him, unable to believe he would give in so easily.

'Rothen . . .'

'It's all right, Sonea.' Rothen's voice was strained. 'Stay where you are.'

Closing the distance between himself and her guardian in a few strides, Akkarin placed his hands against the sides of Rothen's head. He closed his eyes and his face smoothed into an unexpectedly peaceful expression.

Rothen drew in a sharp breath and swayed. The hands at his sides clenched, then opened again. Sonea took a step forward and stopped. She dared not interfere. What if it caused Akkarin to harm Rothen? Frustrated, frightened, she clenched her fists until she felt her nails bite into her palms.

The two magicians remained still and silent for an unbearably long time. Then, without warning, Akkarin drew in a deep breath and opened his eyes. He regarded the man standing before him for a moment, then drew back his hands and stepped away.

Sonea watched anxiously as Rothen took a long, ragged breath and swayed a little. Akkarin crossed his arms, watching the old magician. Sonea cautiously stepped forward and took Rothen's arm.

'I'm fine,' he said wearily. 'I'm all right.' He rubbed his temples and grimaced, then squeezed one of her hands to reassure her.

'Now, Sonea.'

A shock of cold terror rushed through her body. She felt Rothen's hands tighten their grip.

'No!' Rothen protested hoarsely. He put an arm protectively around her shoulders. 'You know everything now. Leave her be.'

'I cannot.'

'But you've seen everything,' Rothen protested. 'She's only a—'

'A child?' Akkarin's eyebrows rose. 'A girl? Come now, Rothen. You know this will not harm her.'

Rothen swallowed hard, then slowly turned to her. He looked into her eyes. 'He knows everything, Sonea. There is nothing to hide from him. Let him confirm it for himself if he must. It will not hurt.'

His eyes, though rimmed with moisture, were steady. Sonea felt him squeeze her hands, then release them. He stepped away. A terrible feeling of betrayal rose.

—*Trust me. We must co-operate. It is all we can do for now.*

She heard Akkarin's footfall behind her. Her heart raced as she turned to face him. The black robes rustled softly as the High Lord moved forward. She backed away and felt Rothen's hands on her shoulders.

Akkarin frowned as he reached toward her. Cool fingers brushed her face and she flinched. Then his palms pressed firmly against her temples.

A presence touched her mind, but it held no personality. She sensed no thoughts or feelings. Perhaps he didn't *have* emotions. The thought wasn't comforting.

Then an image flashed into her mind. She started, realising she had been waiting for him to encounter the barriers in her mind. Somehow he had passed them. Checking, she saw that her defences were intact, but his presence was not tangible enough to meet their resistance.

The same image kept flashing into her mind. It was of

309

the underground room beneath his residence, seen from outside the door. A memory rose of the scene she had witnessed the night she had spied upon him.

Something took hold of that memory and began to sort through the details. Sonea remembered how Lorlen had manipulated her memories, and how she had been able to hide them by willing them out of her thoughts. Perhaps she could do that now. She tried to smother the memory, but the mind-read continued without a pause. Her efforts made no difference, she realised, because Akkarin was in control of the memory, whereas Lorlen had been only guiding and encouraging.

The discovery sent panic through her. In desperation, she tried to drown the memory with other thoughts and images.

Stop this.

An undertone of anger accompanied the words. Sonea paused, feeling a thrill of triumph as she understood she had found a way to hamper him. Her fear hardened into determination. She drew up lessons, lists of facts, images of work she had done. She bombarded him with pictures from text books and nonsense poems that she had discovered in the library. She threw memories of the slum, irrelevant, ordinary bits of her old life.

A mental image of a storm appeared – a funnel of images that kept him trapped at its core. She did not know if the picture was real, or something her mind had created . . .

Pain! Knives ripping through her skull. A cry reached her ears. Realising that she had made it, she opened her eyes and her consciousness swayed between the outer and the inner world. Hands tightened on her shoulders. A voice came from above.

'Stop fighting me,' it commanded.

Hands pressed hard against her temples. She snapped back into the domain of her mind. Disoriented and shocked by the pain, she tried to regain some sense of balance. The presence returned to the task of digging up the memories he sought. He mercilessly called up image after image. This time she found herself reliving the moments in the North Square. Once more she threw the stone and fled from the fire of the magicians. Rooms and corridors of the slums flickered by. The day she had sensed Rothen's searching mind and had instinctively hidden her presence. Cery, Harrin and his gang. Faren of the Thieves. Senfel, the Thieves' magician.

Then she was creeping through the forest in the Guild grounds. The memories sharpened, were examined closely. Once more she climbed the wall of the Healers' Quarters and watched the novices within. Once again she sensed the vibration around the Arena. She peered through windows into the University. Her journey took her around the back of the Guild again to look into the Novices' Quarters and through the forest behind. Then, after Cery left to steal the books, she crept down to the strange, grey two-storey building. The servant came, forcing her to retreat behind the low bushes. Then, seeing light coming through the ventilation holes, she crouched down and peered though.

A faint flicker of annoyance touched her senses. *Yes*, she thought, *I'd be angry, too, if my secrets were discovered so easily.* She saw the bloodstained man remove his clothes, clean himself and move away. Returning clad in black robes, the man spoke to his servant. 'The fight has weakened me. I need your strength.' The man took an elaborate knife and cut the servant's arm, then placed his hand over the wound. Once more she sensed the strange magic.

The memory stopped abruptly, and she sensed nothing from the mind that lurked behind hers. What was he thinking, she wondered . . .?

Have you allowed any to know of this other than Lorlen and Rothen?

No, she thought.

She relaxed, sure that this was all he sought, but a relentless interrogation followed as he quested after further memories. He explored parts of her life, from childhood to her lessons in the University. He sorted through her feelings, from her fondness for Rothen to her lingering loyalty to Cery and the people of the slums, to the new emotions she felt for Dorrien.

And, unbidden, came the anger she felt toward him for doing this to her. He sought her feelings about his practice of black magic, and her mind responded with disapproval and fear. Would she expose him if she could? *Yes!* But only if she knew Rothen and others would not be harmed.

Then the presence vanished and she felt the pressure against her temples stop. She opened her eyes and blinked. Akkarin had turned his back and was pacing slowly away from them. She felt Rothen's hands on her shoulders, steady and reassuring.

'You would both expose me if you could,' Akkarin said. He was silent for a time, then turned to face them. 'I will claim Sonea's guardianship. Her abilities are advanced and, as Lorlen surmised, her strength is unusually high. None will question my choice.'

'No!' Rothen gasped. His grip tightened.

'Yes,' Akkarin replied, turning to face them. 'She will ensure your silence. You will never cause anyone to know that I practice black magic while she is mine.' His eyes shifted to Sonea's. 'And Rothen's wellbeing will be my guarantee that *you* will co-operate.'

Sonea stared at him in horror. She was to be his *hostage*!

'You will not speak to each other except to avoid raising suspicion. You will behave as if nothing more unusual than a change of guardianship has occurred. Do you understand?'

Rothen made a choking noise. Sonea turned to him, alarmed. He glanced at her and she saw guilt in his eyes.

'Don't make me consider an alternative,' Akkarin warned.

Rothen's voice was strained as he answered. 'I understand. We will do as you ask.'

'Good.'

Akkarin took a step closer, and Sonea looked up to find him regarding her intently. 'There is a room in my residence for the High Lord's novice. You will come with me now, and send a servant for your belongings later.'

Sonea looked at Rothen, her throat tight. He searched her eyes.

– *I'm sorry.*

'*Now*, Sonea.' Akkarin gestured at the door. It swung open.

She felt Rothen's hands loosen. He gave her the tiniest push. Glancing at Akkarin, she realised she did not want Rothen to see her dragged away. He would find a way to help her. He would do everything he could. For now, they had no choice but to obey.

Taking a deep breath, she moved away from Rothen and stepped out into the corridor. Akkarin gave Rothen one last measuring look, then started toward the door. As the High Lord turned away, Rothen's eyes narrowed with hatred.

Then the door closed and he was cut off from her sight.

'Come along,' Akkarin said. 'The novice's room in my residence hasn't seen an occupant in many years, but it has always been kept ready for one. You'll find it much more comfortable than those in the Novices' Quarters.'

PART TWO

CHAPTER 20

SONEA'S GOOD FORTUNE

As the door opened, the University Director looked up from his desk to see who had entered his office. For the first time Sonea could remember, Jerrik's sour expression vanished. He leapt to his feet.

'What can I do for you, High Lord?'

'I wish to discuss Sonea's training. I have read your report, and her lack of skills in certain subjects concerns me.'

Jerrik looked surprised. 'Sonea's progress has been more than satisfactory.'

'Her marks in Warrior Skills are average at best.'

'Ah.' Jerrik glanced at Sonea. 'It is not unusual for a novice to show less aptitude for one of the disciplines at this stage. While she is not excelling in Warrior Skills, her results have been acceptable.'

'Nevertheless, I want this weakness addressed. I believe Lord Yikmo would be a suitable tutor.'

'Lord Yikmo?' Jerrik's generous eyebrows rose, then drew together in a frown. 'He does not teach in the evenings, but if Sonea attends evening classes in other subjects that would allow time during the day.'

'I believe she missed her Warrior Skills yesterday.'

'Yes,' Jerrik replied. 'Usually we would arrange for a testing after the break, but I think an assessment by Lord

Yikmo would do instead.' He glanced at his desk. 'I can put together Sonea's schedule for next year now, if you wish. It will not take long.'

'Yes. I'll leave Sonea with you to collect it. Thank you, Director.'

The presence at her side moved away. As the door closed, Sonea drew in a deep breath and slowly exhaled. He was gone. At last.

With a soft thump, Jerrik dropped back into his seat. He waved at a wooden chair near the end of his desk.

'Sit down, Sonea.'

She obeyed. Taking another deep breath, she felt tension ease out of her muscles.

Everything that had happened after leaving Rothen seemed like a bad dream. She had followed Akkarin to his residence, where a servant had shown her to a room on the second floor. Not long after, a chest had arrived with her belongings from the Novices' Quarters. Another servant had brought a plate of food, but Sonea had been too anxious to feel hungry. Instead, she sat by one of the small windows, barely noticing the magicians and novices walking about the grounds, and searched for a way out of her situation.

First, she had considered escaping to the slums. The Thieves would be eager to protect her now that she had Control of her magic. They had managed to hide Senfel, the rogue magician Faren had failed to persuade to teach her. They could hide her, too.

If she disappeared, however, Akkarin would do something to Rothen. But if Rothen had sufficient warning, he could tell the rest of the Guild that Akkarin was practising black magic, before the High Lord realised she'd gone. She would have to warn Lorlen, too, since he would also be in danger if she left. Yes, if she warned both of them she was leaving, and timed it right, Akkarin might not have a chance to prevent Lorlen and Rothen speaking out.

And what then? The Guild would confront Akkarin. Lorlen had believed they couldn't win such a battle, and Lorlen knew Akkarin better than any other magician. So, if she escaped, she could bring about a confrontation that would devastate the Guild, and possibly the whole of Kyralia.

It had occurred to her, then, that the fate of the Guild rested in her hands. Her, a mere slum girl. This sudden power over the Guild's fate gave her no pleasure, however. Instead, she felt ill with frustration and fear.

Long after the gardens had disappeared into the night's shadows, the servant had returned with a drink. Recognising the aroma of a mild, sleep-inducing medicine, Sonea had drunk it all, curled up on the strange, too-soft bed and welcomed the numbness that slowly crept over her.

In the morning, fussing servants had brought new robes and more food. She managed a few bites, but when Akkarin arrived she regretted it. Feeling ill with fear, she had followed him to the University. To Jerrik's office. Had she passed novices on the way? Had they fallen silent when he appeared, as they always did? She couldn't remember.

Jerrik's movements were hurried, his brows lowered in concentration. The few times she had seen the High Lord among other magicians, she had noted that he was treated with respect and even awe. Was this reverence for the position of High Lord? Or was it something else? Did they fear him instinctively, without knowing the reason?

Watching Jerrik, she shook her head. Schedules and tests seemed so trivial now. If Jerrik knew what had really happened, he wouldn't be at all interested in all this shuffling of paper and classes. He wouldn't respect Akkarin at all.

But he didn't know, and she couldn't tell him.

Jerrik rose abruptly. Turning to a cupboard, he took out three boxes: one green, one red and the other purple. He moved to the tall, narrow doors that covered one wall of the room and waved a palm over the handle of the first. There was a click, and the door opened to reveal a stack of shelves.

Running his finger down the first of these, he stopped and pulled out a neat folder. He placed it on the table and Sonea saw her name written neatly on the cover. Curiosity stirred in her as he opened the folder and read through several sheets of paper. *What is in there?* she wondered. *Comments from the teachers, probably. And a report about the pen I was supposed to have stolen.*

Jerrik opened the three boxes. Inside were more sheets of paper with teachers' names and tables drawn on them. He selected some of these, then drew a clean sheet from his desk and began drawing up another table. For several minutes all that could be heard in the room was Jerrik's breathing and the scrape of his pen.

'This is quite a turn of good fortune for you, Sonea,' he said without looking up.

Sonea smothered a sudden, bitter urge to laugh.

'Yes, Director,' she managed.

He looked up at her and frowned, then turned his attention back to his writing. Finishing the table, he drew out another sheet of paper and started making a copy.

'You're not going to have much time to yourself next year,' he told her. 'Lord Yikmo prefers to teach during the day, so you will have to take some private classes in Alchemy instead. You'll have Freedays for study. If you work efficiently, you may be able to keep Freeday mornings free for personal pursuits.' He paused and considered his work with a sad shake of his head. 'If you satisfy Lord Yikmo with your progress you may also regain a few afternoons to yourself.'

Sonea did not answer. What use did she have for free time now? Akkarin had forbidden her to speak to Rothen and she had no friends among the novices. She was dreading the coming few weeks. With no classes to attend until the next year, what was she to do with herself? Stay in her new room in Akkarin's residence? She shuddered. No, she would stay away from there as much as possible.

If he let her. What if he wanted to keep her close by? *What if he wants to use me in his evil work?* She began to push the thought away, then stopped herself. No matter how appalling, she had to consider the possibility. He could make her do anything by threatening to harm Rothen. Her stomach knotted with dread. *Anything . . .*

Her hands were hurting. Looking down, she unclenched her fists. Four sets of crescent-shaped indents marked each palm. Rubbing her hands on her robe, she made a mental note to trim her nails when she returned to her room.

Jerrik remained totally absorbed in his papers. She watched as his pen worked down the page. Reaching the end, he gave a grunt of satisfaction and handed the page to her.

'As the High Lord's favourite you will be given preferential treatment, but you'll also be expected to prove that his choice was well made. Don't hesitate to take advantage of your new position — you'll need to if you are to meet his expectations.'

She nodded. 'Thank you, Director.'

'You may go.'

Swallowing hard, she rose, bowed and moved to the door.

'Sonea.'

Looking over her shoulder, she found a rare smile lifting the corners of Jerrik's mouth. 'I know you will miss having Rothen as your guardian,' he said. 'Akkarin may not be as companionable, but in choosing you he has done much to improve your situation.' The smile vanished. 'You may go.'

She forced herself to nod in reply. As she pulled the door closed, she saw that Jerrik was watching her, his expression thoughtful. Turning away, she slipped the schedule into her box and started along the wide, familiar corridor.

A few novices lingered in doorways. They watched her as she passed. Disturbed by their stares, she quickened her pace. *How many people know?* she wondered. *Probably everyone. They've had an entire day to find out.* The news that the High Lord had finally chosen a favourite would have spread through the Guild faster than the winter cough. A teacher stepped out of a corridor. He looked at her doubtfully, then his eyes dropped to her sleeve. His eyebrows rose and he shook his head slightly as if in disbelief.

She glanced down at the small square of gold on the sleeve of her robe. Incals were family symbols worn by members of the Houses. Magicians did not wear them because once they joined the Guild they were supposed to leave family and political ties behind them. The servant who had brought the robes had explained that the High Lord wore the Guild symbol as an incal because his position was a lifetime commitment. The Guild became his family and House.

And she was his novice. Folding her sleeve against her body to hide the incal, she approached the door of her classroom. She paused just outside to gather her courage.

'Good morning, Sonea.'

Turning, she saw Lord Elben striding down the corridor toward her. He smiled, his mouth widening but his eyes remaining cold.

'Congratulations on your new guardian,' he offered as he reached her side.

Sonea bowed. 'Thank you, Lord Elben.'

He strode into the classroom. Steeling herself, Sonea followed.

'Take your seats, please,' Elben boomed. 'We have much to do today.'

'Ah!' A familiar voice rose above the clatter and drag of chairs. 'The High Lord's favourite has deigned to honour our humble class with her presence.'

The room fell silent. All faces turned toward Sonea. Seeing the disbelief on their faces, she felt a wry amusement. How ironic that her own classmates should be the last to find out. All but one, she amended. Regin was lounging on a table, grinning with satisfaction at the effect his news had on the class.

'Take your seat, please, Regin,' Elben growled.

Regin slid off the table and settled into his chair. Moving to her place, Sonea lifted her box onto her desk. As she did her sleeve fell free, and she heard a small gasp nearby. Glancing up, she saw that Narron was staring at the incal.

'Sonea,' Elben said. 'I have saved a place for you at the front.'

She looked up and realised that there was, indeed, a seat free in the front row of the class. Poril's seat. She turned and saw that her old friend was sitting at the back of the room. He flushed and evaded her eyes.

'Thank you, my lord,' she replied, turning back. 'That was generous of you, but I would prefer to stay here.'

The magician's eyes narrowed. He looked as if he might argue, but he glanced at the class and he seemed to think better of it.

'Very well.' He lowered himself into his seat and placed a hand on a stack of paper on the desk. 'Today you will be tested on your knowledge of Alchemy,' he told the class. 'I will give you a list of questions to answer now, and later I will be giving you exercises to complete. After the midbreak you will be given practical tests.'

As he passed sheets of paper out to the class, Sonea felt an old, almost forgotten anxiety return. The tests. She let her eyes skim across the questions, and sighed with relief. Despite the disdain of the teachers, despite the long hours of study, despite all Regin's attempts to hamper her, she had managed to absorb the lessons. Feeling better, she took a pen out of her box and began to write.

Hours later, when the gong tolled to mark the end of the test, the class let out a unified sigh of relief.

'That will be all,' Elben finished. 'You may go.'

As one the novices rose and bowed to the teacher. Sonea caught several glances in her direction as they filed out of the room. Remembering why, she felt her stomach turn over with dread.

'Wait, Sonea,' Elben said as she passed his desk. 'I would like to speak with you.'

He waited until the room was empty before speaking. 'After midbreak,' he told her, 'I would like you to take the place I have arranged for you.'

Sonea swallowed. Was this what Jerrik had meant when he said the teachers would give her preferential treatment? Should she take advantage of it, as he had suggested?

But what was to be gained by moving to the front of the classroom? Only the knowledge that Poril had lost even more status in the class because of her. She shook her head.

'I prefer the seat by the window.'

Elben frowned. 'It would be more appropriate if you sat at the front of the class now.'

Appropriate? She felt a flare of anger. This was not about helping her learn, this was about being seen to favour the High Lord's novice. He probably expected her to report every little favour to Akkarin. She smothered a bitter laugh. She would be saying as little to her new guardian as possible.

If she had learned anything from the last six months, it was to avoid upsetting the petty social order of the classroom. Taking Poril's place would mean more than just a change of seats. The novices already disliked her, she didn't need to give them more reason to. She looked at Elben, standing with his arms crossed, and felt her anger harden into defiance.

'I'll stay in my usual place,' she told him.

Elben's eyes narrowed, but he seemed to see something

325

in her gaze that made him pause. He pursed his lips thoughtfully.

'It is easier to see and hear at the front,' he pointed out.

'I'm not deaf, Lord Elben, or short-sighted.'

His jaw clenched. 'Sonea,' he moved closer and spoke quietly, 'if you will not take the front seat it might be seen as . . . neglectful of me as your teacher . . .'

'Perhaps I should tell Akkarin that you would not let me sit where I wished.'

His eyes widened. 'You wouldn't bother him over something so small . . .'

She smiled. 'I doubt he would be interested in my seating arrangements at all.'

He regarded her silently, then nodded. 'Very well. You may sit where you wish. Go.'

As she stepped out into the corridor she realised that her heart was racing. What had she done? Novices *never* argued with their teachers.

Then she realised that the corridor was unusually quiet. Looking up, she saw that novices of all years were silently watching her. All satisfaction over her conversation with Elben evaporated. Swallowing hard, she started toward the stairs.

'That's her,' whispered a voice to her right.

'Yesterday,' someone muttered. '. . . no warning at all.'

'. . . High Lord . . .'

'Why *her*?' someone sneered, a comment clearly meant for her to hear. 'She's just a slum girl.'

'. . . not right.'

'. . . should have been . . .'

'. . . insult to the Houses.'

She snorted softly. *If they knew the real reason he chose me,* she thought, *they would not be so—*

'Make way for the High Lord's favourite!'

Her stomach turned as she recognised the voice. Regin stepped out to block her path.

'Great one!' he cried loudly. 'Might I ask a tiny, infinitesimally small favour of one so admired and influential?'

Sonea regarded him warily. 'What do you want, Regin?'

'Would you . . . if it would not be a great offence to your high position, that is,' he smiled cloyingly, 'would you mend my shoes tonight? You see, I know you are skilled in such great and worthy tasks and, well, if I am to have my shoes mended it should be done by the best shoe-mender in the sluh-Guild, wouldn't you say?'

Sonea shook her head. 'Is that all you could come up with, Regin?' She stepped around him and continued down the corridor. Footsteps pursued her.

'Oh, but Sonea – I mean – Oh, Great One. I would be so hon—'

His voice stopped abruptly. Frowning, she resisted the temptation to glance behind.

'She is the High Lord's novice,' someone muttered. 'Are you stupid? Leave her alone.'

Recognising Kano's voice, Sonea caught her breath in surprise. Was this what Jerrik had meant when he had said Akkarin had improved her situation? Reaching the stairs, she descended into the Entrance Hall, stepped out of the doors and started toward the Magicians' Quarters.

Then she stopped.

Where was she going? Rothen's rooms? Standing still, she tried to gather her thoughts.

Hunger decided her. She would go to the Foodhall. And after the afternoon's tests? The library. If she stayed there until it closed, she could avoid returning to the High Lord's

Residence until late. With luck Akkarin would have retired for the night, and she could reach her room without encountering him. Taking a deep breath, she steeled herself for the inevitable stares and whispers, and walked back into the University.

Lorlen's rooms were on the ground floor of the Magicians' Quarters. He spent little time in them, rising early and returning long after the rest of the Guild had retired. From day to day he noticed little more in the rooms than the bed and his clothing cupboard.

But in the last day he had rediscovered much about his private space. There were ornaments and objects on the bookshelves that he had forgotten he owned. These mementos of the past, of family and achievements, brought only guilt and pain. They reminded him of people he loved and respected. People he had failed.

Closing his eyes, Lorlen sighed. Osen would not be concerned yet. Only a day and a half had passed. Not long enough for his assistant to panic at the growing list of unattended work. And Osen had been trying for years to persuade Lorlen to take a break from his duties.

If only it was *a break*. Lorlen rubbed his eyes and wandered into his bedroom. Perhaps he was tired enough to sleep now. He hadn't been able to for two nights, not since . . .

As he lay down the memories returned. He groaned and tried to push them away, but he was too tired to fight them, and he knew they would return again as soon as he relaxed anyway.

How did it start? I said something about the Vindo Ambassador expecting to stay in the residence . . .

'He was surprised to hear that the High Lord does not entertain guests any more, since his father stayed here with your predecessor,' Lorlen remembered explaining.

Akkarin had smiled at that. He had been standing by the little table he served drinks at, gazing out the window at the night-shrouded grounds.

'The best change I ever made.'

'You do value your privacy,' Lorlen had said absently.

Akkarin then placed a finger on a wine bottle, as if considering whether he would have another glass. His face had been turned away, something Lorlen had been thankful for when Akkarin spoke next.

'I doubt that the ambassador would be comfortable with my . . . habits.'

There! Another one of those strange comments. Like he was testing me. I thought I was safe, since his back was turned and he couldn't see my reaction . . .

'Habits?' Lorlen had affected disbelief. 'I doubt he'd care if you had a few late nights, or drank too much. You're just afraid he'll drink all your favourite wine.'

'That, too.' Akkarin had then opened the bottle. 'But we couldn't have anyone discovering all my little secrets, could we?'

An image of Akkarin covered in bloodied beggar's rags had flickered through Lorlen's mind at that point in the conversation. He had shuddered and pushed it aside, thankful again that Akkarin's back was turned.

Was this what Akkarin had sensed? Was he listening to my thoughts at that moment?

'No,' Lorlen had replied and, wanting to change the subject, asked about the news of the court.

At that point, Akkarin lifted an object from the table.

Catching a glitter of gems, Lorlen looked closer. It was a knife. The knife Sonea had seen Akkarin using for the black magic ritual. Surprised and horrified, Lorlen drew in a breath and choked on the wine.

'You're supposed to *drink* wine, my friend,' Akkarin said, smiling. 'Not breathe it.'

Lorlen looked away, hiding behind his hands as he coughed. He tried to regain his composure, yet seeing Akkarin holding the knife had been like reliving Sonea's memory. He wondered why Akkarin had brought it into the guestroom.

Then his blood turned to ice, as the thought came that Akkarin might be intending to use it.

'What news do I have?' Akkarin mused. 'Let me think.'

Lorlen forced himself to regard his friend calmly. As Akkarin turned back to the bottle, Lorlen caught a corresponding movement on the table. A polished silver tray leaning against another bottle had reflected Akkarin's eyes. Eyes that were watching him.

So he had been watching me all along. Perhaps he hadn't tried to read my surface thoughts at that point of the conversation. Only my reaction to his comments, and the knife, would have convinced him that I knew something . . .

'I've heard reports of Dannyl from friends in Elyne and Lonmar,' Akkarin had said next, abruptly moving away from the table. 'They speak well of him.'

'That is good to hear.'

Akkarin had then paused in the centre of the room. 'I've been following his progress with interest. He is an efficient researcher.'

So he knew Dannyl was researching something. Did he know *what* Dannyl was researching? Lorlen had forced himself to smile. 'I wonder what has caught his attention.'

Akkarin's eyes narrowed. 'Hasn't he been keeping you informed?'

'Me?'

'Yes. You did, after all, ask him to investigate my past.'

Lorlen considered his next words carefully. Akkarin might know that Dannyl was retracing his travels, but how could he know why when Dannyl didn't? 'Is that what your friends say?'

'Spies would be a more accurate term.'

Akkarin's hand had moved, and with a flash of fear Lorlen saw that it still held the knife. Realising that Akkarin could not have missed his reaction, Lorlen stared at it openly.

'What *is* that?'

'Something I picked up during my travels,' Akkarin replied, holding it up. 'Something you recognise, I think.'

Lorlen then felt a flash of triumph. Akkarin had all but admitted he had learned black magic during his travels. Dannyl's research might prove useful yet . . .

'It is strangely familiar,' Lorlen said. 'Perhaps I have seen something like it before in a book, or a collection of antiques – and it is such a vicious-looking thing it would be sure to stick in my memory.'

'Do you know what it is used for?'

A memory of Akkarin cutting his servant's arm flashed into Lorlen's mind. 'It's a knife, so something unpleasant, most likely.'

Akkarin, to Lorlen's relief, set the knife down on a side table, but the relief had been short lived.

'You have been strangely cautious of me these last few

months,' Akkarin said. 'You avoid mental communication, as if you are afraid I will detect something behind your thoughts. When my contacts told me of Dannyl's research, I was intrigued. Why did you ask him to investigate my past? Don't deny it, Lorlen. I have proof.'

Lorlen was dismayed that Akkarin had discovered Dannyl's orders. But he had prepared for this question. He pretended to be embarrassed.

'I was curious, and after our conversation about your diary I thought I might restore some of what you lost. You're not free to gather the information again, so . . . It wouldn't be as satisfying as going yourself, of course, but I hoped it would be a pleasant surprise.'

'I see.' Akkarin's voice had hardened. 'I wish I could believe you, but I don't. You see, tonight I have done something to you that I have never done before, and never wanted to. While we spoke I read your surface thoughts. They have revealed much, much more. I know you are lying. I know you have seen things you should never have seen, and I must know how this came about.

'Tell me, how long have you known I practice black magic?'

Just a few words, and everything changed. Was there any remorse or guilt in his voice? No. Just anger . . .

Appalled, and not a little frightened, Lorlen had grasped at a last, desperate evasion. He had stared at his friend in horror.

'You practice *what*?'

Akkarin's expression darkened. 'Don't be a fool, Lorlen,' he had snapped. 'I have seen it in your thoughts. You know you cannot lie to me.'

Realising that he could not deny it, Lorlen glanced at

the knife on the table. He wondered what would happen now. If he was about to die. How Akkarin would explain it. If Rothen and Sonea would suspect the truth and reveal Akkarin's crime . . .

Too late, he realised that Akkarin might have heard his thoughts. He looked up, but Akkarin's expression had showed no alarm or suspicion, only expectation, and that gave him a little hope.

'How long?' Akkarin had pressed.

'Over a year,' he confessed.

'How?'

'I came here one night. The door was open and I saw a light through the stairs, so I started to come down. When I saw what you were doing . . . it was a shock. I didn't know what to think.'

'What exactly did you see?'

With difficulty that he did not need to fake, Lorlen had described what Sonea had seen. As he spoke, he had looked for a hint of shame in the High Lord's expression, but had seen only a flicker of annoyance.

'Does anyone else know about this?'

'No,' Lorlen answered quickly, hoping to avoid betraying Sonea and Rothen, but Akkarin's eyes narrowed.

'You're lying to me, my friend.'

'I'm not.'

Akkarin had then sighed. Lorlen remembered that sigh vividly.

'That is unfortunate.'

Lorlen had then risen to face his old friend, determined to convince Akkarin that his secret was safe. 'Akkarin, you must believe me. I have told no-one about this. It would cause too much strife in the Guild. I . . . I don't know why you are playing with this . . . this forbidden magic. I can only trust that you have good reason. Do you think you would be standing here if I didn't?'

'So you trust me?'

'Yes.'

'Then show me the truth. I must know who you are protecting, Lorlen, and just how much you have learned.'

Akkarin had then reached toward Lorlen's head. With a shock, Lorlen realised Akkarin intended to read his mind. He grabbed Akkarin's hands and tossed them away, appalled that his friend might demand such a thing. 'You have no right to—'

And then the last of Lorlen's trust in his friend had died as Akkarin's fingers flexed in a familiar gesture. A force pushed Lorlen backward. He fell into the chair and felt magic pressing him down.

'Don't do this, Akkarin!'

But Akkarin's mouth was set in a thin line. 'Sorry, my old friend, but I must know.'

Then Akkarin's fingers had touched Lorlen's temples.

It should not have been possible! It was as if he wasn't there, but he was. How does he do this mind-reading?

Shivering at the memory, Lorlen opened his eyes and stared at the walls of his bedroom. As he clenched his fists he felt a warm band of metal press into the skin around one finger. Lifting his hand, he felt his stomach twist as a red gem glinted in the dim light.

Everything had been revealed: what Sonea had witnessed, the truth-read, Rothen's involvement, and all that Dannyl had learned or discovered. No hint of Akkarin's thoughts or emotions had filtered through to him. Only afterward had Lorlen seen hints of the High

Lord's state of mind as Akkarin paced his guestroom, brooding in silence for an hour, perhaps longer. What he had discovered obviously concerned him greatly, but his demeanour had not lost any of its confidence.

Finally, the restraining magic holding Lorlen in the chair had withdrawn. Akkarin picked up the knife from the table. Given more time to think, Lorlen would have feared for his life, but instead he stared in disbelief as Akkarin ran the blade over his own palm.

With blood pooling in one hand, Akkarin took Lorlen's empty glass and smashed it against the table. He picked up one of the fragments and tossed it in the air.

It had halted in front of Akkarin's eyes, and begun spinning, the sharp edges glowing red as it melted. When it had cooled again, it formed a faceted sphere. Akkarin lifted his bleeding hand and curled his fingers around the sphere. When he opened his hand again, the cut had disappeared and a bright red gem lay on his palm.

Next, Akkarin had willed a silver spoon to his hand from the drinks cabinet. It had twisted about, melting and folding until it had formed a thick circle. Akkarin took the gem between two fingers and placed it in the thickest part of the band, which closed about it like a flower.

Then he had held the ring out to Lorlen.

'Put it on.'

Lorlen had considered refusing, but he knew that Akkarin was willing to use force to get his way, and he could imagine a few unpleasant ways that a ring might be permanently attached. He wanted the option of removing it one day, so he took the ring and reluctantly slipped it onto his middle finger.

'I will be able to see and hear everything around you,'

Akkarin had told him. 'And we will be able to communicate without anyone hearing.'

Was Akkarin watching now? Does he observe me pacing in my rooms? Does he feel any guilt for what he's done?

While Lorlen felt hurt and betrayed by Akkarin's actions, it was Sonea's fate that tormented him most. Had Akkarin been watching when, looking out of his window a few minutes ago, Lorlen had seen Sonea leave the University? She had stopped abruptly, the pain in her eyes so clear as she remembered that she could no longer return to Rothen's rooms.

He wasn't sure if he wanted Akkarin to have seen her. He wasn't sure if his 'friend' could feel remorse or guilt. For all Lorlen knew, Akkarin might have enjoyed seeing her misery.

But, despite everything, he still wanted to believe it wasn't so.

CHAPTER 21

THE TOMBS OF WHITE TEARS

As Sonea walked away from the University she imagined she could feel the enormous building shrinking behind her. Her back prickled with lingering warmth and her face stung with cold. Ahead a dark shape loomed larger as she approached.

The High Lord's Residence. Akkarin's house.

She had stretched her evening meal out as long as possible then, unable to bring herself to leave the University, she had gone to the Novices' Library. Now, with the library closed and the rest of the University empty and silent, she had no alternative but to return to her new room.

Her heart was beating too fast by the time she reached the door. She stopped, swallowed hard and reached out to the door handle. As she touched it, the door swung inward.

The room inside was lit by a single globe light. A figure sat in one of the luxurious chairs, holding a book in long, pale fingers. He looked up and Sonea felt her stomach clench.

'Come in, Sonea.'

She forced her legs to move. Once inside, the door swung shut behind her, closing with a soft, but decisive click.

'Did you do well in the tests today?'

She opened her mouth to answer but, not trusting her voice, decided to nod instead.

'That is good. Have you eaten?'

She nodded again.

'Then you should get some rest in preparation for tomorrow. Go.'

Relieved, she bowed and hurried through the door to her left. She created a globe of light and sent it before her as she climbed the curving stairs.

In the light of magic, the staircase reminded her of the one that led down to the underground room where she had seen him practising his black magic. Those stairs lay behind the door on the other side of the guestroom, she guessed. On this side, the stairs led only upward.

At the top she reached a long corridor. Behind the first door was her bedroom. She had seen nothing else of the High Lord's Residence.

As she turned the door handle, she heard footsteps coming from the other end of the corridor. Looking up, she saw a wall illuminated by a slowly brightening light, and the top of the other staircase.

Willing her own light to vanish, she quickly opened the door of her room and slipped inside. She left the door open a crack, but as she peered through she cursed under her breath. Only the corridor wall opposite was visible. To watch him, she would have to open the door further, and he was sure to notice.

Light streaked down the corridor wall. The footsteps stopped and a faint click reached her ears. The light moved again, then all disappeared in darkness as the sound of a door closing echoed down the corridor.

So that's his bedroom, Sonea mused. *Just twenty or so strides down the corridor*. Knowing he was so close was not comforting, but it wouldn't have been much better had he been on the other side of the residence. Just knowing she was in the same building was disturbing enough.

Closing her own door quietly, Sonea turned around and surveyed her room. Moonlight spilled through the two small windows, throwing pale rectangles on the floor. The room seemed almost welcoming in the gentle light.

It was very different to her plain room in the Novices' Quarters. The furniture here was made of a dark red wood, polished to a shine. A large cabinet stood against one wall. A table and chair for study stood beside it. Between the two windows was a bed. Something lay on it.

Sonea walked over to the bed and willed a globe light into existence. A bundle of simple cloth, tied with string, lay on the covers. As she untied the knot, it fell open and green material spilled out.

Her Acceptance Ceremony dress.

As she lifted it, heavier objects fell out of the folds: her silver comb and mirror, and two books of poetry that Rothen had given her. She felt tears spring to her eyes.

No. I am not going to start blubbering like some lost child, she told herself. Blinking the moisture away she put the objects on the study table, then carried the dress to the clothes cupboard.

A faint woody odour wafted out as she slipped the dress onto a hanger. The smell reminded her of the Guildhall. A memory of Rothen speaking the ceremonial words of a guardian flashed into her mind. She remembered her elation as she stood beside him, her new robes in her hands. *But he's not my guardian any more*. Sighing, she closed the cupboard door.

Returning to the bed, she saw a smaller object lying on the cover. Picking it up, she recognised the rough carving of a reber that Dorrien had given to Rothen soon after he arrived. It had fascinated her how something could be so crudely hewn, yet have all the essence of the animal it represented.

Dorrien. She hadn't thought of him since he'd left. It seemed like weeks ago, but it was only two days since they had walked up to the spring, and he had kissed her.

What was he going to think when he heard about her sudden change of guardian? She sighed. Like the rest of the magicians, he would marvel at her 'good fortune' — but she was sure that, had he been here, he would have detected that something wasn't right. He would have noticed her fear and Rothen's distress and anger.

But he wasn't here. He was far away in his little village in the mountains.

Eventually Dorrien would visit the Guild again. When he did, he would want to see her. Would Akkarin let him? Sonea smiled. Even if Akkarin forbade it, Dorrien would find a way. Besides, if Akkarin stopped Dorrien seeing her it would raise suspicions.

Or would it? Akkarin could simply claim that Dorrien was distracting her from her studies. Though Dorrien might find that a bit over-protective, no-one else would question it. She frowned. What if Dorrien *did* notice that something was wrong? What would he do? What would Akkarin do? She shivered. Unlike Rothen and herself, Dorrien lived far from the Guild's sight. Who would question if a Healer working in a distant village died in an 'accident'?

She clutched the carving tightly. She must not give Akkarin reason to notice Dorrien. When Dorrien returned to the Guild, she would have to tell him she had no feelings for him. He had said himself that she might find someone else in the years until graduation. Let him think that she had.

But there could never be anyone else. Not while she was Akkarin's hostage. To make a friend was to bring someone else into danger. And what about her aunt and uncle and her little cousin? For now, Akkarin would not harm Rothen without freeing her to reveal his secret. If he knew where her family was, they could be used against her, too.

Sighing, she lay back on the bed. When had it all started to go wrong? Her thoughts went back to the North Square. Since that day her fate had been in the hands of others: first Cery and Harrin, then the Thieves, then Rothen, and now Akkarin. Before then, she had been a child, protected by her aunt and uncle. Would she ever be in control of her life?

But I'm alive, she reminded herself. *All I can do now is be patient and hope something will happen to fix all this – and make sure I'm ready to help when it does.*

Rising, she went to her study table. If something did happen, it would probably involve magic, so the more prepared she was, the better. Healing tests would be held tomorrow, and she ought to go over her notes one more time.

Moving to the window again, Rothen stared at the High Lord's Residence. Small squares of brightness had appeared by its northern tower during the last two nights. The more he stared at it, the more sure he was that Sonea was behind those windows.

How frightened she must be. How trapped. She must wish she never agreed to join the Guild.

He realised that his fists were clenched. Forcing himself to return to his chair in the guestroom, he sat down and regarded the remains of his half-eaten meal.

What can I do? There must be something I can do.

He had asked himself that question over and over. Each time the answer was the same.

As much as you dare.

Everything depended on Sonea's safety. He wanted to step out into the corridor and scream out the truth to all the magicians who had so blindly accepted Akkarin's decision, but he knew if he did, Sonea would be the first of Akkarin's victims. Her power would be used to fight the Guild; her death would help Akkarin defeat them.

He desperately wanted to talk to Lorlen. While he craved an assurance that Lorlen wasn't about to sacrifice Sonea's life in an attempt to defeat Akkarin, he also wanted to know that the Administrator hadn't abandoned all plans to fight the High Lord.

Akkarin had forbidden any contact between them, but even if Rothen had dared to risk talking to Lorlen, he couldn't. The Administrator had retired to his rooms and was resting. Since hearing this, Rothen had been worried that Lorlen had been injured in his confrontation with Akkarin. The possibility was frightening. If Akkarin could harm his closest friend, what was he capable of doing to those he cared less about?

But the High Lord might be well used to killing and taking power from others. He might have been doing so for years. Rothen frowned. How long had Akkarin been practising black magic? As long as he had been High Lord? Longer?

Since Sonea had told him of Akkarin's secret, Rothen

had considered many times how Akkarin might have discovered black magic. It was commonly understood that the Guild had destroyed all knowledge of it centuries ago. The Higher Magicians were told how to recognise it, but that was all. Nevertheless, it was possible that Akkarin had access to information and instructions from forgotten records somewhere in the Guild.

Or he might have learned black magic years ago, before he set out on his journey. The quest to discover knowledge of ancient power may have been an excuse to find out more, or simply to gain time and freedom to practice. Or perhaps it was during Akkarin's travels that he had discovered black magic. Had Akkarin stumbled upon the knowledge and used it to strengthen himself?

Where knowledge of power could be found, a means to defeat that power often lay beside it. If Akkarin had discovered black magic during his travels, then another might find it again. Rothen sighed. If only he could leave the Guild, he would spend every moment of each day searching for that knowledge. But he couldn't leave. Akkarin was probably watching him closely. He wouldn't want Rothen roaming the Allied Lands, out of his sight.

Someone else must do it, then. Rothen nodded to himself. *Someone free to travel. Someone who will do it without asking too many questions. Someone I can trust . . .*

Slowly, Rothen began to smile. He knew exactly the right person.

Dannyl.

Hundreds of torches flickered in the chill night breeze. Ahead, hundreds more formed a long zigzag that wove back and forth and up toward the sky. The rocky surface of a cliff was illuminated by them and, at intervals, the mouths of caves were circled by flames.

The rowers pulled on their oars in time to the slow beat of the drummer at the prow. Song echoed back from the cliffs as the singers shifted through slow harmonies that sent a shiver down Dannyl's spine. He glanced at Tayend, who was gazing around at the other boats in wonder. After a few weeks of rest, the courtier was looking healthier.

'Are you feeling well?' Dannyl murmured.

Tayend nodded and gestured to the hull of the boat. 'Hardly rocks at all.'

A soft scraping came from the bottom of the boat. The rowers leapt out nimbly and pulled the craft up onto the beach. Tayend stood up and, carefully gauging the rhythm of the waves swirling around the boat, leapt out when the water had withdrawn. He cursed as his fine shoes sank into the wet sand.

Chuckling, Dannyl stepped out and started across the beach toward the torch-lined path. He paused as a large group of mourners started their procession up the stairs carved into the cliff face. Leaving a respectful gap behind the group, Dannyl and Tayend followed.

At the full moon every month, the people of Vin visited these caves. Within them were tombs of the dead. Gifts were laid by the remains of ancestors, and requests were asked of their spirits. Some tombs were so ancient, no descendants remained to visit them, and it was one of the oldest tombs that Dannyl and Tayend had come to see.

Remembering the customs they had been told about, they remained silent as they climbed. They passed several caves, climbing steadily. Tayend was breathing hard when the group of mourners in front of them turned into a cave entrance. After a short rest, he and Dannyl continued up the narrow stairs.

'Wait. Look at this.'

Hearing the whisper, Dannyl turned to find Tayend pointing back at a cave entrance he had walked past without noticing. A slight fold in the cliff had hidden a narrow crack barely wide enough for a man to slide through sideways. Above it was carved a symbol.

Recognising the symbol, Dannyl moved to the crack and peered through. He could see only blackness. Stepping back, he created a globe light and sent it inside.

Tayend gave a half-smothered yelp as the light revealed a staring face. The man squinted at Dannyl and said something in Vindo. Realising that this was a tomb guard, Dannyl spoke the ritual greeting that he had been taught.

The man gave the appropriate reply, then stepped back and beckoned. As Dannyl slipped through, his globe light set the man's polished ceremonial armour and short sword glittering. The guard bowed stiffly.

They stood in a small room. A low corridor led deeper into the cliff side. The walls were covered in paintings. Tayend examined them closely, humming with appreciation.

'You must have watcher,' the guard said. 'So you not get lost. You must not take anything away, not even rock.' He drew out a small flute and blew a single note. After a moment a boy in a simple belted shift appeared in the doorway. He beckoned and, as Dannyl and Tayend stepped through the door, indicated that they should go first. As they started down a narrow tunnel, he followed silently.

Tayend set the pace, walking slowly as he examined the wall paintings.

'Anything interesting?' Dannyl asked when the scholar stopped for the third time.

'Oh, yes,' Tayend breathed. He looked up at Dannyl, then smiled apologetically. 'Just not related to what you're looking for.'

Straightening, he continued at a faster pace, his attention still on the walls, but his expression less distracted. As time passed, Dannyl grew conscious of the weight of earth above him, and the closeness of the walls. If the tunnel was to collapse, he was sure he could prevent them being crushed by throwing up a barrier. He had done much the same thing a year ago when, to prevent him catching Sonea, the Thieves had collapsed one of their tunnels.

But here it was different. There was a lot more rubble and dirt above him. He could probably stop them being crushed, but he wasn't sure what he would do then. Could he shift the earth around and behind his barrier, and so tunnel a way out? Would he have time before the air inside ran out? Did he have the magical strength to do it? If he didn't, he would slowly weaken until the weight of the earth won out.

Disturbed by the thought, he tried to think of something else. The footsteps of the boy following behind were faintly discernible. He wondered whether the boy worried about being buried alive. He found himself thinking of another day, when he had entered the tunnels under the University to see why Fergun had been snooping around down there. He had fought off the suspicion that someone was following him, only to find that that someone was the High Lord.

'Are you all right?'

Dannyl jumped at the question. Tayend was regarding him closely.

'Yes. Why?'

'You're breathing a bit fast.'

'Oh. Was I?'

'Yes.'

After a few more steps, Dannyl quietly took a deep breath and let it out slowly, then started practising a calming exercise.

Tayend glanced at him and smiled. 'Does being underground bother you?'

'No.'

'Lots of people feel uncomfortable in places like this. I've had plenty go all panicky in the library, so I've learned to recognise the signs. You will tell me if you're going to get panicky, won't you? I don't much like the idea of being near a panicky magician.'

Dannyl smiled. 'I'm fine. I'm just . . . remembering a few unpleasant experiences I've had in similar places.'

'Oh? Do tell.'

Somehow, relating the two experiences made Dannyl feel better. Describing how the Thieves came to bury him led to stories about the search for Sonea. As he reached the part where he had entered the tunnels under the University and encountered the High Lord, Tayend's eyes narrowed.

'You're scared of *him*, aren't you?'

'No. Not scared so much as . . . well, it depends on the situation.'

Tayend chuckled. 'Well, if someone as scary as you is afraid of the High Lord, then I'm definitely keeping out of his way.'

Dannyl checked his stride. '*I'm* scary?'

'Oh, yes.' Tayend nodded. 'Very scary.'

'But . . .' Dannyl shook his head. 'I haven't done anything to—' He stopped as he remembered the mugger. 'Well, I guess I have now – but surely you weren't scared of me before then?'

'Of course I was.'

'Why?'

'All magicians are scary. Everyone has heard what they can do – but it's what you *don't* know they can do that is scarier.'

Dannyl grimaced. 'Well, I guess you've seen what I can do, now. And I didn't mean to kill him.'

Tayend regarded him silently for a few steps. 'How are you feeling about that?'

'Not great,' Dannyl admitted. 'You?'

'I'm not sure. It's like I've got two different and opposing views at the same time. I'm not sorry you killed him, but I do think killing is wrong. I suppose it's the uncertainty that bothers me most. Who really knows whether it was right or wrong? I've read more books than most people I know, and none of them agree on anything. But there's one thing I do want to say to you.'

Dannyl forced himself to meet Tayend's eyes. 'Yes?'

'Thank you.' Tayend's expression was sober. 'Thank you for saving my life.'

Something inside Dannyl loosened, like a knot unravelling. He realised he had needed Tayend's gratitude. It did not make his conscience any easier to live with, but it helped him to keep the whole event in perspective.

Looking ahead, he noticed that his globe light was failing to illuminate the walls in the distance. He frowned, then realised they were approaching a larger cavern. As they neared this, a mineral smell caught Dannyl's attention. The tang in the air grew more distinct as they arrived at the opening. Dannyl sent his globe light out and Tayend gasped.

The chamber was as wide as the Guildhall, and filled with glistening curtains and spires of white. The sound of dripping water echoed through the space. Looking closely, Dannyl could see moisture falling from the ends of the stalactites. Between the fang-like stalagmites a shallow stream trickled.

'The Tombs of White Tears,' Tayend murmured.

'Formed by water seeping through the roof, depositing minerals wherever it flows,' Dannyl explained.

Tayend rolled his eyes. 'I knew that.'

A slippery path led down into the chamber. Descending carefully, they made their way along the uneven floor. As they passed the fantastic white structures, more came into sight. Suddenly Tayend stopped.

'The Mouth of Death,' he said in a hushed voice.

Ahead, a row of stalagmites and stalactites crossed the chamber. Some had grown into each other and were slowly thickening to form columns. The gaps between others were so small, it seemed as if they would meet in mere moments. Each was colossal at the floor or ceiling, tapering to fine white points, so that the whole arrangement looked like the teeth of a huge animal.

'Shall we see if there's a stomach?' Tayend asked. Not waiting for an answer, he ducked through two of the teeth and disappeared.

Following, Dannyl found Tayend standing on one side of a tunnel, beckoning furiously. The walls on either side were curtains of glistening white, broken here and there by shallow horizontal alcoves. Moving to Tayend's side, he saw that a skeleton lay within a small alcove. A new curtain of white had formed, half covering the alcove.

'They must have cut the tombs knowing that the walls would grow down to cover them,' Tayend said quietly.

Moving on, they found another tomb, then another. The further they travelled, the older and more numerous the tombs. Eventually there were no skeletons to be seen, just walls that had covered the alcoves completely.

Dannyl knew that hours had passed. The Vindo forbade visitors to the caves during daylight, and he began to worry that they would not return to the beach in time to meet their boat. When they reached the end of the tunnel he breathed a sigh of relief.

'There's nothing here,' Tayend said, casting about.

Around them the walls were unbroken. Dannyl moved closer to the right, examining them carefully. They almost seemed to be translucent in places. Following suit, Tayend peered at the surface of the left-hand wall intently. After several minutes, he called Dannyl's name excitedly.

Moving to his friend's side, Dannyl saw that Tayend was pointing at a small hole.

'Can you get some light in there?'

'I'll try.'

As Tayend moved aside, Dannyl created a tiny spark and sent it into the hole. He watched as it moved through a finger-width of white mineral deposit, then out into darkness.

Brightening the spark to light the space beyond, he felt a smile spread across his face.

'What is it?' Tayend asked excitedly. 'Let me see!'

Stepping aside, Dannyl watched as Tayend bent to peer

in the hole. The scholar's eyes widened. Beyond the curtain of white was a small cave. A carved coffin lay in the centre of the room. The walls inside were partly coated in mineral sediment, but much of the original carved decoration was still visible.

Tayend whipped out sheets of paper and a drawing stick from his coat, his eyes glowing with excitement. 'How long have I got?'

Dannyl shrugged. 'An hour, probably less.'

'That'll be enough for now. Can we come back again?'

'I don't see why not.'

Tayend grinned. 'We've found it, Dannyl! We've found what your High Lord was searching for. Evidence of ancient magic!'

CHAPTER 22

AVOIDING THE HIGH LORD

As Sonea left the Healers' Quarters, novices hurried past her, some running or leaping about and whooping. Sonea listened to the laughter and excitement around her. With the final gong still ringing in their ears, novices of all ages and levels were talking of riding horses, attending court dances and playing games she had never heard of.

For the next two weeks brown robes would be a rare sight in the grounds, as the novices – and not a few magicians – returned to their families for the winter break. *If only I could leave, too.* She thought wistfully of spending the days with her aunt and uncle, and their baby, in the slums. *But he would never let me.*

Reaching the University, she paused as several older novices rushed out. A few stragglers hurried past her as she climbed the stairs. Once she had reached the second floor, however, she found herself abruptly alone.

The silence in the corridor had an emptiness to it that she hadn't experienced before, even late at night. Clasping her box to her chest, Sonea hurried to a side passage.

While the Magicians' Library was on the ground floor of the University, close to the rear of the building, the Novices' Library was reached via a confusing and twisted series of passages on the second level. Sonea hadn't been able to find it the first time she had looked, and had eventually resorted to following other novices.

Reaching the library, she saw that it, too, was empty of novices. Opening the door, she heard footsteps and bowed as the librarian, Lady Tya, appeared.

'I'm sorry, Sonea,' Tya said, 'the library is closing now. I've just finished packing up for the year.'

'Will it be open over the break, my lady?'

The librarian shook her head. Nodding, Sonea backed out of the door and turned away.

At the next crossing of passages she stopped. Cursing, she leaned back against the wall. Where could she go now? Anywhere but the High Lord's Residence. Shivering, she considered the passages to her left and right. The one on the right led back to the main corridor. To the left the passage led to . . . where?

Starting down it, she reached another intersection. She stopped, remembering the confusing journey Dorrien had taken her on to get to the roof of the University. He had said he knew every passage and room in the building. Growing up in the Guild had its advantages, he'd told her.

Sonea pursed her lips. She needed every advantage she could get. It was time she knew her way around this place.

But what if she got lost?

Sonea chuckled. She had hours to fill. For the first time in six months, she didn't need to be anywhere. If she lost her way, she'd find it again.

Smiling grimly, she started walking.

Four firm knocks rapped on the door. Lorlen's blood turned to ice.

This was not Osen's polite rapping, or the timid tap of Lorlen's servant. Nor was it the unfamiliar tap of another magician. It was a knock he had been dreading; a knock he had known would come.

Now that it had he couldn't move. He stared at the door hoping in vain that the visitor would think him absent, and go away.

—*Open the door, Lorlen.*

The communication jolted him. It sounded different, as if an actual voice had spoken within his mind.

Lorlen drew in a deep breath. He would have to face Akkarin eventually. Why prolong the moment? Sighing heavily, Lorlen willed the door to open.

'Good evening, Lorlen.'

Akkarin stepped inside, wearing the same half-smile that he usually greeted Lorlen with. As if they were still good friends.

'High Lord.' Lorlen swallowed. His heart was beating too fast and he wanted to shrink into his chair. He felt a flash of irritation at himself. *You're Administrator of the Guild*, he told himself, *at least be dignified*. He forced himself to rise and face Akkarin.

'Not visiting the Night Room tonight?' Akkarin asked.

'I wasn't in the mood.'

There was silence, then Akkarin crossed his arms.

'I did not harm them, Lorlen.' Akkarin's voice was quiet. 'Nor you. Sonea will actually benefit from my guardianship. Her teachers were neglecting her, despite Rothen's influence. Now they will go out of their way to help her – and she will need their help if she is to fulfil the potential I saw in her.'

Lorlen stared at Akkarin, shocked. 'You *read* her mind?'

An eyebrow rose. 'Of course. She may be small, but she is no child. You know this, Lorlen. You have read her mind, too.'

'That was different.' Lorlen looked away. 'I was invited.' No doubt Akkarin had read Rothen's mind as well. He felt another wave of guilt.

'But that is not why I'm here,' Akkarin said. 'Nothing has ever kept you from the Night Room when so much gossip and speculation was sure to be had. They will expect you to attend. It is time you stopped moping, my friend.'

Friend? Lorlen scowled and looked down at the ring. What kind of friend did this? *What kind of Administrator allows a black magician to take a novice hostage?* He sighed. *One who has no choice.*

To protect Sonea, he must pretend that nothing had happened. Nothing more extraordinary than the High Lord finally claiming a novice's guardianship and surprising all by choosing the slum girl. He nodded.

'I will go. Are you coming?' he asked, though he knew the answer.

'No, I will return to my residence.'

Lorlen nodded again. If Akkarin appeared in the Night Room, his presence would discourage gossip. In his absence, however, the questions that none dared ask the High Lord would be asked of the Administrator. As usual, Akkarin would expect a report.

Then Lorlen remembered the ring and Akkarin's words: *'I will be able to see and hear everything around you.'* Akkarin did not need to wait for a report. He would be listening to all that was said.

Rising, Lorlen moved into his bedroom, splashed water on his face from a bowl, and checked his reflection in the mirror. Two dark smudges under his eyes told of the sleepless nights he'd endured. Smoothing his hair, he combed it to the nape of his neck and tied it neatly. His robes were creased, but a small magical exertion fixed that.

Returning to the guestroom, he met Akkarin's gaze levelly. A faint smile touched the High Lord's mouth. Turning away, Lorlen schooled his expression and willed the door open.

Following Akkarin out, Lorlen saw the magicians in the corridor pause and look at him closely. He nodded politely. They would see the dark circles under his eyes and assume he had been ill. Outside the Magicians' Quarters, Akkarin bade him good night and disappeared into the University.

Continuing to the Night Room, Lorlen greeted two magicians as they, too, reached the entrance. As he expected, they asked if he was well. He assured them that he was, and led them inside.

As the inner doors opened, heads turned to see who had entered. The buzz of voices changed, first diminishing, then growing more intense. Lorlen made his way across the crowded room toward his favourite chair and saw that several magicians, including many of the Higher Magicians, had already gathered around it.

To his amusement, he found Lord Yikmo in his seat. The young Warrior leapt to his feet.

'Administrator Lorlen!' he exclaimed. 'Please sit down. Are you well? You look tired.'

'I'm fine,' Lorlen replied.

'That is good to hear,' Yikmo said. 'We were hoping you would come tonight, but I'd sympathise if you decided to avoid all the questions about Sonea and the High Lord.'

Lorlen managed to smile. 'But I couldn't leave you all wondering, could I?' Lorlen leaned back in the chair, and waited for the first question. Three magicians, including Lord Peakin, spoke at once. They stopped, glanced at each other, then two nodded politely to the Head of Alchemic Studies.

'Did you know Akkarin was thinking of taking on her guardianship?' Lord Peakin asked.

'No,' Lorlen admitted. 'He has shown no more interest in her than in any other novice. We've talked about her from time to time, but otherwise he kept his thoughts to himself. He may have been considering her for weeks, even months.'

'Why Sonea, then?' Lord Garrel asked.

'Again, I'm not sure. Something must have attracted his attention.'

'Perhaps it was her strength,' Lord Yikmo mused. 'Those summer intake novices alerted us all to her potential when they combined their powers against her.'

'Has he tested her, then?'

Lorlen hesitated, then nodded. 'Yes.'

The magicians around him exchanged looks of sympathy.

'What did he find?' Peakin asked.

'He told me he saw great potential,' Lorlen replied. 'He's eager to oversee her training.'

One of the magicians standing nearby straightened and moved away to join a newcomer and no doubt spread this information. Beyond the pair, a familiar face caught Lorlen's eye. As Rothen's eyes met his, Lorlen felt a pang of guilt.

That Rothen was present surprised him. Had Akkarin ordered Rothen to keep up appearances, too?

'Director Jerrik has told me she will be attending evening classes,' Lady Vinara said. 'Do you think this is too much to expect from her?'

Dragging his attention back to the questioners, Lorlen shrugged. 'That is news to me. I didn't know he had already approached Jerrik.'

'Most of her night classes are to cover those displaced by private Warrior Skills,' Lord Yikmo told them.

'Why couldn't she attend those at night?' another asked.

'Because I don't teach during the evening,' Yikmo replied, smiling broadly.

'Forgive me for saying so, but I'd have expected Lord Balkan to teach the High Lord's favourite,' Lord Garrel said. 'But perhaps your unusual teaching style would suit a girl like Sonea.'

'I have found novices with quick minds and less aggressive temperaments respond well to my methods,' Yikmo replied smoothly.

Sensing that Rothen was still watching him, Lorlen turned to look into the crowd. Rothen looked away. Returning to the conversation, Lorlen steered it away from Sonea's classes with Yikmo. *Warriors!* he thought. *Always so competitive.*

Two hours later Lorlen found himself suppressing a yawn. He glanced around at the magicians, then rose.

'Excuse me,' he said. 'It is growing late and I want to have an early night. Good evening.'

Crossing the room was not easy. Every few steps he was approached and questioned. After politely extracting himself several times, he turned around and found himself facing Rothen.

They stared at each other in silence. Heart racing, all

Lorlen could think was that Akkarin had forbidden them to talk to each other. But faces had turned to watch them, and if they didn't speak all kinds of speculation would be generated.

'Good evening, Administrator,' Rothen said.

'Good evening, Lord Rothen,' Lorlen replied.

So we've disobeyed Akkarin already, Lorlen mused. Rothen's face was more lined than he recalled. Suddenly remembering the ring, Lorlen clasped his hands behind his back. 'I wanted to . . . to express my sympathy. It must be distressing to lose the guardianship of a novice who you were clearly very fond of.'

A crease deepened between Rothen's brows. 'It is,' he agreed.

How he wished he could reassure Rothen. Perhaps he could . . .

'I've just heard she has been enrolled in evening classes for her Second Year. She'll be spending most of her time in lessons, so I doubt she'll see much of her new guardian at all – which is probably Akkarin's way of keeping her out from under his feet.'

Rothen nodded slowly. 'That will agree with her, I'm sure.' He hesitated then lowered his voice. 'Are you well, Administrator?'

'Yes.' Lorlen smiled wanly. 'I just need some sleep. I—' He stopped and smiled as a group of magicians passed. 'Thank you for your concern. Good night, Lord Rothen.'

'Good night, Administrator.'

Turning away, Lorlen continued to the doors of the Night Room and stepped out into the chill night air. He allowed himself a shallow sigh. *Do I really believe Akkarin won't harm them?*

—They're safe enough. Reassuring Rothen was a wise move.

Lorlen stiffened in surprise and looked down at the ring. Glancing around, he was relieved to see that the courtyard was empty and no-one had seen his reaction.

—You've told me about Garrel's conversational skills, but I've never seen him in action. Does he do that to everyone?

Lorlen looked down at the ring. It caught the light of the lamps around the courtyard, looking no different to any ordinary ruby.

—I told you, Lorlen. Everything you see and hear.

—And think?

—When I'm listening – but you won't know when I'm listening.

Appalled, Lorlen grasped the ring and began twisting it off.

—Stop, Lorlen. You're tormented with enough guilt already. Don't force me to make it worse.

Letting the ring go, Lorlen clenched his fingers in frustration.

—That's better. Now get some rest. You have work to catch up on.

Breathing heavily with anger and defeat, Lorlen started toward his rooms.

Familiarising herself with the inner passages of the University had turned out to be more difficult than Sonea had expected. The deeper she explored, the easier it was to become lost. So convoluted and unpredictable were the passages, she began to wonder if they had been designed specifically to confuse strangers.

The layout did not follow a predictable or repetitive pattern. Each passage twisted and turned in different ways.

Sometimes they met the main corridor again; sometimes she found a dead end.

Taking a piece of paper out of her box, she began counting her steps and drawing the turns as she walked. After an hour, she had mapped out a small section of passages. Parts were missing, however. Though she retraced her steps, she found no passages leading into the blank sections on her maps.

She stopped and sat on her box to rest and think. She had assumed that the convoluted route Dorrien had taken when he took her up to the roof had been a deliberate ploy to confuse her. Perhaps it hadn't. Thinking back, she remembered an odd little room they had passed through. It had contained a few cabinets with ornaments, but otherwise appeared to have no practical purpose. Perhaps, she thought, its true purpose might be that of a portal or gateway to internal parts of the University.

Rising, she hurried to one of the dead ends she had encountered. The corridor ended at a plain, unmarked wall, but to her left was a door. She gripped the handle . . . and paused.

What if she was wrong and this was an ordinary room? She might walk in on a magician, or interrupt a gathering.

Perhaps that was exactly what she was supposed to think. Most people would feel reluctant to open the closed door of an unknown room uninvited. She took her hand from the door and stepped back to regard it. Was there any sign or indication that this door led to a portal room rather than an ordinary one?

It was made of a dark wood. The surface was plain and undecorated. The hinges were blackened iron. She walked back along the passage to examine other doors. They were the same.

Returning to the first door, Sonea struggled with her reluctance to open it. She imagined herself striding into a room only to find a startled and angry magician staring at her.

But if she did, she could always apologise and say she had made a mistake. Better still, she could knock first and if anyone answered she could say that she had knocked on the wrong door. Obviously, novices were always getting confused and lost.

She rapped lightly, then a little louder. After she had counted to fifty, she turned the handle. The door opened with a click and swung outward.

Stepping through, she entered a room just like the one she remembered Dorrien taking her through. Feeling pleased with herself, she strode across to the other door. It swung inward to reveal another passage.

This one was different to those she had already explored. The walls were panelled with wood, and paintings and relief carvings hung along its length. Even the air smelled different – a mix of wood polish and herbs. Sonea wandered slowly from picture to picture, enjoying the satisfaction of having proved her instincts right.

The portal rooms acted as a barrier, she decided. They kept those who didn't know their purpose out of these inner passages. Most people would not open a door unless they knew what lay beyond, and even if they opened the door by mistake, they would find an uninteresting room beyond. She wondered how many portal rooms there were. Finding out would give her something to do over the next two weeks.

She frowned then. If parts of the University had been designed to deter exploration, was she now in a part that was forbidden to novices?

Hearing a soft creak nearby, she spun about. A door opened a few strides down the passage. Too late to hide, she felt her heart skip as a magician stepped out. He looked up at her and frowned.

Look like you belong here! Straightening her back, she walked toward him as if she had just paused to view a painting. His eyes dropped to the incal on her sleeve. As she neared, she paused and bowed, then moved past.

Hearing his footsteps fade behind her, she sighed with relief. From his reaction to her presence, novices were not allowed into this part of the University. Yet he had accepted her presence after noting the incal on her sleeve. Perhaps he assumed she was on some errand for the High Lord. She smiled at that. So long as she looked as if she had a reason to be there, the magicians would leave her alone.

So where to from here? she asked herself. Unfolding the scrap of paper in her hand, she considered her map again.

CHAPTER 23

AKKARIN'S PROMISE

Returning from the deck, Dannyl found Tayend sitting cross-legged on the narrow bed in his cabin. The scholar's drawings and notes were spread over every flat surface.

'I've translated what I can. There's a phrase on the coffin that I suspect is repeated in several ancient languages. I'll be able to check that when I get back to the library. The third line is in the early Elyne tongue that merged with the Kyralian one a thousand years ago.'

'What does it say?'

'That this woman was fair and honourable. That she protected the islands with high magic. The words for "high magic" were carved deeply. There's a glyph emphasised in the same way in what I think is an old Vindo tongue – which is what was carved on the walls. The same glyph appears on the walls in several places.'

Handing Dannyl a drawing, Tayend pointed out the glyph. Each time the words for 'high magic' occurred, the picture above it represented a figure kneeling before a woman. The woman's hand was extended to touch the supplicant's upraised palm, as if to placate or reward.

'That could imply that she's performing this high magic. What do you think she's doing?'

Dannyl shrugged. 'Healing, perhaps. That would make

sense, since Healing would have been very rare a thousand years ago. It was only through co-operation and experimentation that the Guild managed to develop the skill — and it's still the most difficult discipline to learn.'

'So the term "high magic" is not familiar?'

Dannyl shook his head. 'No.'

'The hole we looked through did not look natural to me. It had to have been made by someone. Do you think it might have been made by magic?'

'Possibly.' Dannyl smiled. 'I think the last visitor did us a favour.'

'Indeed he did.' The ship dropped sharply. Tayend winced and turned a sickly colour.

'You're not going to spend this journey in misery,' Dannyl said firmly. 'Give me your wrist.'

Tayend's eyes widened. 'But . . . I . . .'

'You haven't got any excuses now.'

To Dannyl's amusement, Tayend blushed and looked away. 'I'm still, um, uncomfortable with . . . well . . .'

Dannyl waved a hand. 'This sort of Healing is quick. And I won't be reading your mind. Besides, you have to face the truth. You're not very good company when you're sick. When you're not throwing up everywhere, you're complaining about throwing up.'

'*Complaining* about it!' Tayend protested. 'I did not complain!' He thrust his wrist out. 'Go on then.'

Tayend closed his eyes tightly. Taking the scholar's wrist, Dannyl sent his mind out and immediately felt nausea and giddiness. A small effort of will soothed it away. Letting go of Tayend's wrist, Dannyl watched as the scholar opened his eyes and considered the effect.

'That's much better.' Tayend gave Dannyl a quick,

searching glance, then shrugged and looked down at his notes. 'How long will it last?'

'A few hours. Longer as you get used to the rocking.'

Tayend smiled. 'I knew I'd broght you along for something. What are we going to do when we get back?'

Dannyl grimaced. 'I'll have to spend a lot of time catching up on my ambassadorial duties.'

'Well, while you do that, I'll continue our research. We knew where Akkarin travelled to because of the ships' records. A question here and there will tell us what he did afterward. The Bel Arralade has a party to celebrate her birthday every year and that will be the perfect place to start. An invitation will be waiting at the Guild House for you.'

'How can you be sure? I've barely spent more than a few months in Capia, and I haven't met the Bel Arralade yet.'

'Which is why I'm certain you'll be invited.' Tayend smiled. 'A young, unmarried magician like yourself. Besides, Ambassador Errend always attends. If you didn't get an invite, he'd insist you accompanied him.'

'And you?'

'I have friends who'll take me if I ask nicely.'

'Why not come with me?'

Tayend glanced up and down the corridor between their cabins. He leaned forward.

'If we arrive together, there will be assumptions made you might rather weren't.'

'We've been travelling together for months,' Dannyl pointed out. 'Assumptions may have already been made.'

'Not necessarily.' Tayend waved a hand. 'Not if people observe you treating me as a mere underling. They may assume you don't know about me. After all, you're Kyralian. If you knew, you would have found another assistant.'

'We really have a bad reputation, don't we?'

Tayend nodded. 'But we can use that to our advantage. If anyone says anything about me, you should be outraged that they would slander my name. I'll plead with my friends that they keep you in the dark, because it's important to my work. If we're convincing enough, we'll be able to continue working together without anyone questioning.'

Dannyl frowned. He hated to admit it, but Tayend was right. Though he wanted to shrug and let the gossips talk, any steps they could take to protect his reputation would make both of their lives easier.

'Very well. I'll act like the arrogant Kyralian magician people expect.' He looked at Tayend. 'But I want you to remember, if I say anything harsh or judgmental, I don't really mean it.'

Tayend nodded. 'I know.'

'I'm just warning you. My acting skills are fairly good.'

'Oh, really?'

Dannyl chuckled. 'Yes, really. I have my mentor's words to prove it. He said if I could convince the Thieves I was a poor merchant, I could deceive anyone.'

'We'll see,' Tayend replied. 'We'll see.'

Lord Osen waited patiently as Lorlen finished the letter. With a wave of his hand, Lorlen dried the ink then folded the sheet of paper and sealed it.

'What is next?' he asked as he handed the letter to Osen.

'That is all.'

Lorlen looked up, surprised. 'We've caught up?'

'Yes.' Osen smiled.

Leaning back in his chair, Lorlen regarded his assistant

approvingly. 'I haven't thanked you for looking after everything for me last week.'

Osen shrugged. 'You needed a rest. In my opinion, you should have taken a longer break. Perhaps visited family for a few weeks like everyone else. You still look worn out.'

'I appreciate your concern,' Lorlen replied. 'But leave them all to their own devices for a few weeks?' He shook his head. 'Not a good idea.'

The young magician chuckled. 'Now you're starting to sound like your old self. Shall we start preparations for the next Meet?'

'No.' Lorlen frowned as he remembered. 'I'm visiting the High Lord tonight.'

'Forgive me for saying, but you don't sound particularly enthusiastic.' Osen hesitated, then continued in a quieter tone. 'Have you two had a disagreement?'

Lorlen considered his assistant. Osen rarely missed anything, but he was discreet. Would he believe a denial? Probably not completely.

—*Tell him we have. Something minor.*

Lorlen stiffened at the voice in his mind. Akkarin hadn't spoken to him through the ring since the conversation outside the Night Room over a week ago.

'I guess you could say we have,' Lorlen replied slowly. 'In a manner of speaking.'

Osen nodded. 'I thought so. Was it over Sonea's guardianship? That's what some of the magicians believe.'

'Do they?' Lorlen could not help smiling. He had become an object of gossip.

—*Well?* he projected at the ring.

—*The answer you are considering will do.*

Snorting softly, Lorlen looked up and gave Osen a

warning look. 'I know I can trust you to keep this to yourself, Osen. Speculation is fine, but I do not want the others to know the High Lord and I disagreed. For Sonea's sake.'

Osen nodded. 'I understand. I will keep it to myself – and I hope you two resolve your differences.'

Lorlen stood up. 'That depends on how well Sonea adapts to the change. It is a bit much to expect of her after all she's been through already.'

'I wouldn't want to be in her position,' Osen admitted as he followed Lorlen to the door. 'But I'm sure she'll cope.'

Lorlen nodded. *I hope so.* 'Good night, Osen.'

'Good night, Administrator.'

The University corridor echoed with the young magician's steps as he strode away. Walking into the Entrance Hall, Lorlen felt a cloud of dread gather around him. He stepped between the enormous doors and stopped at the top of the stairs.

Looking across the front of the gardens, he considered the High Lord's Residence. He hadn't been back since the night Akkarin had read his mind. Remembering sent a chill down his spine.

Taking a deep breath, he made himself think of Sonea. For her safety, he must make himself cross the garden and face Akkarin again. The High Lord's invitation was not to be refused.

Lorlen forced himself to move. After a few steps, he quickened his pace. Better to get it over and done with. At the door to the residence he paused, heart beating quickly, then made himself knock. As always, the door swung inward at the first touch. Seeing that the room was empty, Lorlen sighed with relief. He stepped inside.

In the corner of his eye he saw a movement. A shadow

detached itself from the dark rectangle of the right-hand stairway entrance. Akkarin's black robes rustled quietly as he approached.

Black robes. Black magic. Ironically, black had always been the colour of the High Lord. *You didn't have to take it so literally*, Lorlen thought.

Akkarin chuckled. 'Wine?'

Lorlen shook his head.

'Then sit. Relax.'

Relax? How could he relax? And he resented this friendly familiarity. Lorlen remained standing, and watched Akkarin move to the wine cabinet and pick up a bottle.

'How is Sonea?'

Akkarin's shoulders lifted. 'I don't know. I'm not even sure where she is exactly. Somewhere in the University, I believe.'

'She's not here?'

'No.' Akkarin turned and gestured to the chairs. 'Sit.'

'Then how do you . . . you didn't give her one of these rings?'

'No.' Akkarin took a sip of wine. 'I've checked on her from time to time. She spent a few days exploring the University, and now that she's found a few corners to hide in, she fills her time reading books. Adventure stories, from what I can tell.'

Lorlen frowned. He was glad that Akkarin hadn't forced Sonea to stay in her room for the break, but hearing of her hiding in corners of the University confirmed how frightened and unhappy she must be.

'Are you sure you don't want any wine? This year's Anuren dark is very good.'

Lorlen glanced at the bottle, then shook his head. Sighing, he moved to a chair and sat down.

'Taking on her guardianship has not been as trouble-some as I had feared,' Akkarin said quietly as he moved to his chair. 'It complicates everything, but it is better than the alternative.'

Lorlen closed his eyes and tried not to think what the alternative might be. He took a deep breath and let it out slowly, then forced himself to meet Akkarin's eyes.

'Why have you done this, Akkarin? Why black magic?'

Akkarin met his gaze levelly. 'Of all people, Lorlen, you are one I wish I could tell. I saw it change how you regard me. If you had thought defeating me was possible, you would have sent the Guild against me. Why didn't you ask what I was doing when you first learned of it?'

'Because I didn't know what you would do.'

'After all the years we were friends, you didn't trust me?'

'After what I saw in Sonea's mind, I realised I didn't know you at all.'

Akkarin's brows rose. 'That's understandable. It is a powerful thing, this belief that black magic is evil.'

'Is it?'

Akkarin frowned, his eyes focussing far beyond the floor. 'Yes.'

'Then why practice it?' Lorlen demanded. He held up the hand bearing the ring. 'Why this?'

'I cannot tell you. Be assured, I'm not intending to take over the Guild.'

'You don't have to. You're already High Lord.'

The corner of Akkarin's mouth curled up. 'I am, aren't I? Then be assured that I'm not about to destroy the Guild, or anything else you hold dear.' Putting down his glass, he rose and moved to the serving table. Filling another glass, he handed it to Lorlen.

'I will tell you one day, Lorlen. I promise you that.'

Lorlen stared at Akkarin. The dark eyes were steady. Lorlen accepted the glass and reassurance reluctantly.

'I'll hold you to that.'

Akkarin opened his mouth to reply, but stopped at a faint knock from the door. He straightened and narrowed his eyes.

The door swung open. The glow from Akkarin's globe light barely reached Sonea's eyes as she stepped inside, head bowed.

'Good evening, Sonea,' Akkarin said smoothly.

She bowed. 'Good evening, High Lord, Administrator,' she replied in a quiet voice.

'What did you do today?'

She looked down at the books she was holding to her chest. 'Some reading.'

'With the libraries closed, you must have little to choose from. Are there any books you would like to buy?'

'No, High Lord.'

'Other entertainments can be arranged if you wish.'

'No, thank you, High Lord.'

One of Akkarin's eyebrows rose, and then he waved a hand. 'You may go.'

Looking relieved, she hurried to the left-hand staircase. Lorlen felt a pang of guilt and sympathy as he watched her go.

'She must be miserable,' he murmured.

'Hmmm. Her reticence is irritating,' Akkarin said quietly, as if to himself. Moving back to his chair, he retrieved his glass of wine.

'So tell me, have Peakin and Davin resolved their little dispute yet?'

* * *

Leaning against the window, Rothen stared at the little square of light on the other side of the gardens. He had seen the slight figure approach the residence a few minutes before. A moment later the light had appeared. Now he was certain that the room behind that window was Sonea's.

A light tap at the door drew his attention away. Tania walked inside, carrying a jug of water and a small jar. She set them down on the table.

'Lady Indria said you should avoid taking it on an empty stomach,' Tania told him.

'I know,' Rothen replied. 'I've used it before.' He moved from the window and picked up the jar. The soporific was an innocuous grey, but he had never forgotten how vile it tasted.

'Thank you, Tania. You may go.'

'Sleep well,' she said. Bowing, she moved to the door.

'Wait.' Rothen straightened and regarded his servant carefully. 'Would you . . . can you . . .?'

She smiled. 'I'll let you know if I overhear anything.'

He nodded. 'Thank you.'

After she had left, he sat down and mixed some of the powder in water. Forcing himself to swallow it in one draught, he leaned back and waited for the drug to take effect. The taste brought back a memory of a face he sometimes thought he'd forgotten, and he felt a stab of pain.

Yilara, my wife. Even after all this time I still mourn you. But I suppose I would never forgive myself if I stopped.

He had resolved to always remember his wife as she had been when healthy, not as she had been at the end, wasted with her illness. He smiled as happier memories returned.

Still smiling, still in his chair, he slipped into a peaceful sleep.

CHAPTER 24

A REQUEST

As she left the Baths, Sonea thought of the past two weeks and was surprised to feel some regret that the break was over. She had spent most of the time exploring the University, reading or, on warmer days, walking up through the forest to the spring.

In some ways, little had changed. She still planned her movements about the Guild to avoid someone. Akkarin was far easier to avoid than Regin, however. The only time she saw him was in the evenings, when she returned to the High Lord's Residence.

A servant had been assigned to her. Unlike Tania, Viola was distant and businesslike. Having noted Sonea's habit of rising early, she always appeared just after dawn. It had taken several requests before the woman finally brought a jar of raka powder, and her expression when the aroma filled Sonea's room spoke clearly of her distaste for the stimulant so loved by the slum dwellers.

Each morning, Sonea left the High Lord's Residence and headed to the Baths, where she soaked in luxuriously warm water and decided how she would fill the day. Relaxation allowed hunger to catch up with her, and she visited the Foodhall next. A small number of cooks and servers catered for the handful of novices who had remained in the Guild. Bored, and eager to cultivate opportunities for future positions serving the Houses, they encouraged these novices to request favourite meals. Though Sonea had no high connections, the younger cooks indulged her as well, no doubt because of the incal on her sleeve.

After eating, Sonea would pace through the passages of the University to reinforce her memory of the plan. From time to time she would stop in a quiet room and open a book, sometimes reading for hours before she decided to move on again. As evening settled in, however, her dread would slowly return until she could no longer concentrate on reading. She had been given no hour to return by. Though she had tried arriving at the residence later and later, Akkarin was always there, waiting for her. After a week she had resigned herself to this daily encounter, and started to return at a time that allowed her to get a good night's sleep.

Just as she had been getting used to her new routine, the break ended. She had spent most of the previous afternoon at a University window, watching carriages coming and going. On most days, when the Guild was filled with magicians, it was easy to forget that wives, husbands and children also lived in the grounds. Sonea had realised how few she could name. Deciding she ought to know more about her future colleagues, she had begun to note family groups, and the House incals on the carriages they arrived in.

There had been a lack of formality to this homecoming. While servants had been kept busy hauling baggage and tending horses, magicians and their spouses had paused to chat with others. Children had run into the gardens to play in the snow. Novices had gathered in knots of brown robes, their shouts and laughter audible through the University windows.

But today, magicians were striding about the grounds, clearly the masters of their domain. Servants hurried about, but the families she had watched were nowhere to be seen. Novices were everywhere.

Walking toward the University, Sonea felt a familiar uneasiness. Though she was sure Regin wouldn't dare harass the High Lord's favourite, she created a barrier about herself just in case. Reaching the stairs, she noted that the novice in front of her was shivering and rubbing his arms. A newcomer, she mused. Lord Vorel had claimed that the winter intake novices always learned to shield faster than those who started training in summer. Now she understood why.

'That's her.'

'Who?'

The whispers came from behind her. She resisted the urge to glance behind as she continued up the stairs.

'The slum girl.'

'So it's true?'

'Yes. Mother says it isn't right. She says there are plenty of novices as strong as her. Ones that don't have a bad history.'

'My father says it's an insult to the Houses – and even the Administrator didn't . . .'

The rest was lost as Sonea turned into the corridor on the second floor. Pausing, she examined the novices in the corridor ahead, then began to walk. Unlike the first time she had appeared as Akkarin's novice, they did not stare at her. Instead, they looked once, scowled, then turned away. Eyebrows rose and meaningful looks were exchanged.

This is not *good*, she thought.

As she approached her classroom, she felt a rising dread.

She paused at the doorway to take a deep breath, then stepped inside. The teacher who looked up at her was surprisingly young. It could not have been many years since he'd graduated. She glanced at her schedule for his name.

'Lord Larkin,' she said, bowing.

To her relief, he smiled. 'Take a seat, Sonea.'

Only half of the other novices had arrived. A few watched her as she moved to her usual position by the window. Their expressions weren't friendly, but they weren't disapproving, either. The feeling of dread eased.

Larkin rose. Seeing that he was approaching her desk, she sighed. No doubt he would want her to move closer to the front.

'The High Lord asked me to tell you he wishes to see you after the next class,' he told her quietly. 'You are to return to his residence.'

Sonea felt all warmth leave her face. Guessing that she had turned pale, she looked down at her desk, hoping he hadn't noticed. 'Thank you, my lord.'

Larkin turned away and moved back to his desk. Sonea swallowed hard. What did Akkarin want? Frightening scenarios came to mind, and she jumped when Larkin rose and began to address the class. Looking around, she realised that the rest of the novices had arrived.

'The history of magician-designed architecture is a long one,' Larkin told the class. 'Parts are unbearably dry, but I will skip as many of those as possible. Instead, I will begin with the story of Lord Loren, the architect who designed the University.'

Thinking of the map she had drawn up of the University passages, Sonea straightened in her seat. This would be interesting. Taking sheets of paper from his desk, Larkin walked up and down the rows of desks, handing one to each novice.

'This is a rough plan of the top level of the University – a copy of a sketch drawn by the man himself,' Larkin said. 'Lord Loren's early work was often unstable and ridiculous in appearance. He was considered to be an artist obsessed with making large, impractical sculptures rather than habitable buildings, but his discovery of the methods of shaping and strengthening stone with magic changed more than architecture. He began to make buildings that people wanted to live in.'

Larkin waved a hand at the ceiling. 'The University is one of his finest works. By the time Lord Loren was requested to design and construct the new Guild buildings, he was famous throughout the world for his work.' Larkin paused to chuckle. 'The Guild still felt it necessary to stipulate in their guidelines that he wasn't to use spirals in the design – something he was known to do in excess.

'However, the use of spirals can be found in the glass ceiling above the Guildhall and the staircases of the Entrance Hall,' Larkin continued. 'From the diaries and records kept by other magicians of that era, we know Lord Loren was a devious character at the best of times. Over a hundred years later a magician named Lord Rendo wrote a book detailing the architect's career. I have included with the plan a few extracts of this biography and a chronology of his life and works. Read them now. After class you may want to look around the grounds at the buildings he designed. You will, as I did, see much that you had not noticed before. I will expect an essay on his work in three weeks from today.'

As the other novices began to read, Sonea looked down at the plan of the University. The four towers at each corner and the huge room at the centre were clearly drawn, as was the design of the glass ceiling, but the rooms and passages on either side of the main corridor were unmarked.

She took her map out of her box and lay it next to the plan. After staring at both, she started copying the ceiling design onto her own sketch. As she suspected, the lines that marked the spirals in the glass met those showing the passages. Though the passage turns were at right angles, they combined with the ceiling design to form even larger spirals.

'What are you doing, Sonea?'

Realising that the teacher was standing over her desk, she felt her face heat.

'I . . . I thought of what you said about spirals, my lord,' she explained, 'and started looking for them.'

Larkin tilted his head and examined her sketch, then pointed to the inner passages she had marked. 'I've looked at the University plans many times but I've never seen this many. Where did you get this plan?'

'I, ah, made it. I didn't have much else to do over the break. I hope I wasn't going anywhere I wasn't supposed to.'

He shook his head. 'The only place in the University that is forbidden to novices is the Guildhall and the Administrator's office.'

'But . . . those rooms between the normal passages and the decorated ones. They seemed to be a kind of barrier.'

Larkin nodded. 'In the past they were locked, but as more space was needed it was decided that the inner areas should be accessible to all.'

Sonea thought of the disapproving look she had received

from the magician she encountered the first night of exploration. Perhaps he had merely been suspicious of a novice wandering about alone. Perhaps he simply distrusted the slum girl.

'Would you mind if I took a copy of your plan?' Larkin asked.

'I'll draw one for you if you like,' she offered.

He smiled. 'Thank you, Sonea.'

As he moved away, Sonea watched him speculatively. There didn't seem to be any of the disapproval or disdain in his manner that she was used to from the other teachers. Would only the novices resent her now? She glanced around the room and saw several heads turn away, but one caught her gaze.

Regin's eyes bored into her own. Looking away, Sonea shivered. How had she ever earned such unveiled hatred?

Every time she had done well in class, he had managed to equal or surpass her. He was better at Warrior Skills, so if this was about being better than her, he was winning.

But now she had succeeded in a way that he could never match. She had become the High Lord's favourite. To make it worse, he dared not make her suffer for it.

She sighed. *He wouldn't be so jealous if he knew what was really going on. I'd swap places any day. He'd be scared out of his wits . . .*

Or would he? Would Regin, who relished having power and influence and was willing to harm others to get it, be able to resist the lure of black magic? No, he'd probably want to join Akkarin. She shuddered. Regin as a black magician. The idea was truly frightening.

* * *

As Dannyl stepped into the Guild House, Ambassador Errend strolled out of the audience room.

'Welcome back, Ambassador Dannyl.'

'Thank you, Ambassador Errend,' Dannyl replied, inclining his head politely. 'It is good to be back. If I ever get it into my head to go sailing around the world again, please remind me of the last two weeks.'

The Ambassador smiled. 'Ah, sea travel does lose its romance after the first few journeys.'

Dannyl grimaced. 'Especially if you encounter a storm.'

Though Errend's face did not change much, Dannyl was sure he saw a hint of smugness in the man's expression. 'Well, you're on solid ground now,' the man said. 'No doubt you'll want to rest for the remainder of the day. You can tell me of your adventures tonight.'

'Have I missed much?'

'Of course.' Errend smiled. 'This is Capia.' He took a step back toward the audience room, then paused. 'Some urgent letters arrived for you two days ago. Do you want to read them now, or wait until tomorrow?'

Dannyl nodded, curious despite his weariness. 'Have them sent to my room. Thank you, Ambassador.'

The big man inclined his head gracefully, then turned away. Walking down the main corridor of the house, Dannyl considered the work ahead of him. He expected that there was much work to catch up on, and he had a report to compile for Lorlen. It wouldn't be easy to find time to visit the Great Library.

But his research would continue through other means as well. The invitation to Bel Arralade's party would probably be among the letters waiting for him. He had to admit, he was looking forward to it. It had been some time since he'd exercised his gossip-gathering skills.

When he had returned from the small Baths within the Guild House, he found a pile of letters on his desk. Sitting down, he spread them out and immediately recognised the elegant handwriting of Administrator Lorlen.

Breaking the seal, he unfolded the thick paper and began to read.

> *To Second Guild Ambassador to Elyne, Dannyl, of family Vorin, House Tellen.*
>
> *It has been brought to my attention recently that some people believe you have spent less time attending to your ambassadorial duties than you have to 'personal' research. You have my gratitude for the time and effort you have given to my request. The work you have done has been invaluable. However, to prevent further questions arising, I must ask you to cease your research. Further reports will not be needed.*
>
> *Administrator Lorlen.*

Letting the letter fall to the desk, Dannyl stared at it in astonishment. All the travelling and studying of books, and now it was all to be abandoned because of a few gossips? Obviously the research hadn't been that important, after all.

Then he smiled. He had only assumed there was a good reason for reviving Akkarin's quest for ancient magical knowledge. When his own curiosity had lagged in the face of reading some particularly boring old books and the discomfort of sea travel, his enthusiasm had been sustained by the thought that there might be a more significant reason for gathering the information than simply continuing Akkarin's research. Perhaps Akkarin had been on the brink of rediscovering a valuable method of using magic, and Lorlen wanted another to take up the search. Perhaps a lost piece of history was to be found.

But Lorlen had, in just a few scribbled lines, put an end to the research as if it meant nothing after all.

Shaking his head, Dannyl folded the letter and put it aside. Tayend would be disappointed, he mused. They had no reason to attend Bel Arralade's party now. Not that it would keep either of them from going – and he would still visit his friend at the library. Without Lorlen's request as excuse, he would have to find another 'public' reason to talk to the scholar ... perhaps something else to research ...

Dannyl stilled. Was Tayend the reason Lorlen had stopped the research? Had Lorlen heard the gossip about Tayend, and grown concerned that questions about Dannyl's reputation would re-emerge?

Dannyl frowned down at the letters. How could he know if this was the true reason? It was not as if he could ask Lorlen.

Another Guild symbol among the letters caught his eye. Picking up the letter, he smiled as he recognised Rothen's sturdy handwriting. Straightening, he broke the seal and began to read.

To Ambassador Dannyl.

I am not sure when you will read this, as I have heard that you have been visiting other lands. No doubt you are familiarising yourself with the peoples you may need to work with in the future. If I had realised the duties of ambassador included travelling the world, I may have put aside my teaching years ago. I'm sure you'll have plenty of stories to tell me when you visit us again.

I have news, but you may have heard it already. I am no longer Sonea's guardian. She has been chosen by the High Lord. While others believe this to be an extraordinary turn of good fortune for Sonea, I am not pleased. I am sure you'll understand why. Along with the loss of her company, I am left with a feeling of having left a work unfinished.

So, at Yaldin's suggestion, I have adopted a new interest to replace the old. You will, no doubt, be amused to hear of it. I have decided to compile a book about ancient magical practices. It is a task Akkarin began ten years ago, and I am determined to complete it.

From what I recall, Akkarin began his search at the Great Library. Since you are living close to the library, I thought I might ask if you would visit it for me. If you do not have time, is there anyone you have met who might be trusted with such a task? They would need to be discreet, since I do not want to give the High Lord the impression I am investigating his past! It would, however, be satisfying to succeed where he failed. I know you will appreciate the irony.

Yours in friendship, Lord Rothen.

P.S. Dorrien visited for a few weeks. He asked me to forward his congratulations and good wishes to you.

Dannyl read the letter twice, then chuckled. He had never seen Rothen fail to achieve something he had set out to do. Mostly these 'interests' were the novices he took guardianship of. To lose Sonea to the High Lord must sting.

Yet having the High Lord choose her was no failure. Without Rothen's hard work contributing to her success, Sonea may not have caught Akkarin's eye. Dannyl nodded. He must remember to say that in his reply.

He scanned the letter again, slowing as he reread Rothen's request for assistance. He did appreciate the irony, but even more amusing was that Rothen should ask for the same information that Lorlen had just decided he was no longer interested in. Quite a coincidence.

Dannyl picked up Lorlen's letter and unfolded it. Looking from one letter to the other, he felt the skin tingle at the back of his neck. *Was* this a coincidence? He stared at the two letters for some time, noting the hurried marks of Lorlen's and the carefully shaped letters of Rothen's. What was going on here?

If he set aside all speculation, only three certainties remained. Firstly, Lorlen had wanted to know what Akkarin had learned on his journey, and now didn't. Secondly, Rothen now wanted the same information that Akkarin had sought. Thirdly, both Lorlen and Rothen wanted the search to remain a secret, and Akkarin had never made his own discoveries public.

There was a mystery here. Even if Rothen hadn't requested his help, Dannyl might have been curious enough to continue the research for his own interest. Now he was determined to. After all, he hadn't spent several weeks at sea to just abandon everything.

Smiling to himself, he folded the letters and placed them with his notes on Akkarin's journey.

At every step from the University to the High Lord's Residence, the knot in Sonea's stomach tightened. By the time she had reached the door her heart was racing. She paused, took a deep breath, and tapped the handle.

As always, it swung open at the first touch. She felt her mouth go dry as she looked inside the guestroom. Akkarin was sitting in one of the chairs, waiting for her.

'Come in, Sonea.'

Swallowing, she forced herself to step inside and bow, keeping her eyes to the floor. Robes rustled softly as he rose from the chair. Her heart skipped as he walked toward her. She stepped back and felt her heel meet the door behind her.

'I have had a meal prepared for us.'

She barely heard him, conscious only of the hand that reached toward her. His fingers curled around the handle of her box. At his touch she jerked her hand back, surrendering the box. He set it on a low table.

'Follow me.'

As he turned away she took a deep breath and let it out slowly. She started after him, then stopped as she realised he was heading for the stairs that led to the underground room. As if sensing her hesitation, he turned to look at her.

'Come along. Takan will not be pleased if the food goes cold.'

Food. A meal. Surely he didn't eat down there. She sighed with relief as he began to ascend the stairs. Forcing herself to move, she entered the stairwell and followed him up.

Reaching the corridor, Akkarin passed two doors before stopping at a third. The door swung open, and he stepped aside, gesturing for her to enter.

Looking into the room beyond, Sonea saw a large

polished table surrounded by lavishly decorated chairs. Plates, forks and glasses had been laid out on the table.

A formal meal. Why?

'Go on,' he murmured.

She glanced at him, catching a glitter of amusement in his eyes before stepping through the door. He followed and pointed to a chair.

'Please, sit.' Moving around the table, he settled into the opposite chair.

Obeying, she wondered how she was going to eat. Her appetite had fled with Lord Larkin's message. Perhaps she could say she wasn't hungry. Perhaps he would let her go.

She looked down at the table, then caught her breath. Everything before her was made of gold: cutlery, plates and even the rims of the glasses were coated with it. A half-forgotten thrill of temptation ran through her. It would be so easy to slip one of these forks into her clothing when he wasn't looking. Though she was not as quick-fingered as she had once been, she had tested herself now and then by playing tricks on Rothen. Just one of these beautiful forks could fetch a fortune – or, at least, enough to live on until she found some remote place to disappear in.

But I can't leave. Frustrated, she wondered if it would be worth stealing something just to annoy him.

She jumped then, as she realised that Akkarin's servant was standing beside her. Disturbed that she had not heard him approaching, she watched as he poured wine into her glass, then moved around the table to perform the same service for Akkarin.

Since she left her room early, and returned late, she had only glimpsed the servant a few times. Now, looking closer, she shivered as she realised she had seen him before, in the underground room, helping Akkarin perform the black magic ritual.

'How were your lessons today, Sonea?'

Startled, she looked at Akkarin, then quickly evaded his eyes.

'Interesting, High Lord.'

'What did you learn?'

'About magician-designed architecture. Lord Loren's designs.'

'Ah, Lord Loren. Your investigation of the University passages must have familiarised you with some of his peculiarities.'

She kept her eyes lowered. So he knew about her exploration of the University. Had he watched her? Followed her? Despite Lord Larkin's assurances that she had not ventured anywhere forbidden to novices, she felt her face warming. Taking her glass, she sipped at the wine. It was sweet and strong.

'How are your classes with Lord Yikmo going?'

She winced. What should she say? Disappointing? Awful? Humiliating?

'You don't like the Warrior Skills.'

It was a statement. She decided she didn't need to reply. Instead, she took another mouthful of wine.

'Warrior Skills are important. They draw on everything that you learn in the other disciplines, then challenge your understanding of them. Only in battle do you find the limits of your strength, knowledge and Control. It is a pity Rothen neglected to arrange extra training when you first showed a weakness in this part of your education.'

Sonea felt a stab of hurt and anger at his criticism of

388

Rothen. 'I guess he saw no need for it,' she replied. 'We're not at war, or under any threat of it.'

One of Akkarin's long fingers tapped the base of his glass.

'Do you think it is wise to throw away all our knowledge of war during times of peace?'

Sonea shook her head, suddenly wishing she hadn't volunteered an opinion. 'No.'

'Then shouldn't we preserve our knowledge and keep ourselves well practised in its use?'

'Yes, but . . .' She paused. *Why am I arguing with him?*

'But?' he prompted.

'You don't need every magician to do it.'

'Don't we?'

She cursed silently. Why was he even bothering to discuss this with her? He didn't care if she was good at Warrior Skills. He just wanted her occupied and out of his way.

'Perhaps Rothen neglected that part of your training because you are a woman.'

She shrugged. 'Perhaps.'

'Perhaps he was right. In the last five years the few young women who considered becoming Warriors were persuaded otherwise. Do you think that is fair?'

She frowned at this question. He knew that she did not want to join the Warriors, so he could only be asking in an effort to draw her into conversation. If she co-operated, would this lead into dangerous territory? Should she refuse to talk to him?

Before she could decide whether to answer or not, the door behind Akkarin opened and Takan entered carrying a large tray. A delicious smell followed him to the table.

The servant placed bowls and plates in a line between her and Akkarin, then put the tray under his arm and began to describe each dish.

Sonea's stomach stirred with hunger. At each savoury breath the knots within it untied.

'Thank you, Takan,' Akkarin murmured as the servant finished. Takan bowed. As he left, Akkarin picked up a serving ladle and began to select from the dishes.

From a few formal meals with Rothen, Sonea knew that this was the traditional way the Kyralian Houses entertained guests. In the slums, food was eaten with little preparation, and the only utensils used were the knives each person carried. The uniquely Kyralian tradition of serving food in small, bite-sized pieces required more preparation, and the more formal the meal, the more elaborate the food and utensils for eating it.

Fortunately, Rothen had made her memorise the purposes of all the different forks, ladles, tweezers and skewers. If Akkarin had thought he would humble her by drawing attention to her lack of 'proper' upbringing, then he would be disappointed.

She helped herself to the dishes, first ladling onto her plate some of the rassook pieces wrapped in brasi leaves. As she skewered a piece with her fork and placed it between her teeth, she realised Akkarin had paused to watch her.

A delicious flavour filled her mouth. Surprised, she ate another. Soon her plate was empty, and she was eyeing the next dish.

As she sampled each of the dishes, she forgot all else. Slivers of fish were served in a tangy, red marin sauce. Mysterious parcels were stuffed with herbs and harrel mince. Large purple crots, beans she had always hated, were coated with a salty crumb that made them irresistible.

She had never tasted food so delicious. The meals in the University had always been good, and she had listened to the other novices' complaints in disbelief. This meal, however, explained how they could find the Foodhall wanting.

At Takan's return, she looked up and discovered Akkarin watching her, his chin resting on one hand. Averting her eyes, she watched Takan gather the empty plates and bowls, then carry them away.

'What did you think of the food?'

Sonea nodded. 'Good.'

'Takan is an excellent cook.'

'He made all this himself?' She could not hide the surprise in her voice.

'Yes, though he has an assistant to stir the pots for him.'

Takan returned with two bowls, which he set in front of them. Looking down, Sonea felt her mouth water. Pale crescents of pachi fruit glistened in a thick syrup. The first mouthful revealed a sweetness sharpened with an alcoholic tang. She ate slowly, savouring each mouthful. *Meals like this might be worth suffering his company for*, she thought.

'I want you to dine here with me every Firstday night.'

Sonea froze. Had he read her mind? Or was this what he had intended all along?

'But I have evening classes,' she protested.

'Takan is aware of the time allowed for the evening meal. You will not miss your lessons.'

She looked down at the empty bowl.

'But you *will* miss your class tonight, if I keep you any longer,' he added. 'You are dismissed, Sonea.'

Relieved, she all but leapt out of the chair, then put a hand on the table to steady herself as her head began to spin. Still a little dizzy, she bowed then headed for the door.

Pausing in the corridor to catch her balance, she heard a murmur from the room behind her.

'Less wine next time, Takan.'

'It was the dessert, master.'

CHAPTER 25

TURNING UP IN ODD PLACES

Catching sight of Narron and Trassia heading toward the next class, Sonea sighed. For once she wished she was joining them, but only half of her schedule matched theirs now. Her destination for the morning was a small room deep within the University passages where Lord Yikmo was waiting to give her another Warrior Skills lesson.

Turning from the main corridor into a side passage, she walked slowly, feeling a gloom descend over her. The Arena was occupied for all daytime classes, so Yikmo held his lessons in a magically protected room within the University. Only small surges of magic were used, in complicated games that were supposed to sharpen her wits and reflexes.

Turning another corner, she all but collided with a magician. Keeping her eyes down, she started to mutter an apology.

'Sonea!'

Recognising the voice, she looked up at Rothen and felt her heart skip. At once, they both glanced over their shoulders. The passage was empty.

'It's good to see you.' He gazed at her searchingly, his face creasing with lines she could not remember having noticed before. 'How are you?'

She shrugged. 'Still around.'

He nodded, his expression grim. 'How is he treating you?'

'I hardly see him.' She grimaced. 'Too many classes. I think that's what he intended.'

She looked over her shoulder again as she heard distant footsteps drawing near.

'I have to go. Lord Yikmo is expecting me.'

'Of course.' He hesitated. 'According to my schedule, I'm teaching your class tomorrow.'

'Yes.' She smiled slyly. 'I guess it would seem strange if the High Lord's novice wasn't taught by the Guild's best chemistry teacher.'

His face smoothed a little, but he didn't smile. Forcing herself to turn away, she continued down the corridor. She heard no footsteps behind her, and knew he was watching her go.

He looks different, she thought as she turned into another passage. *So much older. Or has he always looked old, but I didn't notice?* Without warning, tears sprang into her eyes. Stopping, she leaned against a wall, blinking furiously. *Not here! Not now! I must get control of myself!* She drew a long, ragged breath and slowly let it out, then another.

A gong rang out, the sound vibrating through the wall behind her. Hoping her eyes weren't red, she hurried down the passage. As she came in sight of the door of Yikmo's room, it opened and, catching a glimpse of a black sleeve, Sonea skidded to a halt.

No. I can't face him. Not now. Dashing back around the last turn, she hurried down the passage to where it intersected with another, then ducked out of sight. Turning, she peered back around the corner. She could hear the murmur of familiar voices, but she could not hear what they were saying.

'Well, well. This is interesting.'

Spinning around, Sonea found Regin standing in the opposite passage, his arms crossed. 'I thought you'd be following your guardian around, not hiding from him.'

She felt her face warming. 'What are you doing here, Regin?'

He smiled. 'Oh, I just happened along.'

'Why aren't you in class?'

'Why aren't you?'

She shook her head. This was pointless. 'Why am I wasting my time talking to you?'

'Because he's still there,' Regin said, smiling slyly. 'And you're too scared to face him.'

She regarded him carefully, weighing up possible responses. He would not believe a denial, and saying nothing would only confirm his suspicions.

'Scared?' She snorted. 'No more than you.'

'Really?' He took a step closer. 'What are you waiting for then? The gong has rung. You're late, and your guardian is around to notice. So why are you still delaying? Or perhaps I should call out and let him know you're hiding down here.'

She glared at him. Would he? Probably, if he thought it would get her in trouble. Yet if she left now, she would be giving in to his goading.

Better to give in, than to have him call out to Akkarin. Rolling her eyes, she turned on her heel and stalked down the passage. As she neared the end, a black figure strode past the passage entrance and she froze.

To her relief, Akkarin didn't notice her. He walked past

and she heard his footsteps fading as he continued along the corridor. She heard a chuckle of satisfaction from behind. Glancing over her shoulder, she saw Regin watching her, smiling.

She turned away and stepped into the corridor. Why was he so interested in whether she was scared of Akkarin or not? She shook her head. Of course, any sign that she was unhappy would give him pleasure.

But why hadn't he been in class? What reason could he possibly have for being in this part of the University?

Surely he hadn't been following her . . .

A gust of cold air greeted Lorlen as he opened the door to his office. The draught picked up a number of messages that had been slipped under the door for him and blew them out into the corridor. Seeing the number of them, he sighed and swept them inside again with a little magic.

Closing the door, he stomped across the room to his desk.

'You're not in the best mood today.'

Jumping at the voice, Lorlen cast around for the owner. Akkarin was sitting in one of the chairs, his dark eyes reflecting the light diffused by the window screens.

How did he get in here? Lorlen stared at Akkarin, tempted to demand an explanation. But the temptation faded as the High Lord returned his stare. Looking away, Lorlen concentrated on the messages scattered around the floor. He sent them fluttering across the room and into his hand, then sorted through them.

'What's bothering you, my friend?'

Lorlen shrugged. 'Peakin and Davin are still at each other's throats, Garrel wants me to allow Regin to resume lessons with Balkan, and Jerrik just passed on another request from Tya for an assistant.'

'All within your ability to solve, Administrator.'

Lorlen snorted at the use of his title. 'What would you have me do, High Lord?' he asked mockingly.

Akkarin chuckled. 'You know our little family better than I, Lorlen.' He pursed his lips thoughtfully. 'Say "yes" to Garrel, "no" to Lady Tya, and as for Davin . . . his idea that we rebuild the Lookout so he can observe the weather is interesting. The Guild hasn't built anything for a long time, and a lookout tower has military value – which would please Captain Arin. He's been trying to persuade me to rebuild the Outer Wall since he became Military Adviser to the King.'

Lorlen frowned. 'Surely you're not serious. A project like that would be expensive and time-consuming. Our time would be better spent . . .' Lorlen paused. 'Did you say "yes" to Garrel? Would you have Regin's punishment for attacking Sonea ended six months early?'

Akkarin shrugged. 'Do you really think he'll cause Sonea trouble now? The boy has talent. It is a shame to waste it.'

Lorlen nodded slowly. 'It would . . . reduce the sting of having his adversary favoured by the High Lord.'

'Balkan would agree.'

Placing the messages on his desk, Lorlen moved to his seat. 'But this isn't what you came to see me about, is it?'

Akkarin's long fingers drummed on the arm of his chair. 'No.' His eyes were thoughtful. 'Is there any way we can take Rothen from Sonea's Second Year schedule without the change looking suspicious?'

Lorlen sighed. 'Must we?'

Akkarin's expression darkened. 'Yes. We must.'

The scrape of her dragging footsteps echoed in the passage. The morning lesson with Lord Yikmo had been a disaster. Her encounters with Rothen and Regin had also left her feeling too edgy and distracted for memorising plant names in medicines, and too tired to grasp the evening mathematics lesson.

All things considered, it had been a day she would be happy to see end.

Remembering Regin's smug expression, she wondered again what he had concluded. Perhaps he simply enjoyed the thought that she was unhappy about her change of guardian.

So what? she thought. *So long as he leaves me alone, I don't care what he thinks.*

But would he leave her alone? If he decided she was too scared of Akkarin to report his harassment, he might start bothering her again. He would have to be careful to do it when other magicians wouldn't see, however . . .

Only a blurred movement in the corner of her eye warned her. She had no time to dodge away. An arm wrapped around her neck, the other around her waist. The attacker's momentum spun them both around, but the arm about her neck did not loosen.

She struggled, but quickly realised that her attacker was too strong for her. Then a trick Cery had taught her flashed into her mind. The memory was so vivid, she could almost hear Cery's voice . . .

If someone does this, brace your legs – that's right – then reach back and . . .

She felt the man toppling and gave a short laugh of

satisfaction as he fell to the floor. He did not sprawl on his face, however, but nimbly rolled aside and sprang to his feet. Alarmed, she backed away, groping for a knife that wasn't . . . then she stopped and stared at her attacker in surprise.

Lord Yikmo looked strangely unfamiliar in ordinary clothing. A plain sleeveless shirt revealed surprisingly muscular shoulders. He crossed his arms and nodded.

'I thought so.'

Sonea stared at him, her surprise slowly turning to annoyance.

The Warrior smiled. 'I may have found the source of your problem, Sonea.'

She swallowed an angry retort. 'What is it, then?'

'From your reaction just now it's clear that your first response to an attack is physical. You learned that defensive manoeuvre in the slums, didn't you?'

She nodded reluctantly.

'Did you have a particular trainer?'

'No.'

He frowned. 'How did you know what to do?'

'My friends taught me.'

'Friends? These would be young people, yes? No older trainers?'

'An old whore once showed me how to use my knife if I was . . . in a certain situation.'

His brows rose. 'I see. Street fighting. Defensive manoeuvres. Little wonder you use it first. It's what you know best, and you know it works. We have to change that.' He waved a hand, gesturing for her to walk beside him, and started down the passage toward the main corridor.

'You have to learn to react magically rather than physically,' he told her. 'I can devise exercises that will help you do that. I have to warn you, though, this kind of relearning can be quite slow and difficult. Persevere, however, and you'll be using magic without thinking by the end of the year.'

She shook her head. 'Without thinking? That's the opposite to what the other teachers say.'

'Yes. That is because most novices are too eager to use magic. They must be taught restraint. But you are no ordinary novice, and so ordinary teaching methods may be discarded.'

Sonea considered that. It made sense. Then something else occurred to her. 'How do you know that I didn't think of using magic first, but decided not to?'

'I know you were acting on your instincts. You went looking for a knife. You didn't stop to think about *that*, did you?'

'No, but that's different. If someone attacks me like that, I have to assume he really wants to hurt me.'

'So you were quite prepared to hurt me in return?'

She nodded. 'Of course.'

His brows rose. 'Few would condemn an ordinary man or woman if he or she killed another in self-defence, but if a magician kills a non-magician it is an outrage. You have the power to defend yourself, so there is no excuse for killing, no matter what your attacker's intent – not even if the attacker is a magician. When confronted with such an attack your first reaction should be to shield yourself. That is another good reason to change your first reaction to a magical rather than physical one.'

As they reached the main corridor, Yikmo smiled and patted her shoulder.

'You're not doing as badly as you think, Sonea. If you'd struck out at me with magic, or simply froze or screamed, I would have been disappointed. Instead, you kept calm, thought quickly, and succeeded in throwing me off. I think that's an impressive start. Good night.'

She bowed and watched him stride down the corridor toward the Magician's Quarters. Turning away, she walked in the other direction.

'You have the power to defend yourself, so there is no excuse for killing, no matter what your attacker's intent – not even if the attacker is a magician.' Yet when she had reached for a knife, she had been prepared to kill. It would have seemed reasonable once, but now she wasn't so sure.

Whatever the reason, the punishment for a magician who deliberately harmed someone, even if by non-magical means, was harsh and that was enough reason to change her thinking. She did not want to spend the rest of her days in prison, with her powers blocked. If her instinctive reaction was to kill, then she had best unlearn it as soon as possible.

Anyway, what use to her were the tricks that she had learned in the slum now? When she considered what she was capable of, she doubted that she would ever need to wield a knife again. If she needed to defend herself in the future, she thought with a shiver, it would be against magic.

CHAPTER 26

A JEALOUS RIVAL

As the carriage moved away from the Guild House, Dannyl considered everything he knew about the Bel Arralade. A widow of middle years, she was the head of one of the richest families in Elyne. Her four children – two daughters and two sons – had married into powerful families. Though the Bel herself had never remarried, rumours told of many amorous encounters between Arralade and other members of the Elyne court.

The carriage turned a corner, then another, and stopped. Looking through the window, Dannyl saw that it had joined a long line of fashionably decorated vehicles.

'How many people attend these parties?' he asked.

Ambassador Errend shrugged. 'Three or four hundred.'

Impressed, Dannyl counted the carriages. The line extended out of view, so he could not guess how long it was. Enterprising street hawkers strode up and down the street, offering their wares to the occupants of the carriages. Wine, sweets, cakes, and all manner of diversions were available. Musicians played and acrobats performed. The best of them were persuaded with a steady stream of glittering coins to linger beside bored courtiers.

'We could walk faster than this,' Dannyl said.

Errend chuckled. 'Yes, we could try, but we would not

get far. Someone would call us over and insist we travel with them, and it would be impolite to refuse.'

He bought a small box of sweets and, as they shared them, told stories about previous parties held by Bel Arralade. It was during times like these that Dannyl was grateful that the First Guild Ambassador was a native to this land, and could explain the Elyne customs. Dannyl was surprised to hear that small children were allowed to attend.

'Children are indulged here,' Errend warned. 'We Elynes like to spoil them when they're young. Unfortunately, they can be little tyrants to magicians, expecting us to perform for them like entertainers.'

Dannyl smiled. 'All children believe a magician's primary role is to amuse them.'

Much later, the carriage door opened and Dannyl followed Errend out to stand before a typical Capian mansion. Well-dressed servants greeted then directed them through a grand archway. A large room followed, open to the elements as the Palace forecourt had been. The air was chilly, and the guests who had arrived before them were hurrying toward doors at the far end.

Beyond was a larger, circular room filled with people. The light of several chandeliers fell on myriad brightly coloured costumes. A constant buzz of voices echoed back from the domed ceiling and the mingled scents of flowers, fruit and spices were almost overpowering.

Heads turned, most only long enough to note who had arrived. Dems and Bels of all ages were present. A few magicians stood among them. Children, dressed in miniature versions of adult clothing, ran about or crowded together on bench seats. Servants were everywhere, each dressed in yellow and carrying platters of food or bottles of wine.

'What a remarkable woman this Bel Arralade must be,' Dannyl murmured. 'If you put this many members of the Kyralian Houses together – outside of the court – swords would be drawn within half an hour.'

'Yes,' Errend agreed. 'But weapons will be drawn tonight, Dannyl. We Elynes find words sharper than swords. They don't make such a mess of the furnishings.'

A grand stairway led up to a balcony that ran around the entire room. Looking up, Dannyl saw Tayend watching him from behind the railing. The scholar gave a slight bow. Resisting the temptation to smile at this stiff formality, Dannyl inclined his head in reply.

Beside Tayend stood a muscular young man. Seeing his companion's half-bow, the man frowned and looked down. As he saw Dannyl, the man's eyes widened in surprise and he quickly looked away.

Dannyl turned back to Errend. The Ambassador was helping himself to the contents of a platter offered by one of the brightly-clad servants.

'Try these,' Errend urged. 'They're delicious!'

'What happens now?' Dannyl asked, taking one of the little pastry scrolls.

'We mingle. Stay with me, and I will introduce you to people.'

So for the next few hours Dannyl followed his fellow Ambassador about the room and concentrated on memorising names and titles. Errend warned him that no meal would be served, that the latest fashion in entertaining was for guests to graze from the platters of delicacies carried around. Dannyl was given a wine glass and it was so regularly topped up that eventually, to keep his mind clear, he slipped it onto one of the platters when a servant wasn't watching.

When a woman wearing an elaborate yellow dress approached them, Dannyl knew instantly that this was the hostess. Her skin had not been as lined in the portrait he had studied while preparing for his new position, but her bright, alert gaze warned him that she was still the formidable Bel he had heard so much about.

'Ambassador Errend,' she said, bowing slightly. 'And this must be Ambassador Dannyl. Thank you for coming to my party.'

'Thank you for inviting us,' Errend replied, inclining his head.

'I could not hold a party without including the Guild Ambassadors on my guest list,' she said, smiling. 'Magicians have always been the most well-mannered and entertaining guests.' She turned to Dannyl. 'So, Ambassador Dannyl, have you enjoyed your stay in Capia so far?'

'I have indeed,' Dannyl replied. 'It is a beautiful city.'

The conversation continued in this way for several minutes. A woman joined them and drew Errend into conversation. Bel Arralade exclaimed that her feet were already tired, and drew Dannyl aside to a bench seat set within an alcove of the wall.

'I've heard you've taken to researching ancient magic,' she said.

Dannyl regarded her with surprise. Though he and Tayend had avoided discussing the subject of their research to anyone but Librarian Irand, it was possible that their interest had been noted by someone they had met on their journey. Or had Tayend decided that it no longer needed to be a secret now that they were not gathering information for Lorlen, but 'helping' Rothen with his book?

If that were so, a denial would only make her suspicious. 'Yes,' he replied. 'It is an interest of mine.'

'Have you discovered anything new and fascinating?'

He shrugged. 'Nothing very exciting. Just a lot of books and scrolls filled with old languages.'

'But haven't you recently travelled to Lonmar and Vin? Surely you have gathered some interesting stories there.'

He decided to be vague. 'I saw scrolls in Lonmar and tombs in Vindo, but they weren't much more exciting than the musty old books I've been reading. I fear I will bore you if I start describing them in detail – and what will people say if the new Ambassador sends the hostess to sleep at her own party?'

'That must be avoided, at all cost.' She laughed, then her eyes grew misty. 'Ah, but the subject brings back pleasant memories. Your High Lord came here on a similar quest, many years ago. He was such a handsome man. Not a High Lord then, of course. He could have talked for hours about ancient magic, and I would have listened just to have the opportunity to admire him.'

Was that, then, the reason for her interest? Dannyl chuckled. 'Fortunately for you, I know I am not handsome enough to compensate for rambling on about my research.'

She smiled, her eyes flashing. 'Not handsome? I would not say so. Others would say quite the opposite.' She paused, her expression becoming thoughtful. 'But do not think the High Lord rude. While I said that I would have listened to him talk for hours, he never did so. He attended my birthday party, but he had barely returned from Vin when he left for the mountains, and I have never seen him since.'

The mountains? This was new. 'Shall I forward a greeting to him from you, Bel?' he offered.

'Oh, I doubt he remembers me,' she said, waving a hand.

'Nonsense! No man can forget beauty, even if it is merely glimpsed in passing.'

She smiled broadly and gave him a light pat on the arm. 'Oh, I like *you*, Ambassador Dannyl. Now, tell me: what do you think of Tayend of Tremmelin? He was your companion on these journeys, was he not?'

Conscious of the way she watched him from between her long eyelashes, Dannyl considered the answers he had discussed with Tayend.

'My assistant? I found him to be most useful. He has an amazing memory, and his grasp of languages is impressive.'

She nodded. 'But what about personally. Did you find him an agreeable companion?'

'Yes.' Dannyl grimaced. 'Though he didn't travel well, I must say. I've never seen anyone so seasick.'

She hesitated. 'They say he has some unconventional interests. Some, particularly the ladies, find him a little . . . disinterested.'

Dannyl nodded slowly. 'Spending days deep underground, surrounded by books and speaking dead languages, would not make a man attractive to ladies.' He gave her a calculating look. 'Are you playing matchmaker, Bel Arralade?'

She smiled coyly. 'And what if I am?'

'Then I should warn you that I don't know Tayend well enough to be of use. If he has a lady in mind, he has kept the matter to himself.'

Again, she hesitated. 'Then we'll leave him his privacy,'

she said, nodding. 'Matchmaking is a habit as evil as gossip when unwanted. Ah, here's Dem Dorlini. I hoped he would come, as I have a few questions for him.' She rose. 'It was a pleasure talking to you, Ambassador Dannyl. I hope we may converse again soon.'

'I would be honoured, Bel Arralade.'

After a few minutes Dannyl discovered the peril of remaining still and alone. A trio of young girls, their child-sized court clothes stained with food, surrounded him. He kept them entertained with illusions until their parents rescued him. Rising, he started toward Errend, then stopped as he heard his name spoken.

Turning, he saw Tayend approaching, the muscular man at his side.

'Tayend of Tremmelin.'

'Ambassador Dannyl. This is Velend of Genard. A friend,' Tayend said.

The young man's mouth curved, but the smile did not reach his eyes. He bowed stiffly and reluctantly.

'Tayend has told me of your travels,' Velend said. 'Though from his descriptions I don't think I'd find Lonmar to my taste.'

'It is a hot and imposing country,' Dannyl replied. 'I'm sure it would be possible to acclimatise, if one stayed long enough. Are you a scholar, too?'

'No,' the man replied. 'My interests are in swordplay and weaponry. Do you practice, Ambassador?'

'No,' Dannyl replied. 'There is little time for such pursuits for young men who join the Guild.' Swordplay, then. He wondered if that was why he felt this instant dislike of the man. Did Velend remind him too much of Fergun, who also favoured hard weapons?

'I've found a few books that might be of interest, Ambassador,' Tayend said, his tone businesslike. As Tayend began to describe the books, their age and general contents, Dannyl observed Velend shifting his weight from one foot to the other and glancing around at the crowd. Finally, the man interrupted Tayend.

'Excuse me, Tayend, Ambassador Dannyl. There is someone I must speak to.'

As he walked away, Tayend smiled slyly. 'I knew it wouldn't take long to get rid of him.' He paused as a passing couple drew closer to them, and returned to the businesslike tone. 'We've been looking at old books, but I decided to try some more recent ones. Sometimes, when a Dem dies, his family sends whatever diaries or visitor books he owned to the library. In one Dem's diary I found some interesting references to . . . well, I won't go into detail now, but they indicate that we may find more information in some of the other Dems' private libraries. I'm not sure who or where, however.'

'Do any of them live in the mountains?' Dannyl asked.

Tayend eyes widened. 'A few. Why do you ask?'

Dannyl lowered his voice. 'Our hostess was just reminiscing about a particular young magician who attended her birthday party ten years ago.'

'Ah.'

'Yes. Ah.' Seeing Velend approaching, Dannyl frowned. 'That friend of yours is coming back.'

'He's not a friend, really,' Tayend corrected. 'More a friend of a friend. He brought me to the party.'

Velend's walk was fluid, like the gait of a limek – the predatory dog that bothered farmers and sometimes killed travellers in the mountains. To Dannyl's relief, the man stopped to talk to another courtier.

'I should warn you,' Dannyl added. 'Bel Arralade might be trying to find you a young lady.'

'I doubt it. She knows me too well.'

Dannyl frowned. 'Then why did she comment on your attractiveness to women, I wonder?'

'She was probably testing you, to see what you knew about me. What did you say?'

'That I didn't know you well enough to guess if you had anyone in mind.'

Tayend's eyebrows rose. 'No, you don't, do you?' he said in a quiet voice. 'I wonder. Would it disturb you to know if there was?'

'Disturb me?' Dannyl shook his head. 'No . . . but perhaps that would depend on who it was. Should I take it, then, that there is someone?'

'Perhaps.' Tayend smiled crookedly. 'But I'm not going to tell you . . . yet.'

Amused, Dannyl looked over Tayend's shoulder at Velend. Surely not . . . A face turned toward him, and a hand waved. Recognising Ambassador Errend, Dannyl nodded in reply. 'Ambassador Errend wants me to join him.'

Tayend nodded. 'And I will be accused of being a bore if I spend the night discussing work. Will I see you at the library soon?'

'In a few days. I think we may have another journey to plan.'

Sonea ran a finger along the spines of the books. She found a gap and slipped the missing volume into it. The other book she was holding was thick and heavy. Realising it belonged on a shelf on the other side of the library, she tucked it under her arm and started across the room.

'Sonea!'

Turning into another aisle, Sonea strode toward the front of the library where Lady Tya was sitting behind a small desk.

'What is it, my lady?'

'A message arrived for you,' the librarian told her. 'The High Lord wants to see you in Lord Yikmo's training room.'

Sonea nodded, her mouth suddenly dry. What did Akkarin want? A demonstration?

'I had better go, then. Would you like me to come back tomorrow night?'

Lady Tya smiled. 'You're a dream come true, Sonea. Nobody believes how much work it takes to maintain this place. But you must have a lot of studying to do.'

'I can spare an hour or two – and it helps to know what's here, and where to find it.'

The librarian nodded. 'If you have some spare time, then I welcome the help.' She shook a finger at Sonea. 'But I don't want to hear anyone saying I'm distracting the High Lord's favourite from her studies.'

'You won't.' Putting down the book, Sonea picked up her box and opened the door. 'Good night, Lady Tya.'

The University passages were quiet and still. Sonea started toward Lord Yikmo's room.

With each step she felt dread growing. Lord Yikmo did not like to teach in the evenings. The Vindo magician's reasons had something to do with the religion of his homeland. A request from the High Lord could not be refused, however.

Even so, it was a late hour to start any kind of lesson or demonstration. Perhaps Akkarin had another reason for calling her to Yikmo's room. Perhaps Yikmo wasn't even going to be there . . .

She jumped as a novice stepped out in front of her from a side passage. As she tried to walk around him, he moved to block her path, and three more novices stepped out to stand beside him.

'Hello, Sonea. Did you get my message?'

Turning around, she felt her heart sink. Regin stood at the front of a small crowd of novices, blocking the passage behind. She recognised a few members of her old class, but the rest were only vaguely familiar. These others, she realised, were older novices. They stared at her coldly, and she remembered the comments she had overheard the day classes had resumed. If so many thought she didn't deserve to have been chosen by the High Lord, it wouldn't have taken much for Regin to persuade some of them to join him.

'Poor Sonea,' Regin drawled. 'It must be so lonely being the High Lord's favourite. No friends. No-one to play with. We thought you might like some company. Perhaps a little game.' He glanced at one of the older boys. 'What shall we play?'

The boy grinned. 'I liked your first idea, Regin.'

'A game of "Purge", then?' Regin shrugged. 'I guess it will be good practice for the work we might have to do later in life. But I think it'll take more than flashy lights and barriers to get this sort of vermin out of the University.' He narrowed his eyes at Sonea. 'We'll just have to use more persuasive means.'

Anger stirred within Sonea at his words, but as his hands rose, it turned to disbelief. Surely he wouldn't strike her. Not here. Not in the University.

'You wouldn't dare . . .'

He grinned. 'Wouldn't I?' As light flashed from his

hand she threw up a shield. 'What are you going to do about it? Tell your guardian? Somehow, I don't think you will. I think you're too scared of him.'

Regin drew closer, and white magic blasted from both palms.

'How can you be sure?' she retorted. 'And what if someone finds us fighting in the corridors? You know the rules.'

'I don't think there's much chance of that.' Regin smirked. 'We've checked. There's nobody around. Even Lady Tya has left the library.'

His strikes were easy to shield. A few blasts of power and she could stop him. But she resisted the temptation, remembering Yikmo's lecture on the responsibility of magicians to avoid harming others.

'So call on your guardian, Sonea,' he urged. 'Ask him to rescue you.'

She felt a shiver of cold run down her spine, but ignored it. 'From you, Regin? That's hardly worth bothering the High Lord for.'

He glanced at the novices around him. 'Did you hear that? She thinks we're not worthy of the High Lord's attention. The best of the Houses, and she a mere slum girl? So let's show her who's worthy. Come on.'

He attacked her again. Feeling her shield assailed also from behind, she glanced back to see that Kano and Issle had stepped to the front of the novices there. But the older novices were frowning. Looking around at their faces, Sonea saw doubt.

'I told you,' Regin said between strikes. 'She won't tell him.'

Still, the older novices hesitated.

'If she does,' Regin added, 'I'll take responsibility. I'm willing to do that, just to prove it to you. What have you got to lose?'

Feeling more strikes, Sonea glanced over her shoulder again to see that more novices had joined in. It took much more power to hold her shield now. Growing worried, she glanced to either side, considering what to do. If she could get to the main corridor . . . She started forward, forcing Regin and his companions back.

'If you don't join us now,' Regin all but shouted to the few still-hesitant novices, 'she'll get away. Just like she's getting away with taking what's rightfully ours. Are you going to put her in her place, or spend the rest of your lives bowing down to a slum girl!'

The novices beside him stepped forward, though with some reluctance, and attacked with forcestrike. Trying to move into forcestrike took more of her strength than simply shielding, and though she managed to advance, progress was slow and costly.

She stopped and reconsidered. Did she have enough strength to reach the corridor? She couldn't say. Better to conserve her strength. Hopefully they would exhaust themselves, and she would be able to push past easily.

So long as she didn't tire first.

To reduce the size of her shield, she pressed her back to the wall. As the attack continued, she considered what their purpose was. She had assumed Regin had gathered such a large group so he would have a bigger audience – and protection if she fought back. Was he hoping to exhaust her, too? If so, what did he intend to do once they had worn her down? Kill her? Surely a slum girl was not worth going to prison for. No, he probably intended for her to be too tired for her lessons the next day.

The strikes were weakening but, to her alarm, she felt her own strength starting to falter. It was going to be close. Too close. As her shield began to waver, Regin raised his arms.

'Stop!'

The strikes ceased. In the silence, Regin looked at the others one by one and grinned.

'See? Now let's put her in her proper place.'

As he turned back to regard her, she saw the malicious glint in his eyes and realised that exhausting her had just been the first part of his plan. She wished she had continued pushing toward the main corridor. But as she did, she knew she would not have made it that far.

Regin sent another, cautious strike at her shield. One by one, the others continued this careful onslaught. Most of the strikes were weak, but as she drew more and more on the source of her power to maintain the shield, she realised she was doomed anyway. Even if they all ended up too exhausted to use their powers, ten novices could still happily torment her without using magic at all.

With growing dread, she felt her power fading. Her shield shimmered away, leaving nothing but air between herself and Regin. He smiled at the others – a tired but triumphant grin.

Then a streak of red light pulsed from Regin's palm. Pain blossomed in her chest and flashed outward, shivering down her arms and legs and stabbing up into her head. She felt her muscles spasm, and her back sliding against the wall.

As the sensation faded she opened her eyes, and found

415

herself curled up on the floor. Heat rushed to her face. Humiliated, she tried to stand up, but another burst of pain took over her senses. She gritted her teeth, determined that she would not cry out.

'Well, I've always wondered what stunstrike did,' she heard Regin say. 'Like to try it?'

Hearing a sound of disgust, Sonea felt a momentary hope as two of the novices exchanged a look of dismay, then turned and walked away. But the others all wore eager expressions and her hope faded as stunstrike after stunstrike sent pain coursing through her again.

Regin's taunt ran through her mind. *'So call on your guardian, Sonea. Ask him to rescue you.'* It would take a brief mental call; an image of Regin and his accomplices . . .

No. Nothing Regin did to her could be as awful as having to ask Akkarin for help.

Rothen then!

Not allowed to talk to him.

There's got to be someone!

But a call for help would be heard by Akkarin – and other magicians. The whole Guild would soon know that his novice had been found exhausted and defeated in the passages of the University.

There was nothing she could do.

Curling into a ball, she waited for the novices to use up the last of their power, or grow bored with their game, and leave her alone.

It was well past midnight when Lorlen finally finished the last letter. He rose, stretched and walked to the door, barely seeing his surroundings as he automatically set the magical lock. As he turned to walk down the corridor he heard a noise in the University Entrance Hall.

He paused, considering whether to investigate. It had been a soft sound, perhaps a dead leaf blown in through the doorway. He had just made up his mind to ignore it when the sound came again.

Frowning, he moved to the Entrance Hall doorway. A movement drew his eye to one of the enormous doors. Something slid along the ancient timber. He took a step forward, then drew in a sharp breath.

Sonea was leaning against the enormous door as if she might fall over without its support. She took a step, then stopped and swayed at the top of the stairs. Hurrying forward, Lorlen grabbed her arm to steady her. She stared at him in surprise and obvious dismay.

'What has happened to you?' he asked.

'Nothing, my lord,' she said.

'Nothing? You're exhausted.'

She shrugged, and it was obvious even that took effort. All her strength was gone. As if . . . as if she had been drained of it . . .

'What has he done to you?' Lorlen gasped.

She frowned, then shook her head. Suddenly her knees buckled and she sank to the stairs. He sat down beside her, releasing her arm.

'It's not what you think,' she told him, then folded forward and rested her head on her knees. 'Not *who* you think. Not *him*.' She sighed and rubbed her face. 'I've *never* felt this tired before.'

'Then what has made you like this?'

Sonea's shoulders drooped, but she didn't answer.

'Was it something a teacher set you to do?'

She shook her head.

'Did you try something that took more power than you expected?'

She shook her head again.

Lorlen tried to think of some other way her powers might have been exhausted. He thought of the few times he had used all his strength. He had to think back many years, to his time in the University. To fighting Akkarin in Warrior Skills. But she had said it wasn't Akkarin.

Then he remembered. Once, the teacher had set several novices against each class member. It had been one of the few times he had been bested.

But it was too late for classes. Why would she be fighting other novices? Lorlen scowled as a name sprang to mind. Regin. The boy had probably gathered his supporters together and waylaid her somewhere. It was bold and risky. If Sonea told Akkarin of the harassment . . .

But she wouldn't. Lorlen looked at Sonea and felt his heart twist. At the same time he felt an unexpected pride.

'It was Regin, wasn't it?'

Her eyelids flickered open. Seeing the wariness there, he nodded.

'Don't worry, I won't tell anyone unless you want me to. I will let Akkarin know what is going on, if you like.' *If he's listening now he'll already know.* He glanced down at the ring, then quickly away.

She shook her head. 'No. Don't. Please.'

Of course. She wouldn't want Akkarin to know.

'I wasn't expecting it,' she added. 'I'll keep away from them now.'

Lorlen nodded slowly. 'Well, if you can't, then know that you can call on me for help.'

The edge of her mouth lifted in a wry smile, then she

drew in a deep breath and started to rise.

'Wait.' She paused as he took her hand. 'Here,' he said. 'This will help.'

He sent a gentle stream of Healing energy out through his palm into her body. Her eyes widened as she sensed it. It would not restore her power, but it did ease the physical weariness. Her shoulders straightened and the pallor left her face.

'Thank you,' she said. Standing up, she looked toward the High Lord's Residence and her shoulders drooped again.

'It won't be like this forever, Sonea,' he said softly.

She nodded. 'Good night, Administrator.'

'Good night, Sonea.'

He watched her as she walked away, hoping that his words would prove true, but wondering how they possibly could.

CHAPTER 27

USEFUL INFORMATION

Sonea shifted the box of books onto her hip as Lady Tya opened the door of the Magicians' Library and walked inside. Setting her burden next to Tya's on Lord Jullen's desk, Sonea looked around the darkened room.

'I haven't been in here for weeks.'

Tya began removing books from the boxes. 'Why not?'

'"No novices allowed unless accompanied by a magician".'

The librarian chuckled. 'I can't imagine your guardian wanting to wait around while you studied. You don't have to ask him, though. You can go almost anywhere you want now.'

Sonea blinked in surprise. 'Even here?'

'Yes, but you still have to carry these for me.' The librarian's eyes twinkled as she held out a stack of books. Taking them, Sonea followed her between bookshelves to the far wall, then through a small door into a room she hadn't seen before. More shelves filled the centre of the room, but the walls were lined with cupboards and chests.

'Is this a storeroom?'

'Yes.' Tya began stacking books on shelves. 'These are duplicates of popular volumes from the Novices' Library or classes, ready for when the old ones wear out. The originals are stored in those chests.'

Taking the books from Sonea, Tya continued along the wall toward the back of the room. They passed a large, heavy cabinet filled with books of many sizes and a small mountain of scrolls. The glass doors were backed by a mesh of wire.

'What's in there?'

The librarian looked back, and a gleam came to her eyes. 'Originals of the oldest and most valuable books and maps in the Guild. They're too fragile to use. I've seen copies of some of them.'

Sonea peered through the glass. 'Have you ever looked at the originals?'

Moving to Sonea's side, Tya regarded the books inside. 'No, the doors are locked by magic. When Jullen was a young man, his predecessor opened the doors for him, but Jullen has never opened them for me. He told me once that he'd seen a map of the passages under the University in there.'

'Passages?' A memory rose of being blindfolded and taken to see her friend Cery, imprisoned beneath the University by Fergun.

'Yes. The Guild is supposed to be riddled with them. No-one uses them these days – though I'd say your guardian does since he's well known for his habit of appearing and disappearing in unexpected places.'

'And there's a map in here?'

'So Jullen said, but I suspect he was just teasing me.'

Sonea looked sideways at Tya. 'Teasing you?'

The librarian's face reddened, and she straightened and turned away. 'It was many years ago, when we were much younger.'

'It's hard to imagine Lord Jullen was ever young,' Sonea

said, following Tya to the end of the room. 'He's so stern and disapproving.'

Stopping at a chest, Tya took the books Sonea was carrying and stacked them inside. 'People change,' she said. 'He's grown much too full of his own importance, as if being a librarian was as important as, say, being the Head of Warriors.'

Sonea chuckled. 'Director Jerrik would say that knowledge is more important than anything else, so as caretakers of the Guild's knowledge, you *are* more important than the Higher Magicians.'

A smile curled the librarian's mouth. 'I think I know why the High Lord chose you, Sonea. Now go fetch me the rest of those books on Jullen's desk.'

Sonea returned to the other room. Over the last two weeks she had spent most nights helping Tya. Thought her real motivation had been to avoid Regin, she found she was growing to like the eccentric librarian. Once the library closed and they began cleaning up, Tya could be as talkative as the washing women who worked down by the Tarali River.

The librarian was an eager listener when Sonea needed to discuss the projects she had been given. If she didn't feel like talking, Lady Tya seemed happy to do it all herself. She was also an endless source of information and recent Guild history, full of tales of infighting and political meddling, scandals and secrets. Sonea had been surprised to learn of the rumours that had circulated about Dannyl when he was a novice, which Tya dismissed, and saddened to hear of the slow death of Rothen's wife from a disease no Healer could cure.

Returning with the books, she passed the cabinet

again, and looked at it thoughtfully. No-one used the passages under the University. Certainly not Regin. And, as Tya had said, she could go anywhere she wanted to now.

As soon as the door to his rooms had closed, Rothen hurried to a chair and pulled the letter out of his robes. It had been hidden there since a messenger had delivered it to him between classes. Though curiosity had tormented him for most of the day, he dared not open it in the University.

It had been seven weeks since he had written to Dannyl. Seven weeks since Akkarin had taken Sonea away. He'd spoken to her only once in that time. When a novice of an influential family had requested Rothen's private tutorship, he had been flattered; but when it turned out that the novice was only available during the time Rothen taught Sonea's class, he began to suspect other reasons behind the arrangement. It would have been rude to refuse, however. And he could not think of a valid reason to explain why, other than the truth.

Rothen looked down at the letter and prepared himself for disappointment. Even if Dannyl had agreed to help him, there was only a slim hope that he would find anything that might lead to Akkarin's downfall. But the letter was large and surprisingly thick. With trembling hands, Rothen broke the seal. As several sheets of paper slid out and Dannyl's handwriting appeared, he grabbed the first sheet and began to read.

To Rothen. It was a pleasant surprise to hear from you, old friend. I have, indeed, been travelling about the lands, meeting people of different races, cultures and religions. The experience has been both educational and enlightening, and I will have plenty of stories to tell you when I return next summer.

Your news about Sonea is remarkable. It is a fortuitous change for her, though I understand your dismay at losing her guardianship. I know that it was your care and hard work that made her into a novice worthy of the High Lord's notice. Her new position must surely have ended her troubles with a certain novice, too.

I was disappointed, however, to hear that I missed Dorrien's visit. Please forward my regards to him.

With this letter is a little information I have gathered from the Great Library and a few other sources. I hope it is of use to you. I do greatly appreciate the irony of your new interest. If my next journey is successful, we may have even more to add to our book.

Your friend, Dannyl.

Leafing through the sheets of paper, Rothen muttered in amazement.

'All this? The Splendid Temple? The Tombs of White Tears!' He chuckled. 'Just a *few* other sources, eh Dannyl?'

Turning back to the first page, he began to read. When he had just reached the third page, a knock on the door interrupted him. He stared at the door, then jumped to his feet, heart pounding. He cast about for a place to hide the bulky letter, then rushed to the bookcase and slipped it between the pages of a large volume. The extra thickness caused the book to bulge, but it wouldn't be noticed unless someone looked closely.

As the knock came again, Rothen hurried to the door. He took a deep breath, steeling himself for the worst.

Opening the door, he sighed with relief as he saw the old couple standing in the corridor beyond.

'Yaldin and Ezrille. Come in.'

They moved into the guestroom. 'How are you, Rothen?' Ezrille asked. 'We haven't seen you in a while.'

Rothen shrugged. 'Well. You?'

'Fine,' Ezrille said. She hesitated, then glanced at Yaldin.

'Would you like a cup of sumi?' Rothen offered.

'Yes, thank you,' Yaldin replied.

The couple sat down, and Rothen set about gathering a tray, cups and jars from a side table. As he started making the hot drink, Yaldin talked about a minor Guild matter. It *had* been too long since he'd talked to his old friends, Rothen decided. Ezrille remained silent until Rothen had poured a second cup of sumi.

'I want you to have dinner with us every Firstday, Rothen,' she said.

'Really?' Rothen smiled. 'That would be nice. But *every* Firstday?'

'Yes,' she said firmly. 'We know it was a shock to you to have Sonea chosen by the High Lord. She never comes to visit, which must be so disappointing after all you did for her. Though she has extra classes, she—'

'Can hardly help it,' Yaldin injected. He smiled at Rothen. 'I'm sure she'll visit when she has more time. In the meantime, we can't have you moping about.'

'He means you shouldn't spend every evening alone.'

'Especially with Dannyl abroad,' Yaldin added. 'You need someone to talk to other than novices and teachers.'

'And Tania says you've started taking nemmin again,' Ezrille added in a low voice. 'Don't be angry at her for telling us. She's concerned about you – and so are we.'

'So will you come?' Yaldin asked.

Rothen looked from one anxious face to another, then chuckled.

'Of course. I'd love to.'

Sonea walked slowly along the University passage, conscious of the tap of her boots on the floor. As she reached a turn, she peered into the next passage cautiously, and sighed with relief as she found it empty.

It was late. Later than usual. She had avoided Regin successfully for two weeks by either accompanying Tya out of the University, or taking long, convoluted routes through the passages. Each time, she had emerged in the main corridor to find a novice waiting there. They didn't try to attack her in the main corridor, however. The risk of being discovered by a magician was too high. The same fear kept them from waiting too close to the library, in case Tya heard them.

Sonea hoped Regin's allies would eventually lose interest. Just to be safe, she had started leaving her box in the library instead of carrying it back to her room. They had made a mess of her notes and books after they had grown bored with tormenting her with stunstrike. And she had been forced to leave it behind, being too exhausted to carry it.

Keeping her footsteps quiet meant walking slowly, when she desperately wanted to hurry. Not for the first time, she wondered if magician boots were made to be noisy. No matter how gently she stepped, their hard soles made a tapping that echoed in the silent passages. She sighed. Only a few weeks ago she had enjoyed wandering around in the passages of the University. Now, she actually felt relief when she entered the door of the High Lord's Residence.

A faint sound reached her ears. A snigger, half smothered. She stopped, realising they had blocked her way to the main corridor. They didn't know that she'd heard them, however. If she ran back and slipped through a portal room into the inner passages, she could make her way to the corridor from another direction.

Turning on her heel, she dashed away.

'Run, Sonea run!' came Regin's voice. The sound of footsteps and laughter filled the passage.

She leapt around a corner, then another. A familiar door appeared. She grabbed the handle and slipped through. Not waiting to see if they followed, she hurried across the portal room to the opposite door and ran along the passage beyond. Behind her she heard the muffled sound of a door closing. She dashed into the first side passage.

It twisted to the right, met another and ended at another door. A novice stood outside this, his mouth stretched into a grin.

Sonea skidded to a halt and regarded the novice with dismay. So they knew about the inner passages now. The novice's grin widened and she narrowed her eyes. Obviously he'd been posted to watch for her. He was alone, however, and easily overcome.

His grin vanished as he read her expression, and he hastily stepped aside. Slipping through the door, she crossed the room and entered the ordinary passages again. As she heard a door opening somewhere behind her, she broke into a run. The main passage was only a few turns away. She threw herself around one corner, then another, then into a rain of red fire.

She hadn't been shielding, hoping to conserve her strength as long as possible. As pain ripped through her body, everything went black. When her sight cleared again, she was lying on the floor and her shoulder felt bruised. Another flash of fire seared her, making it impossible to do anything but grit her teeth. When it stopped, however, she managed to shield.

Rolling over, she tucked her feet under her and stood up. Regin and four other novices stood behind her. Three others blocked her way to the main corridor. Two more novices arrived, then three more. Thirteen novices. More than before. She swallowed hard.

'Hello again, Sonea.' Regin smiled. 'How is it that we keep running into each other like this?'

The novices sniggered. There was no sign of doubt in their expressions now. They hadn't been called to account for ambushing and torturing her, proving that, as Regin had predicted, she wouldn't tell Akkarin about it.

Regin placed a hand on his heart. 'What a strange thing is love,' he said wistfully. 'I thought you hated me, but here you are, following me around!'

One of the novices passed him a paper box. Sonea frowned. Boxes like these usually contained sugared nuts, or other sweets.

'Ah! A gift!' Regin said, flipping the lid open. 'Something to show my regard for you.'

Inside were twists of coloured paper. An odour wafted to Sonea's nose and she felt her stomach turn. Harrel pellets, she guessed, or reber dung – or both. Regin took one out.

'Shall I feed it to you, like young lovers do?' He glanced at his followers. 'But you look as if you might need some warming up first.'

As he blasted her shield, the others joined in. Her stomach sank with dread. With so many novices attacking her, there was no chance of outlasting them. Turning to the ones blocking her path to the main corridor, she started pushing against their attack. Slowly they fell back, but after several paces she felt herself weakening. The novices, however, showed no signs of tiring.

She stopped. It had taken her a long time to crawl down to the University doors last time. She had wished she'd had just a little energy left, enough to be able to stand and walk. To conserve power she could let her shield fall a little early, and pretend to be completely exhausted. Yes, that might work.

But looking at the sweet box, she changed her mind. She would hold out as long as possible. As she felt her strength failing, she resolved to spit them back at him.

She felt the last of her power slowly drain away. As her shield failed, stunstrikes hit her body and she gasped with the pain. She felt her knees buckle and hit the floor. When the fire finally stopped she opened her eyes to see Regin crouching in front of her, crinkling the sweet wrapper between his fingers.

'What is going on here?'

Regin's eyes widened and his face turned a deathly white. He quickly closed his fingers around the 'sweet' and straightened. As he moved away, Sonea saw the owner of the voice and felt heat rush to her face. Lord Yikmo stood in the passage, his arms crossed.

'Well?' he demanded.

Regin bowed and the other novices hastily followed suit.

'Just a little game, my lord,' he said.

'A game, is it?' Yikmo glowered. 'Do the rules of this

game take precedence over those of the Guild? Fighting outside lessons or the Arena is forbidden.'

'We weren't fighting,' one of the novices said. 'Just playing.'

Yikmo's eyes narrowed. 'Really? So you were using stun-strike outside of battle – on a defenceless young woman.'

Regin swallowed. 'Her shield failed before we realised it, my lord.'

Lord Yikmo's eyebrows rose. 'It appears you are neither as disciplined nor as skilled as Lord Garrel claims. I'm sure Lord Balkan will agree.' Yikmo's eyes scanned the group, noting identities. 'Get back to your rooms, all of you.'

The novices hurried away. As Lord Yikmo turned to regard her, Sonea wished she'd had the strength to slip away while his attention had been on the novices. He looked very disappointed. She forced her legs under herself and rose unsteadily.

'How long has this been going on?'

She hesitated, not wanting to admit it had happened before. 'An hour.'

He shook his head. 'The stupidity of these novices. Attack the High Lord's favourite? In numbers, too.' He looked at her, then sighed. 'Don't worry. It won't happen again.'

'Please, don't tell anyone.'

He considered her, frowning. She took a step forward, then swayed as the corridor began to spin. A hand grasped her arm to steady her. She felt a little Healing energy tingle through her arm. As soon as she had regained her sense of balance she brushed his hand from her arm.

'Tell me, did you strike back?'

She shook her head.

'Why not?'

'What use would that be?'

'None, but most people, when outnumbered, will fight back out of pride. But perhaps you refrained for the same reason.'

He regarded her expectantly, but she looked away and remained silent.

'Of course, if you had targeted one or two of the weaker novices, you might have left them as exhausted as you. It would be a discouragement to the others, at the least.'

Sonea frowned. 'But they had no inner shields. What if I hurt one of them?'

He smiled, pleased. 'That is the answer I want to hear. Yet I think there is more to your reluctance to strike than caution.'

Sonea felt a flare of anger. Once again he was pushing and poking her, prying out her weaknesses. But this was not a lesson. Wasn't the humiliation of being found by him enough? She wanted him to leave her alone, and thought of the one subject that made most magicians flinch.

'Would you be so eager to strike, if you'd seen a boy die at the hands of magicians?'

His gaze did not waver, but sharpened instead.

'Ah,' he said. 'So *that's* it.'

She stared at him, appalled. Would he turn even the tragedy of the Purge into another lecture? She felt anger growing, and knew she would not be able to hold her temper much longer.

'Good night, Lord Yikmo,' she said between gritted teeth. Then, turning away, she strode down the passage toward the main corridor.

431

'Sonea! Come back.'

She ignored him. He called after her again, anger and command in his tone. Fighting the weariness in her legs, she quickened her stride.

As she reached the corridor she felt her fury ebb. He would make her regret her rude departure, but for now she didn't care. All she wanted was a warm bed and to sleep for days.

CHAPTER 28

A SECRET PLAN

As the door opened, bright sunlight streamed in to dazzle Lorlen's eyes. He shaded his face with a hand and followed Akkarin onto the University roof.

'We have company,' Akkarin observed.

Following his companion's gaze, Lorlen saw a lone figure in red robes standing by the railing.

'Lord Yikmo.' Lorlen frowned. 'Balkan must have given him access.'

Akkarin made a low, disapproving noise. 'There are so many identities imprinted into the door, I wonder why we bother to lock it.'

He strode toward the Warrior. Lorlen hurried after, worried that Akkarin intended to remove Yikmo's access to the roof.

'Balkan would not have granted him access if he did not regard him highly.'

'Of course. Our Head of Warriors knows that his methods of teaching are not suited to every novice. I'm sure he's aware that Yikmo draws attention away from his own weaknesses.'

Yikmo had't noticed them approaching. The Warrior leaned on the railing, his attention captured by something below. He looked up when Akkarin was a few steps away, and straightened hastily.

'High Lord. Administrator.'

'Greetings, Lord Yikmo,' Akkarin returned smoothly. 'I have not seen you up here before.'

Yikmo shook his head. 'I rarely come up – only when I need to think. I'd forgotten how good the view is.'

Lorlen looked around at the grounds, and at the city to one side. Letting his gaze drop to the gardens, he saw that a few novices had ventured outside for the midbreak. Though snow still covered the ground, the sun held a hint of the coming spring warmth.

Closest to them was a familiar figure. Sonea was sitting on one of the garden seats, her head bent over a book.

'The source of my contemplation,' Yikmo admitted.

'Is she improving?' Akkarin asked.

'Not as rapidly as I hoped,' Yikmo sighed. 'She still hesitates to strike. I'm starting to understand why.'

'Oh?'

Yikmo smiled crookedly. 'She's far too nice.'

'How so?'

'She's worried that she might hurt somebody – even her enemies.' Yikmo frowned and faced the High Lord. 'Last night, I discovered Regin and several other novices tormenting Sonea. They had worn her down to near exhaustion, and were using stunstrike.'

Lorlen felt his heart skip. '*Stunstrike,*' he hissed.

'I reminded them of the Guild rules, and sent them to their rooms.'

Yikmo looked at the High Lord expectantly, but Akkarin did not reply. He stared down at Sonea with a gaze so intense that Lorlen wondered how she could not sense it.

'How many novices were there?' he asked.

Yikmo looked aside as he considered. 'Twelve or thirteen. I can identify most of them.'

Akkarin nodded. 'That won't be necessary. There is no need to bring further attention to the incident.' His dark gaze turned to the Warrior. 'Thank you for informing me of this, Yikmo.'

Yikmo paused as if he might say something more, then nodded and moved away toward the door. When the Warrior had disappeared, Akkarin's gaze fell to Sonea again. The corner of his lips curled upward slightly.

'Twelve or thirteen. Her strength is growing quickly. I remember a novice in my class whose power grew as fast.'

Lorlen regarded Akkarin closely. In the bright sunlight the High Lord's pale skin looked sickly. Shadows lay under his eyes, but his gaze was sharp.

'As I recall, you progressed just as quickly.'

'I've often wondered if we would have, had we not been constantly trying to outdo each other.'

Lorlen shrugged. 'Probably.'

'I don't know. Perhaps the rivalry was good for us.'

'Good for us?' Lorlen gave a short laugh. 'Good for *you*. Believe me, there was nothing good about second place. Next to you, I may as well have been invisible – at least when it came to the ladies. If I'd known we'd both end up bachelors, I wouldn't have been so jealous of you.'

'Jealous?' Akkarin's smile faded. He turned away to stare at the horizon. 'No. Don't be jealous.'

The reply was so faint the Administrator wondered if he had really heard it. Lorlen opened his mouth to ask why he shouldn't be, but Akkarin's gaze had slid to the ruined Lookout.

'How are Davin's plans for the Lookout going?'

Sighing, Lorlen put aside the question and turned his mind back to Guild matters.

By early afternoon, Dannyl and Tayend had left the last of Capia's shabby outer homes behind. Farms and orchards covered the hills with squares of different greens. Occasionally a patch of newly turned soil added a splash of red-brown to the pattern.

Their horses plodded along at a comfortable pace. Servants had gone ahead to announce their arrival at the first stop, the home of Tayend's sister. Dannyl drew in a deep breath and sighed contentedly.

'It is good to be travelling again, isn't it?' Tayend said.

Dannyl looked at his companion in surprise. 'You're actually looking forward to it?'

'Yes. Why shouldn't I?'

'I'd thought our last journey had put you off travelling.'

Tayend shrugged. 'We had some unpleasant experiences, but it wasn't all bad. This time we're staying inside the borders of Elyne, and on solid ground.'

'I'm sure we could find a lake or a river with boats to hire if you start to feel our trip lacks that feeling of adventure you craved.'

'Snooping around in other people's libraries will be adventure enough,' Tayend said firmly. He looked into the distance and narrowed his eyes. 'I wonder which Dem has the books we're after.'

'If any of them do.' Dannyl shrugged. 'For all we know, Akkarin could have visited a Dem somewhere else, and travelled to the mountains for a completely different reason.'

'But where did he go afterward?' Tayend glanced at Dannyl. 'That's what intrigues me the most. We know Akkarin went to the mountains. After that there is no mention of him. Not in the city records, nor in people's recollections. I doubt that he could have slipped back into Capia in secret, and it was several years before he returned to the Guild. Did he stay in the mountains all that time? Did he travel along them, north or south? Or did he go through them?'

'Into Sachaka?'

'It would make sense. The Sachakan Empire wasn't old enough to call ancient, but it was a highly magical society – and he may have discovered references to even older cultures.'

'We have plenty of material in our libraries about the empire,' Dannyl said. 'But I doubt there is much left to find in Sachaka. What the Guild didn't take after the war, it destroyed.'

Tayend's brows rose. 'That was nice of them.'

Dannyl shrugged. 'It was a different time. The Guild was newly formed, and after the horrors of the war the magicians were determined to prevent another. They knew that if they allowed the Sachakan magicians to keep their knowledge of magic, there would be never-ending wars of vengeance between the two countries.'

'So they left it a wasteland.'

'Partly. Beyond the wasteland there is fertile soil, farms and towns. And Arvice, the capital.'

Tayend frowned. 'Do you think Akkarin went there?'

'I've never heard anyone say that he did.'

'So if he visited Sachaka, why did he keep the fact to himself?' Tayend paused, thinking. 'Perhaps he spent all those years researching the Sachakan Empire and found nothing, and was too embarrassed to admit it. Or,' Tayend smiled, 'perhaps he spent the time in idleness and didn't want to admit *that* – or he did something the Guild would not approve of – or he fell in love with a young Sachakan girl, married her, and vowed never to return, except that she died, or left him and he—'

'Let's not get too carried away, Tayend.'

Tayend grinned. 'Or perhaps he fell in love with a young Sachakan boy, and was eventually found out and expelled from the country.'

'This is the High Lord you're speaking of, Tayend of Tremmelin,' Dannyl said sternly.

'Does it offend you that I suggest such a thing?' There was a hint of defiance in the scholar's tone. Dannyl met Tayend's gaze levelly.

'I may be digging up a little of his past to aid my research, Tayend, but that does not mean I have no respect for the man, or his position. If he would be offended, or his position was threatened by speculation, then I would discourage it.'

'I see.' Sobering, Tayend looked down at his reins.

'But even so,' Dannyl added, 'what you suggest is impossible.'

Tayend smiled slyly. 'How can you be so sure?'

'Because Akkarin is a powerful magician. The Sachakans expelled him? Ha! Unlikely!'

The scholar chuckled and shook his head. He was silent for a while, then he frowned. 'What will we do if we learn that Akkarin did travel into Sachaka? Will we go there, too?'

'Hmmm.' Dannyl turned to look back down the road.

Capia had disappeared behind the undulating hills. 'That depends on how much time it takes me to perform my duties as Guild Ambassador.'

When he had heard Errend groaning about his coming bi-yearly tour of the country, Dannyl had offered to take his place, thinking it would be an ideal opportunity to leave Capia and continue his research without raising questions about shirking duties. Errend had been delighted.

To Dannyl's dismay, he had learned that the journey would wind about the entire country, that he would be required to spend weeks in places where there were no private libraries, and that he wouldn't be leaving until summer. Impatient to start, Dannyl had persuaded Errend to arrange the trip earlier, but there was no way he could omit any of the destinations from the schedule.

'So what exactly will you be doing?' Tayend asked.

'Introducing myself to country Dems, checking on magicians, and confirming magical potential in the children the King will be sending to the Guild. I hope you won't find it all very boring.'

Tayend shrugged. 'I get to snoop around private libraries. That's worth ten journeys. And I get to visit my sister.'

'What is she like?'

Tayend's face lit up with a bright smile. 'She's wonderful. I think she worked out I was a lad long before I did. You'll like her, I think, though she has a way of getting to the point that is quite disconcerting.' He pointed down the road. 'See that row of trees on the hill ahead. That's where the road to her property begins. Let's move on. I don't know about you, but I'm hungry!'

As Tayend urged his horse into a trot, Dannyl felt his

own stomach rumble. He looked ahead at the trees Tayend had indicated and nudged his mount's flanks with his boots. Soon they were turning off the road, riding beneath a stone arch and starting toward a distant country mansion.

Returning to the library after her evening lesson, Sonea noted the shadows under Tya's eyes.

'Did you stay much later last night, my lady?'

The librarian nodded. 'When these deliveries come in, I have to. There's no other time to sort them.' She yawned, then smiled. 'Thank you for staying back to help me.'

Sonea shrugged. 'Are these boxes for the Magicians' Library, too?'

'Yes. Nothing too exciting. Just more textbooks.'

They picked up a stack of boxes each and made their way through the passages. Lord Jullen's eyebrows rose as Sonea followed Tya into the Magicians' Library.

'So you've found yourself an assistant,' he remarked. 'I thought Lorlen refused your request.'

'Sonea has offered her time of her own choosing.'

'Shouldn't you be studying, Sonea? I should think the High Lord's novice would have better things to be doing than carrying boxes.'

Keeping her expression neutral, Sonea looked around. 'Can you suggest a better place to spend my spare time, my lord?'

His mouth twitched, then he sniffed. 'So long as the time *is* spare.' He looked at Tya. 'I am retiring now. Good night.'

'Good night, Lord Jullen,' Tya replied.

When the stern magician had left, Tya started toward the storeroom. Sonea chuckled.

'I think he's jealous.'

'Jealous?' Tya turned and frowned. 'Of what?'

'You've got an assistant. The High Lord's novice, no less.'

She lifted an eyebrow. 'You've put a high value on yourself.'

Sonea grimaced. 'That wasn't of my choosing. But I'd lay a bet that Jullen's a bit peeved that you've got a willing helper.'

Tya's mouth tightened, as if she was resisting the urge to smile. 'Hurry up, then. If you're going to be of any help, don't stand around speculating.'

Following Tya to the back room, Sonea set the boxes down on top of a chest and began unpacking them. She resisted the temptation to look at the cabinet of old books and maps, instead concentrating on stacking and sorting. Tya paused to yawn several times.

'How late *did* you stay back last night?' Sonea asked.

'Too late,' Tya admitted.

'Why don't you leave me to do this?'

Tya sent her a disbelieving look. 'You really have too much energy, Sonea,' she sighed. 'I shouldn't leave you here alone – and you'll be locked in. I'll have to come back and let you out.'

Sonea shrugged. 'I'm sure you won't forget me.' She looked down at the books. 'I can help with this, but not the cataloguing work. You may as well go back and finish it.'

Tya nodded slowly. 'Very well. I'll come back for you in an hour.' She smiled. 'Thank you, Sonea.'

Following the librarian to the door, Sonea watched her walk away. She felt a growing excitement as Tya's footsteps faded into the distance. Turning, she regarded the library. Dust hung in the air, tinged yellow by the glow of her globe light. The shelves of books extended into darkness, as if they stretched on forever.

Smiling to herself, she returned to the storeroom and stacked up the textbooks as quickly as possible. She counted the minutes, conscious that she only had an hour. Once the boxes were unpacked, she abandoned them and moved to the cabinet.

She inspected the lock carefully, both with her eyes and her mind. Tya had spoken of a lock, and it made sense that an important store of knowledge would be protected by magic. Her search proved her suspicions right.

Though the physical lock was no more complicated than any she had picked before, she had no idea if it was possible to foil a magical one. Even if she managed to, the meddling might be detectable, and the meddler identifiable.

When Cery had taught her how to pick locks, he had told her to look for another way first. Sometimes there were quicker ways to get into something than picking. She looked for hinges on the doors, and cursed softly as she saw they were on the inside of the cabinet.

She began to examine the entire unit, inspecting the joints and edges carefully. The cabinet was old, but sturdy and well made. She pursed her lips thoughtfully, then fetched a chair and stood upon it so she could check the top of the cabinet. No weaknesses there, either. Sighing, she stepped down to the floor again.

That left the back and the base. To look underneath, she would have to lift it with magic, then crawl under to examine the bottom. Though she had recovered enough from the previous night's exhaustion to tackle her lessons, she wasn't sure if she could lift and hold the cabinet steadily. Did she really want to find the map that badly?

She peered through the glass at the books and rolled papers. A thin sheet of glass and wire mesh was all that lay between herself and a possible escape from Regin. She chewed her lip in frustration.

Then she noticed something odd about the wooden back. She could see two lines running down the length, too straight to be natural cracks in the wood. The back of the cabinet obviously wasn't made from one large sheet of wood. Crouching a little, she checked to see if the lines extended all the way to the base. They didn't.

Moving to one side of the cabinet, she peered along the gap between it and the wall. Using a tiny globe light, she illuminated the narrow space and discovered something strange.

Something about the size of a textbook, but made of wood, was attached to the wall behind the cabinet.

Stepping back, she took a deep breath and slowly extended her power out and around the cabinet, taking care that her magic did not touch that of the lock. With the gentlest flexing of will, she lifted the cabinet upward. It swayed slightly as it rose. Frowning with concentration, she turned it away from the wall like a door and carefully set it down again, a few faren scampering away from their webs in alarm.

Sonea let out the breath, and realised that her heart was beating fast. If anyone discovered what she was doing now, there would be no end of trouble for her. Looking through the glass, she was relieved to find none of the cabinet's contents was out of place. Walking around the back she found that the object behind the cabinet was only a small painting. She looked at the back of the cabinet and drew in a breath in amazement.

A small square had been cut into the back. She slipped her fingernails into the crack, and the square of wood slipped out easily, revealing the ends of rolled up papers and a few books.

Her heart was racing now. She hesitated, wary of reaching inside. This square hole had been created by someone. Had it been there all along? Or had someone cut it later, so that they could take something unnoticed? Her senses did not detect a barrier over the hole, or any other magic. She slipped a hand in and gently pulled out one of the scrolls.

It was a plan of the Magicians' Quarters. She inspected it carefully but could find no hidden passages marked. Replacing it, she drew forth another. This time it was a plan detailing the Novices' Quarters. No secret passages there, either.

The third scroll she pulled out showed a map of the University and her pulse quickened. But nothing mysterious or unusual was marked on it. Disappointed, Sonea replaced it and was about to pick up another when something caught her eye.

Jutting up from between the pages of one of the books was a slip of paper. Curious, she eased the book out from between its neighbours.

'*The Magiks of the Werld*,' she read aloud. It was one of the early texts used in history class. Under the title was written, in faded ink: 'High Lord's copy'.

A chill went through her. Suddenly she wanted to replace the book, put the cabinet back in place, and get out of the library as quickly as possible. Taking a deep breath, she pushed her fears aside. The library was locked. Even if Jullen or Tya returned, she would hear them coming. Though she would have to move fast, she could probably put the cabinet back before they entered the storeroom.

Opening the book where the slip of paper lay, she examined the pages and recognised some of the text. Nothing strange or unusual explained the marker. Shrugging, she lay the paper bookmark back over the page.

Then her heart skipped. Three tiny, hand-drawn maps of the University had been sketched on the slip of paper – one for each level. Looking closer, she felt a thrill of excitement. On other maps the walls were thick lines, on this they were hollow and doors were indicated in them where she knew there were none. Mysterious little crosses had been marked *inside* the walls. The third map, of the ground floor, showed a spider's web of passages *outside* the University walls.

She had found it! A map of the passages under the University. Or, more accurately, a map of passages *throughout* the University.

Clutching the map, she stepped back from the cabinet. Should she take it, or would someone notice it missing? Perhaps she could copy it. How much time did she have left? Could she memorise it?

Looking down at the map, she traced the passages with her eyes. She noted a little symbol drawn on one of the inner walls next to the Magicians' Library. Looking closer, she realised it was the wall she was standing next to, marking a place just about . . .

Turning, she stared at the painting hanging behind the cabinet. *Why hang a painting behind a cabinet?* Sonea took the frame, lifted it and caught her breath.

A neat square hole had been cut into the wall. Peering inside, she could see a corresponding square of light illuminating a stone wall beyond, an arm's length away.

Hastily, she let the painting fall again. Her heart was pounding now. This was no coincidence. Whoever had made that hole had created it to reach the cabinet.

It might have been done centuries ago. Or it might have been made recently. Looking down at the map again, she knew she could not memorise it, and now that she knew that someone might return to the cabinet and notice it missing, she dared not take it with her. But she couldn't leave empty-handed. An opportunity to get into the cabinet might not come again.

Running to Lord Jullen's desk she found a thin sheet of paper, a pen and his inkwell. Laying the paper over the map, she began tracing as quickly as she could. Her mouth was dry as she worked, her breathing unsteady. It seemed to take much too long, but finally she was done. Folding the tracing up, she put it in a pocket in her robe.

Only then did she hear the faint sound of footsteps approaching the library. Cursing softly, she hastily cleaned Jullen's pen and put it away. Running to the storeroom, she replaced the map in the book and slid it back on the shelf. As she pressed the square of wood back into place she heard the footsteps pause at the library door. Dancing away from the wall, she focussed her mind on the cabinet.

Steady. Taking a deep breath, she lifted it and turned it back against the wall.

The library door clicked shut.

'Sonea?'

Realising she was shaking, Sonea decided she didn't trust her voice.

'Mmm?' she replied.

Tya appeared in the storeroom doorway. 'Are you done?'

Nodding, Sonea picked up the empty boxes.

'I'm sorry I took so long.' Tya frowned. 'You look a bit
. . . unsettled.'

'It's a bit spooky in here,' Sonea admitted. 'But I'm
fine.'

Tya smiled. 'Yes, it can be. But, thanks to you, it's all
done and we can finally get some sleep.'

As Sonea followed Tya out of the library, she placed a
hand over the pocket where the map was hidden, and
smiled.

CHAPTER 29

A REVELATION

Sonea took a deep breath as she entered Yikmo's practice room. Keeping her eyes lowered, she stopped just inside the door.

'My lord,' she began. 'I apologise for disobeying you the other night. You helped me and I was rude.'

Yikmo was silent for a moment, then he chuckled. 'You don't have to apologise for that, Sonea.'

Looking up, she was relieved to see that he was smiling. He pointed to a seat and she obediently sat down.

'You have to understand that this is what I do,' he told her. 'I take novices who are having difficulties with Warrior Skills training and find out why. In all cases but yours, however, the novices I have taught have sought my help willingly. When they realise that I am going to raise personal matters that may be the cause of their problems, they have three choices: accept my method of teaching, find another teacher, or choose another discipline.

'But you? You're here only because your guardian wishes it.' He looked at her directly. 'Am I right?'

Sonea nodded.

'It's hard to like what one is not good at.' The magician regarded her levelly. 'Do you want to be better at this discipline, Sonea?'

She shrugged. 'Yes.'

His eyes narrowed. 'I suspect you are saying only what you believe you ought to say, Sonea. I will not repeat your answer to your guardian, if that is what you fear. I will not regard you badly if you say you do not. Consider the question carefully. Do you *really* wish to master this art?'

Looking away, Sonea thought of Regin and his followers. Perhaps if what Yikmo taught her helped her to defend herself . . . but with so many novices allied against her what use was there in skill and strategy?

Was there any other reason to improve? She certainly didn't care about gaining the High Lord's approval – and even if she became as proficient as Yikmo or Balkan, she would never have the strength to fight Akkarin.

But one day the Guild might discover the truth about the High Lord. She wanted to be there to lend her strength in the fight. It would only increase the chances of beating him if she was good at Warrior Skills, too.

She straightened. Yes, *that* was a good reason to improve her skills. She might not enjoy Warrior Skills classes, but if they helped the Guild oust Akkarin one day she should learn all she could.

She looked up at Yikmo. 'If it's hard to like what one isn't good at, will I like it more when I am better at it?'

The Warrior smiled broadly. 'Yes. I promise that you will. Not all the time, though. We all have to suffer defeat from time to time, and I don't know anyone who enjoys that.' He paused, his expression sobering. 'But first we have some tougher matters to attend to. You have many weaknesses to overcome, and what you witnessed during the Purge has brought about most of them. Fear of killing has made you reluctant to strike and knowing that you are stronger than others makes you even more cautious.

You have to learn to trust yourself. You have to learn the limits of your strength and Control – and I have devised some exercises that will help you do that. This afternoon we have the use of the Arena.'

Sonea stared at him in surprise. 'The Arena?'

'Yes.'

'Just me?'

'All to yourself – and your teacher, of course.' He took a step toward the door. 'Come along, then.'

Rising, she followed him out of the room and into the passage.

'Isn't the Arena used by other classes every day?'

'Yes,' Yikmo replied. 'But I convinced Balkan to find something else for his class to do this afternoon.' He glanced at her, smiling. 'Something fun that took them outside the Guild, so they would not resent your intrusion.'

'What are they doing?'

He chuckled. 'Blasting rock out of an old quarry.'

'What will they learn from that?'

'To respect the destructive potential of their powers.' He shrugged. 'It also helps to remind them of the damage they could do to their surroundings should they ever fight outside the Arena.'

They reached the main corridor and continued to the rear stairway. As they left the building and started on the path to the Arena, Sonea looked up at the University windows. Though she could see no faces, she was suddenly conscious that her 'private' lesson was not going to be at all private.

Descending into the Arena's portal, they moved through darkness and into the sunlight again. Yikmo pointed toward the Healers' Quarters.

'Strike at the barrier.'

She frowned. 'Just . . . strike?'

'Yes.'

'What kind?'

He waved a hand dismissively. 'Any. It doesn't matter. Just strike.'

Taking a deep breath, she focussed her will and sent a firestrike toward the invisible shield. As it hit, hundreds of fine threads of energy rippled out between the curved spires of the Arena. The air vibrated with a muted tinkling.

'Strike again, but stronger.'

This time lightning covered the entire domed barrier. Yikmo smiled and nodded.

'Not bad. Now put all your strength into it.'

Power flashed through and out of her. It was an exhilarating sensation. The shield crackled with light and Yikmo chuckled.

'Now give it *all* your strength, Sonea.'

'I thought I had.'

'I don't think you did. Imagine everything that matters to you depends on one immense effort. Don't hold back.'

Nodding, she imagined that Akkarin stood in front of the barrier. She pictured Rothen standing beside her, the target of Akkarin's immense power.

Don't hold back, she told herself as she let loose her magic.

The Arena barrier glowed so brightly she had to shield her eyes. Though the tinkling was no louder, her ears vibrated with the sound. Yikmo crowed quietly.

'That's more like it! Now do it again.'

She looked at him. 'Again?'

'Stronger, if you can.'

'What about the Arena barrier?'

He laughed. 'It would take much more than *that* to break the Arena barrier. Magicians have been strengthening it for centuries. I expect to see the supports glowing red by the end of this lesson, Sonea. Go on. Give it another blast.'

After another few strikes, Sonea realised she was beginning to enjoy herself. Though battering the Arena barrier posed no challenge, it was a relief to be able to strike without worrying about precautions or restrictions. Each strike was a little weaker, however, and soon all she could do was send a few ripples of light across the barrier.

'That will do, Sonea. I don't want you falling asleep in your next class.' He looked at her questioningly. 'How do you feel about this lesson?'

She smiled. 'It wasn't as hard as your usual ones.'

'Did you enjoy it?'

'I guess.'

'In what way?'

She frowned, then suppressed a smile. 'It's like . . . seeing how fast I can run.'

'Anything else?'

She couldn't tell him that she had imagined she was blasting Akkarin to ashes. But he had noticed her hesitation. Something similar, then? Looking up at him, she smiled mischievously. 'It's like throwing stones at magicians.'

His eyebrows rose. 'Is it really?' Turning, he gestured for her to follow him to the Arena portal. 'We've tested your limits today, but not in any way that will measure your strength against others. That will be the next step. Once you know how much power you can safely use against another, then you should stop hesitating before you strike.'

He paused. 'It is two days since Regin exhausted you. Were you tired yesterday?'

'A little, in the morning.'

He nodded slowly. 'Go to bed early tonight, if you can. You'll need your strength tomorrow.'

'So what do you think of my sister?'

Seeing that Tayend was grinning broadly, Dannyl chuckled. 'Rothen would say she speaks plainly.'

'Ha!' Tayend replied. 'That's putting it mildly.'

Mayrie of Porreni was as plain as her brother was handsome, though both were slim and small-boned. She had a forthright manner and a bold sense of humour that made her easy to like.

The estate her husband managed produced horses, some food crops, and wines that were sought after in all of the Allied Lands. The house was a sprawling single-storey mansion with a verandah all around. After dinner, Tayend had taken a bottle of wine and some glasses and led Dannyl out under the verandah where chairs were arranged to take in the view of the vines.

'So where is her husband, Orrend?' Dannyl asked.

'In Capia,' Tayend said. 'Mayrie manages everything here. He only comes out to visit once every few months.' He looked at Dannyl and lowered his voice. 'They don't get along very well. Father married her off to someone he decided she'd be suited to. But, as always, the Mayrie he has in his mind is vastly different to the Mayrie she actually is.'

Dannyl nodded. He'd noticed how Mayrie had tensed when her husband's name had been mentioned by one of the dinner guests.

'Mind you, the man she would have chosen had her

marriage not been arranged would have been an even bigger mistake,' Tayend added. 'She'll admit that these days.' He sighed. 'I'm still waiting for father to select some appropriately disastrous wife for me.'

Dannyl frowned. 'He'd still do that?'

'Probably.' The scholar toyed with his glass, then looked up abruptly. 'I've never asked before, but do you have someone waiting for you in Kyralia?'

'Me?' Dannyl shook his head. 'No.'

'No lady? No sweetheart?' Tayend seemed surprised. 'Why not?'

Dannyl shrugged. 'I've never had time. Too much to do.'

'Like what?'

'My experiments.'

'And?'

Dannyl laughed. 'I don't know. When I think back, I wonder how I managed to fill my time. Certainly not by attending those court gatherings that seem designed for finding a wife or husband. They don't attract the sort of woman I'd be interested in.'

'So what sort of woman are you interested in?'

'I don't know,' Dannyl confessed. 'Never met one that interested me enough.'

'But what about your family? Haven't they tried to find you a suitable wife?'

'They did once, years ago.' Dannyl sighed. 'She was a nice enough girl, and I planned to go ahead with the marriage just to keep my family happy. But one day I decided I couldn't do it, that I'd rather remain alone and childless than marry someone I didn't care for. It seemed crueller to do that to her, than refuse the marriage.'

Tayend's eyebrows rose. 'But how did you get out of it? I thought Kyralian fathers arranged matches for their children.'

'Yes, they do.' Dannyl chuckled, 'but one privilege that magicians have is the right to refuse an arranged marriage. I didn't refuse outright, but I found a way to persuade my father to change his mind. I knew the girl admired another young man, so I made sure that certain events occurred that convinced all that he was a better match. I played the part of the disappointed suitor, and everyone felt sorry for me. She is quite happy, I am told, and has had five children since.'

'And your father didn't arrange another match?'

'No. He decided that – how did he put it? – if I chose to be contrary, then so long as I didn't scandalise the family by choosing some low-born servant, he'd leave me alone.'

Tayend sighed. 'Sounds like you got more out of the affair than being able to choose your wife. My father has never accepted my choices. Partly because I am his only son, so he's worried there will be no-one to inherit after me. But mostly he disapproves of my . . . well . . . inclinations. He thinks I am being wilful, that I am enchanted with perverse things, as if it's only about physical gratification.' He frowned then drained his glass. 'It's not, in case you're wondering. At least, not for me. There is a . . . a *certainty* in me about what is natural and right for me that is as strong as his own certainty about what is natural and right. I've read books about eras and places where being a lad was as ordinary as being . . . I don't know, a musician or a swordsman. I . . . I'm ranting, aren't I?'

Dannyl smiled. 'A little.'

'Sorry.'

'Don't apologise,' Dannyl said. 'We all need to rant a little now and then.'

Tayend chuckled and nodded. 'Indeed, we do.' He sighed. 'Well, that's enough for now.'

They gazed out over the moonlit fields, the silence stretching comfortably between them. Suddenly Tayend drew in a sharp breath. Leaping out of his chair, he hurried inside the house, swaying a little from the effect of the wine. Wondering what had caused his friend's sudden departure, Dannyl considered going after him, but decided instead to wait and see if he returned.

As he was pouring himself another glass of wine, Tayend appeared again.

'Look at this.'

The scholar spread one of the drawings of the tomb over Dannyl's lap, then held out a large book. On the pages of the book was a map of the Allied Lands and neighbouring countries.

'What am I looking at?' Dannyl asked.

Tayend pointed to a row of glyphs at the top of the tomb drawing. 'These say something about a place – the place the woman came from.'

His finger tapped at a particular glyph: a crescent and a hand surrounded by a square with curved corners. 'I didn't know what this meant, but it was familiar, and it took a while before I remembered what it reminded me of. There's an old book in the Great Library that's so old the pages crumble into dust if you touch them too roughly. It belonged to a magician many centuries ago, Ralend of Kemori, who ruled part of Elyne before Elyne was one country. Visitors would write their names and titles, and purpose for visiting, in this book – though most of it was in the same handwriting so I suspect a scribe was hired to take the names of those who couldn't write themselves.

'There was a symbol similar to this on one page. I remember it, because it was a mark made by a stamp, not a pen. And it was red – faded but still visible. The scribe had written "King of Charkan" next to it.

'Now, it's not unreasonable to think that the woman in the tomb came from the same place – the glyph is so similar to the stamp. But where is this place called Charkan?' Tayend smiled broadly and tapped the map. 'This is an old atlas Orrend's great-grandfather owned. Look closely.'

Dannyl lifted the book out of Tayend's hands and brought his globe light closer. Near the end of Tayend's finger was a tiny word and a drawing.

'Shakan Dra,' Dannyl read aloud.

'I might have missed it if it weren't for that little crescent moon and hand.'

Looking at the rest of the map, Dannyl blinked in surprise. 'This is a map of Sachaka.'

'Yes. The mountains. It's hard to tell from this, but I'd bet twenty gold that Shakan Dra is close to the border. Are you thinking what I'm thinking about a certain unmentioned person making a trip to the mountains some years ago?'

Dannyl nodded. 'Yes.'

'I think we have a new destination to explore.'

'We still need to follow our planned route,' Dannyl reminded him. He did not much like the idea of entering Sachaka. Considering its history, he had no idea whether the locals would welcome him. 'And Sachaka is not one of the Allied Lands.'

'This place is not far from the border. No more than a day's travel.'

'I don't know if we have time.'

'We can be a little late returning to Capia. I doubt anyone would question if we were delayed.' Tayend returned to his chair, and collapsed into it.

'A few days, perhaps.' Dannyl regarded his friend carefully. 'But I wouldn't have thought you'd want to be delayed.'

Tayend shrugged. 'No. Why not?'

'Isn't there someone waiting for your return?'

'No. Unless you mean Librarian Irand? He won't be concerned if I'm a few days late.'

'Nobody else?'

Tayend shook his head.

'Hmmm.' Dannyl nodded to himself. 'So you don't have your eye on somebody, as you hinted at Bel Arralade's party.'

The scholar blinked in surprise, then looked at Dannyl sideways. 'I've got you curious, haven't I? What if I said that there's no-one waiting for my return because this person doesn't know of my interest?'

Dannyl chuckled. 'You're a secret admirer, then.'

'Perhaps.'

'You can trust me to keep your secret, Tayend.'

'I know.'

'Is it Velend?'

'No!' Tayend looked at him reproachfully.

Relieved, Dannyl shrugged apologetically. 'I've seen him at the library a few times.'

'I'm trying to discourage him,' Tayend said, grimacing, 'but he thinks I'm only doing it because I'm keeping up appearances for you.'

Dannyl hesitated. 'Am I keeping you from pursuing the one you're interested in?'

To his surprise, Tayend winced. 'No. This person is, ah . . .'

Hearing footsteps, they looked up and saw Mayrie walking toward them carrying a lantern. From the sound of her steps, she was wearing heavy boots underneath her dress.

'I thought I'd find you here,' she said. 'Would either of you like to accompany me on a walk through the vines?'

Dannyl rose. 'I would be honoured.' He looked at Tayend expectantly, but was disappointed to see that the scholar was shaking his head.

'I've drunk too much, sister dear. I'm afraid I'll step on your toes or tumble into the vines.'

She clucked her tongue disapprovingly. 'Then stay where you are, drunkard. Ambassador Dannyl will be more suitable company.' She hooked her arm into Dannyl's and steered him gently toward the vineyard.

They walked in silence for a hundred paces or so, then turned into the gap between the vines. Mayrie questioned Dannyl about the people he had met at court, and what his opinion of them was. Then, as they reached the end of the row of vines, she gave him a measuring look.

'Tayend has told me much about you,' she said, 'though not of your work. I get the impression that is a secret matter.'

'He probably doesn't want to bore you,' Dannyl replied.

She glanced at him sideways. 'If you say so. Tayend has told me everything else, however. I would not have expected a Kyralian magician to be quite so . . . well, I would not have expected you to remain friends, at least not such comfortable friends.'

'We have quite a reputation for intolerance, it seems.'

She shrugged. 'But you are an exception. Tayend told me of the rumours that caused you so much trouble as a novice, and that the incident has given you a greater understanding than most magicians have. I think that has also given him cause to count himself lucky for being born Elyne, too.' She paused. 'I hope you do not mind me talking about this?'

Dannyl shook his head and hoped he was managing to look unconcerned. It did make him uneasy, however, listening to someone he had just met talk about his private past in such a matter-of-fact way. But this was Tayend's sister, he reminded himself. Tayend would not have mentioned anything to her if he didn't think she could be trusted.

They reached the end of the vineyard. Turning to the left, she started back toward the house along the last row of vines. Looking back at the house, Dannyl noted that the chair Tayend had been sitting in was empty. Mayrie stopped.

'Being Tayend's sister, I am very protective of him.' She turned to face him, her expression serious and intent. 'If you do think of him as a friend, have a care. I suspect he is besotted with you, Dannyl.'

Dannyl blinked in surprise. *Me?* I'm *Tayend's secret love-interest?* He looked at the empty chair. No wonder Tayend had been so evasive. He felt . . . strangely pleased. *It's flattering to be admired by someone,* he told himself.

'This is a surprise to you,' Mayrie said.

Dannyl nodded. 'I had no idea. Are you sure?'

'More sure than not. I would not have told you, except that I worry for him. Don't lead him to believe anything of you that isn't true.'

Dannyl frowned. 'Have I?'

'Not that I can tell.' She paused and smiled, but her eyes remained hard. 'As I said before, I am very protective of my younger brother. I only wish to warn you – and to let you know that, if I hear that he has been hurt in any way, you may find your stay in Elyne less comfortable than you would like it to be.'

Dannyl regarded her closely. There was a steeliness to her gaze, and he didn't doubt that what she said was true.

'What would you have me do, Mayrie of Porreni?'

Her face relaxed, and she patted his hand. 'Nothing. Just take care. I do like what I've seen of you, Ambassador Dannyl.' Taking a step forward, she kissed him on the cheek. 'I'll see you at the morning meal tomorrow. Good night.'

With that, she turned and walked away toward the house. Dannyl watched her go, then shook his head. Clearly, her purpose for leading him out here had been to give him this warning.

Had Tayend suggested the visit so his sister could access Dannyl? Had he planned for his sister to perceive so much, and reveal it?

'He is completely besotted with you, Dannyl.'

Moving to the seat Tayend had vacated, he sat down. How was this going to change their friendship? He frowned. If Tayend didn't know his sister had revealed his interest, and Dannyl continued to behave as if he didn't know, then everything should remain the same.

But I know, he thought. *That does change things.*

Their friendship depended on how well Dannyl took this news. He considered his feelings. He was surprised, but not dismayed. It even pleased him a little to know someone liked him that much.

Or do I like the idea for other reasons?

Closing his eyes, he pushed that thought away. He had faced those questions before, and their consequences. Tayend was and could only ever be a friend.

The entrances to the secret passages were surprisingly easy to find. Most were located in the inner part of the University, which made sense since the original designers would not have wanted mere novices stumbling upon them. The mechanisms for opening the doors in the wood panelling lay behind paintings and other wall ornaments.

Sonea had started looking for them as soon as her evening class had finished, instead of going to the library. The corridors were quiet, but not completely deserted, which was why she never encountered Regin and his friends at this time. They preferred to wait until after she left the library, when they were sure the University was empty.

Even so, she felt as tense as a bowstring as she moved through the passages. She inspected several of the hidden doors before she drew up the courage to try one. Though it was late, she could not help worrying about being observed. Finally, in a little-used part of the inner passages, she dared to flick the lever behind a painting of a magician holding drawing instruments and a scroll.

The panelling swivelled inward silently, and cold air rushed out to chill her. Thinking back to the night Fergun had blindfolded and led her into the tunnels to meet Cery, she recalled how she had felt this change of temperature.

Looking inside, she saw a dry, narrow passage. She had expected it to be dripping with moisture like the tunnels under the city. The Thieves' Road was under the level of the river, however; the University was on higher ground

– and, of course, there wouldn't be any moisture up on the third floor.

Worried that someone would see her standing next to the open door, Sonea stepped inside. As she let go of the door it swung shut, plunging the tunnel into darkness. Her heart skipped, then she winced as the globe light she willed into existence flared brighter than she had intended.

Inspecting the passage, she noted that the floor was thick with dust. In the centre the dust was thinner where the traffic of feet had scuffed it aside, but her boots had left faint footprints, indicating that no-one had come this way for some time. All her doubts evaporated. She would not encounter anyone else in the passages; they were hers to explore. Her very own Thieves' Road.

She pulled out her plan of the passages and started forward. As she moved along, she found and noted other entrances. The secret ways were restricted to the larger walls of the University, so they were set out in a simple pattern that was easy to remember. Soon she had circled the entire top floor of the building.

She hadn't seen any stairs, however. Examining her map again, she noted the little crosses here and there. She moved to the location of one of them and examined the floor. Brushing dust aside with her toe, she uncovered a crack.

Dropping into a crouch, she pushed the dust away with light sweeps of magic. As she suspected, the crack turned at right angles, once, twice . . . forming a hatch in the floor. Standing back, she concentrated on the slab of wood, willing it to rise.

It hinged upward, revealing another passage below, and a ladder attached to the side wall. Smiling to herself, Sonea climbed down to the second floor.

The layout of the passages of the second level was almost identical to those on the third. When she had checked all of the side passages, she located another hatch and descended to the ground floor. Again, the ways were similar, though there were fewer side passages, but here she found staircases leading even further down, under the ground.

Excitement grew as she discovered that the foundations of the University were riddled with tunnels and empty rooms, indicated by dashed lines on the map of the ground floor. Not only did the tunnels roam under the building, but they extended out beyond the walls and under the gardens. Heading away from the University, Sonea noted how the passage sloped down, deeper under the ground. The walls changed to brick, and roots hung from the ceiling. Remembering the size of some of the trees above, she realised she must be deeper underground than she thought.

A little further on the passage ended where its roof had caved in. As she turned back, she considered how much time she had spent exploring. It was late. Very late. She did not want to give Akkarin reason to come looking for her – or worse, to order her to return to the residence after classes each night.

So, satisfied with her success, she started back up into the University walls and emerged at a place where she knew the chance of being seen leaving the secret ways was remote.

CHAPTER 30

A DISTURBING DISCOVERY

As Tania cleared empty sumi cups from the table, Rothen yawned. He was taking smaller quantities of nemmin now, but that meant he often woke early and spent the last hours of the night worrying.

'I spoke to Viola again this afternoon,' Tania said suddenly. 'She's still aloof – the other servants say she's put a high value on herself since becoming Sonea's servant. But she's warming to me because I can tell her how best to please the High Lord's favourite.'

Rothen regarded her expectantly. 'And?'

'She told me that Sonea is well, though some mornings she looks tired.'

He nodded. 'That's no surprise with all the extra lessons. I've heard that she's been helping Lady Tya, too.'

'Viola also said that Sonea has dinner with the High Lord on Firstdays, so perhaps he's not neglecting her as much as you fear.'

'Dinner, eh?' Rothen's mood darkened as he thought of Sonea eating meals with the High Lord. It could be worse, he reminded himself. Akkarin could have kept her close by, could have . . . but no, he knew how stubborn she could be. She would not allow herself to be corrupted. Still, he could not help wondering what they talked about.

—Rothen!

Surprised, Rothen straightened in his seat.

—*Dorrien?*

—*Father. How are you?*

—*Well. And you?*

—*I am well, but some here in my village are not.* Rothen could sense his son's concern. *We have had an outbreak of black-tongue disease here – an unusual strain of it. When it has passed, I will be coming back for a short visit, to bring a sample for Vinara.*

—*Will I see you?*

—*Of course. I could not come all the way without speaking to you! Can I stay in my old room?*

—*You're always welcome to.*

—*Thank you. How is Sonea?*

—*Well, from what Tania tells me.*

—*You haven't spoken to her yet?*

—*Not often.*

—*I thought she would be visiting you all the time.*

—*She is busy with her studies. How soon will you be visiting?*

—*I can't tell you exactly. It could take weeks or months for this disease to run its course. I'll let you know when I have a better idea.*

—*Very well. Two visits in a year!*

—*I wish I could stay longer. Until then, Father.*

—*Take care of yourself.*

—*I will.*

As Dorrien's mind-voice faded, Tania chuckled. 'How is Dorrien?'

He looked up, surprised. 'Well. How did you know it was him?'

She shrugged. 'You get a certain look on your face.'

'Do I?' Rothen shook his head. 'You know me far too well, Tania. Far too well.'

'Yes,' she agreed, smiling. 'I do.'

She turned at a knock on the door. Rothen waved a hand and willed the door open, and was surprised when Yaldin stepped inside.

'Good evening,' the old magician said. He glanced at Tania, who bowed and slipped out of the door, pulling it closed behind her. Rothen gestured to a chair and Yaldin sat down with a relieved sigh.

'I've been doing some of this "listening" you taught me,' Yaldin said.

Abruptly, Rothen remembered that it was a Fourday. He had completely forgotten about the Night Room gathering. It was definitely time to stop taking nemmin. Perhaps he would try to sleep without it tonight.

'Hear anything interesting?'

Yaldin nodded, his expression growing serious. 'It's probably just speculation. You know what gossips magicians are – and you have a gift for choosing novices that get themselves into trouble. But I wonder if he can afford such rumours surfacing again. Especially n—'

'Again?' Rothen interrupted. His heart had begun to pound at Yaldin's words. Now he could hardly breathe. Had something happened in the past to cause people to question Akkarin's integrity?

'Yes,' Yaldin said. 'The Elyne court is all abuzz with speculations – you know what they're like. What do you know about this assistant of Dannyl's?'

Taking in a deep breath, Rothen let it out slowly. 'So this is about Dannyl, then?'

'Yes.' Yaldin's frown deepened. 'You do remember the rumours that circulated about the nature of his friendship with a certain novice?'

Rothen nodded. 'Of course – but nothing was ever proven.'

'No, and most of us dismissed the rumours and forgot about the whole thing. But, as you may know, the Elynes are more tolerant of such behaviour. From what I've heard, Dannyl's assistant is known for it. Fortunately, most of the Elyne court believe that Dannyl is unaware of his assistant's habits. They seem to find this quite funny.'

'I see.' Rothen shook his head slowly. *Ah, Dannyl,* he thought. *Isn't Sonea enough for me to worry about? Must you cause me sleepless nights, too?*

But perhaps this wasn't as bad as it first sounded. As Yaldin had said, the Elynes tolerated much, and loved to gossip. If the Elynes thought that Dannyl was unaware of his assistant's preferences, and thought his ignorance merely amusing, there mustn't be any proof that there was more to the relationship.

And Dannyl was an adult now. He could handle himself in the face of public scrutiny. If anything, his past experience would have prepared him for it.

'Do you think we should warn Dannyl?' Yaldin asked. 'If he doesn't know about this assistant . . .'

Rothen considered this suggestion. 'Yes. I'll write him a letter. But I don't think we should be too concerned. I'm sure he'll know how to deal with the Elynes.'

'But what about the Guild?'

'Nothing will stop the gossip here but time, and neither you nor I – nor Dannyl – can do anything about that.' Rothen sighed. 'I think this sort of speculation is going to follow Dannyl around all his life. Unless anything is proven, it'll sound more tired and ridiculous every time it does.'

The older magician nodded, then yawned. 'You're probably right.' He stood up and stretched. 'I'll be off to bed, then.'

'Dannyl would be proud of your spying success,' Rothen added, smiling.

Yaldin shrugged. 'It's easy once you get the trick of it.' He walked to the door. 'Good night.'

'Good night.'

Rising, Rothen moved into his bedroom and changed into his night clothes. As he lay down, the inevitable questions started running through his mind. Was he right? Would this gossip about Dannyl blow over?

Probably. But only if nothing was proven.

Trouble was, while he knew Dannyl better than anyone else, there was a side to the man that was still unknown to him. The novice he had adopted had been full of self-doubt and fear. Rothen had respectfully kept his distance, avoiding certain subjects and making it clear he did not intend to question Dannyl about the incident with the other novice. He knew that anyone who'd had their personal life publicly discussed – especially at such a young age – needed their privacy respected.

All novices thought about their desires, about things Dannyl had been accused of. That was how the mind worked. It did not mean they were guilty of acting upon those thoughts.

But what if those early rumours were true?

Rothen sighed, rose and returned to the guestroom. When he had taken on Dannyl's guardianship, he had approached the Head of Healers, Vinara's predecessor, for advice. Lord Garen had told Rothen that the occurrence of men taking male lovers was more common than generally thought. The old Healer had been surprisingly accepting of the practice, saying in his typical clinical fashion that there was no physical harm in an adult male relationship if both were free of disease.

But the social consequences, however, were far worse. Honour and reputation mattered more than anything else to the Houses, and the Kyralian court was painfully conservative. While Dannyl couldn't be thrown out of the Guild for such a 'crime', he would become a social outcast. He would probably lose his ambassadorial position, and would never be offered a role of importance again. He would not be included in Guild projects, and none of his own experiments would receive funding or attention. He would be the butt of jokes and the victim of . . .

Stop it. Nothing has been proven. It's just a rumour.

Rothen sighed and reached for the jar of nemmin. As he mixed the powder with water, he thought wistfully of the past year. How could so much have changed in a few short months? How he wished everything was still as it was a year ago, before Dannyl left for Elyne, and Sonea started at the University.

Bracing himself for the bitter taste, he put the glass to his lips and gulped down the drug.

At the knock on his office door, Lorlen looked up in surprise. He was rarely disturbed this late. Rising, he walked to the door and opened it.

'Captain Barran,' he exclaimed in surprise. 'What brings you to the Guild this late?'

The young man bowed, then smiled thinly. 'Forgive me for the late visit, Administrator. I'm relieved to find you awake. You said I should contact you if evidence of magic was found in connection with the murders.'

Lorlen felt a stab of alarm. He opened the door wider and stepped aside. 'Come in and tell me what you have found.'

Barran followed Lorlen into the room. Indicating with a wave that the young guard should sit down, Lorlen stepped around his desk and returned to his seat.

'So tell me why you believe this murderer is using magic,' he prompted.

Barran grimaced. 'The burns on one of the bodies – but let me first describe the scene.' He paused, obviously sorting through details in his mind. 'We were alerted to the murders about two hours ago. The house is in the Western Quarter, in one of the wealthier areas – which was a surprise. We found no sign that anyone had forced their way into the house. One window was wide open, however.

'Inside a bedroom we found two men, a young man and his father. The father was dead, and had all the marks we've come to associate with this murderer: wrists cut and marked with bloody fingerprints. The younger man was alive, though barely. He had typical strike burns across his chest and arms and his ribcage was crushed. Despite this, we were able to question him before he died.'

Barran's expression was strained. 'He said the murderer was tall and dark-haired. He was dressed in dark, strange clothing.' Barran glanced up at Lorlen's globe light. 'And one of those was floating in the room. He had arrived home and heard his father shouting. The murderer had been surprised at his discovery, and had struck out without hesitation, then had fled through the window.' Barran paused and looked at Lorlen's desk. 'Oh, and he was wearing a . . .'

Seeing the guard's surprised expression, Lorlen looked down. He caught his breath as he realised that Akkarin's ring, glinting red in the light, was in plain sight. Thinking quickly, he lifted his hand to give Barran a better view.

'A ring like this?'

Barran's shoulders lifted. 'I can't say exactly. The young man didn't have time to describe it in detail.' He frowned and grew hesitant. 'I don't remember you wearing this before, Administrator. May I ask where you acquired it?'

'It was a gift,' Lorlen answered. He smiled wryly. 'From a friend who wasn't aware of that detail about the murders. I felt I had to wear it, even if just for a little while.'

Barran nodded. 'Yes, ruby is not a popular stone at the moment. So, what will you do now?'

Lorlen sighed and considered the situation. With such obvious evidence of magic, he ought to alert the Higher Magicians. But if Akkarin was the murderer, and an investigation led to this discovery, it would bring about the confrontation with Akkarin that Lorlen feared.

Yet if Lorlen tried to hide the evidence of magic, and it turned out that Akkarin wasn't the killer, people would continue to die at the hands of a rogue magician. Eventually the murderer would be found, the truth would come out, and people would question why Lorlen hadn't done anything—

—*You must investigate it yourself.*

Lorlen blinked in surprise. Akkarin's mind-voice was as quiet as a whisper. He managed to stop himself staring at the ring.

—*Tell Barran that the evidence of magic must remain secret.*

If the public knows that a magician has turned into a killer it will generate panic and distrust.

Nodding, Lorlen looked up at Barran. 'I will need to discuss this with my colleagues. For now, don't let any word that this murderer uses magic spread further than necessary. Better that we can deal with this man without the public knowing he is a rogue. I will contact you tomorrow.'

Barran nodded. As Lorlen rose the young guard quickly got to his feet.

'There is one other piece of information that might interest you,' Barran said as he followed Lorlen to the door.

'Yes?'

'Word is going around that the Thieves are looking for this man, too. Seems they don't much like having a killer about who isn't in their control.'

'No, I imagine they wouldn't.'

Barran stepped out of the door. 'Thank you for seeing me at such a late hour, Administrator.'

Lorlen shrugged. 'I am often up late. Though I doubt I'll be getting much sleep during the rest of the night after this piece of news. Still, I thank you for bringing it to me so soon after receiving word yourself.'

The young guard smiled, then bowed. 'Good night, Administrator.'

Watching Barran walk away, Lorlen sighed. He looked down at the ring on his hand. *Are you the murderer?* he projected at it.

There was no answer.

The passage turned again and Sonea paused to get her bearings. At first she tried to picture the plan in her memory, but after several tries she gave up and reached into her robe pockets.

It was a week since she had first entered the passages. She had visited them every night, each time leaving the map in her robes until she was forced to use it. She wanted to memorise it all in case Regin and his allies ambushed her and looked through her box or pockets once they had exhausted her.

Sonea's searching fingers found nothing. The map wasn't there. Her heart skipped and started racing. Had she lost it? Had she dropped it somewhere in the passages? She didn't think there'd be much hope of retracing her steps. All those turns and intersections behind her . . .

Then she remembered that she had hidden the map inside the fraying cover of one of her medicine books, which was in her box – and she had left her box at a passage entrance, not wanting to lug it around while exploring.

She cursed herself for forgetting and started back the way she had come. After several hundred paces she stopped, shaking her head. She should have reached familiar ground by now, but the turns and intersections were all wrong.

She was lost.

She didn't feel frightened, only annoyed at herself. The Guild grounds were big, but she doubted the tunnels would go far beyond the area covered by the buildings. If she kept going, she was bound to find herself under the University eventually. So long as she didn't wander aimlessly, and paid attention to the general direction they took her, she would find her way out.

So she started walking. After several twists and turns, and the discovery of a small complex of rooms including one with a blocked fireplace and a tiled room that must have once been a bath, she came to a dead end where the roof had collapsed. It was not one of the dead ends she had encountered before. Doubling back, she chose another path.

Eventually she found herself in a straight passage with no side entrances. Her curiosity grew stronger as she continued down this passage. A straight tunnel like this must lead to something. Perhaps another Guild building. Or perhaps it led out of the Guild altogether.

After a few hundred paces she encountered an alcove. Stepping into it, she discovered the mechanism for a hidden door. She found the spy hole that all of the doors contained and put her eye to it.

A room lay beyond, but she could not see much of it. Not only was the room dark, but a piece of dirty glass had been placed over the hole, blurring the view.

But she could see enough to know that the room was empty. Reaching for the mechanism, she pulled a lever and the door swung open. She looked around the room and felt her blood turn to ice.

It was the room underneath the High Lord's Residence.

For what seemed an age all she could do was stare around, her heart hammering in her chest. Then slowly her legs obeyed her need to get away. Her hands groped for the lever that would close the door and found it.

As it slid shut her muscles unfroze and went limp. She sagged against the wall, heedless of faren or other insects, and slid to her knees.

If he'd been there . . .

It was too terrifying to think about. Taking a deep breath, she willed herself to stop shaking. She looked up at the door and down at herself. She was kneeling next to a secret entrance to Akkarin's room. Not a good place to be, particularly if he was in the habit of using these passages.

Strengthened again by fear, she stumbled to her feet and hurried away. Though the passage continued past the alcove, she no longer felt any need to know where it led. Breathing quickly, she broke into a run and fled in what she hoped was the direction of the University.

CHAPTER 31

AN UNPLANNED ENCOUNTER

The road twisted about, following the curve of the land as it wound through the foothills of the Grey Mountains. As Dannyl, Tayend and their servants rode around a corner, a striking building came into sight. It rose straight up from the edge of a precipice. Tiny windows dotted the walls, and a narrow stone bridge led to an unadorned opening.

Dannyl and Tayend exchanged glances. By Tayend's expression, Dannyl knew the scholar found the building as unwelcoming as he did. He turned to the servants.

'Hend, Krimen. Go ahead and see if Dem Ladeiri will grant us a visit.'

'Yes, my lord,' Hend replied. The two servants nudged their horses into a trot and disappeared beyond the next turn of the road.

'Not a friendly looking place,' Tayend muttered.

'No,' Dannyl agreed. 'More like a fort than a house.'

'It *was* a fort once,' Tayend said. 'Centuries ago.'

Dannyl slowed his horse to a walk. 'What can you tell me of Dem Ladeiri?'

'He's old. About ninety. He has a few servants, but lives alone otherwise.'

'And he has a library.'

'Quite a famous one. His family has collected all sorts

of oddities over the last few hundred years, including some books.'

'Perhaps we'll find something useful here.'

Tayend shrugged. 'I'm expecting to find much that is strange, and little that is useful. Librarian Irand said he knew the Dem when they were both young men, and called him an "amusing eccentric".'

Dannyl watched for glimpses of the building through the trees as they continued along the road. They had been travelling for three weeks, staying no more than a night in any place. Introducing himself to country Dems and testing their children was becoming a chore, and none of the libraries they visited contained anything they had not already learned.

Of course, this may have been the case for Akkarin as well. His quest for knowledge of ancient magic had ended without him producing any great discoveries.

At last the bridge appeared before them. It spanned a dizzying drop to a ravine far below. Deep within an opening in the front wall of the building were two large wooden doors, hanging from hinges so rusted that Dannyl wondered why they hadn't yet given way. A thin, white-haired man wearing clothes that looked a size too large stood between the doors.

'Greetings, Ambassador Dannyl.' The old man's voice was thin and wavering. He bowed stiffly. 'Welcome to my home.'

Dannyl and Tayend dismounted and handed the reins to their servants. 'Thank you, Dem Ladeiri,' Dannyl replied. 'This is Tayend of Tremmelin, scholar of the Great Library.'

The Dem turned and peered short-sightedly at

Tayend. 'Welcome, young man. I have a library too, you know.'

'Yes, I've heard. A library famous throughout Elyne,' Tayend replied with convincingly affected eagerness. 'Full of curiosities. I would love to see it, if you do not mind.'

'Of course you can!' the Dem exclaimed. 'Come inside.'

They followed the old man into a small courtyard, then through a rusty iron door into a hall. Though the furnishings were luxurious, a smell of dust hung in the air.

'Iri!' the old man called shrilly. Footsteps hurried to a doorway and a middle-aged woman wearing an apron appeared. 'Bring my guests some refreshments. We'll be in the library.'

The woman's eyes widened as she saw Dannyl's robes. She bowed hastily and backed out of sight.

'There's no need to take us to the library straightaway,' Dannyl said. 'We do not wish to inconvenience you.'

The Dem waved a hand. 'It's no inconvenience. I was in the library when your servants arrived.'

They followed the old man into a corridor, then down a long, spiral staircase that looked as if it had been carved out of the rock wall. The last section of the staircase was made of sturdy wood, and opened out into the middle of a vast room.

Dannyl smiled as he heard Tayend's gasp. Clearly, the scholar had not expected to be impressed.

The room was carefully divided by rows of shelving. Spread before them were stuffed animals, bottles of preserving liquid containing organs and creatures, carvings made from all manner of materials, strange contraptions, lumps of rock and crystal, countless scrolls, tablets, and shelf after shelf of books. Huge sculptures stood here and there, making Dannyl wonder how they could have been brought down the stairs into the library – or even transported through the mountains. Charts of stars and other mysterious diagrams hung from the walls.

They followed the Dem through these marvels, too amazed to speak. As he led them down an aisle between the books, Tayend peered at the small plaques engraved with subjects and numbers attached to each shelf.

'What are these numbers for?' the scholar asked.

The Dem turned and smiled. 'Cataloguing system. Each book has a number and I keep a record of them all on paper.'

'We don't have anything this detailed at the Great Library. We keep books on the same subject together . . . as best we can. How long have you had this system in place?'

The old man glanced at Tayend sideways. 'My grand-father invented it.'

'Did you ever suggest the Great Library adopt it?'

'Several times. Irand did not see any value in it.'

'Really.' Tayend looked amused. 'I would love to see how it works.'

'You will,' the old man replied, 'since that is what I am about to show you.'

They left the shelves and arrived at a large desk surrounded by wooden chests of drawers.

'Now, is there any particular subject you would like to explore?'

'Have you got any books on ancient magical practices?' Tayend asked.

The old man's eyebrows rose. 'Yes. But can you be more specific?'

Dannyl and Tayend exchanged a glance.

'Anything to do with the King of Charkan or Shakan Dra.'

The Dem's eyebrows rose higher. 'I will check.'

He turned and pulled open a drawer to reveal rows of cards. Flicking through, he called out a number. Then, closing the drawer, he moved down to the end of the shelves and turned into an aisle. Stopping at one of the bookcases, the Dem ran a finger along the spines then tapped one.

'This is it.' He drew out the book and handed it to Tayend.

'It's a history of Ralend of Kemori.'

'There must be a reference to the King of Charkan in there, or my cards would not have led me to this book,' the Dem assured him. 'Now, follow me. I believe we have some artefacts, too.'

They followed the Dem out of the bookshelves to several rows of drawers. These, too, were numbered. The old man pulled out a drawer and set it on a nearby table. As he peered inside he gave a low exclamation.

'Ah! That's right. This was sent to me five years ago. I remember thinking that your High Lord would have wanted to see it.'

Once more Tayend and Dannyl exchanged a glance.

'Akkarin?' Dannyl asked looking into the box. It contained a silver ring. 'Why would he be interested?'

'Because he came to me many years ago looking for information about the King of Charkan. He showed me this symbol.' The Dem held up the ring. Set into it was a dark red gem, and carved into the surface of the gem was a crescent moon next to a crude hand. 'But when I sent him a letter telling him what I had received, he replied that he was unable to visit because of his new position.'

Taking the ring, Dannyl examined it closely.

'The person who sent it said that, according to legend, magicians can use it to communicate with each other without fear of being overhead,' the Dem added.

'Really? Who was this generous donor?'

'I don't know. He – or she – didn't give their name.' The Dem shrugged. 'Sometimes people don't want their family to know they've given something valuable away. In any case, it's not a true gem. It's only glass.'

'Try it,' urged a voice at Dannyl's shoulder.

Dannyl looked at Tayend, surprised. The scholar grinned. 'Go on!'

'I'd need to be communicating with another magician,' Dannyl pointed out, as he slipped the ring on his finger. 'And have a third to test if he could detect our conversation.'

Dannyl looked down at the ring. He felt nothing to indicate anything magical was happening.

'I can't sense anything from it.' He pulled it off and gave it back to the Dem. 'Perhaps it had once held some magical properties, but has lost them over time.'

The old man nodded and put the box away. 'The book may be more enlightening. There are chairs over here for reading,' he said, waving them across the room. As they reached the chairs, the woman they had seen earlier arrived with a tray laden with food. Another followed carrying glasses and a bottle of wine. Tayend sat down and began leafing through the history of Ralend of Kemori.

'"The King of Charkan spoke of his path,"' he read. '"He came by the mountains, stopping to offer gifts at

Armje; the city of the moon."' Tayend looked up. 'Armje. I've heard that name.'

'It is a ruin now,' the Dem said, his mouth still full of savoury bun. 'Not far from here. I used to climb up there all the time, in my younger days.'

As the Dem began to describe the ruins enthusiastically, Dannyl saw that Tayend wasn't listening. The scholar's gaze sharpened as he continued to read the book. Knowing that look, Dannyl smiled. The Dem's library hadn't turned out to be the collection of useless oddities that Tayend had been expecting.

In the two weeks since she had first entered the secret passages, Sonea hadn't once encountered Regin. While she hoped discovery by Lord Yikmo had put off Regin's allies, she suspected it hadn't.

She had heard nothing to indicate they had been punished. Yikmo had not mentioned the incident again, and no-one else seemed to know of it, so she guessed he had respected her request to keep silent. Unfortunately, this would only give Regin's allies more confidence that they could harass her and get away with it.

Since Regin had always waylaid her somewhere on the second level, where the library was, she had been careful to exit the secret passages on the lower floor. The previous evening, she saw the first sign that he had worked this out. Entering the main corridor on the lower floor, she had seen a novice standing at the far end and, a few steps later, in the Entrance Hall, came face to face with one of the older boys. Though he hadn't dared to attack her, he had smiled smugly as she passed.

So this evening she had exited the secret passages on

the third level instead. Keeping her footsteps as quiet as possible, she cautiously made her way toward the main corridor.

If she encountered Regin and his friends, she could still run away and escape into the secret passages. If she wasn't cornered before she could get to an entrance, that is, and if she could get into the passages without them seeing.

Rounding a corner, she glimpsed a flash of brown material around the next turn and felt her heart sink. As she backed away, she heard a faint whisper. Footsteps echoed from the direction she had come. She cursed under her breath and began to run. Darting into a side passage, she collided with a lone novice. A blast of magic hit her shield, but he was alone and she easily pushed him away.

Three turns later she encountered two more novices. They tried to block her path, but gave up after a moment. At the door to a portal room, she was delayed when four novices stepped out to fight her. Pushing past them, she placed a magical lock on the door.

Keep them separated, she thought, *Yikmo would approve.*

Moving into the inner passages, she hurried toward the nearest portal room. When she was in sight of it, she willed the door to open and close, then quickly retraced her steps.

Still alone, she thought. Slowing to quieten her footsteps, she took a winding path, finally coming to a door to the secret passages. Checking to make sure no-one could see, she slipped a hand under a painting and felt the lever.

'She went this way,' a voice called.

Her heart skipped a beat. She yanked the lever down and stumbled through the opening, then pushed the door closed.

Surrounded by darkness, she peered through the

peephole, breathing heavily. Through the little hole, she saw several novices pass. Counting them, she felt ill. Twenty novices.

But she had evaded them. Her heartbeat slowed and her breathing quietened. A little warm air touched her neck.

Sonea frowned. *Warm* air?

Then, beneath the sound of her own breathing, she heard another, softer, breath. She spun around and willed a light into existence . . . then choked down a cry of terror.

Dark eyes bore into hers. His arms were folded across his chest, the incal glinting gold against the black of his robes. His face was set in a disapproving scowl.

Swallowing hard, she edged sideways, but an arm rose to block her path.

'Get out,' he snarled.

She hesitated. Couldn't he hear the novices? Didn't he understand that she would be walking into a trap?

'Now!' he snapped. 'And don't enter these passages again.'

Turning, she fumbled with the lock, her hands shaking. Checking the peephole, she was relieved to see the passage outside was clear of witnesses. She stumbled through and felt a whisper of cold air on the back of her neck as the door closed behind her.

For several heartbeats she stood there, shivering. Then she thought of him watching her through the peephole and forced herself to move. As she rounded a corner twenty pairs of eyes turned to stare at her in surprise.

'Found her!' someone cried joyfully.

Sonea threw up a shield against the first strikes. She backed away and then, as Regin barked orders for half to circle around and block her escape, turned and ran.

As she fled past the hidden door, she felt shock fall away and anger rising.

Why doesn't he stop them? Is this my punishment for going where I wasn't supposed to go? She skidded to a halt as novices leapt out of a side passage and then, throwing up a barrier to hold them there, she dashed down the only other exit.

Won't people question why he didn't . . . but of course, nobody knows he was there but me. Feeling her barrier fail under the onslaught of the novices, she cursed. As she turned a corner she slammed into an invisible wall. She broke the barrier easily and hurried past only to meet another. This, too, fell quickly, but she found herself blocked by another, and another. Her heart sank as footsteps signalled the approach of novices in front and behind. In the next moment she was shielding a relentless shower of strikes.

What was he doing in the hidden passages, anyway? I never saw any sign of footprints . . . unless he has been smoothing the dust as he passed . . . but why would he do that when nobody else uses the passages?

Novices blocked her escape. Trapped, she could only wait as they wore her down. With so many attackers, her strength failed rapidly. As her shield began to waver, Regin stepped to the front and smiled broadly. He held a small bottle in his hand, filled with a dark liquid. At a signal from him the attack stopped.

'Sweet Sonea,' he said, sending a bolt of power at her shield. 'How my heart lifts to see you.' Another strike. 'It has been so long since we met.' Her shield began to crumble, but she drew up more power from somewhere. 'Absence does nurture regard, as they say.' The next strike broke it easily. She braced, waiting for the stunstrikes to come.

'I have brought you a gift,' Regin continued. 'A perfume of the most exotic variety.' He plucked the cork from the bottle. 'Urgh! Such sweet fragrance. Would you like to try it?'

Even from a few steps away, she recognised the smell. Her class had extracted oil from the leaves of the kreppa bush for a medicine project. The remaining juice smelled like rotting vegetation and could cause stinging blisters.

Regin waved the unstoppered bottle carelessly. 'But one tiny bottle is too small a token of my regard. Look, I have brought more!'

Bottles appeared in the other novices' hands. They opened them gingerly and the corridor filled with the sickening odour.

'Tomorrow, we will know where you are by your sweet perfume.' Regin nodded to the others. 'Now!' he barked.

Hands thrust forward, sending several streams of the vile juice toward her. She threw up her hands, closed her eyes and from somewhere managed to draw together a last surge of power.

No liquid touched her skin. Nothing. She heard someone cough, then another, then suddenly the passage was filled with curses and exclamations. Opening her eyes, she blinked in amazement. The walls, the ceiling, and the novices were splattered with fine brown droplets. The novices were wiping at their hands and faces frantically. Some were spitting on the floor. Others were rubbing their eyes and one had begun to wail with pain.

Looking at Regin she saw that, being the closest, he had suffered the worst. His eyes were streaming, and his face was raw with red spots.

A strange feeling was bubbling up inside her. Realising

she was going to laugh, she covered her mouth. Hauling herself away from the wall, she swayed, then made herself straighten.

Don't let them see how tired I am, she thought. *Don't give them time to get ideas of revenge into their heads.*

She started walking through the group of novices. Regin's head snapped up. 'Don't let her get away,' he growled.

A few novices looked up, but the rest ignored him.

'Forget it. I'm getting these robes off now,' one novice said. Others nodded, and began to move away. Regin blinked at them, his face darkening with fury, but he did not argue.

Sonea turned her back and forced her tired legs to carry her past the novices and away.

CHAPTER 32

A LITTLE SIDE TRIP

Rothen yawned as he climbed the stairs of the Magicians' Quarters. Even a cold bath hadn't done much to wake him up. He found Tania waiting for him in his guestroom, laying out plates of cakes and buns.

'Good morning, Tania,' he said.

'You're a little late this morning, my lord,' she replied.

'Yes.' He rubbed his face, then started making sumi. Realising she was still watching him, he sighed. 'I've cut down to a tenth of the dosage.'

She didn't say anything, just nodded approvingly. 'I have some news.' She paused, and when he gestured for her to continue, she grimaced apologetically. 'You won't like it.'

'Go on.'

'The University cleaners were complaining this morning that some foul-smelling liquid was splattered all over one of the passages. I asked them what they thought had happened, and they started grumbling about novices fighting each other. They were a bit reluctant to say which novices – reluctant to say in front of me, that is. So I bribed it out of one of the serving girls who had already heard the story.

'Regin has been gathering together other novices and waylaying Sonea at night. I asked Viola about it, and she said she hadn't seen anything to suggest that Sonea had been harmed at all.'

Rothen frowned. 'It would take a lot to wear Sonea out.' He felt a spark of anger as he realised what this meant. 'Once she had, though, Regin could do anything to her. She'd be too tired to even fight him off physically.'

Tania drew in a sharp breath. 'He wouldn't dare hurt her, would he?'

'Not in any way that would do lasting damage, or have him expelled.' Rothen scowled at the table.

'Why doesn't the High Lord put a stop to it – or hasn't he heard about it? Perhaps you should tell him.'

Rothen shook his head. 'He knows. It's his place to know.'

'But—' Tania stopped at a knock on the door. Relieved at the interruption, Rothen willed it open. A messenger stepped inside, bowed, and handed Rothen a letter, before retreating from the room again.

'It's for Sonea.' Rothen turned the letter over and felt his heart skip. 'It's from her aunt and uncle.'

Tania moved closer. 'Don't they know she isn't living in your rooms any more?'

'No. Sonea thought Regin might get hold of her mail if it came to her in the Novices' Quarters, and she probably hasn't contacted them since she moved to the residence.'

'Would you like me to take it to her?' Tania offered.

Rothen looked up, surprised. It was easy to forget that others had no reason to fear Akkarin. 'Would you?'

'Of course. I haven't spoken to her in such a long time.'

Akkarin might grow suspicious if he saw Rothen's servant delivering a message to Sonea, however. 'She'll want to read this as soon as possible. If you deliver it to her room, she won't get it until tonight. I think she spends Freedays in the Novices' Library. Could you give it to Lady Tya?'

'Yes.' Tania took the letter and slipped it into the front of her uniform. 'I'll drop by the library after dropping these dishes off at the kitchen.'

'Agh! My legs hurt!' Tayend complained.

Dannyl laughed quietly as the scholar collapsed onto a boulder to rest. '*You* wanted to visit the ruins. It wasn't my idea.'

'But Dem Ladeiri made them sound so interesting.' Tayend pulled out his flask and drank a few mouthfuls of water. 'And closer.'

'He just neglected to say we'd have to scale a few cliffs to get here. Or that the rope bridge wasn't safe.'

'Well, I suppose he did tell us it had been a long time since he had come up here. Levitation must really come in handy at times.'

'At times.'

'Why aren't you breathing hard?'

Dannyl smiled. 'Levitation isn't the only useful trick the Guild teaches us.'

'You're *healing* yourself?' Tayend threw a small stone at him. 'That's cheating!'

'Then I assume you would refuse my assistance if I offered it.'

'No, I feel it would be only fair that I have the same advantage as you.'

Dannyl sighed in mock resignation. 'Give me your wrist, then.' To his surprise, Tayend offered his arm without hesitation, but as Dannyl placed his palm against the scholar's skin, Tayend looked away and closed his eyes tightly.

Sending a little Healing magic into Tayend's body, Dannyl soothed the stressed muscles. Most Healers would frown at this waste of magic. There was nothing wrong with Tayend, he was simply unused to the strain of trekking across mountainous territory.

As Dannyl released Tayend's arm, the scholar stood and looked down at himself.

'That is amazing!' he exclaimed. 'I feel like I did this morning, before we left.' He grinned at Dannyl, then began striding up the path. 'Come on; then. We haven't got all day.'

Bemused, Dannyl followed. Only a few hundred paces on, Tayend reached a rise and slowed to a stop. As Dannyl caught up with the scholar, the ruins came into view. Spread over a gentle slope were low walls, marking the outlines of buildings. Here and there an ancient column had survived, and at the centre of the small deserted city a larger, roofless structure still stood intact, its walls constructed of huge slabs of stone. Grass and other vegetation grew over and around everything.

'So this is Armje,' Tayend muttered. 'Not much left.'

'It is over a thousand years old.'

'Let's take a closer look.'

The path, as it curved around to meet the city, widened into a grassy road. As it reached the first of the buildings it straightened, leading to the large building. Dannyl and Tayend paused to examine some of the exposed rooms of the smaller buildings.

'Do you think this was some kind of public washroom?'

Tayend asked at one point, standing by a stone bench that had holes cut into it at regular intervals.

'Perhaps some kind of kitchen,' Dannyl replied. 'The holes might have held pots over a fire or brazier.'

When they reached the large structure at the centre, Dannyl noticed a stillness in the air. They passed beneath a heavy lintel into a wide room. The floor was hidden beneath dirt and waist-high grass and herbs.

'I wonder what this place was,' Tayend mused aloud. 'Something important. A palace, perhaps. Or a temple.'

Moving into a smaller room, Tayend suddenly darted to one side. He peered at the wall, which was carved with a complex pattern.

'There are words in this,' he said. 'Something about laws.'

Dannyl looked closer, then felt his heart skip a beat as he saw a carved hand. 'Look.'

'That's the glyph for magic,' Tayend said dismissively.

'A hand is the sign for magic in ancient Elyne?'

'Yes – and it is in many ancient writings. Some scholars believe that the modern letter "m" is derived from the symbol of a hand.'

'So half of the Charkan King's title indicates magic. What does the crescent moon mean, then?'

Tayend shrugged and moved further into the ruin. 'Moon magic. Night magic. Does magic ever follow the cycles of the moon?'

'No.'

'Perhaps it has something to do with women. Women's magic. Wait – look at this!'

Tayend had stopped before another carved wall. He was pointing at a section high up where some of the stone had fallen away, leaving only part of the carving behind. Then Dannyl drew in a sharp breath. The scholar wasn't pointing at one of the carved glyphs. He was pointing at a familiar name written in modern lettering.

'Dem Ladeiri didn't mention anything about Akkarin coming up here,' Tayend said.

'Perhaps he forgot. Perhaps Akkarin didn't tell him.'

'But he really wanted us to come here.'

Dannyl stared at the name, then looked at the rest of the wall. 'What does the ancient writing say?'

Tayend looked closer. 'Give me a minute . . .'

As the scholar examined the glyphs, Dannyl stepped back and looked around the room. Below Akkarin's name was a relief carving of an archway. Or was it? He scuffed the dirt and grass away from the base and smiled as he uncovered a crack.

Tayend drew in a sharp breath. 'According to this, this is a—'

'Door,' Dannyl finished.

'Yes!' Tayend tapped the wall. 'And it leads to a place of judgment. I wonder if it can still be opened.'

Looking at the door, Dannyl extended his senses. He detected a simple mechanism, designed to be opened from the inside only – or by magic.

'Stand back.'

As Tayend moved out of the way, Dannyl exerted his will. The mechanism turned reluctantly, straining against the dirt, dust and grass clogging the doorway. A loud rumble and scraping noise filled the room as the stone door swivelled inward, revealing a dark passage.

When the door had opened wide enough for a man to slip through sideways, Dannyl released the mechanism, afraid he would do lasting damage if he forced it further. He exchanged a look with Tayend.

'Shall we go in?' the scholar whispered.

Dannyl frowned. 'I will go first. It might be unstable.'

Tayend looked as if he would protest, but seemed to change his mind. 'I'll continue translating this.'

'I'll come back as soon as I know it's safe.'

'You'd better.'

As Dannyl slipped through the door, he willed a globe light into existence and sent it ahead. The walls were unadorned. At first he had to brush aside fine cascades of roots and faren webs, but after twenty steps the way was clear. The floor sloped downward slightly, and the air grew rapidly colder.

There were no side passages. The roof was low and soon Dannyl felt a familiar uneasiness stealing over him. Counting his steps, he had passed two hundred when the walls ended. The floor continued, however, as a narrow ledge leading into utter darkness. Cautiously, he stepped out on this ledge, ready to levitate if it should collapse under his feet. From the way his footsteps echoed, the drop on either side was considerable.

The ledge widened to form a circular platform after about ten paces. Willing his globe light to brighten, Dannyl gasped as the light reflected off a glittering dome. The surface sparkled and shimmered as if covered by innumerable gemstones.

'Tayend!' he called. 'Come look at this!' Glancing back at the black opening of the passage, Dannyl flexed his will, creating small globe lights along the length of it.

Something shifted in the corner of his eye. He turned to see that a section of the dome was glittering brighter than the rest. Rivulets of light appeared, shivering toward each other. Staring in fascination, he watched as they raced to meet. It looked like the Arena barrier when it had been struck, except in reverse . . .

Some instinct warned him and he threw up a shield just in time to meet the streak of power from the dome. He exclaimed in surprise at the strength of it – then again in shock as he felt another attack from behind. Turning, he saw a second starburst of power in the stones . . . and two more rapidly forming.

He took a step toward the passage entrance, then another, and felt the sting of a barrier blocking his way. *What is going on! Who is doing this?*

But there was nobody else here. Only Tayend. Dannyl looked at the passage, but it was empty. As more attacks came, Dannyl spread his hands before the barrier and sent out a bolt of magic. The barrier held. Perhaps, if he put all his strength into it . . . but he needed power to shield.

He felt panic rising. Every strike tired him further. He had no idea how long this attack would continue. If he waited, this place – this trap – might kill him.

Think! he told himself. The strikes from the walls were directed at a point above the centre of the platform. If he squeezed himself up against the barrier, the strikes might miss him when his shield failed. And if he let his shield drop and put all his power into breaking the barrier it might fall before the next strike hit.

It was all he could think of. He had no time to come up with a better idea. Closing his eyes, he ignored the sting of magic as he pushed up against the barrier. He drew in a breath, then simultaneously dropped his shield and blasted out all his power.

He felt the barrier waver. At the same time, he was conscious of the last of his strength leaving him. He braced himself for pain, but instead felt himself falling. He opened his eyes, but all he could see was darkness . . . a darkness he continued to fall into long after he ought to have hit the ground . . .

'Lady Sonea.'

Looking up, Sonea felt her heart skip. 'Tania!'

As the servant smiled, fond memories of early morning chats brought an ache of longing. Sonea patted the seat next to her, and Tania sat down.

'How are you?' Tania asked. Something about the way the servant looked at Sonea suggested she didn't expect a favourable answer.

'Well.' Sonea forced a smile.

'You look tired.'

Sonea shrugged. 'Too many late nights. There's so much to learn now. How are you? Is Rothen keeping you run off your feet?'

Tania chuckled. 'He's no trouble, though he misses you terribly.'

'I miss him, too – and you.'

'I have a letter for you, my lady,' Tania said. She drew it out of her clothes and put it on the table. 'Rothen said it was from your aunt and uncle and said you might want to read it straightaway, so I offered to deliver it to you here.'

Sonea picked up the letter eagerly. 'Thank you.' She tore it open and began to read. The script was formal and stilted. Since her aunt and uncle could not write, they would hire a scribe whenever they wanted to send her a letter.

'My aunt is going to have another child!' Sonea exclaimed. 'Oh, I wish I could see them.'

'Of course you can,' Tania said. 'The Guild isn't a prison, you know.'

Sonea considered the woman. Of course, Tania didn't know about Akkarin. But Akkarin had never said that he forbade family visits. Nor had he told her she must never leave the Guild. The guards at the gate wouldn't stop her. She could just walk out into the city and go where she pleased. Akkarin wouldn't like it, but since he had forced her out of the secret passages and left her at the mercy of Regin's gang, she hadn't cared too much about being co-operative.

'You're right,' Sonea said slowly. 'I'll visit them. I'll visit them today.'

Tania smiled. 'I'm sure they'll be delighted to see you again.'

'Thank you, Tania,' Sonea said, rising. The servant bowed and, still smiling, walked away toward the library door.

Packing her books back into her box, Sonea felt a growing excitement, but as she considered where she was going, she sobered again. She could move through the city easily. Nobody would think twice about the presence of a magician on the streets, not even a novice. But once in the slums her robes would draw attention, possibly hostile attention. It was a problem she hadn't needed to consider on her previous visits because she hadn't been a novice then. While she could protect herself from any missiles or harassment with magic, she did not want to be followed around, or draw that sort of attention to her aunt and uncle.

The law said she must wear the uniform at all times, however. She was not too worried about breaking the law, but where was she going to change into the sort of shabby clothing that would disguise her in the slums, even if she managed to find some?

She could buy a coat or cloak from the Market when she got to the North Quarter. For that, however, she needed money, and she kept her money in her room in the High Lord's Residence. Looking down at her box, she reconsidered her plan. Was she going to let her fear of Akkarin stop her visiting her family? No. He was rarely in the residence during the day. She probably wouldn't encounter him.

Picking up her box, she bowed to Lady Tya and left the library. As she walked through the passages of the University, she smiled. She would buy a present for her aunt and uncle, too – and she might drop by Gollin's inn to see Harrin and Donia afterward, and ask after Cery.

As she entered the High Lord's Residence, she felt her heartbeat quicken. To her relief, Akkarin was not inside, and Takan, his servant, appeared only long enough to give her a respectful bow and disappear again. Leaving her box, she tucked a money bag into her robes and left her room. When the door of the residence shut behind her, she straightened her back and headed for the gates.

The gate guards glanced at her with curiosity as she passed between them. They had probably never seen her before, since she had only left the Guild a few times in a carriage with Rothen. Perhaps it was simply odd to see a novice leaving on foot.

Once in the Inner Circle, she felt strangely out of place. Looking up at the grand homes that lined the streets, strong memories returned of her few visits to this part of the city years before, to deliver repaired shoes and clothing to servants of the Houses. During those visits the well-dressed men and women of the Inner Circle had regarded her with suspicion and disdain, and she had been forced to show her token of admission several times.

Now those people smiled and bowed politely as she passed them. It felt strange and unreal. The feeling increased as she passed through the gates into the North Quarter. The gate guards stopped and saluted, and even stopped a carriage of House Korin so she could pass without delay.

Once in the North Quarter, polite bows and smiles changed to stares. After several hundred paces, Sonea changed her mind about visiting the Market. Instead, she stepped up to a house advertising 'Quality Clothing and Alterations'.

'Yes?' A grey-haired woman answered the door and, upon seeing a young magician on her doorstep, she gasped with astonishment. 'My lady! What can I do for you?' she asked, bowing hastily.

Sonea smiled. 'I would like to buy a cloak, please.'

'Come in! Come in!' The woman opened the door wide and bowed again as Sonea stepped inside. She ushered Sonea into a room, where racks of clothing hung all around the room.

'I'm not sure if I have anything good enough,' the woman said apologetically, as she lifted several cloaks from the racks. 'This one has limek fur around the hood, and that one has a beaded hem.'

Unable to resist, Sonea inspected the cloaks. 'This is good work,' she said of the beaded cloak. 'I doubt this fur is limek, however. Limek have a double coat.'

'Oh dear!' the woman exclaimed, snatching the cloak back.

'But they're not what I'm looking for, anyway,' Sonea added. 'I need something old and a bit worn – not that I expected to find anything of low quality here. Do any of your servants have a cloak that looks as if it ought to be thrown out any day?'

The woman stared at Sonea in surprise. 'I don't know . . .' she said doubtfully.

'Why don't you ask them now,' Sonea suggested, 'while I admire some of your work.'

'If that's what you want . . .' Curiosity had crept into the woman's gaze now. She bowed, then disappeared into the house calling a servant's name.

Moving to the hangers, Sonea looked at some of the clothing. She sighed wistfully. With the law restricting her to robes, she was never likely to wear anything like this, even though she could now afford to.

Hearing hurried footsteps approaching, she turned to see the seamstress enter the room, her arms laden with clothing. A servant followed her in, looking pale and harassed. Seeing Sonea, the girl's eyes widened.

Looking over the cloaks, Sonea chose one with a long, neatly repaired rip down one side. The hem had come unstitched from the lining, too. She looked at the serving girl.

'Is there a garden here? Perhaps a poultry yard?'

The girl nodded.

'Take this cloak and rub the hem in some dirt for me – and throw a little dust over it.'

Looking bemused, the girl disappeared with the cloak. Sonea pressed a gold coin into the seamstress's hand, then as the servant returned with the soiled cloak, slipped a silver into the girl's pocket.

Who would have thought I'd end up using my pick-pocketing skills to give money away rather than steal it? she mused as she left the house. With the cloak covering her robes, she received no more stares as she continued toward the Northern Gates.

The guards gave her only a cursory glance as she entered the slums. They were more concerned about dwells leaving the slums, than who was going in. A smell, both unpleasant and comfortingly familiar, enveloped her as she moved into the winding streets. Looking around, she felt herself relax a little. Here, Regin and Akkarin seemed like distant, petty worries.

Then she noted a man eyeing her from the door of a bolhouse and tensed again. This was still the slums, and though she could protect herself with magic, it would be better to avoid having to. Keeping alert and within the shadows, she made her way quickly along the streets and alleys.

Jonna and Ranel now lived in a more prosperous part of the slums, where the residents lived in sturdy wooden houses. She slipped into a Market to buy some blankets and a basket filled with vegetables and fresh bread. She wished she could buy something more luxurious, but Jonna had always refused such gifts saying: 'I don't want anything with the look of the Houses in my home. People will get strange ideas about us.'

As she arrived at the street her family lived in, she tossed a few savoury buns to a small gang of boys sitting on some empty crates at the corner. They called out their thanks. She realised she hadn't enjoyed herself so much for months.

Not since Dorrien visited, she thought suddenly. *But best not to think of Dorrien.*

Reaching the house of her aunt and uncle, she sobered. Since she joined the Guild, they had been uneasy and awkward. They had witnessed her lose Control of her powers over a year before, and Sonea would not have been surprised if they were still afraid of her. But she knew that she would never overcome their fear or awkwardness if she didn't keep visiting them. They were still her only family and she was not going to let them disappear from her life.

She knocked. A moment later, the door opened and Jonna stared at her in surprise.

'Sonea!'

Sonea grinned. 'Hello, Jonna.'

Jonna pushed open the door. 'You look different . . . but I see what you've done with the cloak. Is that legal?'

Sonea snorted. 'Who cares? I got your letter today, and had to see you. Here, I brought you a present to celebrate.'

Handing over the basket and blankets, Sonea moved into the small, simply furnished guestroom. Ranel stepped into the room and laughed with delight.

'Sonea! How's my little niece?'

'Well. Happy,' Sonea lied. *Don't think about Akkarin. Don't spoil the afternoon.*

Ranel hugged her. 'Thank you for the money,' he murmured.

Sonea smiled and started to take off the cloak, then thought better of it. Seeing a cot at one side of the room, she moved over to it and looked down at her sleeping cousin.

'He's growing well,' she said. 'No problems?'

'No, just a bit of a cough,' Jonna said, smiling. She patted her belly. 'We're hoping for a girl this time.'

As they talked, Sonea was relieved to find them more relaxed in her presence. They ate some of the bread, played with the baby when he woke, and discussed names for the next one. Ranel told Sonea news about old friends and acquaintances, and other events that had concerned the slum dwellers.

'We weren't in the city, but we heard when the Purge happened,' Ranel said, sighing. He glanced at her. 'Did you . . .?' he asked reluctantly.

'No.' Sonea scowled. 'Novices don't go. I . . . I guess it was stupid, but I thought they wouldn't have one, after what happened last year. Perhaps, when I've graduated . . .' She shook her head. *What will I do? Talk them out of it? As if they'd listen to a slum girl.*

She sighed. She was still a long way from ever being able to help the people she had once felt she belonged among. The idea of persuading the Guild to stop the Purge seemed naive and ridiculous now, as did the hope that they'd ever offer Healing to the dwells.

'What else have we got in here?' Jonna said, poking among the vegetables in the basket. 'Are you staying for dinner, Sonea?'

Sonea straightened in alarm. 'What time is it?' Looking through one of the high, narrow windows, she saw that the light outside was subdued and golden. 'I'll have to go back soon.'

'You be careful going home,' Ranel said. 'You don't want to run into this murderer everyone's talking about.'

'He won't be any rub for Sonea,' Jonna said, chuckling.

Sonea smiled at her aunt's confidence. 'What murderer?'

Ranel's eyebrows rose. 'I'd have thought you'd have known about it already. Been all over the city.' He grimaced. 'They say the murderer isn't one of the Thieves – I've heard the Thieves are out for him. Had no luck, though.'

'I can't see him evading the Thieves for long,' Sonea mused.

'But it's been going on for months,' Ranel said. 'And some dwells say they remember similar killings happening a year ago, and before that.'

'Does anyone know what he looks like?'

'Stories are all different. But most say he wears a ring with a big red gem.' Ranel leaned forward. 'The strangest story I heard was from one of our customers. He said that his sister's husband owns an inn down Southside. This man heard someone yelling in one of the rooms one night, so he checked on them. When he opened the door, the murderer jumped out the window. But instead of falling to the ground, three storeys down, he fell *upward* like he was flying!'

Sonea shrugged. Many people of dubious employment used the paths across the rooftops of the slums, known as the High Road. It was possible the man had swung out on a handhold and climbed up to the roof.

'That wasn't what was strange,' Ranel continued. 'What spooked the innkeeper was that the man staying in the room was dead, but all he had on his body were shallow cuts.'

Sonea frowned. Dead, but without any wounds except a few shallow cuts? Then her blood turned to ice. A memory flashed into her mind of Akkarin in the underground room.

Takan dropped to one knee and offered his arm. In Akkarin's hand was a glittering dagger. He ran the blade over the servant's skin, then placed a hand over the wound . . .

'Sonea. Are you listening?'

She blinked, then looked at her uncle. 'Yes. Just remembering something. From a long time ago. All this talk of murderers.' She shivered. 'I must go.'

As she stood, Jonna enveloped her in a hug. 'It is good knowing you can protect yourself, Sonea. I don't have to worry about you.'

'Hmph. You could at least worry about me a bit.'

Jonna laughed. 'All right. If it makes you feel better.'

Sonea said goodbye to Ranel, then stepped out into the street. As she continued through the slums, she could not help remembering Lorlen's words during the truth-read.

'I fear that, though I do not like to think it, you may be an attractive victim for him. He knows you have strong powers. You would be a potent source of magic.'

But Akkarin could not kill her. If she disappeared, Rothen and Lorlen would tell the Guild of his crime. Akkarin would not risk that.

Yet, as she walked through the city gates into the North Quarter, Sonea could not help worrying. Had he made the slums his hunting ground? Were her aunt and uncle in danger?

He will not kill them, either, she told herself. *Then I would tell the Guild the truth.*

But then it suddenly occurred to her that visiting her aunt and uncle was the worst kind of foolishness. She had all but disappeared; only Tania knew where she had gone. If Lorlen and Rothen had heard she was missing, they might decide it was Akkarin's doing. Or Akkarin might have concluded that she had left the Guild, and be preparing to silence the others right now.

Shivering, she realised she would not feel safe until she was back in the Guild, even though it meant living under the same roof as the man who might be the very murderer the slum dwellers feared.

CHAPTER 33

THE HIGH LORD'S WARNING

The sound of birdsong and wind greeted Dannyl as he woke. He opened his eyes and blinked at his surroundings, momentarily confused. Stone walls stood on all sides, but there was no roof above. He lay on a thick bed of pulled grass. The air had the feel of morning.

Armje. He was in the ruins of Armje.

Then he remembered the chamber, and the domed ceiling that had attacked him.

So I survived.

He looked down at himself. His robes were charred around the hem. The skin around his calves above where his boots had been was red and stinging. Looking up, he saw his boots standing neatly together a few steps away. They were blistered and charred.

He had come very close to dying, he realised.

Tayend must have taken him out of the cavern to this place. Dannyl looked around, but saw no sign of the scholar. Catching a splash of colour on the ground nearby, he recognised Tayend's blue jacket lying folded beside another bed of grass.

He considered getting up and looking for his friend, but remained on his grass bed. Tayend would not be far away, and he felt an overwhelming reluctance to move. He needed rest – not because his body needed it, but because he needed to recover magically.

Focussing on the source of his power, he found he had almost no magic to draw upon. Normally, he would have slept until at least partially recovered. Perhaps the lingering memory of danger had woken him as soon as he had regained enough strength to pull out of his exhausted slumber. Knowing that he lacked magic should have made him feel vulnerable and uneasy, but instead he felt freer, as if released from something.

Hearing footsteps, he drew himself up onto one elbow. Tayend stepped into the room and smiled when he saw that Dannyl was awake. The scholar's hair was a little ruffled, but otherwise he still managed to appear well groomed despite having slept on a bed of grass.

'You're awake at last. I just refilled our flasks. Thirsty?'

Realising he was, Dannyl nodded. He accepted his flask and drained it.

Tayend crouched beside him. 'Are you all right?'

'Yes. A bit cooked around the ankles, but nothing worse.'

'What happened?'

Dannyl shook his head. 'I was about to ask you that same question.'

'Your part comes first.'

'Very well.' Dannyl described the chamber, and how it had attacked him. Tayend's eyes widened as he listened.

'After you went in, I kept reading the glyphs,' the scholar said. 'The writing said that the door led to a place called the Cavern of Ultimate Punishment, and a little further I worked out that it was made to execute magicians. I tried to call to you – to warn you – then I heard you call me and you made the lights. Before I could reach the end of the passage, they went out.'

Tayend shivered. 'I kept going. When I got to the cavern, you were pressed up against something invisible. Then you fell forward and you didn't move. I could see more of those lightning things on the walls. I ran forward and grabbed your arms, and pulled you off the platform. The lightning touched it, then everything went dark. I couldn't see, but I kept pulling you along, into the passage and back outside. Then I carried you here.' He paused, and his mouth curled into a half-smile. 'You're really heavy, by the way.'

'Am I?'

'It's your height, I'm sure.'

Dannyl smiled, and suddenly felt overwhelmed with affection and gratitude. 'You saved my life, Tayend. Thank you.'

The scholar blinked, then smiled self-consciously. 'I suppose I did. Looks like I've returned the favour. So, do you think the Guild knows about this Cavern of Ultimate Punishment?'

'Yes. No. Maybe.' Dannyl shook his head. He didn't want to discuss the Guild, or the cavern. *I'm alive*, he thought. He looked around, at the trees, the sky, then Tayend. *He really is a beautiful man*, he thought suddenly, remembering how he had been struck by the scholar's fine looks that first day, at Capia's docks. He felt something at the edge of his thoughts, like a memory just out of reach. It grew stronger as he concentrated on it, and he felt a familiar uneasy feeling steal over him. He tried to push it away.

Suddenly he was acutely aware of his lack of magical

strength. He frowned, wondering why he had reached for his powers unconsciously. Then realisation came. He had been about to use his Healing powers to take away the uneasiness, or at least the physical reaction that had caused it. *As I always do, without realising it.*

'What's wrong?' Tayend asked.

Dannyl shook his head. 'Nothing.' But that was a lie. All these years he had been doing this: turning his mind from the thoughts that had caused him so much trouble and anguish, and using his Healing power to stop his body from reacting in the first place.

Memories came rushing back. Memories of being the object of scandal and rumour. He had decided that, if how he felt was so unacceptable, then it was better not to feel at all. And perhaps, with time, he would begin to desire what was right and proper.

But nothing had changed. The moment he lost the ability to Heal, there it was again. He had failed.

'Dannyl?'

Looking at Tayend, Dannyl felt his heart skip. How could he look at his friend, and consider that being like him was a failure?

He couldn't. He remembered something that Tayend had said. *'There is a . . . a certainty in me about what is natural and right for me that is as strong as his own certainty about what is natural and right.'*

What *was* natural and right? Who really knew? The world was never so simple that one person could have all the answers. He had fought this for so long. What would it be like to stop fighting? To accept what he was.

'You've got the strangest look on your face. What are you thinking?'

Dannyl regarded Tayend speculatively. The scholar was his closest friend. Even closer than Rothen, he realised suddenly. He had never been able to tell Rothen the truth. He knew he could trust Tayend. Hadn't the scholar protected him from the Elyne gossips?

It would be such a relief just to tell *someone,* Dannyl thought. He drew in a deep breath, and let it out slowly.

'I'm afraid I haven't been completely honest with you, Tayend.'

The scholar's eyes widened slightly. He sat back on his haunches and smiled. 'Really? How so?'

'That novice I befriended years ago. He was exactly what they said he was.'

Tayend's lips curled into a half-smile. 'You never said he wasn't.'

Dannyl hesitated, then continued. 'So was I.'

Watching Tayend's face, Dannyl was surprised to see the smile change to a grin.

'I know.'

Dannyl frowned. 'How could you know? *I* didn't even . . . remember until now.'

'Remember?' Tayend sobered and tilted his head to one side. 'How would you forget something like that?'

'I . . .' Dannyl sighed, then explained about the Healing. 'After a couple of years, it became a habit I suppose. The mind can be a powerful thing, particularly for magicians. We're trained to focus our minds and achieve deep levels of concentration. I pushed away every dangerous thought. It mightn't have worked, if I hadn't been able to smother my physical feelings with magic as well.' He grimaced. 'But it didn't change anything. It made me empty of any feelings of attraction. I desired neither men nor women.'

'That must have been terrible.'

'Yes, and no. I have few friends. I suppose I was lonely. But it was a dull kind of loneliness. There isn't as much pain in life if you don't let yourself become entangled with others.' He paused. 'But is that really living?'

Tayend didn't answer. Looking at the scholar, Dannyl read a wariness there.

'You knew,' Dannyl said slowly. 'But you couldn't say anything.' *Otherwise I would have reacted with fear and denial.*

Tayend shrugged. 'It was more like a guess. If I was right, though, I knew there was a chance you'd never confront it. Now that I know the effort you went to, it is amazing that you have at all.' He paused. 'Habits are hard to break.'

'But I will.' Dannyl stilled as he realised what he had said. *Can I really commit to that? Can I accept what I am, and face this fear of discovery and rejection?*

Looking at Tayend, he heard a voice deep within answer: *Yes!*

The path to the High Lord's Residence was dusted with tiny fragments of colour. As the wind rustled the trees, more blossoms flitted down to join them. Sonea admired the colours. A lighter mood had stayed with her since visiting her aunt and uncle the previous day. Even Regin's stares in class hadn't diminished it.

When she reached the door, however, a familiar gloom settled over her. It swung inward at her touch. She bowed to the magician standing in the guestroom.

'Good evening, Sonea,' Akkarin said. Was she imagining it, or was there a difference in his tone?

'Good evening, High Lord.'

The Firstday evening meals had become a predictable routine. He always asked her about her lessons; she replied as succinctly as possible. They didn't talk about much else. The night after he had discovered her in the passages she had expected him to raise the subject but, to her relief, he hadn't mentioned it once. Obviously, he felt that she needed no further rebuke.

She trudged up the stairs. Takan, as always, was waiting for them in the dining room. A delicious, spicy odour lingered about him, and she felt her stomach growl with impatience. But as Akkarin sat down opposite her she remembered Ranel's story about the murderer and her appetite fled.

She looked down at the table, then stole a glance at him. Was she sitting opposite a murderer? His eyes slid to hers, and she quickly averted her gaze.

Ranel had said that the murderer wore a ring with a red gemstone. Looking at Akkarin's hands, she was almost disappointed to see they were bare. Not even a mark to hint that a ring might have been worn regularly. His fingers were long and elegant, yet masculine . . .

Takan entered with a platter of food, drawing her attention away. As Sonea began to eat, Akkarin straightened and she knew his usual questions were about to start.

'So how are your aunt and uncle, and their son? Did you have a pleasant afternoon with them yesterday?'

He knows! She sucked in a breath, and felt something catch in her throat. Grabbing a napkin, she covered her face and coughed. *How does he know where I went! Did he follow me? Or was he in the slums, hunting for victims, and happened to see me there?*

'You're not going to die on me, are you?' he asked dryly. 'That would be inconvenient.'

Pulling the napkin away, she found Takan standing beside her, offering a glass of water. Taking it, she gulped a mouthful.

What should I say? He knows where Jonna and Ranel live. She felt a stab of fear, but pushed it aside. If he had wanted to, he could have found that out easily enough without following her. He might even have read their location from her – or Rothen's – mind.

He didn't seem to expect an answer, or gave up waiting for one. 'I don't disapprove of you visiting them,' he told her. 'I do, however, expect you to ask me for permission if you intend to leave the Guild grounds at any time. Next time, Sonea,' he stared at her directly, his eyes hard, 'I'm sure you'll remember to ask me first.'

Looking down, she nodded. 'Yes, High Lord.'

The door opened just as Lorlen reached the High Lord's Residence. He stopped as Sonea stepped out, box in hand. She blinked at him in surprise, then bowed.

'Administrator.'

'Sonea,' he replied.

She glanced down at his hand, then her eyes widened. Her gaze flickered to his, her expression questioning, then she quickly looked away and hurried past, toward the University.

Looking down at the ring on his hand, Lorlen felt a sinking feeling in his stomach. Clearly, she had heard about the murderer and his red ring. What did she think of him now? Turning to watch her, he felt his chest tighten. Each day she moved from one inescapable nightmare to another. From the shadow of Akkarin to the torments dealt out by the novices. It was a cruel situation.

And an unnecessary one. Clenching his fists, he advanced on the door and stepped through. Akkarin sat in one of the luxurious armchairs, already sipping from a wineglass.

'Why are you letting the novices gang up on her?' he demanded before his anger and courage failed.

Akkarin's eyebrows rose. 'I gather you mean Sonea? It does her good.'

'*Good?*' Lorlen exclaimed.

'Yes. She has to learn to defend herself.'

'Against other novices?'

'She ought to be able to defeat them. They're not well co-ordinated.'

Lorlen shook his head and started to pace the room. 'But she *isn't* defeating them, and some magicians are wondering why you do not step in and put a stop to it.'

Akkarin shrugged. 'It is up to me how my novice is trained.'

'Trained! This isn't *training*!'

'You heard Lord Yikmo's analysis. She's too nice. Real conflict will teach her to fight back.'

'But this is fifteen novices against one. How can you expect her to stand up to that many?'

'Fifteen?' Akkarin smiled. 'The last I saw it was near twenty.'

Lorlen stopped pacing and stared at the High Lord.

'You've been *watching* her?'

'Whenever I can.' Akkarin's smile widened. 'Though it's not always easy to keep up with them. I would like to know how that last one ended. Eighteen, perhaps nineteen, and she still managed to free herself.'

'She got away?' Lorlen suddenly felt lightheaded. He moved to a chair and sank into it. 'But that means . . .'

Akkarin chuckled. 'I'd advise you to think twice if you were planning to take her on in the Arena, Lorlen, though her lack of skill and confidence would ensure you won the fight.'

Lorlen didn't answer, his mind still struggling to accept that a novice as young as Sonea could already be so powerful. Akkarin leaned toward him, his dark eyes glittering.

'Every time they attack her she stretches herself,' he said quietly. 'She's learning to defend herself in ways neither Balkan or Yikmo can teach her. I'm not going to stop Regin and his accomplices. They're the best teachers she has.'

'But . . . why do you want her stronger?' Lorlen breathed. 'Aren't you afraid she will turn against you? What will you do when she graduates?'

Akkarin's smile vanished. 'She is the High Lord's chosen novice. The Guild expects her to excel. But she will never grow strong enough to be a threat to me.' He looked away and his expression hardened. 'As for graduation, I'll decide how to deal with that when the time comes.'

Seeing the calculating look in Akkarin's eyes, Lorlen shivered. A memory of his visit to the Guard House returned. The images of the bodies of the murdered young man and his father were hard to forget. Though more gruesome, the young man's death had not chilled Lorlen as much as the other. The father's wrists had shallow cuts, and he had lost little blood. Yet he was dead.

At Akkarin's instruction, Lorlen had explained to Barran he would not be sending magicians out in a hunt for the rogue, as he had done with Sonea. The previous search had driven Sonea to seek the help of the Thieves, and they had kept the Guild from finding her for months. Though the Thieves were rumoured to be hunting for the murderer as well, it was not impossible that they would strike a deal if he came to them for help. So it was better that the Guild gave the murderer no reason to hide himself too carefully. The Guard must locate him, then Lorlen would arrange for magical assistance to capture him. Barran had agreed that this was the wisest action.

But this would never happen if the murderer was Akkarin. Lorlen considered the black-robed man. He wanted to ask Akkarin directly if he had anything to do with the murders, but he was afraid of the answer. And even if the answer was no, could he believe such a denial, anyway?

'Ah, Lorlen,' Akkarin sounded amused. 'Anyone would think Sonea was *your* adopted novice.'

Lorlen forced his mind back to the subject. 'If a guardian is neglecting his obligations, it is my duty to correct the situation.'

'And if I tell you to leave this alone, will you?'

Lorlen frowned. 'Of course,' he said reluctantly.

'Can I trust you to?' Akkarin sighed. 'When you have not done as I have asked concerning Dannyl.'

Surprised, Lorlen frowned at Akkarin. 'Dannyl?'

'He has continued his investigations.'

Lorlen could not help feeling a trickle of hope at this news, but it quickly evaporated. If Akkarin knew this, whatever good might have come from it was already lost. 'I sent him orders to abandon the work.'

'Then he hasn't followed them.'

Lorlen hesitated. 'What will you do?'

Akkarin drained his glass, then rose and walked toward

the drinks table. 'I haven't decided. If he goes where I fear he may go, he will die – and not by my hand.'

Lorlen's heart skipped a beat. 'Can you warn him?'

Placing his glass on the table, Akkarin sighed. 'It may be too late already. I shall have to weigh the risks.'

'Risks?' Lorlen frowned. 'What risks?'

Akkarin turned and smiled. 'You are full of questions tonight. I wonder if there is something in the spring water lately. Everyone seems to have grown so bold.' He turned away and refilled his glass, and another. 'That is all I can tell you, for now. If I was free to tell you what I know, I would.'

He crossed the room and handed Lorlen a glass.

'For now, you'll just have to trust me.'

CHAPTER 34

IF ONLY IT WAS THAT SIMPLE

As they reached the curve of the road from where they had first seen Dem Ladeiri's home, Dannyl and Tayend halted their mounts and turned to regard the building one last time. Their servants continued ahead, their horses walking slowly down the winding road.

'Who would have thought we'd find the answers to so many questions in that old place?' Tayend said, shaking his head.

Dannyl nodded. 'It has been an interesting few days.'

'Now *that's* an understatement.' Tayend's lips curled up at one side, and he gave Dannyl a sidelong glance.

Smiling at the scholar's expression, Dannyl looked up at the mountains above the Ladeiri house. The ruins of Armje lay beyond one of the ridges, hidden from sight.

Tayend shivered. 'It makes me nervous, knowing that cavern is up there.'

'I doubt any magicians have visited Armje since Akkarin,' Dannyl said. 'And that door can't be opened without magic – or without breaking down the whole wall. I would have warned the Dem, but I didn't want to tell him before consulting the Guild.'

Tayend nodded. He nudged his horse forward, and Dannyl's followed. 'We have some more information on this Charkan King, anyway. If we had a few weeks to spare, we could travel into Sachaka.'

'I'm still not sure that's wise.'

'Akkarin probably went there. Why shouldn't we?'

'We don't know for sure if that's where he went.'

'If we went there we might find evidence that he did. The Sachakans are sure to remember if a Guild magician passed their way. Have any other magicians visited Sachaka in the last ten or so years?'

Dannyl shrugged. 'I don't know.'

'If one had, surely he would have heard that another Guild magician had been in the country before him.'

'Perhaps.' Dannyl felt a nagging uneasiness. The thought of being around other magicians reminded him that, one day, he would have to return to the Guild. As if his colleagues might be able to see . . .

But, of course, they wouldn't – couldn't – know that from just *looking* at him. So, as long as he and Tayend were careful about discussing the matter, and he never allowed anyone to truth-read him, and he was cautious during mental communication, who could ever prove anything?

He looked at Tayend. *Rothen would say I was cunning enough to discover – or hide – any secret*, he mused.

—Dannyl.

Startled, Dannyl sat up straight in the saddle. Then he recognised the personality behind the mental call and was paralysed by disbelief.

—Dannyl.

He felt panic rush over him. Why was Akkarin calling him? What did the High Lord want? Dannyl glanced at Tayend. Or had he heard that . . . but, no, surely that was not important enough to—

521

—Dannyl.

He had to answer. He could not ignore a call from the High Lord. Dannyl swallowed hard, took a deep breath and let it out slowly. Then he closed his eyes and sent out a name.

—Akkarin?

—Where are you?

—In the mountains of Elyne. He sent an image of the road. *I offered to take over Ambassador Errend's biannual rounds of the Dems so that I might familiarise myself with the country.*

—And so that you could continue your research despite Lorlen's orders.

It was not a question. Dannyl was surprised at the relief he felt. If Akkarin had heard rumours about Tayend and . . . but he quickly turned his thoughts from that.

—Yes, he confirmed, deliberately thinking of the Tomb of White Tears and the mystery of the Charkan King. *I continued out of my own interest. Lorlen did not indicate that I shouldn't.*

—Clearly your duties as Ambassador are not overly time consuming.

Dannyl winced. There was a definite feeling of disapproval behind Akkarin's communication. Was he simply concerned that Dannyl was spending too much time on research or did he resent that another magician was continuing work he had abandoned? Or was he annoyed that someone was tracing a part of his own past? *Does he have something to hide?*

—I want to discuss what you have found in person. Return to the Guild at once, and bring your notes with you.

Surprised, Dannyl hesitated before asking:

—What of the rest of my journey to visit the Dems?

—*You will return to complete your duties afterward.*

—*Very well . . . I will have to—*

—*Report to me when you arrive.*

A tone of dismissal told Dannyl that the conversation was over. He opened his eyes and cursed.

'What happened?' Tayend asked.

'That was Ak – the High Lord.'

Tayend's eyes widened. 'What did he say?'

'He has learned about our research.' Dannyl sighed. 'I don't think he's happy about it. He ordered me to return.'

'Return . . . to the Guild?'

'Yes. With our notes.'

Tayend stared at him in dismay, then his expression hardened.

'How did he find out?'

'I don't know.' *How had he?* Remembering the tale of Akkarin's ability to read unwilling minds, Dannyl shivered again. *There was a moment there, when I thought of Tayend . . . did he detect anything?*

'I'll go with you,' Tayend said.

'No,' Dannyl said quickly, alarmed. 'Believe me, you don't want to be dragged into this.'

'But—'

'No, Tayend. Better he doesn't learn how much you know.' Dannyl tapped the flanks of his horse with his heels, urging it into a trot. He thought of the long weeks of riding and sailing that lay between this day and facing Akkarin. He ought to wish he could delay that moment, but instead he wanted to hurry toward it because one thought bothered him more than any other.

What would happen to Tayend if Akkarin took exception to Dannyl continuing his research? Would the High

Lord's disapproval extend to the scholar? Could Tayend lose access to the Great Library?

Dannyl did not care what consequences he might suffer, so long as Tayend was not affected. Whatever happened, Dannyl would make sure the blame rested entirely with himself.

The garden seat was warm. Putting down her box, Sonea closed her eyes and enjoyed the heat of the sun on her face. She could hear the chatter of other novices, and the deeper voices of older magicians, coming nearer.

Opening her eyes, she watched as several Healers strolled down the path toward her. She recognised a few as younger graduates. They burst into laughter, then as the two at the front of the group stepped apart Sonea glimpsed a familiar face.

Dorrien!

Her heart skipped. Standing up, she hurried along one of the side paths, hoping he hadn't seen her. She moved into a small area surrounded by hedges, and sat down on another garden seat.

She had forced Dorrien out of her thoughts, knowing that it would be months, possibly more than a year, before he visited the Guild again. But here he was only a few months after he had left. Why had he come back so soon? Had Rothen told him about Akkarin? Surely not. But perhaps he had unintentionally given Dorrien the feeling that something wasn't right during one of their mental conversations.

She frowned. Whatever the reason, Dorrien would probably seek her out. She would have to tell him she was no longer interested in him as anything more than a friend.

Now *that* was a conversation she would have to prepare herself for.

'Sonea.'

She jumped and looked up to find Dorrien standing in the entrance of the little garden.

'Dorrien!' She fought down panic. He must have seen her, and followed. At least she hadn't needed to feign surprise. 'You're back already!'

He smiled and moved into the garden. 'Just for a week. Didn't Father tell you?'

'No . . . but we don't see much of each other now.'

'So he said.' His smile disappeared. Sitting down, he regarded her questioningly. 'He tells me you're attending lessons at night, and spend most of your time studying.'

'Only because I'm a hopeless Warrior.'

'Not from what I've heard.'

She frowned. 'What have you heard?'

'That you've been fighting several novices at once, and winning.'

Sonea winced.

'Or have I got the winning part wrong?'

'How many people know about this?'

'Most.'

Sonea cradled her head in her hands, and groaned. Dorrien chuckled and patted her lightly on the shoulder.

'Regin is at the head of this, isn't he?'

'Of course.'

'Why hasn't your new guardian done anything about it?'

Sonea shrugged. 'I don't think he knows. I don't want him to know.'

'I see.' Dorrien nodded. 'I suppose if Akkarin came to

your rescue all the time, people would say you weren't a good choice. The novices are all jealous of you, not realising that they would be in the same situation if *they* were the High Lord's favourite, even if they are from the Houses. Any novice he chose would be a target. Always expected to prove themselves.'

He fell silent, and she could see from his expression that he was thinking hard. 'So it's up to you to stop these novices.'

She laughed bitterly. 'I don't think baiting Regin will make any difference this time.'

'Oh, I wasn't thinking of that.'

'So what were you thinking?'

Dorrien smiled. 'You have to prove you *are* the best. That you can beat him at his own game. What have you done so far to get him back?'

'Nothing. I can't do anything. There are too many of them.'

'There must be novices who don't like him,' he pointed out. 'Persuade them to help you.'

'Nobody talks to me at all now.'

'Even now? I'm surprised. Surely some have seen an advantage in being a friend of the High Lord's favourite.'

'I wouldn't want their company if that's all they wanted from me.'

'But so long as you know that is the reason they're around, why not take advantage of the situation?'

'Perhaps because Regin arranged an accident for the last novice who did.'

Dorrien frowned. 'Hmmm, I remember that now. Something else, then.' He fell silent again. Sonea struggled with a vague feeling of disappointment. She had hoped Dorrien would find some inventive way to end Regin's ambushes, but perhaps the problem was beyond him this time.

'I think what Regin needs,' he said suddenly, 'is a thorough, public beating.'

Sonea's heart stopped. 'You're not going to—'

'Not from me. From you.'

'*Me?*'

'You are stronger than him, aren't you? Quite a bit stronger, if the rumours are true.'

'Well, yes,' Sonea admitted. 'That's why he gets so many others to help him.'

'Then challenge him. A formal challenge. In the Arena.'

'A *formal* challenge?' She stared at him. 'You mean . . . fight him in front of everybody?'

'Yes.'

'But . . .' She remembered something Lord Skoran had said. 'There hasn't been one for over fifty years – and it was between two adult magicians, not novices.'

'There's no rule against novices making formal challenges.' Dorrien shrugged. 'Of course, it *is* a risk. If you lose, the harassment will probably get worse. But if you're so much stronger than him, how can you lose?'

'"Skill can overcome strength",' Sonea quoted.

'True, but you're not unskilled.'

'I've never beaten him before.'

Dorrien's eyebrow rose. 'But if you are as strong as they say, your powers will have been limited in class, am I right?'

She nodded.

'They won't be in a formal battle.'

Sonea felt a tiny spark of hope and excitement. 'Is that so?'

'Yes. The idea is for the combatants to face each other as they are, no restraints or enhancements. It's a ridiculous way to solve a dispute, really. No battle ever proved a man – or a woman – right or wrong.'

'But that's not what this is about,' Sonea said slowly. 'This is about persuading Regin that it's not worth bothering me. Once he's suffered a humiliating defeat, he won't want to risk another.'

'You've got the idea.' Dorrien smiled. 'Make your challenge as public as possible. He will be forced to accept it or dishonour his family name. Give him the most public thrashing you can bring yourself to deal on the stupid boy. If he harasses you afterward, challenge him again. He'll give you no reason to keep putting him in such a position.'

'Nobody else gets dragged into it,' Sonea breathed. 'No-one will get hurt and I won't have to wheedle myself into any false friendships.'

'Oh, yes, you will,' he said soberly. 'You'll still need those supporters. He might decide that people will admire his determination if he fights you over and over, in search of a way to beat you. Gather other novices around yourself, Sonea.'

'But . . .'

'But?'

She sighed. 'I'm not like that, Dorrien. I don't want to be the leader of some petty gang.'

'That's fine.' He smiled. 'You don't have to be like Regin. Just be enjoyable company, which you shouldn't have any difficulty with. I think your company is very enjoyable.'

She looked away. *I should say something to put him off now,* she thought. But she could not think of anything. Looking at him again, she saw a wary, disappointed expression on his face, and realised she had told him enough by not saying anything.

He smiled, but this time there was no twinkle in his eyes. 'What else have you been up to?'

'Not much. How is Rothen?'

'He misses you terribly. You know he considers you like a daughter, don't you? It was hard enough on him when I left, but he knew I was going and had got used to the idea by the time it happened. With you, it was a bigger shock.'

Sonea nodded. 'For both of us.'

Entering the classroom, Rothen directed the two volunteers toward the demonstration table. As the novices set down their burdens, he unlocked the supply cupboard and checked that there were enough utensils for the next class.

'Lord Rothen,' one of the boys said.

Looking up, Rothen followed the boy's gaze toward the door. His heart skipped as he saw who was standing there.

'Lord Rothen,' Lorlen said. 'I wish to speak to you in private.'

Rothen nodded. 'Of course, Administrator.' He looked at the two novices and nodded toward the door. They hurried out of the room, pausing to bow to Lorlen.

As the door closed behind them, Lorlen strolled forward to the window, his expression taut and worried. Rothen watched him, knowing that only something very important would have brought the Administrator to him in defiance of Akkarin's order that they not talk to each other.

Or had something happened to Sonea? Rothen felt dread

rising. Had Lorlen come to bring the awful news, knowing that it would free him to confront Akkarin?

'A short time ago I saw your son in the garden,' Lorlen began. 'Is he visiting for long?'

Rothen closed his eyes, relieved. This was about Dorrien, not Sonea.

'A week,' he replied.

'He was with Sonea.' Lorlen frowned. 'Did they become . . . familiar when Dorrien visited last?'

Rothen drew in a sharp breath. He had guessed – and hoped – that Dorrien's interest in Sonea had been more than just curiosity. From Lorlen's question, enough was apparent between the pair for the Administrator to suspect something more. Rothen might have been pleased, but instead he felt only alarm. What would Akkarin do if he discovered this?

Rothen chose his words carefully. 'Dorrien knows that it will be many years before Sonea is free to leave the Guild – and that she may not want to join him when that time comes.'

Lorlen nodded. 'He may need a little more discouragement than that.'

'With Dorrien, discouragement is often taken as encouragement,' Rothen said wryly.

The look that Lorlen gave him was humourless. 'You're his father,' he snapped. 'You of all people should know how to convince him.'

Rothen looked away. 'I don't want him involved in this any more than you do.'

Lorlen sighed and looked down at his hands. He wore a ring, and the ruby in the setting glittered in the light. 'I'm sorry, Rothen. We have enough to worry about. I trust you will do everything you can. Do you think Sonea will see the danger and turn him away?'

'Yes.' Of course she would. Rothen felt a pang of sympathy for his son. Poor Dorrien! He would have half-expected Sonea to lose interest anyway, considering the years of study ahead of her and his long absences. But if Dorrien knew the real reason, it would probably drive him to do something foolish. Better that he didn't know.

How did Sonea feel about this? Was it difficult to turn Dorrien away? Rothen sighed. How he wished he could ask her.

Lorlen moved to the door. 'Thank you, Rothen. I will leave you to your preparations.'

Rothen nodded and watched the Administrator leave. Though he understood Lorlen's resigned manner, he resented it. *You're supposed to find a way out of this*, he thought at the man's back. Then resentment changed to a feeling of hopelessness.

If Lorlen couldn't find a way, then who could?

It's still late, Sonea thought fuzzily. *Not long past midnight. Why am I awake? Did something wake me . . .?*

A faint chill touched her cheek. A breeze. Opening her eyes, she took a moment to register the square of darkness where there should have been a door. Something pale moved within that darkness. A hand.

By the next heartbeat she was completely awake. A pale oval floated above the hand. Otherwise, he was invisible in his black robes.

What is he doing? Why is he here?

Her heart beat so loudly she was sure he could hear it. She forced her breathing to slow and stay even, afraid of what he might do if he realised she was awake and aware of him. For an excruciatingly long time he stood there. Then, between one blink and the next, he was gone and the door was closed.

She stared at the door. Had it been a dream?

Better to believe it was. The alternative was too frightening. Yes, it must have been a nightmare . . .

When she woke next it was morning. The memory of dreams filled with dark figures and foreboding had joined the one of the night watcher, and she dismissed them all as she rose and dressed in her robes.

CHAPTER 35

THE CHALLENGE

At first glance there was nothing wrong, but when Sonea looked closely she saw that the chemical in one vial was cloudy and the other's contents had dried into a brown lump. The intricate arrangement of rods and weights in the timer were a shambles.

From the doorway behind her Sonea heard a low and familiar chuckle, followed by half-smothered sniggers. She straightened, but did not turn around.

After her conversation with Dorrien she had been full of confidence and ready to challenge Regin at the first opportunity, but as the day had continued, doubts had begun to grow. Every time she had thought about actually fighting Regin, the idea had seemed less brilliant and more foolish. Warrior Skills was Regin's best subject, and her worst. She would never see the end of his harassment if she lost. It was not worth the risk.

By the end of the week, she had decided it was the worst move she could make. If she put up with him long enough, he might grow bored with her. She could endure being called names or being waylaid and tormented outside classes.

But not this. As she considered the ruin that was left of her work she felt a dark fury begin to simmer. When Regin did something like this, even if the teachers didn't penalise her for failing an exercise, he stopped her from learning. And when he stopped her from learning, he lessened the chances that she might, one day, be skilled enough to help the Guild defeat Akkarin.

She felt something shift inside as her fury grew stronger. Suddenly she wanted nothing more than to blast Regin into ashes.

'Give him the most public thrashing you can bring yourself to deal on the stupid boy. If he harasses you afterward, challenge him again. He'll give you no reason to keep putting him in such a position.'

A formal battle. It was a risk. But waiting was a gamble, too. He might never grow bored and leave her alone. And she didn't like waiting . . .

'Make your challenge as public as possible.'

Slowly, she turned to see that Regin and the novices from the earlier class were standing in the doorway, watching her. Walking toward them, she pushed her way through and out of the classroom. Novices and teachers filled the corridor outside. The buzz of voices was loud, but not too loud for a single voice to be heard above it. A magician in purple robes appeared, heading toward the classroom. Lord Sarrin, Head of Alchemy. Perfect.

'What's wrong, Sonea?' Regin sneered. 'Didn't your experiment work?'

Sonea spun about to face Regin.

'Regin, of the family Winar, House Paren, I challenge you to a formal battle in the Arena.'

Regin's face froze into open-mouthed surprise.

Silence seemed to spread outward like smoke. In the edges of her vision, Sonea saw faces turning in her direction. Even Lord Sarrin had stopped. She forced aside a nagging feeling that she had just done something she would always regret. *Too late now.*

Regin managed to close his mouth. His expression became thoughtful. She wondered if he was going to refuse, to say she was not worth fighting. *Give him no time to think of it.*

'Do you accept?' she demanded.

He hesitated, then smiled broadly. 'I accept, Sonea of no family of consequence.'

At once a whispering and murmuring began in the corridor. Afraid that her courage would fail if she looked around, Sonea kept her eyes on Regin. He glanced back at his companions, then laughed. 'Oh, this is going to be—'

'The time is yours to choose,' she snapped.

His smile vanished for a second, then returned.

'I guess I had better give you some time to catch up,' he said lightly. 'Freeday, a week from tomorrow, an hour before sunset. That sounds generous enough.'

'Sonea,' another older voice said.

She turned to see Lord Elben striding toward her. He glanced at the audience that had gathered, and frowned. 'Your experiment has failed. I checked it last night, and this morning, and I can see no cause. I will give you another day to attempt it again.'

She bowed. 'Thank you, Lord Elben.'

He considered the novices lingering in the doorway. 'Enough chatter, then. Classes are held *inside* the rooms as far as I'm aware.'

'You drink more siyo than last time, eh?'

Dannyl handed the flask to Jano and nodded. 'I think I'm getting a taste for it.'

The sailor looked a little worried. 'You not going to do magic wrongly from drink, are you?'

Dannyl sighed and shook his head. 'I'm not that drunk yet, but I wouldn't want us to encounter any sea leeches.'

Jano patted his shoulder. 'No eyoma this far south, remember.'

'I'm not likely to forget,' Dannyl muttered. His comment was smothered as the sailors cheered. A member of the crew had just entered the room. The man grinned and moved to his hanging bed. Pulling a small pottery wind instrument from a bag, he strolled over to take his place at the head of the table.

As the man began to play, Dannyl thought of the last week. He and Tayend had made it back to Capia within three days, travelling directly and changing horses several times. Tayend had remained at his sister's home, while Dannyl continued to the city. Stopping at the Guild House only long enough to pack a small chest of clothing, Dannyl had found and boarded a ship leaving for Imardin that night.

He'd been pleased to find himself back on the *Fin-da*. Jano had greeted him like an old friend, and assured him that the journey home would be swifter, as they would catch the spring winds.

Jano hadn't mentioned that the spring winds made for a rougher ride. Dannyl would not have cared, except that the unpleasant conditions kept him inside for most of the day, where he spent hours worrying about the reception that awaited him at the Guild.

His fears that Akkarin had sensed something of his feelings toward Tayend had grown since boarding the ship. During his stop at the Guild House, Errend had handed

Dannyl some letters to read. Finding one from Rothen, Dannyl had opened it eagerly, only to find it contained a warning.

. . . I would not be overly concerned about these rumours. In any case, they concern your assistant, not yourself. But I thought you should be told so that you may judge for yourself whether this might cause you trouble in the future . . .

Rothen clearly thought that Dannyl didn't know about Tayend. This was exactly what they had wanted the Elyne court to believe, but now that he had been 'informed', the Elynes – and Kyralians – would expect him to avoid Tayend's company.

Unless no-one knew that Rothen had told him. He could pretend he hadn't received the letter . . . but no, as soon as he arrived in the Guild, Rothen would want to know if he had received it, and would repeat the warning if he hadn't.

But what of Akkarin? Dannyl wasn't sure how the High Lord had learned of his research. What if those sources had also spoken of Dannyl's 'friendship' with Tayend? What if Akkarin's suspicions had been confirmed during their brief mental communication?

Dannyl sighed. For a few days, everything had been wonderful. He had been happier than he had ever been in his life. Then . . . *this*.

As the flask was passed to him again, he took another sip of the potent liquor. *So long as Tayend doesn't suffer for knowing me*, he thought, *I will be content.*

The Night Room was crowded. Not since the hunt for Sonea had Lorlen seen it so full. Magicians who rarely joined in the weekly social gathering were present now.

The most notable of these was the man at his side. The sea of red, green and purple robes parted before Akkarin as he made his way to the chair that was, unofficially, his.

Akkarin was enjoying himself. To others, his neutral expression suggested indifference, but Lorlen knew better. If Akkarin didn't wanted to participate in a discussion about his favourite novice challenging another, he wouldn't be here. The three Heads of Disciplines were already seated around Akkarin's chair, and a small crowd began to gather as the High Lord settled into his seat. Among them, Lorlen noted, was Rothen's son, Dorrien.

'It appears your favourite novice has found a way to entertain us yet again, Akkarin,' Lady Vinara said. 'I'm beginning to wonder what we can expect from her after she has graduated.'

The corner of Akkarin's mouth curled upward. 'As am I.'

'Was this challenge your idea or hers?' Balkan rumbled.

'It was not mine.'

Balkan's brows rose. 'And did she seek your approval?'

'No, but I believe there is no rule that requires it, though perhaps there should be.'

'Then you would have refused, had she asked?'

Akkarin's eyes narrowed. 'Not necessarily. If she had sought my view on the matter, I might have advised her to wait.'

'Perhaps this was a spontaneous decision,' suggested Lord Peakin, who was standing behind Vinara's chair.

'No,' Lord Sarrin replied. 'She chose a moment when she was assured of numerous witnesses. Regin had no option but to accept.'

Seeing the Head of Alchemists glance pointedly to one

side, Lorlen followed his gaze. Lord Garrel was standing among the gathered magicians, wearing a slight frown.

'So if she planned this, she must be confident of winning,' Peakin concluded. 'Do you agree with her, Lord Balkan?'

The Warrior shrugged. 'She is strong, but a skilled opponent might overcome her.'

'And Regin?'

'He is more skilled than the average Second Year.'

'Skilled enough to win?'

Balkan glanced at Akkarin. 'Skilled enough that the outcome will not be easily predicted.'

'Do you believe she will win?' Vinara asked of Akkarin.

The High Lord paused before answering. 'Yes.'

She smiled. 'But of course you do. She is your novice, and you must be seen to support her.'

Akkarin nodded. 'That is true, as well.'

'She is, no doubt, doing this to please you.' Hearing Garrel's voice, Lorlen looked up in surprise.

'I doubt it,' Akkarin replied.

Surprised at this admission, Lorlen glanced at Akkarin, then carefully noted the other magicians' expressions. None looked surprised. Only Rothen's son, Dorrien, looked thoughtful. Perhaps it had been noted that Sonea was not at all fond of her guardian.

'Then what is her motivation?' Peakin asked.

'If she wins, Regin will not bully her again for fear of another challenge, and another defeat,' Vinara answered.

There was a pause, in which glances were exchanged. By speaking of the bullying openly in front of both Akkarin and Garrel, Vinara had drawn attention to the potential for conflict between the two guardians. While none usually baulked at raising the subject of feuding novices around their guardians, few would dare to do so when one of the guardians was the High Lord. It put Garrel in an interesting position.

Neither guardian spoke.

'That depends on how the battles progress,' Balkan said, breaking the silence. 'If she wins with mere brute strength, none will respect her.'

'That makes no difference,' Sarrin argued. 'No matter how she wins, Regin won't bother her again. I doubt she cares whether anyone else respects her fighting skills.'

'There are methods of defeating a stronger magician,' Balkan reminded him. 'Regin knows this. He has already sought my instruction on such tactics.'

'And Sonea? Will she receive extra instruction from you as well?' Vinara asked Balkan.

'Lord Yikmo is her teacher,' Akkarin replied.

Balkan nodded. 'His teaching style is better suited to her temperament.'

'Who will oversee the fight?' another magician asked.

'I will,' Balkan said. 'Unless anyone protests. Lord Garrel will protect Regin. Will you be protecting Sonea?' he asked Akkarin.

'Yes.'

'Here's Sonea's tutor,' Lord Sarrin observed, pointing. Lorlen turned to see that Lord Yikmo had just strolled into the room. The Warrior stopped and looked around, clearly surprised by the crowd. As his eyes rested on the magicians gathered around Akkarin, his eyebrows rose. Sarrin beckoned.

'Good evening, High Lord, Administrator,' Yikmo said as he reached the chairs.

'Lord Yikmo,' Peakin said. 'You must be planning for a few late nights.'

Yikmo frowned. 'Late nights?'

Peakin chuckled. 'So she's that good, is she? Doesn't need the extra practice?'

The young magician's frown deepened. 'Practice?'

Vinara took pity on the man. 'Sonea has challenged Regin to a formal battle.'

Yikmo stared at her, then at the faces watching him, his own slowly turning white.

'She did *what?*'

Sonea paced her room, wringing her hands. *What have I done? Let my anger get the better of me, that's what. I don't know anything about fighting. All I'm going to do is make a fool of myself in front of—*

'Sonea.'

Turning, Sonea blinked in surprise at the man standing in the doorway of her room. No-one had ever visited her in the High Lord's Residence before.

'Lord Yikmo,' she said, bowing.

'You're not ready yet, Sonea.'

She flinched, suddenly fearful. If Yikmo didn't think she could win . . .

'I was hoping you'd help me with that, my lord.'

Several expressions ran across Yikmo's face. Consternation. Thoughtfulness. Interest. He frowned and ran his hands through his hair.

'I understand why you're doing this, Sonea. But I don't have to remind you that Garrel is an accomplished Warrior and that Regin's skills are better than yours – despite all I have taught you. He has a week to prepare, and Balkan has agreed to tutor him.'

Balkan! This is only getting worse! Sonea looked down at

her hands. They weren't shaking, she was relieved to see, but her stomach was fluttering so much she felt sick.

'But I am stronger, and the rules of a challenge don't require any limits on strength,' she pointed out.

'You can't rely on your strength to win the match for you, Sonea,' Yikmo warned. 'There are ways around it. I'm sure Balkan will ensure Regin knows them all.'

'Then you had better ensure I do, too,' she retorted. Surprised at the determination in her own voice, she grimaced apologetically. 'Will you help me?'

He smiled. 'Of course. I could hardly abandon the High Lord's favourite now.'

'Thank you, my lord.'

'But don't think I'm doing this only out of respect for your guardian.'

Surprised, she looked at him closely and was amazed to see approval in his gaze. Of all the teachers, she would never have expected to gain the respect of a Warrior.

'You do realise that people will watch me teaching you,' he said. 'They will report everything to Regin and Lord Garrel.'

'I have thought about that.'

'And?'

'What . . . what about the Dome?'

Yikmo's eyebrows rose, then he grinned broadly. 'I'm sure it can be arranged.'

CHAPTER 36

THE BATTLE BEGINS

As the carriage passed through the Guild Gates, Dannyl looked up at the University. The Guild buildings were so familiar, but now they seemed foreign and forbidding. He looked toward the High Lord's Residence.

Especially that one.

He glanced at the satchel lying on the seat beside him, then picked it up. In it was a copy of the notes that he and Tayend had gathered, rewritten so that nothing in them read like a retracing of Akkarin's journey. He chewed on his lip. *If Akkarin believes any of this was an investigation of his past, this could infuriate him further. But I'll be in trouble anyway, so it's worth the risk.*

The carriage stopped and rocked a little as the driver clambered down to the ground. The door opened. Dannyl stepped out and turned to the driver.

'Send my travel chest to my rooms,' Dannyl ordered. The man bowed, and moved to the back of the carriage where the chest was roped to a narrow tray.

Tucking the satchel under his arm, Dannyl started down the path to the High Lord's Residence. As he walked, he noticed that the gardens were empty, which was unusual for a sunny Freeday afternoon. *Where is everyone?*

By the time he reached the door of the Residence, his mouth was dry and his heart was beating too fast. Taking a deep breath, he reached out to the door handle. Before he could close his fingers around it, the door swung inward.

A servant stepped forward and bowed. 'The High Lord is waiting for you in the library, Ambassador Dannyl. Please follow me.'

Stepping inside, Dannyl glanced appreciatively around the luxuriously decorated guestroom. He had never entered the High Lord's Residence before. The servant opened a door, ushering Dannyl up a spiral staircase. At the top, he walked down a short corridor to a pair of open doors on the right.

The walls of the room inside were lined with books. *What secrets might I find in them?* Dannyl wondered. *Any information about—?*

Then he saw the desk at one side of the room, and the black-robed magician sitting behind it, watching him. He felt his heart skip a beat, then start racing.

'Welcome home, Ambassador Dannyl.'

Get a hold of yourself! Dannyl thought sternly. He inclined his head politely to Akkarin. 'Thank you, High Lord.'

Hearing the doors close, Dannyl glanced back to see that the servant had left. *Now I'm trapped* . . . He pushed the thought away, stepped forward and placed the satchel on Akkarin's desk.

'My notes,' he said. 'As you requested.'

'Thank you,' Akkarin replied. One pale hand picked up the satchel, the other waved toward a chair. 'Sit down. You must be tired from the journey.'

Dannyl sank into the chair gratefully and watched as Akkarin leafed through his notes. Dannyl soothed away a nagging headache. The previous evening he had drunk a little too much siyo in an attempt to stop imagining what he might face the next day.

'You visited the Splendid Temple, I see.'

Dannyl swallowed. 'Yes.'

'Did the High Priest allow you to read the scrolls?'

'He read them to me – after I vowed to keep their contents a secret.'

Akkarin smiled faintly. 'And the Tomb of White Tears?'

'Yes. A fascinating place.'

'Which led you to Armje?'

'Not directly. If I had continued the course of my research, I might have entered Sachaka, but my duties as Ambassador did not allow for such a journey.'

Akkarin stilled. 'Crossing the border would be . . . inadvisable.' He looked up and met Dannyl's eyes, his expression disapproving. 'Sachaka is not part of the Allied Lands and, as a member of the Guild, you should not enter unless under orders of the King.'

Dannyl shook his head. 'I hadn't considered that, but I was not about to go blundering into an unknown land without making some enquiries here first.'

Akkarin regarded Dannyl thoughtfully, then glanced down at the notes. 'So why did you visit Armje?'

'Dem Ladeiri suggested I see the ruins while I was visiting him.'

Akkarin frowned. 'He did, did he?' He fell silent then, reading the notes. After several minutes he made a small noise of surprise, then looked up and stared at Dannyl.

'You *survived*?'

Guessing what Akkarin was referring to, Dannyl nodded. 'Yes, though it exhausted me.'

As Akkarin continued reading, Dannyl wondered if he

had ever seen the man express astonishment before. He decided he hadn't, and felt a strange pride that he, of all people, had managed to surprise the High Lord.

'So you overcame the barrier,' Akkarin mused. 'Interesting. Perhaps the chamber is losing strength. The power must dwindle eventually.'

'May I ask a question?' Dannyl ventured.

Akkarin looked up, one eyebrow raised. 'You may ask.'

'If you had encountered this Chamber of Ultimate Punishment before, why didn't you tell anyone here about it?'

'I did.' The corner of Akkarin's mouth twitched upward. 'But since it was impossible for anyone to investigate without triggering an attack – and for additional reasons of a political nature – it was decided that its existence should be known by only the highest magicians. Which means that I must order you to keep your knowledge of it to yourself.'

Dannyl nodded. 'I understand.'

'It is unfortunate, indeed, that my warning had crumbled away.' Akkarin paused, his eyes narrowing. 'Was there any sign that it might have been removed deliberately?'

Surprised, Dannyl thought of the wall, and what had been left of Akkarin's name. 'I couldn't say.'

'Someone must investigate. That place could too easily become a death trap for magicians.'

'I will return there myself, if you wish.'

Akkarin regarded him thoughtfully, then nodded. 'Yes. It would probably be best that no others learn of the place. Your assistant knows, does he not?'

Dannyl hesitated, and again he wondered how much

546

Akkarin had sensed during their brief mental communication. 'Yes – but I believe Tayend can be trusted.'

Akkarin's gaze flickered slightly, and he opened his mouth to speak, but closed it again as a knock sounded on the library door. His eyes shifted to the door, alert. The doors swung inward.

The servant stepped inside and bowed. 'Lord Yikmo has arrived, High Lord.'

Akkarin nodded. As the doors closed again, he regarded Dannyl speculatively. 'You may return to Elyne in a week.' He closed the satchel. 'I will read these, and may wish to discuss them with you again. But for now,' he stood up, 'I have a formal battle to attend.'

Dannyl blinked in surprise. 'A *formal* battle?'

The High Lord almost seemed to smile. 'My novice has, perhaps foolishly, challenged another to a fight.'

Sonea challenged Regin to a fight! As the possibilities and consequences of this dawned on Dannyl, he chuckled. 'This I have to see.'

Akkarin strode out of the library. Dannyl followed, feeling surprised and relieved. There had been no hard questions about the reasons for the research. It almost seemed as if Akkarin was pleased with Dannyl's progress. Dannyl and Tayend – and Lorlen – hadn't earned themselves the High Lord's disapproval. Neither had Rothen, though hopefully Akkarin didn't know about Rothen's new 'interest' in ancient magic.

And nothing had been said about Tayend.

All that remained was to face Rothen. Dannyl's mentor would be surprised to see him. Dannyl hadn't warned Rothen of his visit, since no letter could have travelled faster than he had, and he would not risk communicating by mind. Rothen had always been able to read more of Dannyl's thoughts than was intended. Dannyl did not know how well Rothen might take the news that his former novice was guilty of being what Fergun had claimed he was. He did not want to lose his only close friend in the Guild.

Yet he had decided he would not deny the rumours concerning Tayend. It would be too easy for Rothen to discover the lie. He would just have to reassure Rothen that he was not risking his honour by association. The Elynes were a tolerant people, and he was expected to be the same.

In a few weeks he would be back in Elyne with the High Lord's permission to investigate Armje between fulfilling his ambassadorial duties. And he would be with Tayend.

If anything, his situation was better than before.

Sonea reknotted the sash of her robe and smoothed the material. It seemed too thin and flimsy today. *I feel like I ought to be donning armour, not robes.*

Closing her eyes, she wished she had someone fussing about her while she prepared. Naturally, Yikmo could not be in her room while she changed into fresh robes. Neither could Akkarin, for which she was profoundly grateful. No, it was Tania she missed now. Rothen's servant would have made Sonea promise to come out of this day the victor, and at the same time reassured her that losing wouldn't matter to the people who loved her.

She drew in a deep breath and, finding the sash too constricting, loosened it a little. Today she might need more freedom of movement. She glanced at the tray of sweets and savoury buns Viola had brought earlier. Feeling her stomach clench, she turned away and started pacing again.

She had an advantage – or two. While Yikmo's 'spies' had reported everything that Regin had been doing in the Arena for the past week, her own training had been hidden within the claustrophobic confines of the Dome. Yikmo had shown her every strategy that a weaker magician could use against a stronger one. He had drilled her in all the methods that he knew Garrel and Balkan had taught Regin, plus a few more.

Of her own guardian, she had seen little. But his influence was everywhere. The protests against novices involving themselves in formal battles had ended within a day. Balkan obviously disapproved of Sonea using the Dome, but had not forbidden it. And when Sonea first entered the Dome, Yikmo had told her that the High Lord had strengthened the spherical structure to ensure that she would not accidentally damage it.

It hadn't occurred to her until the following evening that the magic he had used might have been gained through black magic. She had lain awake, her conscience uneasy at the possibility that the magic that aided her petty squabble with another novice might have come from some stranger's death.

But she could not refuse Akkarin's help, not without raising suspicion. Even if she pretended she did not want it out of pride, he had nominated himself as her protector during the battle. His magic would form the inner shield that would save her if her own failed. The thought made her more than a little uneasy. If it weren't for Rothen and Lorlen, she would have been worried that he might use the battle as an opportunity to be rid of her.

At a knock on her door, she spun around, heart suddenly racing again. *It must be time at last*, she thought. Relief was quickly replaced with a rush of terror. She took a deep breath and let it out slowly as she approached the door. Opening it, she felt her heartbeat quicken once more as she faced Akkarin, but, seeing another man behind him, her fear was replaced with surprise as she recognised Dannyl.

'High Lord,' she said, bowing. 'Ambassador Dannyl.'

'Lord Yikmo has arrived,' Akkarin told her.

Taking another deep breath, Sonea hurried down the stairs. She found Lord Yikmo pacing back and forth in Akkarin's guestroom. His head snapped up as she entered the room.

'Sonea! You're ready. Good. How are you feeling?'

'Fine.' She smiled, conscious of the magicians still descending the stairs. 'How can I not be after all you have taught me?'

He smiled crookedly. 'Your confidence in me is . . .' He paused, sobering as Akkarin and Dannyl stepped into the room. 'Good morning, High Lord, Ambassador Dannyl.'

'I gathered you were here for my novice,' the High Lord said. 'So I sent her down.'

'Indeed I am,' Yikmo replied. He looked at Sonea. 'We'd best not keep Regin waiting.'

The main door swung open, and Akkarin gestured toward it. Feeling the magicians' eyes on her, Sonea crossed the room and stepped out into the sunlight.

As she started down the path to the University, Yikmo fell into step on her right, and Akkarin on her left. Footsteps from behind told her that Dannyl was following. She resisted an urge to look back, wondering what business he had with Akkarin. Something important, or he would not have returned from Elyne.

Her companions were silent as they walked toward the University. Sonea glanced at Yikmo once, but he only smiled in reply. She didn't look at Akkarin, but was acutely aware of his presence. Never before had she *felt* like the High Lord's favourite. It made her too conscious of the Guild's expectations. If she lost . . .

Think of something else, she told herself. As they neared the University, she turned her mind to remembering Yikmo's lessons.

'*Regin will try to make you waste your power. The best way to do that is through deception and trickery.*'

Trickery was certainly part of Regin's fighting style. He had surprised her many times during the First Year Warrior Skills classes with false strikes.

'*Much of what you have learned will be irrelevant. You will not need to use projection in the Arena: there is nothing in there to move. Stunstrike is allowed, but considered ill-mannered. Mindstrike is forbidden, naturally, though it would only be useful as a distraction.*'

Regin had never used mindstrike against her, since they hadn't yet learned how to do it.

'*Don't gesture! You give away your intentions. A good Warrior does not move during a battle, not even the muscles in his face.*'

Yikmo always referred to 'the Warrior' as 'he', which she found amusing at first, then irritating. When she had complained he had laughed. 'Lady Vinara would approve,' he had said. 'But Balkan would tell you, "When more Warriors are women than men, I will mend my ways".'

Sonea smiled at the memory, and so was smiling when

she walked past the University into the view of the crowd of magicians waiting outside the Arena.

'Is *everyone* here?' she gasped.

'Probably,' Yikmo said lightly. 'Regin chose a Freeday to face you, so that there would be a large crowd to witness his defeat.'

Sonea felt the blood drain from her face. Novices and magicians stood watching her. Even non-magicians – wives, husbands, children and servants – had come along for the spectacle. There were hundreds of people watching her. Heads turned to watch as she, flanked by her teacher and guardian, entered the crowd. The Higher Magicians stood in a line. Yikmo guided her toward them, and as he stopped she bowed. Formal greetings were exchanged, but she was too distracted to pay much attention until her name was spoken.

'Well, Sonea. Your adversary awaits your pleasure,' Lord Balkan said, gesturing.

Following his motion, she saw Regin and Lord Garrel standing by a hedge clipped into an archway. The path that ran through it led directly to the Arena.

'Good luck, Sonea,' Lorlen said, smiling.

'Thank you, Administrator.' Her voice sounded small, and she felt a flash of annoyance at herself. She was the challenger. She ought to be striding into this battle with eager confidence.

As she started toward the Arena, Yikmo placed a hand on her arm. 'Keep your wits about you, and you'll do fine,' he murmured. He stepped away, and waved her on.

With only Akkarin beside her now, she approached the archway. As she met Regin's eyes his face twisted into a sneer, bringing back a memory of the first time she had seen him, before the Acceptance Ceremony. She stared back defiantly.

Sensing the gaze of Lord Garrel, she turned her attention to him. The magician was staring at her with unconcealed dislike and anger. Surprised, she wondered why he was so angry. Did he resent the extra time he'd had to spend preparing his novice for this fight? Had it offended him that she'd had the audacity to challenge his nephew? Or did he resent her for putting him in a position of opposition with the High Lord?

Do I care? No. If he'd had any foresight, he would have stopped Regin from harassing her after she had become the High Lord's favourite. The thought that this challenge might have caused him inconvenience brought a smile to her face once more. Turning away, she stepped through the arch and strode toward the Arena.

With Akkarin at her side, she descended into the Arena portal. Emerging, she walked to the centre of the sandy floor and stopped. Garrel, Regin and Balkan had followed her in. Outside the circle of spires, the crowd of magicians and novices was spreading around the structure, some sitting down on the tiered stairs.

She glanced at Regin. He was looking out at the crowd, his expression unusually sober. She let her eyes skim the watchers, then stopped as she saw Rothen standing among them, Dorrien at her side. Dorrien grinned and waved. Rothen managed a thin smile.

Balkan stepped between her and Regin, raised his arms and waited as the buzz of voices from the audience faded.

'It has been many years since two magicians have seen fit to resolve a dispute or prove their skill by formal battle in the Arena,' Balkan began. 'Today we will witness the first such event in fifty-two years. To my right stands the challenger, Sonea, favoured novice of the High Lord. To my left stands the adversary, Regin, of the family Winar, House Paren, favoured novice of Lord Garrel.

'The combatants' guardians have nominated themselves as protectors. They may now form an inner shield around their novices.'

Sonea felt a hand touch her shoulder lightly. She shivered at the sensation, then looked down at herself. Akkarin's shield was almost undetectable. She resisted an urge to test it.

'The protectors may now leave the Arena.'

She watched as Akkarin and Garrel strode into the portal. As the pair emerged outside the Arena, she saw that Garrel's face was dark with anger and Akkarin looked bemused. Clearly, something had been said to upset Regin's guardian. Had Akkarin made some jibe? Despite herself, she felt an unexpected satisfaction at the thought. But the feeling evaporated as Balkan spoke again.

'The combatants may take their positions.'

At once, Regin spun on his heel and began to walk to the other side of the Arena. Turning away, Sonea started in the other direction. She took a few slow, deep breaths. Soon she would need to focus all her attention on Regin. She would have to ignore all the people who were watching and think only of the fight.

A few steps from the edge of the Arena, she turned around. Balkan was walking toward the portal. Then he was inside it. Then he appeared at the top of the stairs outside the Arena and stepped on top of the portal.

'The victor must win the majority of five bouts,' he told the watchers. 'A bout is over when an inner shield is struck with a force counted as a fatal hit. Mindstrike is forbidden. If a combatant uses magic before a battle has officially commenced, he or she cedes that bout. A battle commences when I say "begin" and ends when I say "halt". Do you understand?'

'Yes, my lord,' Sonea replied. Regin echoed her words.

'Are you ready?'

'Yes, my lord.' Again, Regin's answer followed hers.

Balkan lifted a hand and placed it close to the Arena's barrier. He sent out a pulse of power, which flashed over the dome. Sonea looked at Regin.

'Begin!'

Regin stood with his arms crossed, but the mocking smile she had expected wasn't there. She saw the air ripple with power as he let loose the first strike. It struck her shield a heartbeat after she sent her reply.

His shield remained strong, but he did not strike again. She could see his brow creased in a frown. No doubt he was considering how best to trick her into wasting her powers.

The air between them wavered again as he sent magic toward her, this time in a multiple attack. The strikes flashed faintly white, sensed more than seen. They looked like forcestrike . . . but either they were strong enough to gain the tint of white, or they . . .

Sonea felt the first strikes hit her shield with a soft patter and chuckled. He was trying to trick her into strengthening her shield too much. She almost reduced it, but a difference in the way the air shimmered between them alerted her to something new. As a full forcestrike battered her shield she thanked her instincts, for it was strong enough to push her back a step.

The rain of weak strikes continued, so she sent one powerful beam of energy in return. Regin abandoned his attack and threw up a strong barrier, but an instant before her strike hit she exerted her will and the heatstrike suddenly split into a shower of red stunstrikes that vanished against Regin's shield.

Regin's face twisted with anger. Sonea smiled as she heard murmuring around the Arena. The joke was not lost on the magicians. They must have heard how Regin had used stunstrike on her.

The next attack from Regin was quick but easily evaded. Sonea played on his anger, returning only with stunstrike. She didn't bother to disguise it; he was alert to that trick now. Though this meant the battle was going nowhere, she could not resist taunting him. She had plenty of energy to spare, and anger might spur him into making a foolish move. Using stunstrike in battle was considered bad mannered, however, and was not going to endear her to anyone in the Guild.

Regin suddenly threw a steady rain of strikes at her. Forcestrike, heatstrike, all of varying intensity. Sonea's shield glowed faintly with their power. She returned with her own barrage, recognising the simple ploy. When so many varying strikes were dealt out, the defender had two choices: hold a shield that could block the most potent of the strikes while keeping watch for anything stronger, or try to conserve strength by modifying the shield for each strike.

She matched his attack with her own, and saw that he was modifying his shield. It took a great deal of concentration to do this while attacking at the same time. His face was rigid and his eyes darted from strike to strike, showing the effort it was taking.

He might wear her down eventually this way. She knew that one potent strike would force him to break off the attack, but that would use even more of her power, which was what he wanted.

But his ploy was also his weakness. His defence would only work if he noticed every strike she sent. *So I need to do something unexpected.*

Changing the direction of a strike once it had been let loose took extra effort, but not as much as a strong blast of power. Concentrating, she turned the path of one of her forcestrikes so that, at the last moment, it shot around and struck him from behind.

Regin staggered forward. His eyes widened, then narrowed and burned with anger.

'Halt!'

Sonea abandoned her attack and let her shield fall. She looked up at Balkan expectantly.

'The first victory goes to Sonea.'

The air filled with voices as magicians turned to each other to debate what they had just seen. Sonea tried to smother a smile, then gave in to it. *I won the first bout!* She looked at Regin. His face was dark with fury.

Balkan lifted his arms. The chatter ceased.

'Are you ready to begin the second battle?' he asked Sonea and Regin.

'Yes, my lord,' she answered. Regin's reply was curt.

Balkan placed a hand against the Arena's barrier.

'Begin!'

CHAPTER 37

THE HIGH LORD'S FAVOURITE

Lorlen smiled as the two novices turned to face each other again. Sonea's first victory had been everything it needed to be. She hadn't won by strength, but by finding a hole in Regin's defence. Glancing at Lord Yikmo, he was surprised to find the Warrior frowning.

'You don't look pleased, Lord Yikmo,' Lorlen murmured.

The Warrior smiled. 'I am. This is the first time she's beaten Regin. But it is easy to lose focus in the elation of winning a battle.'

As Sonea attacked Regin with obvious eagerness, Lorlen felt a little of Yikmo's concern. *Don't be overconfident, Sonea*, he thought. *Regin will be wary now.*

Regin defended himself easily, then attacked. Soon the air within the Arena was sizzling with magic. Suddenly Sonea threw her arms wide and looked down, her attack faltering. Lorlen heard the sharp intake of breaths around him, but Sonea's shield held under Regin's increased attack.

Looking at the ground under Sonea's feet, he saw that the sand was shifting about. A disc of power was discernible beneath the soles of her boots. She was levitating just above the ground.

Lorlen knew the tactic. A magician might expect a strike from any direction but not from below. It was tempting to end one's shield where it met the ground to save power.

Sonea's shield had obviously extended below her feet, and her knowledge of levitation had saved her from the indignity of being sent sprawling across the Arena by the shifting and bucking sand. Levitation, he recalled, wasn't taught until the Third Year.

'Wise move, teaching her that,' Lorlen said.

Yikmo shook his head. 'I didn't.'

Sonea's face was tense. The concentration required to levitate, shield and attack was demanding, and her attack had changed to a simple pattern of strikes that was easy to block. Lorlen knew she ought force Regin to use just as much power and concentration. The sand under Regin's feet began to boil, but he simply stepped sideways. At the same time, Sonea threw her arms out again from another subterranean onslaught, and her attack faltered.

'Halt!'

'The second victory goes to Regin.'

A faint cheer went up from the novices. While Regin grinned and waved at his friends, Sonea frowned, obviously annoyed with herself.

'Good,' said Yikmo.

Bemused, Lorlen looked at the Warrior questioningly.

'She needed that,' Yikmo explained.

In the short pause between bouts, Rothen looked for Dannyl among the magicians on the other side of the Arena. He had disappeared from his previous place among the Higher Magicians. Rothen frowned, torn between watching the battle and seeking out his friend.

He had been astonished to see Dannyl arrive with Sonea, Yikmo and Akkarin. Dannyl had sent no word that he would be visiting the Guild, not even a brief mental communication. Did that mean his return had been a secret?

Obviously it was a secret no longer. By appearing with Sonea and the High Lord, Dannyl had revealed his presence to everyone watching. But it was his appearance in company with the High Lord that bothered Rothen most. And Dannyl had sent no notes or letters for several weeks now.

Questions followed questions. Had Rothen's request been discovered by Akkarin? Or was Dannyl merely assisting the High Lord in an ambassadorial matter? Or was it a darker matter, and Dannyl was unaware that he was helping a black magician? Or had he discovered the truth about Akkarin?

'Hello, old friend.'

Jumping at the voice at his shoulder, Rothen turned around. Dannyl smiled, obviously pleased with himself for startling his mentor. He nodded to Dorrien, who greeted him warmly.

'Dannyl! Why didn't you tell me you were coming back?' Rothen demanded.

Dannyl smiled apologetically. 'I'm sorry, I should have let you know. I was ordered back unexpectedly.'

'For what?'

The young magician looked away. 'Just to report to the High Lord.'

Called back unexpectedly *just* to report to the High Lord? Hearing Balkan call the start of the next bout, Rothen was torn between questioning Dannyl and watching Sonea. He turned back to watch the battle. If Dannyl was willing to discuss his meeting with Akkarin, he probably wouldn't want to while standing in a crowd

560

of magicians. *No*, Rothen decided. *I will question him later.*

Regin had adopted a bold and risky defence. Instead of shielding, he directed his strikes at Sonea's. As his magic hammered into hers the Arena filled with shattered streaks of energy, each too weak to bother the two novices. A few reached the Arena's barrier and sent shivers of lightning across it. Through all this, Regin was also sending extra strikes directly at Sonea. Though she defended herself easily, it was clear that she was using more power than Regin simply by keeping her shield up.

She countered this by increasing her attack. Regin's ploy would only work if he caught all the strikes aimed at him. If he missed any he would have to create a shield very quickly.

As Rothen watched, this happened: one of Sonea's strikes slipped through. Before Rothen could suck in a breath of anticipation the strike encountered a hastily raised shield.

Sonea began to advance on Regin, shortening the distance between them so he was forced to react faster. When the pair were only ten strides apart, Regin's strikes suddenly appeared to reverse. He staggered backward and gave a shout of surprise. The Arena was abruptly empty of magic.

'Halt!'

Silence followed Balkan's call, then a low murmuring began among the watchers.

'The third victory goes to Sonea.'

Magicians voiced their confusion. Rothen frowned and shook his head. 'What happened?'

'I believe Sonea's strikes were doubled,' Dorrien said. 'So that each had another strike following a moment behind it. They would have looked like a single strike from Regin's

561

vantage point. Regin's defensive strikes stopped the first ones, but he didn't have time to see the doubles.'

Several magicians had overheard Dorrien, and were nodding to each other, impressed. Dorrien glanced at Rothen, looking smug. 'She really is wonderful to watch.'

'Yes.' Rothen nodded, then sighed as Dorrien turned away. Clearly his son was growing more enthralled with her. He had never expected to be so eager for Dorrien to return to his village.

Balkan's voice boomed over the buzz of voices.

'Please return to your positions.'

Sonea backed away from Regin.

'Are you ready to begin the fourth bout?'

'Yes, my lord,' the pair replied.

A flash of light shivered over the Arena's barrier.

'Begin!'

Sonea began this battle far from triumphant. The method she had used to defeat Regin had used a lot of magic. If Regin's victory depended on him making her waste her energy, then he was winning.

She would have to be more cautious this time. She must refuse to let herself be drawn into his tricks. She had to save her energy, for if she lost this battle she would need to survive another.

For a while she and Regin watched each other, both of them shieldless and motionless. Then Regin's eyes narrowed and the air filled with a thousand near-invisible heatstrikes, each only just strong enough to be counted a fatal hit if they met her inner shield. Within the rain of weaker strikes she saw some more potent ones, and created a shield strong enough to deter them all.

But just before the strikes reached her they faded into nothing. Annoyed at Regin's trick, she sent an identical barrage of strikes, only she let some stronger strikes batter his shield, hoping he would think she was using the same trick in return.

He didn't fall for it, of course, but he staggered backward, his expression strained. She felt a surge of triumph. He was tiring!

A careful attack followed, complex yet economical. He filled the air with light, as if hoping to disguise a few stronger strikes in the dazzle of brightness. At each returning strike, she saw small signs of effort in Regin's face and manner. He was trying to hide it, but it was clear he would be no great threat to her now.

Watching him through the glare, she saw him wince as one of her stronger strikes reached him. Then, from above, she felt an unexpected force slam into her shield. It wavered, and then another strike, timed to come only a moment after the first, broke her shield before she could strengthen it.

'Halt!'

Disbelief and dismay washed over her as she realised that he had only been faking his weariness. Looking at his smug expression, she felt anger at herself for being such a fool.

'The fourth victory goes to Regin.'

But she knew his limits. He *had* to be tiring after all this time.

She closed her eyes, seeking the source of her power. It was a little diminished, but in no danger of depletion.

Yikmo had counselled against defeating Regin with sheer strength. '*If you want respect, you must show both skill and honour.*'

I've shown them enough skill and honour, she thought. Whatever happened in this last bout, she was not going to risk losing again by trying to conserve her strength. If she won this bout, it would only be by lasting longer than Regin.

Which meant she would win it by strength anyway, so why not end it quickly with one ferocious attack?

'Are you ready to begin the fifth bout?' Balkan called.

'Yes, my lord,' she answered, Regin echoing her reply.

'Begin.'

She began by attacking with powerful strikes, hoping to gauge Regin's stamina. Regin neatly sidestepped all, her strikes flashing harmlessly into the Arena's barrier.

Sonea stared at Regin, who returned her look with feigned innocence. Dodging and ducking were considered bad form in battle, but no rules existed against them. She was surprised that he would resort to either, but that was what he'd anticipated. He had done it simply so that she used up her power in a useless attack. Regin smiled. The sand around his feet stirred.

A murmuring began in the crowd as sand began to rise from the floor of the Arena. Sonea watched, wondering what Regin was doing – and why. Yikmo hadn't mentioned any tactic that involved *this*. In fact, he'd said that projection was irrelevant in a formal battle.

Sand was whipping around the Arena now. It thickened rapidly, filling the air with a thin wailing. Sonea frowned as Regin disappeared from sight. Soon she could see nothing but white.

Then something more potent buffeted her shield. Judging the direction, she threw out a strike, but another attack hit her from behind, then a third from above.

He's blinded me, she realised. Somewhere beyond the sand, he was moving around the Arena, or directing his strikes to curve and hit from different directions. She couldn't fight back when she didn't know where he was.

But that wouldn't matter, if she aimed in all directions at once.

Drawing on her power, she sent out a spray of potent strikes. The sand abruptly dropped around her, forming a ring on the ground. Regin had centred the sandstorm on her. *So that was how he knew where I was.*

He stood on the other side of the Arena, watching her carefully. Seeing him, she knew he was trying to judge how tired she was.

I'm not.

As she attacked, he dodged again. She felt a smile pull at her lips. If Regin wanted to waste her power, she would have him running all over the Arena like a frightened rassook. Eventually she would catch him.

Or she could *curve* her strikes around the Arena so he had nowhere to run.

Yes. Let's finish this.

She half-closed her eyes and focussed on the source of her power. Drawing on all but a little of the magic she had left, she formed in her mind a pattern both beautiful and deadly. Then she lifted her arms. It didn't matter if she let her intentions show now. As she released the magic, she knew it was the most potent force she had ever let loose. She sent it outward in three waves of forcestrikes, each more powerful than the previous.

She heard a low sound from the audience as the strikes rayed out like a bright, dangerous flower, then curved down toward Regin.

Regin's eyes widened. He backed away, but there was nowhere to go. As the first strikes hit, his shield shattered.

A heartbeat later the second wave hit the inner shield. Regin's expression changed from surprise to terror. He glanced at Lord Garrel, then threw up his arms as the third wave of strikes hit.

As they did, Sonea heard an exclamation. She recognised the voice as Garrel's. The inner shield around Regin wavered . . .

. . . but remained in place.

Turning to stare at Regin's guardian, Sonea saw him press his hands to his temples and sway. Akkarin's hand rested on the magician's shoulder.

Then a soft thump drew her attention back to the Arena. Sonea felt her heart skip as she saw Regin lying on the sand. All was silent. She waited for him to move, but he remained still. Surely he was just exhausted. He couldn't be . . . *dead*.

She took a step toward him.

'Halt!'

Frozen by the command, she looked up at Balkan questioningly. The Warrior frowned as if in warning.

Then Regin groaned and the watching magicians let out a collective sigh. Closing her eyes, Sonea felt relief rush over her.

'Sonea has won the challenge,' Balkan announced.

Slowly, then with more enthusiasm, the watching magicians and novices began to cheer. Surprised, Sonea looked around.

I've won, she thougt. *I actually won!*

She surveyed the cheering magicians, novices, and nonmagicians: *perhaps more than just the fight*. But she wouldn't be certain of that until later, when she walked down the University corridor and heard what the novices were muttering, or when she encountered Regin and his friends in one of the passages late at night.

'I declare this formal contest concluded,' Balkan announced. Stepping down from the portal, he joined Garrel and Akkarin. Garrel nodded at something the Warrior said, then began to walk around the Arena toward the entrance, his eyes on the still prone figure of Regin.

Sonea regarded Regin thoughtfully. Moving closer, she saw that his face was white and he appeared to be asleep. Clearly he was exhausted, and she knew how awful that felt. But never in all the times she had been exhausted had she fallen unconscious.

Hesitantly, in case he was faking, she crouched beside him and gingerly touched his forehead. His exhaustion was so extreme, his body was in shock from it. She let a little Healing energy flow from her hand into his body to strengthen it.

'Sonea!'

She looked up to find Garrel staring down at her disapprovingly.

'What are—?'

'Ngh . . .' the boy groaned.

Ignoring Garrel, she looked down to see Regin's eyes fluttering open. He stared at her, then his brow creased into a frown.

'*You?*'

Sonea smiled wryly and rose. She bowed to Garrel, then walked past him and into the cool of the Arena's portal.

Though most of the audience was leaving, the Higher

Magicians lingered beside the Arena. They had gathered into a rough circle to discuss the fight.

'Her powers have grown faster than I would have thought possible,' Lady Vinara said.

'Her strength is astounding for one her age,' Sarrin agreed.

'If she is so strong, why didn't she simply wear Regin down at the beginning?' Peakin asked. 'Why did she try to conserve her strength? It lost her two bouts.'

'Because the object of this was not for Sonea to win,' Yikmo said quietly. 'But for Regin to lose.'

Peakin regarded the Warrior dubiously. 'And the difference is?'

Lorlen smiled at the Alchemist's confusion. 'If she had simply beaten him down, she would not have gained anyone's respect. By winning and losing bouts based on skill, she showed that she was willing to fight fairly despite her advantage.'

Vinara nodded. 'She didn't know how strong she really was, did she?'

Yikmo smiled. 'No. She didn't. Only that she was stronger. If she'd known just how strong she was, it would have been difficult for her to allow herself to lose.'

'So how strong is she?'

Yikmo looked pointedly at Lorlen, then over Lorlen's shoulder. Turning, Lorlen saw that Balkan and Akkarin were approaching. He knew it was not Balkan that Yikmo had been looking at.

'Perhaps you have taken on more than even you can handle, High Lord,' Sarrin said.

Akkarin smiled. 'Not likely.'

Lorlen watched the others exchange glances. Not one

face expressed disbelief. A lack of comprehension, perhaps.

'You'll have to start teaching her yourself soon,' Vinara added.

Akkarin shook his head. 'All she needs, she can learn in the University. There is nothing else that I can teach her that she would care to learn – for now.'

Lorlen felt a sudden chill creep up his body. He looked closely at Akkarin, but nothing in the High Lord's expression hinted at what he feared.

'I can't see her understanding or liking the battles and intrigues of the Houses,' Vinara agreed, 'though the idea of the Guild electing its first High Lady is quite interesting.'

Sarrin frowned. 'Let's not forget her origins.'

As Vinara's gaze sharpened, Lorlen cleared his throat. 'Hopefully that will not be an issue for many years.' He glanced at Akkarin, but the High Lord's attention was elsewhere. Lorlen followed his gaze and saw Sonea approaching.

As the circle of magicians parted to receive her, Sonea bowed.

'Congratulations, Sonea,' Balkan rumbled. 'It was a well-fought battle.'

'Thank you, Lord Balkan,' she replied, her eyes brightening.

'How are you feeling?' Lady Vinara asked.

Sonea tilted her head, considering, then shrugged. 'Hungry, my lady.'

Vinara laughed. 'Then I hope your guardian has a celebration banquet waiting for you.'

If Sonea's smile became a little forced, the others did

not appear to notice. They were looking at Akkarin, who had turned to face her.

'Well done, Sonea,' he said.

'Thank you, High Lord.'

The pair regarded each other in silence, then Sonea lowered her eyes. Watching the others carefully, Lorlen noted Vinara's knowing smile. Balkan looked amused and Sarrin was nodding approvingly.

Lorlen sighed. They saw only a young novice awed and intimidated by her powerful guardian. Would they ever see anything more? He looked down at the red gem on his finger. *If they do, I won't be the one to show them. I am as much a hostage as she is.*

He looked at Akkarin and narrowed his eyes. *When he gets around to explaining himself, he'd better have a very good reason for all this.*

Opening the door to his room, Dannyl gestured for Rothen to enter then followed and closed the door. Inside, it was dark, and though it all looked clean and free of dust there was a smell of neglect in the air. His trunk had been deposited just inside the bedroom.

'So what was so pressing that the High Lord ordered you back to Imardin?' Rothen asked.

Dannyl regarded Rothen closely. No 'how are you' or 'how was your journey'. He might have been annoyed, if it hadn't been for the disturbing changes in his friend's appearance.

Dark shadows hung under Rothen's eyes. He seemed older, though Dannyl might simply be seeing his friend through eyes less familiar with the deep creases across Rothen's brow, or the grey in his hair. The slightly hunched, tense way his mentor walked was definitely new, however.

'I can tell you some of it,' Dannyl said, 'but not all. It seems Akkarin learned of my research into ancient magic. He . . . are you all right, Rothen?'

Rothen had grown very pale. He looked away. 'Was he . . . offended by my interest?'

'He wasn't,' Dannyl assured him, 'because he doesn't know you have any interest in ancient magic. He had learned of *my* research, and it appears he approves of it. In fact, I have his permission to continue.'

Rothen stared at Dannyl in surprise. 'Then that must mean . . .'

'You can write your book without worrying about stepping on his toes,' Dannyl finished.

From Rothen's dismissive frown, Dannyl guessed this wasn't what had surprised his friend.

'Did he ask you to do anything else?' Rothen asked.

Dannyl smiled. 'That is the part I can't tell you about. Ambassadorial matters. Nothing too dangerous, however.'

Rothen regarded Dannyl speculatively, then nodded. 'You must be tired,' he said. 'I should leave you to unpack and rest.' He moved to the door, then hesitated and turned around again. 'Did you get my letter?'

Here we go, Dannyl thought.

'Yes.'

Rothen made an apologetic gesture. 'I thought I should warn you in case it stirs up the gossips again.'

'Of course,' Dannyl said dryly. He paused, surprised at the lack of concern in his own voice.

'I don't think it will be a problem,' Rothen added. 'If this assistant of yours is what they say he is, that is. People aren't speculating about you, they just think it's amusing in light of what you were accused of as a novice.'

'I see.' Dannyl nodded slowly, then steeled himself for an unpleasant response. 'Tayend *is* a lad, Rothen.'

'A lad?' Rothen frowned, then his eyes widened with understanding. 'So the rumour is true.'

'Yes. The Elynes are a more tolerant people than Kyralians – most of the time.' Dannyl smiled. 'I'm endeavouring to adapt to their ways.'

Rothen nodded. 'Part of the role of Ambassador, I expect. Along with secret meetings with the High Lord.' He smiled for the first time since they had met that day. 'But I am keeping you from your unpacking. Why don't you have dinner with Dorrien and I tonight? He's returning to his village tomorrow.'

'I'd like that.'

Rothen moved to the door again. At a flexing of Dannyl's will, the door swung open. Rothen stopped, pushed it closed again, and sighed. He turned to stare into Dannyl's eyes.

'Be careful, Dannyl,' he said. 'Be very careful.'

Dannyl stared back. 'I will,' he assured his friend.

Rothen nodded. Opening the door again, he stepped out into the corridor. Dannyl watched his friend and mentor walk away.

And shook his head as he realised he had no idea whether his friend was warning him about his affairs with Tayend, or with Akkarin.

EPILOGUE

The full moon bathed the path to the High Lord's Residence in blue light. Walking toward the building, Sonea smiled.

Four weeks had passed since the challenge, and not once had she encountered Regin and his allies in the University passages after class. No sniggers had reached her ears in the corridors and not one of her projects had been ruined.

Today she had been paired with Hal in Medicines and, after an awkward start, they had started arguing about the right treatment for nailworm. He had told her about a rare plant his father, a village Healer in Lan, used to treat the disease. When she told him that the dwells used tugor mash, left over from distillation of bol, he had laughed. They started exchanging superstitions and unlikely cures from their homes, and when the lesson ended she realised they had been talking for an hour.

Reaching the door to the Residence, Sonea touched the handle. Expecting the door to swing open immediately, she stepped forward and banged her knee.

Surprised and annoyed, she touched the handle again, but the door remained closed. Was she to be locked out tonight? Grasping the handle, she turned it and was relieved when the door swung inward.

Closing the door behind her, she turned toward the stairs, then froze as she heard a crash from somewhere beyond the other staircase. A muffled shout reached her ears, then the floor vibrated beneath her feet.

Something was going on below her, in the underground room. Something magical.

Her whole body went cold. Frozen, she considered what to do. Her first thought was to escape to her room, but she realised that if there was a magical battle happening beneath her she would be no safer in her bedroom.

She should leave. Get as far away as possible.

But curiosity kept her still. *I want to know what is going on*, she thought. *And if someone has come to confront Akkarin, they might need my help.*

Taking a deep breath, she moved to the door of the stairs and opened it a crack. The staircase beyond was dark, so the door to the room below must be closed. Slowly, every muscle tensed ready for a fast retreat, she crept down the stairs. Reaching the door, she searched for a keyhole or some way to see into the underground room, but found nothing. A man's voice yelled something. A stranger's voice. It took her a moment to realise she hadn't understood him because he was speaking in another language.

The reply was spoken harshly, also in another language. Sonea went cold as she recognised Akkarin's voice. Then a high wail of desperation sent her heart racing and she backed up the stairs, suddenly convinced she ought to be anywhere but there.

The door flew open.

Takan looked up at her and stopped. She didn't see his expression, however. Her attention had been caught by the scene beyond.

Akkarin stood over a man dressed in simple clothing. His hand was wrapped about the man's throat, and blood trickled through his fingers. In his other hand was a jewelled knife – a knife that was horribly familiar. As she watched, the stranger's eyes glazed over and he slumped to the floor.

Then Takan cleared his throat, and Akkarin's head snapped up.

Their gaze locked – like in her nightmares in which she relived the night when she had witnessed him in this room, only he saw her watching and she couldn't move . . . then woke up with her heart racing.

But this time she wouldn't wake up. This was *real*.

'Sonea.' He spoke her name with unconcealed annoyance. 'Come here.'

She shook her head, backed away, and felt the sting of magic as her shoulder encountered a barrier. Takan sighed and retreated into the room. Feeling the barrier press against her back, Sonea realised it was going to push her down the stairs. She pushed aside panic with an effort, straightened her shoulders and forced her legs to carry her into his domain.

As she stepped through the doorway the door closed behind her with a solid finality. She looked down at the dead man and shuddered at his empty staring eyes. Akkarin followed her gaze.

'This man is – was – an assassin. He was sent to kill me.'

So he says. She looked at Takan.

'It is true,' the servant said. He gestured. 'Do you think the m— High Lord would mess up his own rooms?'

Looking around, she realised that the walls were scorched and one of the bookcases was a shambles of broken wood and scattered books. She had sensed and heard enough from the guest room to suspect there had been some kind of magical battle going on below her.

So the dead man must have been a magician. She looked at him again. He was not Kyralian, or of any of the races belonging to the Allied Lands. He looked like . . . she turned to stare at Takan. The same broad face and gold-brown skin . . .

'Yes,' Akkarin said. 'He and Takan are of the same people. Sachakan.'

That explained how the man could have magic, but not be of the Guild. So there were still magicians in Sachaka . . . but if this man was an assassin, why did he – or his employer – want Akkarin dead?

Why indeed? she mused.

'Why did you kill him?' she asked. 'Why not hand him over to the Guild?'

Akkarin's smile was humourless. 'Because, as you've no doubt guessed, he and his kind know much about me that I'd rather the Guild did not.'

'So you killed him. With . . . with . . .'

'With what the Guild calls black magic. Yes.' He took a step toward her, then another, his eyes level and un-wavering. 'I have never killed anyone who did not mean me harm, Sonea.'

She looked away. Was that supposed to reassure her, when he knew she would expose his secret if she could? That would certainly do him harm.

'He would be satisfied, indeed, if he knew the harm he has done by coming here and causing you to see what you have seen,' Akkarin said softly. 'You must be wondering who these people are, who want me dead, and what their reasons are. I can tell you only this: the Sachakans still

576

hate the Guild, but they also fear us. From time to time they send one of these, to test me. Do you really think it unreasonable of me to defend myself?'

She looked up at him, wondering why he was telling her this. Did he really expect her to believe anything he said? Surely, if the Sachakans were a danger, the rest of the Guild would know. Not just the High Lord. No, he practised evil magic to strengthen himself and this was only a lie to ensure her silence.

His gaze moved over her face, then he nodded to himself.

'It does not matter if you believe me or not, Sonea.' He narrowed his eyes at the door, which swung open with a faint creak. 'Only remember that, if you speak a word of this, you will bring about the destruction of everything you hold dear.'

She sidestepped to the door. 'I know,' she said bitterly. 'You don't have to remind me.'

Reaching the doorway, she hurried up the stairs. As she reached the door to the guestroom, a voice drifted up from the room below.

'At least the murders will stop.'

'For now,' Akkarin replied. 'Until the next one comes.'

Twisting the handle, Sonea stumbled into the guestroom. She stopped, breathing heavily as relief swept over her. She had faced the nightmare and survived. But she knew she would not sleep easily now. She had seen him kill, and that was not something she would ever forget.

LORD DANNYL'S GUIDE TO SLUM SLANG

blood money – payment for assassination

boot – refuse/refusal (don't boot us)

capper – man who frequents brothels

clicked – occurred

client – person who has an obligation or agreement with a Thief

counter – whore

done – murdered

dull – persuade to keep silent

dunghead – fool

dwells – term used to describe slum dwellers

eye – keep watch

fired – angry (got fired about it)

fish – propose/ask/look for (also someone fleeing the Guard)

gauntlet – guard who is bribeable or in the control of a Thief

goldmine – man who prefers boys

good go – a reasonable try

got – caught

grandmother – pimp

gutter – dealer in stolen goods

hai – a call for attention or expression of surprise or inquiry

heavies – important people

kin – a Thief's closest and most trusted

knife – assassin/hired killer

messenger – thug who delivers or carries out a threat

mind – hide (minds his business/I'll mind that for you)

mug – mouth (as in vessel for bol)

out for – looking for

pick – recognise/understand

punt – smuggler

THE HIGH LORD

Book Three of The Black Magician Trilogy

By Trudi Canavan

Sonea has learnt much in the Magicians' Guild. Over
the past year Regin has come to ignore her and the
other novices treat her with a grudging respect. But she
can never forget what she has witnessed in the high
Lord Akkarin's underground room, or his warning that
Kyralia's ancient enemy is watching the Guild closely.

As Akkarin reveals more of his knowledge, Sonea does
not know who to believe, or what she fears most.
Could the truth be as terrifying as the High Lord
claims? Or is he trying to trick her into assisting him
with his dark schemes?

orbit

www.orbitbooks.co.uk

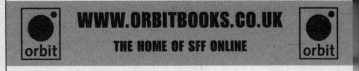

right-sided – trustworthy/heart in the right place

rope – freedom

rub – trouble (got into some rub over it)

shine – attraction (got a shine for him)

show – introduce

space – allowances/permission

squimp – someone who double-crosses the Thieves

style – manner of performing business

tag – recognise (also means a spy, usually undercover)

thief – leader of a criminal group

watcher – posted to observe something or someone

wild – difficult

visitor – burglar

GLOSSARY

ANIMALS

aga moths – pests that eat clothing

anyi – sea mammals with short spines

ceryni – small rodent

enka – horned domestic animal, bred for meat

eyoma – sea leeches

faren – general term for arachnids

gorin – large domestic animal used for food and to haul boats and wagons

harrel – small domestic animal bred for meat

limek – wild predatory dog

mullook – wild nocturnal bird

rassook – domestic bird used for meat and feathers

ravi – rodent, larger than ceryni

reber – domestic animal, bred for wool and meat

sapfly – woodland insect

sevli – poisonous lizard

squimp – squirrel-like creature that steals food

zill – small, intelligent mammal sometimes kept as a pet

PLANTS/FOOD

anivope vines – plant sensitive to mental projection

bol – (also means 'river scum') strong liquor made from tugors

brasi – green leafy vegetable with small buds

chebol sauce – rich meat sauce made from bol

crots – large, purple beans

curem – smooth, nutty spice

curren – course grain with robust flavour

dall – long fruit with tart orange, seedy flesh

gan-gan – flowering bush from Lan

580

iker – stimulating drug, reputed to have aphrodisiac properties

jerras – long yellow beans

kreppa – foul-smelling medicinal herb

marin – red citrus fruit

monyo – bulb

myk – mind-affecting drug

nalar – pungent root

pachi – crisp, sweet fruit

papea – pepper-like spice

piorres – small, bell-shaped fruit

raka/suka – stimulating drink made from roasted beans, originally from Sachaka

sumi – bitter drink

telk – seed from which an oil is extracted

tenn – grain that can be cooked as is, broken into small pieces, or ground to make a flour

tugor – parsnip-like root

vare – berries from which most wine is produced

CLOTHING AND WEAPONRY

incal – square symbol, not unlike a family shield, sewn onto sleeve or cuff

kebin – iron bar with hook for catching attacker's knife, carried by guards

longcoat – ankle-length coat

PUBLIC HOUSES

bathhouse – establishment selling bathing facilities and other grooming services

bolhouse – establishment selling bol and short term accommodation

brewhouse – bol manufacturer

stayhouse – rented building, a family to a room

PEOPLES OF THE ALLIED LANDS

Elyne – closest to Kyralia in position and culture, enjoys a milder climate

Kyralia – home of the Guild

Lan – a mountainous land peopled by warrior tribes

Lonmar – a desert land home to the strict Mahga religion

Vin – an island nation known for their seamanship

OTHER TERMS

cap – coins threaded on a stick to the value of the next highest denomination

dawnfeast – breakfast

midbreak – lunch

simba mats – mats woven from reeds